By: Neri Lopez

Other books by this author:
Path Series
Book 1: Red Path
Book 2: Unconquered Path

American Indian Cultural Center

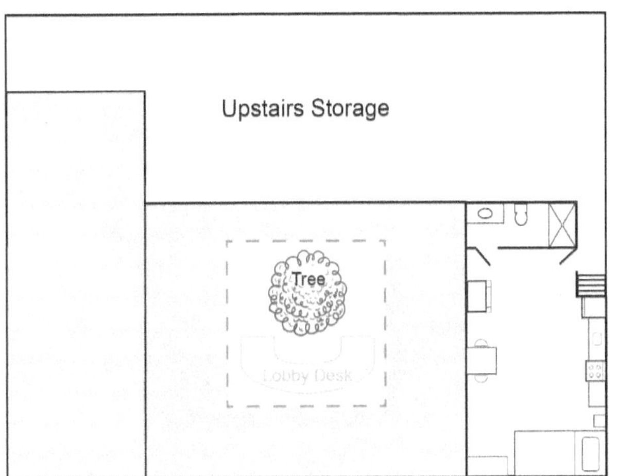

Second Floor

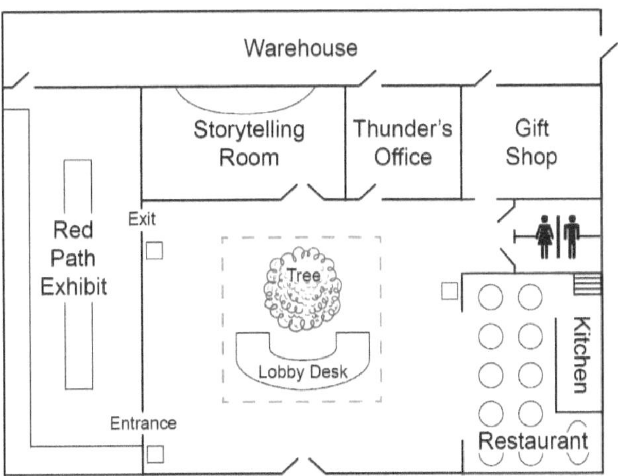

First Floor

Rock 'n' Roll Resort & Casino

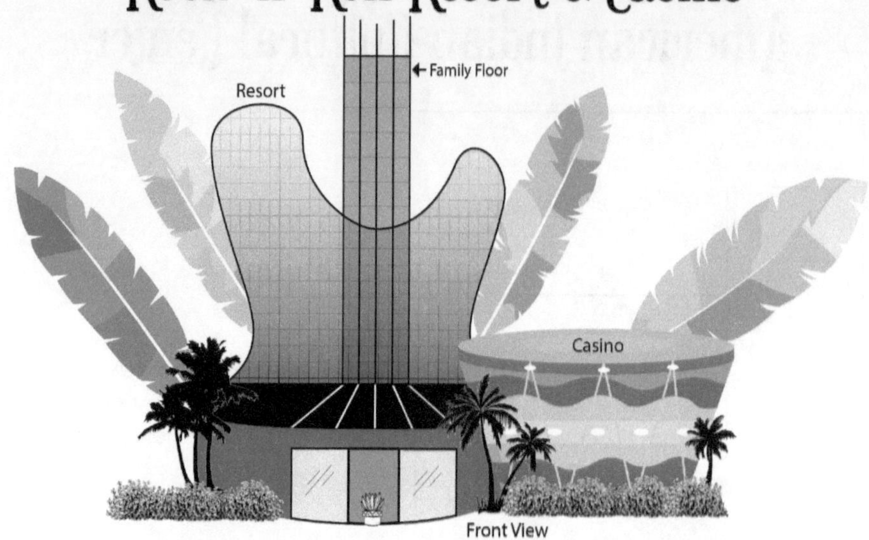

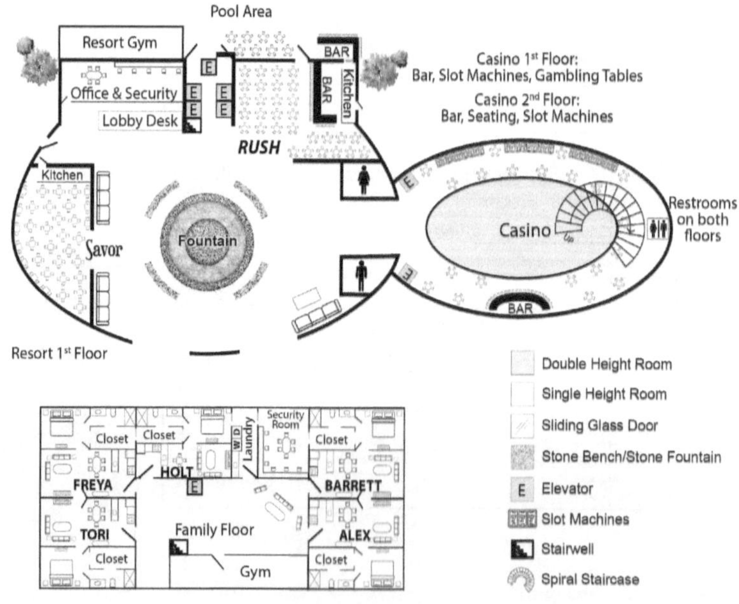

Lakota Translations

lekší – uncle

toján - niece

wíŋyaŋ mitáwa– my woman

Seminole Translations

chackshosti - daughter

chacteka - father

chakpootsi - son

chatski - mother

cheh moka is cheh - I love you

enca - yes

eny - my or mine

estonko - hello

Hesakitaemisi- God

helittah ma hich - handsome, very

Spanish Translations

Hola niña – Hello girl

Contents

Chapter 1

Elementary School...20 years earlier

Frey

F rey was playing on the monkey bars with her friend Jenny when she noticed a skinny boy sitting alone against the wall, reading a book by the water fountain. Dave, the resident bully, and his gang were spitting water on him and cracking up. Dave ensured no one was watching before sneakily kicking the boy's foot.

The boy's ability to read, move his foot, and completely ignore them, amazed Frey. Dave and his gang of bullies constantly harassed anyone smaller than them, including Frey and her friends, unless they spotted one of her brothers nearby. Barrett and Alex kept an eye out for Dave's gang.

She glanced around and saw Barrett, her twin brother, on the other side of the portables, throwing a football with his friends. Alex was in fifth grade and didn't have the same recess time. Frey knew if Barrett saw what Dave was doing, he would storm over there and stop him. Once Dave saw Barrett or Alex, he would back down and leave her alone. Having a pair of overbearing brothers came in handy sometimes.

Frey tried to get Barrett's attention by waving her hands at him from the top of the monkey bars, but he wasn't looking in her direction.

"Frey?" Jenny looked at her like she was crazy. "What are you doing?"

"Trying to get Barrett's attention." Frey lifted her foot to stand on the monkey bars.

Jenny grabbed her arm. "Are you crazy? You're gonna fall and die!"

"I'm not gonna die, Jenny." Frey rolled her eyes. "I just need Barrett to look this way." Frey tried waving again with one arm since Jenny held her other one.

"Why are you trying to get his attention?" Jenny turned and faced where Frey was waving.

"He can't see me. Dave is bullying that boy by the water fountain, and I want to tell Barrett so he can save him." Frey hated seeing other kids being bullied. She'd never confronted Dave. She usually got Barrett, Alex, or a teacher. But no one was nearby, and she felt bad for the skinny boy.

"Go tell him," Jenny shrugged her shoulders.

"That'll take too long." Frey stopped waving at Barrett, turned around and sucked in her breath. "Did you see that? Dave spit on him again. That's it." Despite her fear of Dave, she decided to stop Dave herself. She would stand tall, stick out her chest, and talk to Dave just like she'd seen her brothers do. If she stood her ground and showed no fear, he would stop, right? Heart thumping, Frey dropped to the ground, ready to defend the scruffy boy.

"Jenny," Frey placed her hands on her hips and looked up at her friend. "I'll be right back. I'm gonna go stop Dave." Frey pointed at the boy being bullied.

"Wait, Frey." Jenny eyed the commotion by the water fountain, then looked down at Frey and said in a hurry. "Don't go over there. What if he calls you names and embarrasses you in front of everyone? Or worse, what if they trip or push you again?"

"If they do, I'll run and get Barrett." Frey pointed to the back field. "Sorry, Jenny, but I'm tired of letting them get away with it. It's not right."

Frey left Jenny and marched angrily toward the boy, positioning herself between him and Dave. "Dave," Frey placed her hands on her hips. "Stop bullying him."

"Why?" Dave looked back at his friends and laughed. "Are you going to stop me, Uglayya?" Dave crossed his arms and sneered at her.

Dave liked to combine her name with "ugly" and draw it out to make sure everyone got the joke. It bothered her the first thousand times he used it, but not so much anymore. Sticks and stones and all that. But then he got in her face. Not wanting to show weakness, she stood her ground. Then Dave took another step toward her. He towered over her. Frey was pretty sure if he hit her, it would hurt. At that moment, she realized confronting him on her own may have been a mistake, but her survival skills were telling her to not back down even though on the inside she was terrified of Dave.

"Yes." Frey stood still although her heart was racing, and her breaths were coming in quicker. She needed to calm down and be brave for the boy. "You know, if you hit me, my brothers will hit you back. Leave him alone."

Frey felt a hand on her elbow and a whisper in her ear.

"Please stop." The boy was standing behind her.

"Ooo." Dave uncrossed his arms and shoulder bumped his friends. "Look, he's letting her defend him. What a wimp! I bet I could kick his ass."

"If you don't stop, Dave" –Frey looked around and saw that her teacher was closer than Barrett. Dave had looked mean when he crossed his arms, so she crossed her own and glared at him– "I'm gonna tell my teacher."

"So now you're a snitch, Uglayya?" Dave laughed, then got serious and leaned into Frey's face. "You know snitches get stitches."

Even though Frey was trembling on the inside, she held her ground and said, "I'd like to see you try."

Dave pretended to jump at her and hit her. At the same time the scraggly boy pulled her back.

"Oh yeah, I'm scared, Uglayya," Dave and his friends laughed. "Let's go, boys. These guys are losers. I don't want to waste the rest of my recess on them."

Dave and his gang walked away, still laughing. With a deep breath, Frey pivoted to the scraggly boy.

"Why did you do that?" he asked.

"How could you just sit there?" Frey countered his question with one of her own.

"They're bullies. Eventually they'll stop."

"Well, I felt bad for you" –Frey's jaw clenched– "What's your name?"

"Holt."

"Come on Holt," Frey grabbed his arm. "Let's go tell the teachers."

Holt pulled his arm out of her grasp and stared at her. "No, absolutely not."

"Why not?" Frey was stunned by his reaction. "They need to know Dave and his friends were picking on you."

"Don't make this worse." Holt's eyes darted behind Frey. "My teacher's coming. Don't say anything," Holt insisted. Frey turned to see Ms. Burnett approaching them.

"Holt," Ms. Burnett announced her arrival. "Are you okay?"

"Yes ma'am," Holt looked up and answered her.

"Were those boys bothering you?" Ms. Burnett laid her hand on Holt's shoulder.

"No ma'am," Holt shook his head vehemently and stepped back out of her touch. "I don't know what you're talking about."

Frey's mouth dropped open as she spun to face Holt. "Those boys were spitting water on you, and Dave kicked your foot."

"They were just playing around trying to get my attention." Holt held up his book. "I'm okay. They wanted me to play with them, but I wanted to stay here and read."

"Okay." Ms. Burnett pursed her lips and looked from Holt to Frey. It didn't look like she believed him. "But if anyone is bullying you, you need to tell me. This school has a zero-tolerance rule for bullying, and I won't stand for one of my students being picked on, okay?"

"Yes ma'am." Holt nodded.

Frey watched Ms. Burnett walk back to the other teachers. She was mad at Holt for not telling on Dave but didn't want to yell at him in front of his teacher.

As soon as Ms. Burnett was far enough away, Frey spun toward him. "Why did you lie to her? She could've helped you."

"It's no big deal." Holt shrugged his shoulders. "I asked you not to say anything. You made it worse."

"I was trying to help you." Frey placed her hands on her hips. "Dave isn't going to stop messing with you if you don't tell someone or stand up to them."

"Yeah right." Holt pointed at her. "You stood up to him and he still made fun of you."

"That wasn't a very nice thing to say when I was trying to help you." Frey pushed his finger away. "At least I'm trying."

"Sorry," Holt held his hands up in surrender. "Thanks, but I don't want to be a snitch."

"Whatever." Frey rolled her eyes.

"Just leave me alone, okay?" Holt glared at Frey.

"No." Frey shook her head. "I think you need a friend and I like having friends. I'm Freya, but everyone calls me Frey."

"Hi, Frey," Holt sighed.

"Are you new?" Frey turned around and looked for Dave and his friends.

"Yeah," Holt mumbled. "I just moved here from New York."

"Wow." Frey would love to go to the Big Apple. All the hustle and bustle of a big city life had always fascinated her. "I bet it was cool to live there. Riding the subway seems like fun. Why did you move?"

"My parents divorced, and my mom wanted to get away to a warm place" –Holt shrugged again– "so here we are."

"So, your dad doesn't live here?"

"No."

"Do you have any brothers or sisters?"

"No."

"I have a twin brother, Barrett. He's over there throwing the football with his friends. He's the one with the red shirt and black shorts." Frey pointed toward the group. "My other brother is in 5th grade."

"Cool." Holt's gaze lingered on the boys playing in the playground.

"Do you wanna go meet Barrett?" Frey tried to engage Holt in a conversation, but he was frustrating her with his one-word answers.

"No." Holt shook his head and sat back down. "I'm good here."

"Hmm." Frey bent down and grabbed his hand. "Come on. You're gonna meet him anyway. He's popular. Dave won't bother you if you hang out with Barrett and his friends."

Frey watched Holt's eyes widen and his body tense.

"Ugh, really Frey, I'm okay here."

"I don't think so," Frey pulled on his hand. She was going to introduce him to Barrett if it was the last thing she did. Everyone needed to have at least one friend. Besides, Barrett could help him with Dave like he always helped her. "Let's go. You don't want to hurt my feelings, do you?"

"Ugh" –Holt rolled his eyes– "fine. I'll go."

Holt closed his book and allowed Frey to help him up. Frey grabbed his forearm and dragged him toward Barrett.

"Barrett," Frey tapped her brother's shoulder after he threw the ball.

"Hey, Frey." Barrett held up his hand in a stop motion to his friends and turned around. "What's up?"

"Barrett, this is Holt. He's new. Can he play with you guys?"

"Sure." Barrett waved his friends to come over. "Hey guys, this is Holt. He's new. Holt, this is Josh and Kenny."

"Hey, man," Josh and Kenny said almost simultaneously.

"Hi." Holt nodded.

"Well, my work is done. See ya later, guys." Frey smiled at everyone, turned around and headed back to Jenny on the monkey bars.

As Frey walked to Jenny, she looked over her shoulder and noticed that Holt was now smiling as he threw the ball with them. She knew Barrett would include him. Barrett and Alex were both outgoing and kind to others, but Holt was Barrett's age. She would have to introduce Holt to Alex too, since he was older and more aware of bullies.

"Is Dave mad at you?" Jenny asked, as Frey approached. "Is that boy nice?"

"He seems nice, but quiet. Not sure about Dave." Frey shrugged. "Let's go to the swings before recess is over."

Chapter 2

Back to Work

Frey

F rey stared at herself in her bathroom mirror dressed in her signature black collared long sleeve shirt, black pants, black high-heeled shoes, and guitar pick shaped name tag on her shirt. Frey had been a blackjack dealer as long as she could remember because her parents managed the casino.

The female dealers at the Rock 'n' Roll Resort & Casino pulled their hair back in a bun and wore heavy makeup while working the tables. They needed to enhance their assets to attract male guests, but also remain professional and blend into the background. Normally, Frey didn't mind, but tonight she was a little apprehensive about attracting attention. However, she put on all her heavy makeup and was looking for a bright lipstick when she saw the red lipstick she used on Tori. *That damn red lipstick bet.*

A few weeks ago, Frey bet Tori that if she wore her sexy red lipstick, she would pick up a guy in ten minutes. Big mistake. Frey should have sent Tori to Alex and convinced her to give him a chance, especially since she knew Alex liked her. But Tori had co-worker zoned Alex because she was afraid to date someone she worked with. Trying to cheer her up, Frey came up with that damn red lipstick bet.

Tori, being the good friend that she was, took the bet and met a monster. Winston had originally targeted Frey. She hadn't known what a monster he truly was, but she noticed him watching her all the time. It gave her the creeps. When he finally got the hint that Frey wasn't interested, he went after Tori and charmed her into dating him. Even though Frey had warned Tori about Winston, she didn't listen and continued to date him until the unthinkable happened.

After Tori's traumatic incident, she moved in with Alex. She was frightened and reluctant to enter the room where the horrible act occurred. Who could blame her? Frey and Tori's rooms shared an adjoining door and Frey was terrified to be in the room next door, let alone go into Tori's room.

She knew it was irrational to blame the lipstick for what happened, but it would forever remind her of that stupid bet. Frey threw the lipstick away. She never wanted to see that color again. Instead, Frey reached for a lighter pinkish red.

Finishing up, she grabbed her keycard, and tucked it into her bra. She didn't want anyone to steal it out of her back pocket. Sometimes guests had slippery fingers for wallets or keycards. Some men were real scumbags and didn't take no for an answer. The dealers were always getting hit on, regardless of their gender.

Aggressive customers made her mad and scared. If they didn't stop when she either ignored their sexual comments or tried to let them down professionally, she would push the red button under her table and ask for help from their security officers. That button signaled all the security officers through their cell phones. Barrett and Holt usually answered her call and would escort the irate customer out of the casino. Luckily, nine times out of ten, they would get the hint and leave her alone.

Frey found her mom before starting work.

"Hi, *chatski*," Frey walked behind the lobby desk and gave her mom a hug. "Thank you for giving me several days off work."

"*Chackshosti*, I would do anything for you and Tori. How is she doing?" Sehoy grimaced.

"As good as can be expected, considering what she's been through." Frey leaned against the desk.

"How are you doing?" Sehoy rubbed her arm.

"I'm good, *chatski*. I'm not the one that was violated." Frey looked down and pulled a piece of lint from her pants. She wasn't good and if her mom looked in her eyes, she would know she lied. Frey was having a hard time sleeping. She had recurring nightmares of being held down and raped by Winston.

"That's true, but since your room is next to hers, I just wanted to make sure you were okay. Barrett told me about the bet and that Winston had been after you first." Sehoy ran her hand down Frey's arm to stop her fidgeting. Firmly holding Frey's hand with a squeeze. "You know none of this is your fault, right?" With her other hand, Sehoy cradled Frey's chin and raised her face. Frey knew she was trying to help, but she didn't want to talk about it.

Putting on a brave face and fake smile, Frey looked at her mom and said, "I'm okay, *chatski*, really."

"Okay, but if you need to talk, I'm here for you—always. I love you." Sehoy pulled her in for a hug. "All of us will feel better once they find Winston."

"You're right." Frey kissed her mom on the cheek. "I love you too. I'll see you later. My shift starts in a couple of minutes, and I want to know if there's anything I've missed these last few days. Do you know if Barrett is working?"

"No, *chackshosti*. We've been so busy I haven't checked the schedule." Sehoy moved to her computer and typed in some keys. "I can look it up for you."

"No, it's okay." Frey stepped away from the desk. "If he's working on the floor, I'll see him at some point. See you later."

Frey walked away before she broke down. Work was a great distraction, and she had a dealer to replace. Once she opened the door to the casino, she instantly felt at home with all the slot machine noises and the contagious excitement of the guests as they pleaded with the slot machines to give them a win. She looked around, expecting to find Barrett or Holt. She knew one of them would monitor cameras on the family floor and the other would walk the casino floor.

She stood by the slot machines, inhaling the intense and various perfume scents that always comforted her. Some people love to go to a garden and smell the flowers, others like the smell of books in used bookstores. Frey loved the different scents of strong perfume in the casino. She was sure she looked crazy standing there taking several deep breaths through her nose with her eyes closed and smiling like a loon. Growing up in the casino, all these smells and sounds were home.

"Hey, are you okay?" Frey opened her eyes and saw Holt standing in front of her, his brow furrowed. "Are you ready to be back at work?"

"Yup, it's time." Frey looked around. "Anything I should know about?"

"Nope, same old same old." Holt's eyes darted around her face as he watched her closely.

Frey broke eye contact and turned toward her table. "Who's at my table?"

"Anastasia's been working your shifts." Holt answered and scanned the casino for any signs of trouble.

Frey didn't look at him again, afraid he would see how tired she was from not sleeping. She knew she was safe once he focused his attention back on the guests. Holt was still listening to her, even though he wasn't facing her. Barrett and Holt were both very good at handling the casino activity and a conversation.

"Great, I'll go relieve her. I'm sure she would like to have a few days off." Frey looked around and froze. *Was that Winston by the roulette table?*

"Sounds good. I'll see you around. I'm on the floor tonight."

"Holt." Frey reached out and grabbed his arm, afraid her weak knees wouldn't hold her up. She placed her hand over her throbbing heart. *Breathe or you're going to pass out,* she told herself firmly, but the panic drowned her rational voice out. *Was that him? Did he come back for her?*

"What's wrong?" Holt instantly faced her, holding her biceps gently. "What is it?"

"I thought I saw Winston." Frey blinked and released her breath. False alarm. The minute he turned around and laughed with the man behind him, she saw it wasn't him. Frey placed her palm on her forehead. Now she was seeing things. It was bad enough to see him in her nightmares, but for her mind to play tricks on her at work, just sucked.

"Where?" Holt's head turned and focused on the direction she had been looking.

"It wasn't him." Frey took a few deep breaths to calm herself.

"Are you sure? I can head over there." Holt pointed in that direction.

"I'm sure. I thought it was him from behind. But when he turned around, I was wrong." Frey felt like a basket case.

"Hey." Holt pulled her into his arms for a hug and rubbed her back. "I promise Winston is never stepping foot on this property ever again. Everyone knows what he looks like and is taking what happened seriously. We don't want anything like that to happen here ever again. You have my word. I'm here if you need to talk."

"Thanks, Holt." Frey could stay in his warm embrace forever. She loved the smell of his cologne. He'd worn the same one since high school. One year, she bought him a bottle for his birthday. She still had the paper sample the department store employee had given her tucked under her pillow. Lately, she'd been taking it out every night just to feel like she wasn't alone. If only he liked her as more than a sister.

She pulled out of his arms and tried for a smile, but only managed a slight quirk at the corner of her. "I gotta go to my table. See you later."

Chapter 3

What is Love?

Holt

H olt noticed Frey wasn't her normal sassy self. She looked tired and jumpy. He recognized that look from when he was young and lived with Betty in the trailer. Her boyfriends loved to use him as their personal punching bag. He'd learned to be aware of his surroundings and run to his room as soon as he got home. Holt sighed. The last thing he wanted was for Frey to be terrified everywhere she went.

Holt would have to keep an eye on her table tonight, more so than usual. He had been in love with her for so long but knew he couldn't act on it. All through middle and high school, they flirted with each other.

Frey would always be with him and Barrett. She'd tutored him in Math and constantly touched his shoulder. She always laughed at his jokes or teased him about girls. Barrett must have noticed because one day in high school he got the courage to talk to Barrett about asking Frey out. Barrett got mad and told him Frey was like a sister to Holt and he couldn't date his sister. Then Barrett made him promise to never date her. Holt hadn't expected such an anger filled reaction.

That day he rode the bus home instead of getting a ride from Mrs. Panther to the casino like he normally did to do his homework with Barrett and Frey. He needed time to think and figure out a way to be near Frey, but not want her. His hormones were raging, and they only wanted Frey.

Holt lived in a trailer with his mother, Betty. His mom and dad were divorced, and his father didn't want to have anything to do with them. Betty was sitting on the couch in a robe. A strung-out man in his boxers sat next to her as they took turns snorting cocaine from the cocktail table.

"Get me a beer!" The man looked up and yelled at Holt as he walked in the door.

Holt just wanted to escape to his room and lock the door.

"Hey, asshole? Did you hear me?" the man stood and yelled again.

"Yeah, asshole, I heard you." Holt grumbled and turned to walk to the refrigerator.

"Did your shit kid just talk back to me?" the man turned to Betty and slapped her face. "Train him right Bitch or I'm not bringing you this shit again."

Holt heard the slap, stopped, and turned back around. Ready to defend Betty even though she wasn't a good mom. No man should ever hit a woman.

"I'm sorry, Jack." His mom cried from the couch.

It would figure his mom would bring home a man named Jack. That was his father's name and she regularly cursed him, but still loved him. Holt didn't know how she could've loved him when she cheated on him all the time. But he didn't know what love was anyway. He thought it was what he saw when he visited the Panther family.

"Just don't hit his face!" Betty screamed out. "I don't want social services coming here to ask questions."

Holt shouldn't have spaced out because when he looked up Jack had pulled his arm back and punched him hard in the stomach. Son of a bitch, that punch had hurt. Bending over holding his stomach, he glanced at his mom. She was snorting another line without a care in the world that her sleezy boyfriend was hitting her son. Unfortunately, Jack wasn't done. He continued to kick and punch me in my stomach and kidneys until I fell and must have hit my head on something because when I woke up Jack, my mom, and two other men had now moved on to shooting up.

There were used needles on the table. Holt sat up slowly and noticed he had a tourniquet on his left arm with a loaded needle on the floor next to him. He immediately tore it off and looked for any puncture wounds on his arm. The assholes found it funny and laughed at him. Holt scooted back and ran from the room. Locking his bedroom door, he pushed his small dresser in front of it so no one could follow him.

That was the day he started calling his mom by her first name, Betty. Moms were supposed to love and take care of you, not let men beat you and pretend to shoot you up. That had been the worst day of his life. Not only did he realize his mom didn't love him, but he couldn't have the girl of his dreams. He'd felt so much despair. He crawled out through his bedroom window and ran for a couple of miles.

He couldn't run fast enough or far enough to escape his demons. Not to mention, he probably had a concussion and shouldn't have been running. Looking back, he realized running had been a mistake, but he hated staying home.

The next day, he went home with the Panthers after school. Going there was better than going home. He also asked Barrett and Alex if he could use their gym and start lifting weights. He never wanted to be a punching bag for one of Betty's men ever again. Coming home later in the evening meant that Betty and her crew would be passed out. A better chance of them not hearing him enter the trailer.

He also vowed to stop flirting with Frey and distanced himself from her. At first, she seemed confused by his behavior, but later she got mad at him when he kept ignoring her. It was for the best. *Why would she want to date someone like him?* He didn't even know what love was. She deserved someone who had the capacity to love. Not someone who was a damaged bastard. Barrett had been right in making him promise not to date her and continue to think of her like a sister.

So many hard feelings from that time until now, but Holt never stopped wanting to protect her. Their friendship was still on shaky ground. They had good and bad days, but were always civil to each other with respect to Barrett and her parents. But Holt still remembered and treasured their three musketeers era. Those were the good ole days.

Chapter 4

A Mother's Concern

Sehoy

Sehoy had followed Frey into the casino and saw her freak out while she was with Holt. She waited until Frey walked away from Holt to go to her table before she approached Holt. She wanted to talk to Holt without Frey overhearing.

"*Chakpootsi*, how is she doing?" Sehoy laid her hand against Holt's arm to get his attention. Holt turned to face her, his eyes immediately growing softer as he looked at her.

"She says she's okay. I'm not sure I believe her." Holt looked in her direction. "She thought she saw Winston and panicked."

"Was it him?" Sehoy's eyes darted around the room.

"No." Holt rubbed the back of his neck. "I'll keep an eye on her," Holt promised.

"I know you will." Sehoy hugged him. "Let me know if anything happens or you notice her getting upset."

"I will. Are you working tonight?"

"Only for about another hour until Osceola wraps up his shift," Sehoy grabbed his hands. "Thank you. I didn't see Barrett."

"I think he's upstairs. Do you need him? I can radio him." Holt placed his hand over his earpiece.

"No, it's okay." Sehoy stopped him from calling Barrett. "Just look after Frey and call me if you think she needs me. I'll see you tomorrow."

"Will do. See you tomorrow." Holt turned to walk the floor.

Sehoy went back into the conference room to wait for Osceola. The whole time thinking about how grateful she was for having Holt in their lives. He'd lived a rough life with his mom until that fateful day in high school, when he got suspended for defending Frey. That was the day *Hesakitaemisi* blessed her with another son.

Sehoy noticed her children upset when they came home from school and found her in the lobby, but she couldn't understand a word they were saying with them all talking over each other.

"Whoa, whoa, what happened?" Sehoy held her hand up and walked around the desk, approaching them. "One at a time, please. Frey, you go first."

"I was by my locker minding my own business, when Tami came up behind me and called me a snitch and shoved me into my locker. I told her to get over herself. I mean, she was talking about something that happened between me and Dave in elementary school, for goodness sakes." Frey waved her hands around while she continued her story. "Just because they're dating now doesn't mean she has to avenge every slight he's ever faced. And I told her that, I said, 'I'm sorry your boyfriend's obsessed with me, but he needs to get over it.' She didn't like that. So, then she said she didn't ever think or talk about me when she was with Dave, but I beg to differ. I mean, she was bringing something up that happened a long time ago. Then Dave shows up, and he's calling me a snitch bitch and I called them assholes. Next thing I know, he's in my face and he shoved me."

Frey was practically hyperventilating by the end, her mouth moving a mile a minute. Sehoy placed her hands on her daughter's cheeks and said, "Calm down, chackshosti."

"How can I when I got Holt suspended?" Frey screeched.

"You didn't start it," Barrett jumped into the conversation when Frey started tearing up. "Holt shoved Dave back, away from Frey. But Dave, being the bully that he is, he threw his books at Frey. They hit her in the chest and had I not been there to catch her, she would've fallen on the floor."

"Oh, no." Sehoy pulled Frey into her arms. "Are you okay?" Frey shook her head.

"You would've been proud of Holt for defending Frey. He just punched Dave in the face, knocking him to the ground. His face bleeding all over the floor." Barrett said, reenacting the punch, complete with sound effects.

"What?" Sehoy turned to Holt.

"I'm sorry, Mrs. Panther. He made me so angry when he threw those books at Frey. I wasn't thinking straight." Holt avoided Sehoy's eyes. "Tami called me an asshole and accused me of hitting him to Mr. Calhoun, a teacher at school. When Mr. Calhoun asked me, I confessed to hitting him."

"We tried to explain to him that Holt was defending me, but he still told Dave and Holt to follow him to the dean's office. Chatski, Holt would've never done that if Dave hadn't provoked him. Dave started it. You've gotta help Holt," Frey pleaded with her mom.

"If you ask me," Barrett hmphed, "the asshole deserved it."

"Barrett Panther," Sehoy scolded him, "fighting is not the answer."

"Well, it shut him up," Barrett murmured.

"Anyway, they wouldn't let me go with Holt to tell them our side." Frey stepped in front of her mom, gaining her attention. "Holt wouldn't let me talk to the dean, and then he got suspended."

"Frey," Holt sighed as if they had this argument before, "I needed you to go to class and take notes so you could share them with me."

"*Holt.*" *Sehoy walked to him and put her arm around him. "Come talk to me in my office for a minute.*"

"*Mrs. Panther.*" *Holt tensed and rubbed the bridge of his nose. "I'm sorry. I'll understand if you don't want me to be here, I can go home.*"

"*Nonsense,*" *Sehoy side hugged him. "I always want you here. That's what I want to talk to you about.*"

Sehoy and Holt entered her office behind the lobby in the security area

"*Holt.*" *Sehoy sat at the edge of her seat and reached out to hold his hands. "Osceola and I have been talking about you moving in here with us. We know about your mom's drug use and the men. We don't think you should be around all of that craziness.*"

Holt's body jerked suddenly, his eyes widening in surprise.

"*I know things at home haven't been good for a long time. I see how troubling it is whenever anyone brings up the subject of your mom. You say nothing, but your body language says it all. Your situation has been on our minds for several years. We should have done this sooner and for that, I'm sorry.*"

"*You want me?*" *Holt whispered. "No one's ever wanted me.*"

"*Oh, Holt,*" *Sehoy sighed, her vision blurred. "We've always wanted you. We just didn't know how to go about doing it. But enough is enough. I will get Osceola and we will go talk to your mom ASAP.*"

"*But how can you leave here? You're both working.*" *Holt broke eye contact and looked at their hands.*

"*This is important. I will not have you going back there for three days. At least when you had school, you were gone most of the day. Do you want to come with us when we talk to her?*"

"*No,*" *Holt raised his eyes and the corner of lips lifted, "but I will, so I can get my clothes.*"

"*Okay, go get a snack with Barrett and Frey and as soon as I find Osceola, we'll come get you.*"

"*Yes ma'am,*" *Holt stood up with Sehoy. "Mrs. Panther, I can't thank you enough for this. I hope it all works out. There is nothing I would like better than to live here with all of you.*"

"*It will work out Holt, I promise. Now, go get something to eat. We should be ready to leave in about twenty minutes.*"

Sehoy called Osceola to let him know it was time to save Holt. They had discussed it many times over the years but didn't know how. They didn't want Betty to fight them.

"*Enca, helittah ma hich eny,*" *Sehoy smiled at Osceola. "Thank you for coming so quickly. I need to talk to you about something that we need to take care of right away.*"

Sehoy guided Osceola to the conference room and gave him an overview of what happened to Holt at school.

"*It's time to bring him home with us. I want to take him over there and get his things. He can room with Barrett. It will give us time to turn the kids' playroom next to the laundry room into a bedroom for Holt.*"

"*I agree that it's time to get him out of there. Let's go talk to that poor excuse of a mother and bring our son home.*" *Holt spent so much time with the Panthers they had thought of him as their son for many years.*

"Cheh moka is cheh," Sehoy said before she kissed her husband.
"Cheh moka is cheh," Osceola whispered against her lips.
Sehoy and Osceola walked to RUSH to get Holt.
"Holt." Sehoy walked up to him and patted his back. "Time to go."
"Chatske," Frey spoke up. "Holt told us what you are going to do. Do you think it will work?"
"Enca," Osceola answered for Sehoy, "when your mom puts her mind to something, it always works. Come on, son, let's take care of this so we can be home by dinner."
"Thank you, sir," Holt mumbled.
"No need to thank me. I've been wanting to do this for a long time. I'll go get the car and bring it to the front," Osceola stated and walked away.
"We'll be in my room doing our homework," Barrett stood up. "Come find us when you get back. I'll take your backpack with us."
"Okay," Holt answered, "thanks."

That had truly been one of the best days of her life. They drove to Betty's trailer and convinced her to let Holt live with them. Sehoy always knew Betty didn't treat Holt like a mother should treat her child, but she couldn't prove it until that day when she entered that trailer and saw the half-naked man, drugs, and alcohol. She was glad Betty let him leave without much of a fight. Over the following weeks, Sehoy had seen a change in Holt. He was no longer an angry teen ready for a fight. Living upstairs with Barrett, Alex, and Frey gave him some independence and control over his life and he flourished. Working in the casino after he graduated and turned eighteen as part of the security staff gave him a purpose. He was always eager to take on more work and challenges.

That had been a great day in the end.

*** Holt ***

After speaking with Sehoy, Holt went looking for Barrett to let him know his mom's concerns about Frey. Between the two of them and the other security officers, they would make sure she was safe.

"Hey," Holt found Barrett leaning over the railing, watching the tables on the first floor from a higher position.

"How's it going down there?" Barrett gave Holt a nod.

"Good." Holt stopped next to him. "Your mom came by downstairs to ask me about Frey. I told her she freaked out when she thought she saw Winston, but calmed down when it wasn't him. Frey seemed okay after that. Have you noticed anything lately?"

"No. She hasn't said anything to me." Barrett shook his head.

"Me neither. But *chatski* wants us to keep an eye out for Frey. She's waiting for Osceola, and then they're leaving for the night. She wants one of us to call her if we think Frey might need her." Holt tapped the railing. "I gotta get downstairs, but I wanted to let you know."

"Sounds good. Hey, check those two out." Barrett pointed to two giggling girls by a blackjack table. "What do you think? You can be my wingman. We can tag team them tonight. They look hot."

"Nah, man. Not tonight." Holt turned to leave.

"Why the hell not? You've been avoiding girls lately. Are you turning celibate on me?" Barrett looked like he didn't believe him.

"I just want to find something meaningful," Holt sighed. "I'm tired of all the girls coming onto me for one-night stands. I mean, shit, it's not like we're in our early twenties anymore."

"You talk like we're headed straight for the nursing home." Barrett pounded on his back. "Live it up Holt, we're not even thirty yet.

"Yeah, yeah, yeah, I'll see you later." Holt left and headed back downstairs. He knew he wasn't old, but growing up with Betty felt like he'd lived a lifetime. He'd had to deal with so much shit, living with his mom. Plus, the one girl he wanted he couldn't have. Speaking of his girl, he walked by her table to make sure everything was going well for her tonight. Frey had worried him when she panicked earlier. If he couldn't date her, he could at least be a good friend to her – even if it killed him to hold her and not be able to go any further.

Chapter 5

Freaked Out

Frey

F rey headed to her table and smiled at Anastasia.

"Hey Stasia, thanks for covering for me," Frey whispered in her ear and waited for her to finish out the game with her customers.

"No problem, Frey." Anastasia collected the cards.

"Take the next couple of nights off." Frey placed her hand on Stasia's arm as she turned. "I'll take your shifts."

"Thanks girl, I could use the break. I'll see you Saturday?"

"Yup, see you then." Frey opened a new deck of cards, faced her players, and dealt them each their two cards before placing her card face up. At their casino, whenever the dealers switched, they always cracked open a new deck of cards.

"Place your bets."

None of her players had an immediate blackjack, so she looked at each one individually to see if they wanted to 'draw' or 'stay'. Some of them wanted to draw, and a couple stayed. After handing out cards to those who wanted them, she played her hand and, as usual, the house won. Frey smirked. She knew eventually her luck would run out, but at least the house won on her first game back.

Frey always watched carefully to make sure no one at her table was counting cards. Sometimes she would catch them and push the red button under her table to alert the security officers. Other times, the security officers watching the cameras caught them and came down to escort them out of the casino. Under the table, she also had a blue button to call the roaming dealer – an extra dealer that floated around the room in case one of them working the tables needed a break.

She dealt several hands before needing to use the restroom. Pushing the blue button she waited for the roaming dealer. Everything was going smoothly until a customer followed her.

"Hey baby, your ass looks just as good as your tits. Can I join you in the bathroom for a little fun?" Frey heard him right before he grabbed her ass.

Whirling around, ready to give him a piece of her mind, she watched Holt grab the guy by the back of his shirt and pull him away from her.

"Hey asshole, hands off our dealers. Watch your mouth and show her some respect."

"Fuck man, what's your problem? We were just talking. She is one fine piece of ass."

"My problem is that you don't talk to women like that, and you definitely don't grab their ass. You have two choices: you either walk out on your own or I'll throw your ass out." Holt released his shirt at the same time as he shoved him back and stood between the idiot and Frey.

"Fine, man. I'm going."

Frey held her shaking body as she watched Holt follow him to the door. The jerk's voice told her it wasn't Winston, but she was still jumpy and pissed that a guy got close enough to touch her. She had been doing so well and now that man had messed with her head.

When Holt was out of sight, she turned and placed her hand against the bathroom door to push it open. That's when she noticed how badly she was shaking. She needed to calm down before she went back to her table. Some men were verbally aggressive to the female dealers, but none had ever been so brazen as to touch her. It wasn't uncommon for a guest to get flirtatious, but they usually did it at the table. They rarely followed the dealers.

Men could be such assholes. Why would a woman want a man that said that to her and grabbed her ass? Frey was glad Holt had been there before things got ugly. When that guy grabbed her, her reaction was to turn around and give him a piece of her mind, but the way he looked at her held her frozen. The naked desire and entitlement in his expression gave her flashbacks to when Winston would ask her out. She hated feeling like a helpless female. Maybe she needed to talk to Holt and Barrett about teaching her some self-defense moves, like they were teaching Tori.

Frey rushed into the stall and locked the door. She pressed her hands on the stall door to catch her breath. She felt nauseous as her blood pounded in her ears and her heart throbbed so hard in her chest, she thought it would burst through. Needing to calm down, she turned around, leaned on the stall door and slid to the floor as her vision blurred. Lifting her knees toward her chest, she wrapped her arms around them and dropped her head on her knees. Tears running down her cheeks, shoulders shaking as she quietly sobbed.

What was happening to her? She'd never felt like this before. She needed to pull herself together. Her family would never leave her alone if they saw her like this. She was the happy go lucky girl, not the weak girl sitting on a dirty casino bathroom floor where drunk females missed the toilet or dropped feminine products on the floor. It felt like she was sitting there for an hour, but when she checked her watch, it had only been about five minutes.

She couldn't leave work now. She'd just told Stacia to take the night off. Besides, she always had to be on her toes when she dealt cards. Her job was not only a great distraction from her thoughts, it also soothed her. There was comfort in doing something familiar that you loved. Finally, taking deep regular breaths, she stood up and wiped the seat of her pants, grateful she hadn't sat in a puddle of water or worse, pee. Thank goodness their cleaning crew was constantly sanitizing their bathrooms. Using the toilet and glad that it was to pee and not to throw up, Frey did her business and stepped out of the stall.

While washing her hands, she glanced at her face in the mirror. *Shit.* Her face was a mess from crying. Using a paper towel, she did the best she could to fix her makeup. There was no time to run back to her room for a touch up and she never brought her makeup bag to her table. No place to store it. Finally satisfied with her results, she stepped out of the bathroom and saw Holt standing with his arms crossed, legs shoulder width apart by the door, watching everyone.

"Are you waiting for me?" Frey was surprised to see him. *How long has he been standing there?*

"Yup." Holt dropped his arms and looked at her. "Are you okay? Did that guy hurt you?"

"No," Frey sighed, "you came just in time, like usual. Thank you." Frey's smile was a little wobbly.

"You're welcome. Come on, I'll walk you to your table."

Holt placed his hand on the middle of her back, leading her back to her table. She was really hoping that guy wouldn't show up again. Holt stayed with her for a few minutes, monitoring the guests seated at her table, but when everything seemed back to normal, he left to walk around.

Chapter 6

Things are Looking Up

Frey

Frey opened a new deck of cards and was shuffling them when she heard a man's voice.

"Miss, are you okay? I saw that creepy guy follow you and grab you. I'm glad that security officer escorted him out." The man's brow and forehead were creased.

The handsome man had dark short hair paired with dark brown eyes and a manly square jaw. She would best describe him as a pretty boy, not as rugged as Holt. She compared every man she saw to Holt. She needed to stop doing that. After what happened last month, Frey knew it was time to move on from her childish crush. He wore a business suit without a tie and left a couple of buttons undone.

"Hi, yes, I'm good," Frey answered him and dealt the cards.

The handsome man won some hands and lost some, but during the night, he was laughing and talking with his fellow players. Frey couldn't help but notice Holt and Jake, another security officer, sticking by her table all night. The handsome man stayed at her table until she ended her shift. Their casino was open twenty-four hours a day, seven days a week. Frey, Anastasia, Abigail, and Janie worked on that blackjack table. Frey always took this shift unless she needed to cover for someone else. She saw Janie coming to relieve her, so she finished the game and picked up her cards.

"So, Freya, are you done for the night? Can I buy you a drink?" The handsome man asked Frey after she greeted Janie and watched her open a new deck.

"How do you know my name?" Frey stared at him wide-eyed.

"Uh, your nametag." He pointed toward Frey's shirt.

"Right." Frey winced and placed her hand over her chest. Yep, she had her nametag on. "Not tonight."

"I promise I'll keep my hands to myself." He stood and placed his hands inside his pockets. "Just one drink. It'll help you relax after such a crazy night."

Frey wasn't going to take him up on his offer, but he seemed genuine. A drink would help her relax and, hopefully, sleep. She rarely slept all night anymore. Janie was standing behind her, ready to take over.

"Okay. But just one, and only if we can get a drink from upstairs?" Frey didn't want to avoid life and Holt wasn't making a move, so she figured having one drink with this handsome, nice guy would be fine. Besides, Carl usually worked the bar upstairs, so she knew her drink would be safe. "Have a good night, Janie."

"Goodnight, Frey," Janie spoke as she dealt her players in.

"By the way," Frey turned to face the handsome man when she heard his voice. "My name's Ted." Ted reached his hand out for a handshake.

"Nice to meet you, Ted. My friends call me Frey," Frey shook his hand, "Let's get that drink upstairs." Frey led the way. Ted walked beside her, which made her feel better. If he was behind her, she would feel like he was staring at her ass and remind her of the jerk from earlier today. So far, he was staying true to his word—he hadn't touched her. Upstairs, he pulled out a stool for her when they reached the upstairs bar.

"Hey, Frey, what'll you have?" Carl asked while placing a napkin in front of her and Ted.

"Hey, Carl, I'll have a frozen margarita, please."

"And for you?" he asked Ted.

"Any beer you have on tap is fine with me." Ted pointed toward the beer handles on the dispenser.

"So, Ted, what do you do?" Frey set her crossed arms on the bar and glanced at Ted.

"I work at an insurance company. I'm an insurance agent."

"Cool." Frey was glad he was a man who kept his word with a decent job. At least she knew she could attract nice guys who weren't stalkers or assholes. "Do you like it?"

"I do. I love helping my clients buy insurance protection they can afford. Too many uninsured motorists live here. My mom became paralyzed from an accident with a drunk driver who didn't have insurance a few years ago. My parents had worked so hard to save for retirement. They wanted to travel but ended up having to use most their savings to pay medical bills. I would like to help others so no one will be stuck in the same situation as they were."

"I'm so sorry to hear that." Frey felt horrible for him.

"Thanks," Ted nodded. "My sister and I help them as much as we can. We've also been saving money to gift them a trip to Italy for next year. But enough about me."

Carl placed both their drinks in front of them and they both thanked him.

"How do you like being a dealer? Do you get a lot of assholes like that guy at our table tonight?" Ted pointed behind him with his thumb.

"Unfortunately, I do. Although usually they don't touch us." Frey rolled her eyes. "But our security officers are quick to help us."

"That's good. Any chance you'll go out with me sometime?"

Wow, he went right for the prize. Frey was surprised at how quickly he asked her for a date and got right to the point. It was enough to give her mental whiplash.

"Not soon. I recently took a lot of days off for a family emergency and now I have to cover several shifts," Frey tried to let him down gently. He seemed nice, but she wasn't ready to go out somewhere with him.

"Is everything okay now?" Ted's forehead crinkled.

"I think so, but only time will tell." Frey finished her drink and stood up.

"Can I give you my number and you can call me when you're ready to go to dinner or something?" Ted fiddled with the napkin under his beer.

The longer they talked, the more Frey liked him. He wasn't pushy, seemed to care about her situation, and he was close to his family.

"Sure. Carl?" Frey called out, "can I borrow a pen?"

Carl tossed her one and headed back to the other side of the bar. Frey grabbed a napkin and wrote Ted on it.

"Old school, huh?" Ted smiled at her.

"Yeah, with everything happening with my family, I left my room without grabbing my phone." Frey passed him the napkin and pen. She would let him give her his number and think about calling him. That's what most men usually did when they got a girl's number. Except some girls sat by the phone, hopelessly waiting for that call. Ted was cute and wouldn't have any trouble getting a girl. After a couple of days, he'd just forget and move on. No harm, no foul.

"It's not safe for you to be driving home without a phone. I'll walk you to your car." Ted leapt up from the stool.

"Oh, you don't have to walk me." Frey shook her head. "I live here."

"In the hotel?" Ted raised an eyebrow.

"Yes, my parents run it and my brothers, and I live in it."

"Well, that's cool." Ted took another sip of his beer. "How many brothers do you have?"

"I have a younger twin brother and an older brother." Frey enjoyed talking to him. Their conversation flowed easily, and he seemed to genuinely want to get to know her. "How about you?"

"I have a sister, but she lives in Virginia with the rest of my family," Ted finished his beer. "It must be cool to live in a hotel. I've had to stay in several hotels during some insurance disasters when they've needed my help, but never long term."

"It is nice and convenient. Do you travel a lot?" Frey yawned.

Ted laughed. "Okay so either I'm boring you or you're exhausted."

"I'm sorry," Frey smiled at him. "It's not you. I haven't been sleeping well lately."

"I'm sorry to hear that. A beautiful girl like you shouldn't have anything to worry about." Ted winked at her.

Frey cringed. "Nice line, but a little cheesy."

"Sorry." Ted laughed. "I didn't mean it to come out like that. Anyway, to answer your question. No, I don't travel a lot. Maybe a couple times a month, but never for more than a few days." Ted pulled the napkin over, grabbed the pen, and wrote his phone number. "Here's my number. I'm not going out of town anytime soon. I would love to see you again."

"Thank you, Ted. I'll call you when things settle down," Frey said, not committing to a date.

"That would be great. I think we should say goodnight so you can try to get some sleep, and I should be going. Clearly, I have to practice my pickup lines."

Frey laughed with him.

"I have an early morning meeting and it's way past my bedtime." Ted smiled and lifted his hand to get Carl's attention.

"Can I have the bill for myself and the lady?" Ted asked Carl.

"I'll give you your bill, but the lady is free," Carl smiled and went to the register to ring him up.

"Free, huh? Perks of working and living here, I take it." Ted took out his wallet to pay his bill.

"Yup," Frey nodded.

Carl gave him his bill and took his credit card to ring him out.

"So, since you live here, can I at least walk you to your door?"

"Not to my door, but you could walk me to the elevator?" Even though he seemed nice, no one was walking her to her door.

"Elevator it is," Ted signed the bill and gave Carl his tip. "After you."

Ted placed his hand on Frey's lower back and guided her downstairs and toward the elevator in the lobby. His hand has a more tentative light touch as opposed to Holt's earlier tonight. Holt always spread his hand wide and rubbed her back when he guides her. *Stop it Frey!* She yelled at herself, needing to stop comparing everything to Holt.

"Well goodnight, Frey. It was a pleasure playing at your table, although I lost more than I won." Ted laughed. "But it was all worth it because I got to know you better. Call me when things settle down."

"I will." Frey smiled at him. "Have a good night."

"Goodnight." Ted leaned in and gave her a quick peck on the cheek before he turned and walked away.

Frey was glad her mom didn't see that kiss. Not that it was particularly passionate, but any kiss would have been cause for an inquisition. Sehoy would question her until morning, and Frey was tired. After having a few days off, her feet were killing her. Unfortunately, she saw Holt heading toward her and he looked angry.

Chapter 7

Oh, Hell No!

Frey

"**W**hat the fuck was that?" Holt grabbed her arm above her elbow.

"Lower your voice." Frey pulled her arm away from him, grabbed her key card from her bra, and placed it on the elevator scanner. "I don't need the whole resort knowing my business."

"Fine, we'll discuss this in your room," Holt followed her into the elevator.

"Don't you still have to work?" Frey slammed her finger on the family floor button. *Why was he so fucking angry?*

"No, I finished when you did and had the privilege of watching you flirt with that guy over drinks. Are you crazy? After what happened to Tori?"

"You asshole!" Frey stepped out of the elevator as soon as the doors opened. "You know I'm still freaked out about that."

"Then how can you go with some stranger?"

"I only went upstairs. It's not like I left the premises. Besides, Carl was making my drink and I trust him." Frey opened her door and tried to close it in Holt's face, but he placed his foot in the doorway and shoved the door open.

"Are you going to see him again?" Holt stepped into her room and shut her door. "I'm assuming he gave you his number on that fucking napkin." Holt pointed to the napkin in Frey's hand.

"That is none of your business, Holt. I will not beg you to date or fuck me again. I stay out of your business, so you need to stay out of mine."

That day was imprinted in Frey's mind as one of the lowest moments of her life. She'd finally gotten the courage to seduce Holt, and he'd acted like an asshole.

Frey's crush on Holt had grown exponentially since high school. Holt had grown well over six feet, muscular, short brown hair longer at the top, dark smoky blue eyes, and he had a great smile. His full smile lit up his eyes, welcoming anyone to approach him, but his muscular physique said, 'Don't fuck with me'. He had a mesmerizing effect on any female who saw him.

Holt always treated her like a little sister. Although Frey gave him hints as to her feelings, he never got it. She decided tonight was the night to confess her attraction to Holt. She checked their schedules and saw they were both off work. A few days ago, Frey bought a see-through baby doll nightie that showed her breasts and a tiny thong, waiting for the right moment to put it on and go to Holt.

Every time Holt left with a girl, Frey wanted to stop him and let him know she liked him. Watching him wrap his arms around them was like a dagger to her heart. Tonight, she would put an end to his revolving door. Once Holt saw her as a woman and not a little sister, she knew he would fall for her and make love to her. She wanted Holt to be her first and last boyfriend ever.

Putting on her nightie empowered her to feel strong, confident, and sexy. For tonight, she applied mascara, a light blush on her cheeks, and some lip gloss. She turned around in her bathroom mirror to admire the results. Frey had long wavy dark brown hair to the middle of her back, sparkling dark brown eyes, a brilliant smile with rosy cheeks and high cheekbones. Everyone always told her she had a sweet, angelic face. She wasn't feeling very angelic in her baby doll see-through nightie.

After checking herself out, she walked to their connecting door. Years ago, when they were young, the Panther kids used Holt's room as their playroom, so they installed an adjoining sliding door from Frey's closet to Holt's closet.

Frey took a deep breath and slowly slid the door open, listening for any sounds. It was quiet and dark in the closet. She could see a dim light coming from his bedroom. Holt always left his closet door open in case she needed anything and tonight it had been closed. She should have stayed in her room, but hindsight was 20/20. Frey strode through Holt's closet and peaked into his bedroom. She'd assumed he was in bed, but he was sitting on the bed with his pants down to his ankles and his legs spread wide enough for the girl to be on her knees giving him a blow job.

Frey's stomach dropped as tears sprang to her eyes. Knowing Holt was with other girls was not the same as seeing it. She needed to step away and save her sanity, but she stood frozen in shock, staring at Holt's face.

Holt leaned back on his elbows and watched the girl between his knees. A small, disappointed sound escaped her lips, and she covered her mouth. She thought she had been quiet, but at that moment Holt's eyes snapped to her standing like a creeper in the closet. She watched him swallow and groan, but his eyes never left Frey while the girl sucked him off. Finally, he closed his eyes and moaned his release. Frey quickly turned around and ran back into her room.

Shit, shit, shit, that was more than she bargained for. Holt had seen her and didn't stop. How could he do that to her? Now she knew where she stood in his life. Carrying a torch for someone who clearly didn't return your feelings sucked. Saving herself for him had been a big mistake. She would find some random guy and lose her virginity. It was obvious Holt wasn't interested in the job. It hurt her every time she wanted to talk to him, and she opened their connecting door only to hear a girl moaning in his bed. She needed to stop opening that fucking door when it was shut. This time she thought it was safe, since it was quiet. She had been so wrong...ugh. Her heart shattered. It was obvious he didn't want her if he could get a blow job from a girl while looking at her.

The least he could've done was ask the girl to pop off and come after her, but no, the asshole let the girl finish. Frey ripped her nightie off and put on her comfy pajamas, curled up in bed, and silently cried.

Holt came into her room before she fell asleep and tried to talk to her, but she didn't want to hear anything he had to say.

"Frey?" Holt walked up to her bed. Frey was lying in bed, facing away from him. "Why did you come into my room without announcing yourself like we always do?"

"I didn't hear any noise, so I thought you were asleep. I guess I was wrong."

"What did you need? Are you okay?" Frey felt the bed dip, and he touched her shoulder.

"Yeah, I'm fine," Frey shrugged her shoulder. "Please go away."

"Frey, I think we need to talk," Frey stiffened at Holt's words. "Please roll over and talk to me." Holt massaged her shoulder with his hand.

"There's nothing to talk about," Frey shrugged her shoulders, pulling away from his touch. She wiped her face. "Don't touch me. Please go."

"I'm not leaving until you talk to me, Frey." Holt let out a frustrated breath as his hand dropped from her shoulder to the bed. "Shit, you were standing in my closet looking sexy as hell. You looked so fucking beautiful, but we can't go there. Barrett would not like it, and I can't alienate my best friend and family. I know you've had a crush on me, but I just can't. Didn't I shut the fucking door?"

"I know you've had a crush on me too, jerkface." Frey couldn't believe he was admitting to being attracted to her. Since when did he know she had a crush on him? Refusing to admit the door was shut, she spun around, ready for a fight. "You're a coward. I could be the best thing that has ever happened to you, but you won't even give us a chance. You'd rather fuck around with every girl who hits on you. I hate you."

Then Holt got mean with his verbal attack. Words she would never forget.

"I can't be with you, sweetheart. You need to look elsewhere because this" –Holt pointed between the two of them– "will never happen. Besides, you're not my type." Holt internally winced right after he said that.

"You're an asshole!" Frey yelled at him. "We both know you fuck anything with a pussy."

"Yeah, well, this asshole is not fucking your pussy."

"Get the fuck out of my room! You pretend to be so nice, but deep down, you are just like every other jackass fuck boy." Frey bolted out of the bed and continually shoved Holt back to his room and pulled the sliding door shut that connected their rooms.

Frey glared at Holt, the memories swimming in her eyes as she waited for his response.

"You never begged me to fuck you, so you can't say that to me." Holt crossed his arms.

"No? What about a few months ago when I was in your closet practically naked, and you couldn't stop your fabulous blow job? Pretty sure I wanted you to fuck me. I think my actions made it obvious." Frey wondered how he was going to explain himself now.

Chapter 8

Surprise!

Holt

S hit, he knew he was acting irrationally, but Frey was pushing his patience. Didn't she realize that guy could hurt her just like Winston hurt Tori? *Did Frey still have a crush on him? Did she still want to fuck him?* He thought she had gotten over him after that night. He knew he'd broken her heart and severed their relationship. *By bringing that up now, it was obvious she was still hurt and yet; she was going on a date with another man? What the fuck?*

Over the years, he knew she dated, and he always ignored it. Thinking back, he probably ignored it because she never brought anyone to Sunday Brunch to meet the family. No one was special to her. Why was he so livid about it now? Fuck! Everything changed after that fucking night. He'd sunk to a new low with the ugly things he said to her. That was months ago. They were back to being friendly. Not like best friends, but they weren't enemies. He wanted to tell her the truth about why he'd stayed away from her all these years and beg for her forgiveness for his behavior that night. But he'd made a promise to his best friend back in high school and brothers didn't break promises.

"Well," Frey snapped at him, bringing him back from his thoughts. "Are you going to deny what happened?" Frey stood, arms crossed, tapping her foot on the floor.

"Fine, you're driving me fucking crazy. You want me to fuck you? Take off your clothes and get in the bed." Dammit, she was going to be the death of him. He'd fought his feelings for so long. He was tired and just wanted to sink into her so he could feel some joy for once. To have something that was his, if even just this one time.

Holt was sure he crossed the line until Frey stared into his eyes and undid her pants, letting them drop to the floor, stepping out of them and kicking them off to the side. Shit, he was not expecting her to do that. He watched as she dared him to walk away. She unbuttoned her shirt one button at a time, slow as fuck. Holt was finding it hard to swallow.

Frey took off her shirt and threw it on the floor. She smirked at him right before she turned around and undid her bra, tossing it over her shoulder. *Fuck Me!* Holt couldn't stop himself from following her into the bedroom. It was like an invisible rope pulling him toward her. He was salivating just from watching her ass sway from side to side in her thong. Damn, her legs were long and sexy in those heels.

Upon entering the bedroom, his nostrils flared when he saw her sweep her tongue over her lips. She was sitting on the end of the bed with her legs wide open. Daring him to come closer, she leaned back on her elbows and stared at him with her pupils dilated. She looked like every man's vision of a wet dream pin-up girl. She was exquisite.

"Keep the heels on," he mumbled, watching her every move.

"What about the thong?" Frey slipped her thumb under the sides and stretched the band away from her hips.

"I'll take care of that." Holt leaned over her as he slowly took off her thong. Enjoying every moment of unveiling his dessert, he was panting by the time he tossed her thong on the floor. His cock was hard as a rock and trying to break free of his pants. "If you want this, scoot back on the bed and spread your legs wide for me," Holt whispered.

Frey followed directions, which made Holt even harder, if that was even possible. He was behaving like a dominant alpha male, and she was bringing him down to his knees with her submissive behavior.

"Cup your breasts." Holt wasn't sure she would do it, but to his surprise, she followed directions like a good little girl. "Now, tweak your nipples." He heard her sharp breath intake. "Take one of your fingers into your mouth and wet it with your saliva, then rub it all over your areolas. I want them glistening when I suck them into my mouth." With her nipples now nice and wet for him, Holt leaned down and sucked them one at a time into his mouth.

"Mm," Holt lifted his head and gazed into her eyes. "Take your hand and slide your finger into that sweet pussy while I play with my girls."

"Oh my God, Holt." Frey gripped the sheets.

Holt loved finally being able to see Frey's breasts. He'd dreamed about them since he saw them through her sheer nightie that night. They were the perfect size for his hands. He enjoyed rolling his tongue around her nipple, then sucked them hard while she writhed beneath him.

"Now, put your hands above your head and leave them there. I'm gonna drive you so crazy, you won't think about any other man but me. You are gonna come so hard you might even pass out."

Holt watched Frey's eyes widen, but she listened to every word he said. She slowly raised her arms up and gripped the pillow.

"Holt," Frey whispered, "there's something I need to tell you."

"Not now, sweetheart. The time for talking is over." Holt crawled down her body and slid his hands under her smooth, firm ass, lifting her glistening pussy up to his mouth. "Unless you want to tell me to stop?" He peered at her from between her legs, waiting for her answer.

"I don't want you to stop," Frey muttered.

Holt stared into her eyes, making sure she was okay with him eating her out. Frey nodded and Holt latched onto her pussy. Licking and sucking her clit, with no mercy, until he heard her scream her first orgasm. She tasted sweet with a hint of spice, just like her personality. Now let's see how many more he could wring out of her before she passed out.

This might be the only chance he had to imprint himself in her memories forever. He knew he was acting like a caveman, but damn, she was so fucking beautiful and tasted so good. He just couldn't stop. Frey squirmed and tried to move away. Holt was not having any of that. He didn't want a to-go meal—he wanted to savor a buffet. Moving one hand off her ass, he placed it on her belly and held her down, continuing to lap her come and suck her clit.

Holt was now on a mission to see how responsive her breasts were to his attention. His hand on her belly slid up and cupped her breast. His thumb and pointer finger rolled, tweaked, and squeezed her nipple. And holy shit, she came again into his mouth. Her body tightened as she screamed out to a higher power. Once her orgasm passed, he licked his way up her body to her beautiful breasts, suckling them while he slipped a finger into her pussy.

"One more sweetheart," Holt murmured around her areola.

"Holt," Frey's body was shaking. "I can't."

"Yes, you can. Fuck my fingers now, Frey." Holt stared into her eyes as he slipped another finger and curled them inside her.

That was all it took for Frey to move against his hand like she couldn't get enough. It was a beautiful sight to see her fucking his hand. Holt found her special spot and continued to rub it until she lost control for a third time. This time Holt covered her mouth with his and swallowed her scream. Frey's hands gripped the pillow under her head.

"My turn, sweetheart." Holt got up off Frey and stripped out of his clothes. He had waited long enough to have her, and he wasn't waiting anymore. Lying on top of Frey, he positioned his cock at her entrance between her legs.

"Slide me in, sweetheart, bring me home," Holt said between kisses to her neck.

Frey reached down and grabbed his cock, pumping it a few times before guiding him into her pussy. Holt's self-control broke, and he rammed inside her. Frey screamed out in pain.

"Shit, Frey!" Holt froze and looked up into her eyes. "Was there something you should have told me?" He'd felt a barrier when he pushed through, but he'd gone so fast by the time his head registered what was happening he'd already broken through.

"I tried." Tears streaked out of her eyes. "You didn't want to talk."

"Shit, fuck!" Holt hollered and made a move to get off her, but Frey tightened her legs around his waist and wrapped her arms around his neck. Holt dropped his head into her neck. She was a virgin. He'd taken something from her she'd never given anyone else before. He knew most girls treasured their virginity. Never in his wildest dreams had he imagined taking it from her. Okay, maybe had they dated in high school it would've happened, but not now? Hell, he'd seen her date other guys, and she was twenty-five. *Who was still a virgin at twenty-five?* Someone who wasn't a man whore like him, he supposed. Holt lifted his head and glared at her. He was furious with himself—not with her.

"Don't you dare stop now, Holt Adams! I've waited forever for this. Don't deny me this moment. Just give me a minute." Frey glared at him while she caught her breath.

"I will not fuck you in anger," Holt said through gritted teeth, bracing his hands on the bed beside her head, lifting his upper body off her and attempting to break out of her hold on his neck

"No, you won't. You will get over yourself and realize I wanted you to be my first." Frey's anger dissipated and tears formed in her eyes. "I trust you," she whispered. "Please do this for me."

Holt's eyes searched her face for any signs of deception. There weren't any. If anything, she was going to get upset if he didn't give her what she wanted. "I'm not angry at you being a virgin. Fuck! I'm glad I'm your first," Holt sighed and dropped his head onto her neck. She smelled like lavender mixed with her natural Frey aroma. *God, he loved that scent.* "What I meant was that I don't want to fuck you when I'm angry about you going out with someone else."

"Please finish what you started, Holt. You can't go back, so make it good for me now." Frey ran her fingers through the back of his hair.

"Fuck, sweetheart. I would have been gentler with you. I would've gone slower." Holt didn't know what to do. *Was he an asshole if he continued? But if he didn't, she just might hate him for the rest of his life. Fuck! He would be gentle now and go slow to ease her back into the mood and give her the best orgasm he could.* Holt withdrew slowly, leaving the end of his cock barely inside as he sucked and played with her nipples. Frey bucked her pelvis against his, attempting to slide him back into her body. Holt pulled back and ran his hand down her body to play with her clit. The wetter she was, the easier it would be to take him with as little pain as possible.

Frey grabbed the back of his hair and yanked his head back, staring into his eyes. "I don't want you to be gentle. You're not my boyfriend. Now fuck me and finish it."

"Dammit, Frey, is that what you want?" He glared at her.

"Yes."

Holt didn't break eye contact as he moved inside of her. Slowly at first, he wanted her first time to end well and didn't want to ram into her like he had before. She needed to adjust to his girth. He tried to show her with his body how much she meant to him, but Frey wouldn't have that and moved against him, encouraging him to go faster and harder.

"Holt, stop holding back and fuck me, dammit!"

That did it. If she wanted him to fuck her, he would fuck her. He'd tried to be nice, but she was pissing him off all over again. Holt pulled out and rolled her onto her stomach.

"On your knees, Frey," Holt commanded right before he slammed into her. He was fucking her so hard they kept sliding up the bed. Not wanting her to get away from him, he gripped her hips with one hand, and he wrapped his other hand around her hair, holding her in place. Fuck, he wasn't gonna last long, and he wanted, no, needed, her to come one more time. The hand that held her hair was now firmly pushing her chest onto the bed. While his other hand released her hip and reached around to her pussy, pinching her clit. Frey exploded onto his cock as she screamed into the pillow. Holt couldn't hold it in any longer and exploded inside her. Draining himself dry, he fell on top of her, but quickly rolled sideways, still holding her back against his chest.

Chapter 9

Friends with Benefits...Yeah, No!

Holt

"**S**hit, that was incredible." Holt had never felt like that before. He held her in his arms while his racing heart slowed to a normal rate.

"Uh huh, I think you fucked me dumb." Frey lay limp in his arms.

"Sweetheart" –Holt smirked– "you could never be dumb. Stay here, just like this. I'll be right back."

Getting off the bed, Holt walked into the bathroom to get a washcloth. It being her first time—he knew there was some clean-up to do. Not to mention, a warm cloth might make her pussy feel good after he'd ravished it. Even though he got rougher with her, he was still aware of her reactions, so he wouldn't hurt her. He rolled her onto her back and applied the warm washcloth to her pussy.

"I can't do it again. I'm too tired." Frey yawned.

"We are not doing it again," Holt chuckled. "Although, I could rise to the occasion because you look so beautiful laying there spread open for me. But I think you're probably sore, since that was your first time."

"Okay," Frey mumbled sleepily. "I'm liking you being my friend with benefits."

"We have to keep this between the two of us." Holt finished cleaning her up and threw the washcloth toward the bathroom. "We can't tell anyone that we're friends with benefits."

"Why not?" Freya turned toward him, a deep frown on her face.

"Ah, because Barrett will flip his lid." Holt pulled the covers up around them and pressed her back against his chest. *Is that what they were now friends with benefits? Barrett would kick his ass if he thought Holt was using Frey.* They would have to talk about this. Frey was not just another lay. He didn't want to be her friend with benefits. He wanted to be her boyfriend, but he needed to talk to Barrett first.

"It's none of his business," Freya yawned and tucked further back into Holt's embrace.

"You're his sister. He loves you." Holt raised his head next to Frey and whispered in her ear. "He just wants to protect you." Giving her a quick kiss on her cheek before he tucked her head under his chin. Her magnolia scented shampoo floated up to him with every breath he took. Frey always smelled like some type of flower. The scent calmed his mind and made him feel like he was home.

"I know." Frey mumbled.

"Why do you have a chair under that door?" Holt squeezed Frey to get her attention before she fell asleep. He'd noticed the door when he followed Frey into her room, but he'd been busy focusing on her. Now seemed like the right time to ask.

"I don't want to talk about it. I just want to sleep." Frey yawned.

"Did you put it there because you're scared of Winston coming from Tori's room?" Holt wanted her to answer him so he could reassure her he would protect her.

"Yeah." Frey sighed. "But I feel better now that you're here."

"I won't let him come anywhere near you. I promise to protect you." Holt kissed her neck and held her close.

"I wish you had told me about being a virgin," Holt whispered. After a few minutes of her not saying anything, he realized she was asleep. "But I guess I understand."

Holt couldn't sleep. He was too busy replaying everything that had happened, trying to figure out how he ended up taking his best friend's sister's virginity and then telling her to keep it a secret. It all started when that asshole grabbed her ass. Anger rose inside of him like a wave crashing to the shore. His overprotective instincts kicked in, and he stormed to her before the guy could hurt her. He wanted to beat the shit out of him, but he didn't want to attract attention and embarrass Frey any further. All he could do was throw him out. He would keep an eye out for him in the future.

Then, when everything calmed down at Frey's table. Holt thought he was in the clear, but he'd been wrong, very wrong, because one man at her table went with her upstairs for a drink. Holt was livid. Why was she going up there with him instead of going to bed after her shift? This guy was a stranger she met at her table? Was she insane?

Holt finished his shift upstairs while he watched Frey and the guy at the bar. He almost lost it when he saw the guy give her his number. What the fuck? *Who was this guy and why was Frey talking to him?* Holt stayed close to them because he wouldn't be able to live with himself if anything happened to her. Frey wasn't a one-night stand type of girl, but what if she made an exception for this asshole?

After having their drink, they left, and Holt followed them out of the casino. It gutted him to watch the guy kiss her cheek by the elevator. He knew he didn't have a say in Frey's dates, but he'd become accustomed to seeing her single. Then the guy left, and Holt felt like he could breathe again.

Holt ran up to her without thinking about picking a fight. One thing led to another and now he was staring down at his perfect girl, all worn out and sleeping soundly in his arms.

Holt was glad one of them had been fucked into oblivion, because he wasn't gonna be able to sleep the rest of the night. He was so screwed. He couldn't go back to being friends now, and he still had to keep it from Barrett. What the hell was it she said about friends with benefits? Fuck! What had he done? He would have to talk to her in the morning and let her know they had to stay quiet about what happened until he could figure out a way to talk to Barrett because of that fucking promise.

To this day, Holt couldn't believe he made it. He wasn't totally clueless. He knew Frey was flirting with him when she stood close to him, brushing her hand on his arm or twirling her long hair between her fingers. She always gazed at him with stars in her eyes and he loved it, but he wanted Barrett's approval. God knows his mother never asked for his approval of her conquests. Holt wasn't even an afterthought. If there was one thing his mother had done for him, it was to be a model for what *not* to do. He'd vowed a long time ago not to be anything like her.

Plus, he remembered the night Frey appeared in his closet while Candy had his cock in her mouth. That had been a clusterfuck. In a matter of minutes, he'd lost any chance with the girl he'd been obsessing over for years and one of his best friends. Holt remembered that day as if it was yesterday. How could you forget the dumbest thing you've ever done?

Holt was getting head from some chick that came onto him while he was downstairs eating dinner at RUSH. He could never have the girl of his dreams because she was family, so he went through girls like underwear, always trying to erase Frey from his mind.

He was trying to get into what was happening below his waist, but the girl wasn't very good. He opened his eyes and looked down, ready to tell her to stop, when he heard a low cry coming from his closet. Holy shit. *Frey stood in the closet in a tiny see-through nightie, staring at him. He could see the hurt in her eyes. Holt wanted to go to her, but knew Barrett would beat the shit out of him, so he stayed put. Unfortunately for the girl sucking his cock, he grew harder in her mouth, almost gagging her. Frey's nipples were hard as a rock as she watched.*

Holt knew he should stop, but he was now picturing Frey sucking him off and he was too far gone. At that point, Frey turned around and ran into her room while he shot his load into the girl's mouth.

Leaning his head back, he took some deep breaths and slowly pushed the girl away from his softening cock.

"Darlin','" he called her because he couldn't remember her name, "thank you, but it's time for you to go."

"What?" she cried out. "What about me?"

"I'm sorry," Holt pretended to look at his watch. "I forgot I have to go back to work tonight."

"What time do you get off?" she whined. "I can wait for you here. Naked and in your bed."

"As great as that sounds, I don't have a specific time. Shit goes wrong all the time, and I don't have a set schedule." Holt stood and pulled his pants back up, helping her get up from her knees. "Why don't you give me your number and I'll call you when I get a day off?"

"Yeah right." The girl harrumphed. "Never mind. I'll go find someone else who has time for me. You don't know what you're missing. You'll regret this. No

one treats Candy like trash. Asshole. The least you could have done was satisfy me before I left."

"I'm sorry," Holt said again while she continued to call him many shitty names and talked about herself in the third person. Who does that? Holt tried to tune her out as he walked her out of his room. He wanted to make sure she got on the elevator, so he followed her and pressed the down button when she got in.

"Fucking asshole," was Candy's parting remark just before the elevator doors closed. Shit, now he really needed to go talk to Frey and make sure she was okay. Hell, he wasn't. He had slept with a lot of women, but never felt like a bigger dick as when Frey watched him get blown. Holt walked back into his room and carefully slid open the closet door.

"Frey," Holt whispered. As he walked closer to the bed, he saw Frey curled up in a fetal position, crying. He felt as if someone had ripped his heart out. This was torture. Maybe if he talked to her and explained everything, they could sort things out. They could start out by dating. He struggled between his secret love for the girl and the promise he made to his best friend.

He thinks about all his mom and dad's broken promises. His father called him trash, and he'd been acting like it. Frey was a bright light in his dim life. Why would he want to drag her down to his level? He would never amount to anything, and she deserved so much better than him. If she knew all the sordid thoughts he'd had seeing her in that nightie in his closet, she'd slap the shit out of him and run far away from him.

The only way out was to get Frey pissed off at him, so she would really hate him and stop flirting with him. He had to do this right and be convincing, no matter how much it hurt him. Holt knew he was being arrogant, and cruel, but his mouth continued to vomit things he didn't mean. Holt couldn't believe the words coming out of his mouth. He was acting like a dickhead.

Frey had been livid as she shoved at his chest—understandably so—and even though it had been his plan all along, his heart shattered with every push. But he needed to allow her to get angry with him, so he stepped back every time she smacked his chest. When he entered his closet, she pulled the door shut in his face. He stood there, staring at the door, and listened to her cry on the other side. He'd never hated himself more.

Holt still hated himself now for what he did and said to her that night. He'd have to talk to Barrett and fight for Frey. He was tired of ignoring his feelings for her. Because no matter how many girls he slept with, he always wished they were Frey. His feelings for her never changed, even though he tried to deny them. She made him want to be a better man.

Maybe he could ease Barrett into accepting them as a couple, starting with only holding hands in front of him and not being all over each other. After all, Barrett knew Holt had been celibate for the past few months. He had told Barrett well before today he was tired of all the girls coming onto him. He was ready to settle down. Barrett didn't believe him, but over time, Barrett would come around.

Armed with a plan to get his girl and keep his best friend—he felt better. Being Frey's first meant he needed to protect her. She had given him a special part of herself, and it humbled him. He wanted to be her first and last. No other man was going to touch her like he did. What they'd just shared was so much more than just sex. Their passion and sexual chemistry were off the charts. Now that he'd had her, he wasn't going to let her go. He would convince her to give them a shot and not be "friends with benefits". That shit was not acceptable.

Chapter 10

FUBAR

Holt

He woke up before Frey and smiled as he tilted his head down to see her sleeping peacefully. Frey held him like she would a body pillow with her head on his chest, one leg draped between his, and her arm wrapped around his waist. Holt would be her pillow anytime she wanted.

Waking up like this felt like heaven. Taking a deep breath, he laid his head back on the pillow and closed his eyes. He didn't want to disturb her. Suddenly, he heard a sound coming from his room and his head snapped up. Terrified that it might be Barrett, he carefully untangled Frey from his body and slid a pillow under her arm. He didn't want to wake her, but he had to make sure Barrett didn't catch them. After the pillow was in place, he jumped out of Frey's bed, pulled on his pants, darted through their closets, and froze when he spotted Candy in his bedroom.

"Uh, what are you doing here?" Holt looked around to see if she was alone. How the hell had she gotten into his room? Shit, he needed to get rid of her before Frey saw her.

"I came to see you, baby," Candy sashayed to Holt and threw her arms around his neck.

"Why?" Holt reached up behind his neck to pull her arms off him. *He hadn't seen her in several months. Why now when things were getting better with Frey?*

"Don't be like that, baby. I brought you breakfast." Candy nodded to the living room, where Holt saw a paper bag with two coffees sitting on his table.

"I'm not hungry." Holt looked back toward the closet. "I think you should leave."

Candy pouted when he removed her arms. Thinking it was over, Holt tried to push her out of his room. She surprised him by undoing the tie on her wraparound dress and letting it drop to the floor. Shit, she was naked. Holt knew he had to get her out of his room before Frey woke up and came looking for him.

Holt attempted to push Candy away by placing his arms at her sides, but she kept leaning into him, trying to press her breasts against his chest. He could've shoved her away, but he didn't want to hurt her like he'd seen so many of Betty's men hurt him and his mom. Holt vowed to himself that when he grew up, he would never behave like a coward and pick on women and children when dealing with any situations. He released her arms and took a step back.

To his surprise, she grabbed his crotch. Holt was ready to set her straight, but Candy seized the opportunity and jumped on him, placing her arms tightly around his neck while her legs wrapped around his waist. She was clinging to him like a koala bear in a tree. *What the hell?*

Shocked, he grabbed her hips ready to pull her off. Opening his mouth to ask her what the fuck she was doing, she pushed her tongue into his mouth. *Fucking shit, what was wrong with this girl? Could she not take a hint?* He guessed he had to stop being Mr. Nice Guy and get her the fuck away from him.

With her body pressed against him, Holt had been hard from sleeping next to Frey, but Candy probably thought it was from seeing her. He had to get Candy out of his room before Frey saw her or he'd be screwed and anything Holt wanted to build with Frey would blow up in his face.

Frey

Frey hadn't slept that well in a long time. As she straightened her arms and legs in a full body stretch, she reveled in the slight ache from a night of being well loved. It wasn't a painful ache, but a throbbing one. An ache that wanted some attention from her sexy man. Who knew all she needed was to be fucked by Holt to get a good night's sleep? Feeling fully awake and ready for round two, she reached out next to her and felt an empty bed. Not a hunky man. Ugh, I guess he woke up first. Maybe he's in the bathroom. Frey dragged herself out of bed and walked into the bathroom. He wasn't there, but as she relieved her bladder. Hearing noises coming from his room, she put on her robe.

Frey walked through her closet to Holt's and froze. Motherfucker! Holt was in his room kissing that blow job bitch from a few months ago. *What the hell? Had they been seeing each other all this time? Was she the other woman?* Shocked, Frey covered her mouth and backed up before Holt saw her. Tears of anger and despair ran down her face as she stumbled back into her room. She was so stupid to think that what happened had meant anything to him.

She knew he had been with other girls. Dreaming about him all these years was nothing like what they shared in bed. She had not been prepared for all the feelings he stirred up in her and said they could be 'Friends with Benefits' so she could eventually convince make him fall in love with her. In her mind, they would keep fucking until he developed feelings for her. They would be exclusive, marry, have kids, and live happily ever after. A fantasy she'd had since she met him in elementary school. Unfortunately, he must have believed her friends with benefit idea and thought he was a free agent leaving her to go back to that girl.

How could he do that? He'd been so good to her last night. She thought he was finally coming around to seeing her as a woman and maybe loving her. After witnessing the scene in his room, anger took over and, in that moment, she decided to stop putting her future on hold, waiting for Holt. Clearly, he wasn't worth it. What an asshole! Not having her virginity hanging over her head as a barrier, she would find a man worthy of her. Frey remembered she still had Ted's number, and he seemed like a nice guy. She should give him a chance.

Frey stripped her bed of the soiled sheets and put them in a trash bag. Seeing some of Holt's clothes on the floor, she gathered them and threw them in the trash bag, too. Fucking cheater! She would throw him away in the trash bag too, if she could. A trip to the hardware store was in her near future to find a lock to attach to the sliding adjoining door. Because she would not let Holt use it to enter her room anymore. Damn man whore!

She got dressed in a pair of shorts and t-shirt, grabbed her keys, threw the trash bag over her shoulder, and stormed out of her room. The hardest part was avoiding her mom in the lobby. As she crept out of the elevator, she looked around, making sure not to run into anyone in her family. When the coast was clear, she dashed out the side door, throwing the bag in the dumpster on her way to her car.

Holt

Holt withdrew her hand from his cock and used one hand to keep her at a distance, while he bent down to pick up her dress from the floor. He pushed the dress into her hands and guided her backwards into the living room.

"I think you should put that on before I open the door. There is nothing going on between us, Candy, and there never will be. Please do not come back. How did you get in here, anyway?"

"Barrett let me in. I told him we were dating." Candy put her dress on while her eyes shot daggers at him. "Why are you so mad?"

"I'll have to talk to Barrett," Holt murmured as he ran his hand down his face. "I don't want to hurt you, Candy, but I'm dating someone."

"What do you mean? Were you dating her when you let me suck your dick?" Candy was getting hysterical again and Holt had to get rid of her before Frey heard her.

"That was months ago!" Holt screamed. "Things have changed. I'm in love with someone else, so don't come up here again or look for me."

"Fine!" Candy stomped to the kitchen table, "but I'm taking breakfast with me. You don't deserve me or this food."

Candy forcefully pushed past him and slammed the door on the way out. Holt needed to talk to Barrett, but first he was going to check on Frey. Walking through his closet, he burst into her room. *Where was she? Did she hear Candy? Was she mad at him?* She couldn't possibly think he was fucking around with Candy after last night. Besides, she said they weren't serious. As he burst into her room, he noticed the sheets were stripped off the bed and she was not there. Fuck! He'd wanted to be there when she woke up. He would've helped her with the sheets. And where the hell were the rest of his clothes? Shit, that was his work shirt. Fuck, now he had to order a new one if he couldn't find it.

Candy's words would anger Frey if she heard them. He needed to find Frey and make her understand nothing had happened with Candy. *Would Frey believe him if he told her he didn't invite Candy to his room?* Holt took a shower, got dressed, and went in search of Frey. His stomach tied up in knots, thinking about what she might have seen or heard.

Frey

Frey drove to the hardware store for some retail therapy in the form of a lock for her door. Not knowing what she was looking for, she hoped someone there would have a suggestion for her.

Walking down the lock aisle, she quickly became overwhelmed with her choices. In her free time, she watched home improvement shows, but she'd never installed a lock or done any home improvement. But dammit, she was smart and could do anything she put her mind to. She saw a gentleman with a vest heading her way.

"Excuse me, sir," Frey spoke up as he got near her.

"Yes, ma'am. Can I help you?"

"Yes, I need to install a lock on a door, but I don't have experience doing it."

"Okay," the store clerk said, "is this for a door that leads to the outside or for a door inside the house?"

"I need to put a lock on a sliding door." *If that's even possible*, Frey thought.

"A glass door?" The man raised his eyebrow at her.

"No, sir. It is a sliding wooden door that leads from one room to another." Frey didn't want to get into too many details with a stranger. She was sure she already sounded crazy.

"You mean a pocket door? How about this?" The store clerk held up a packaged lock. "This is a chain lock and all you need to do is screw in these plates. One on the sliding door and the other on the wall or door frame. If you put it on the wall, make sure you find the stud, otherwise it won't be sturdy. Do you know what I mean by that?"

"I do," Frey nodded. "I'll take it. Where can I find a small power drill and a stud finder?"

"Follow me."

After Frey paid for her supplies, she headed back to the resort to fortify her door. She lucked out and didn't run into Holt. Laying all the supplies down in her closet, she got to work. Using the stud finder she had bought because she didn't want to explain anything to her dad or maintenance, she drilled the slider part to the wall, put the chain in, and then drilled the bracket with the other part of the chain to the closet door.

Perfect, she was so proud of herself. She cleaned up her trash and then laid in bed watching TV. She would've gone to find Tori, but Tori had gone to work with Alex.

Now that Holt was officially out of her life, Frey fished the napkin with Ted's number out of her trash can and placed it on her bedside table. Originally, she didn't think she would need it, but being rejected by Holt made her want to be with someone who would appreciate her. Ted found her attractive and had asked her for a date.

She would wait until she calmed down and then call him. Her date with him would have to be at the resort. She was still a little leery of strange men after Winston's actions with Tori. Laying down on the bed, she closed her eyes, took some deep breaths, and started binge-watching a home improvement show until she had to get ready for work.

Chapter 11

Locked Out

Holt

Unable to find Frey anywhere, Holt headed to the family security room to look for Barrett.

"Hey, asshole," Holt walked up to Barrett and slapped him on the back of the head.

"What the fuck?" Barrett bolted up from his chair. "What the hell is wrong with you? You should be happy after I sent you a morning gift."

"I didn't want that morning gift. I wanted..." Holt stopped himself before he got his ass kicked.

"You wanted what? Who wouldn't want a morning fuck?"

"I wanted a morning to myself. Shit, the last time I saw Candy was a few months ago when she sucked me off. I wasn't interested in a relationship with her then and I'm not interested now." Holt pointed his finger at Barrett's face. "Don't fucking let girls up into my room."

"Well, how the fuck was I supposed to know, Romeo? You usually tell me, but you haven't talked to me in a while about your conquests. She looked familiar, so I thought I was sending you a happy gift."

"She is not a gift I'd ever want. I haven't talked to you about 'my conquests' because I haven't had any." Holt lied right to his best friend's face. Could he dig a bigger hole for himself? What if Barrett found about his night with Frey?

"Fine, Mr. Celibate. You do you, man," Barrett laughed. "More girls for me."

"Have you seen Frey? Is she with Tori?" Holt knew Barrett wouldn't think anything of his question. They had all been taking turns hanging out with Tori because she was afraid to be alone.

"Nope, I haven't seen Frey. But I know she's not with Tori, because Tori went with Alex to work at the cultural center."

"Okay, cool. I'm sure I'll see her later." Holt didn't want to make a big deal out of finding Frey to Barrett.

"If I see her, do you want me to send her your way?" Barrett asked.

"Yeah, that'd be great. I'll see you later. I'm gonna put on some shorts and go work out."

"Maybe I'll see you there," Barrett sighed. "I haven't had my run yet."

"Sounds good."

Holt returned to his room and tried to slide the closet door open, hoping to find Frey there. What the fuck? Why was the door not opening? It only budged a little and then stopped.

"Frey, are you in there?" Holt knocked but heard nothing. So, he knocked louder. Still not hearing Frey on the other side, he began banging on the door.

"Frey!"

"What!" Frey screamed from the other side.

"Are you okay? Why is this door not opening?" Holt hollered through the door.

"Because I put a lock on it."

"And why would you do that?" Holt braced his hands on his waist.

"Because I don't want you in my room."

"What the fuck is going on?" Holt wanted to talk to her in person, not through some fucking door.

"You're an asshole Holt. Leave me alone."

"Frey, can you please open the door so we can talk about whatever is going on in that beautiful head of yours?" *What did she put on the door that he couldn't open it?*

"No, why don't you call your whore girlfriend and talk to her?" Holt heard her voice closer to the door. It sounded like she had walked into her closet to have this conversation.

"What are you talking about?" Holt ran his hand down his face. Shit, Frey must have seen or heard Candy.

"Don't play stupid with me." Holt heard her sniffling. *Oh shit, was she crying?* He tried to open the door again.

"Sweetheart, please open the door." Maybe if he spoke gently, he could get her to open the door. He knew Frey would shut down when she was angry.

"No. I gave you something special, and you threw it in my face. I'm done. The next man I fuck will be someone who can love me and not hide our relationship."

Frey was now full out crying. Holt banged his head on the door. He loved her; he just couldn't say anything yet until he could talk to Barrett.

"Frey, please open this damn door," he begged. "I didn't throw anything in your face, sweetheart. It was special for me too. Let me in so we can talk."

"If it had been special, you wouldn't want to hide our relationship. And you wouldn't have been with that slut just hours after me! I'm done!"

"What the hell are you talking about? Why are you so mad?" Holt threw his arms up, like she could see him. "You were the one that said we were just friends. I didn't think you'd want your brothers to know I was just fucking around with you." As soon as the words flew out, he knew he fucked up. Throwing that in her face was not the way to change her thinking about a relationship with him. *Why did he keep saying the wrong thing at every pivotal moment with her?*

"Ugh! You are such an asshole!" Yep, he fucked up.

"Sweetheart, you realize I can break down this door, right?" Holt was getting madder by the moment. His blood boiled faster with every word she said. He debated kicking the sliding door out of the track.

"Yes, but then you would have to explain to my parents and brothers why you did it."

Fuck her sassy answer. Well, she got him there. "I'd give them some bullshit answer that I thought you were in trouble."

"You'd lie to them?" Holt heard the surprise in her voice. "When they took you in and have provided for you all these years? You really are an asshole."

Holt stumbled back and placed his hand over his heart. Wow, direct hit. Holt couldn't believe she was throwing something like that in his face. That comment hurt more than anything she had ever said to him. He loved her parents. They were the only family he had that he could count on. These insults were getting out of control. He needed her to open the door so they could look at each other and discuss this like adults.

"Frey, open the damn door!" Holt was losing patience, and she was right. He wasn't about to break down the door unless it was an emergency.

"No."

"Frey?" Holt couldn't hear a peep coming out of her room. She must've left the closet. Well shit, he had to talk to her before their attitude continued into the workday and anyone noticed she was mad at him. That would cause a lot of questions he wasn't ready to answer. He grabbed his master key and left his room. He'd never used his key for this purpose, but he really needed to talk to Frey. Opening her front door, he walked in.

"Sweetheart?" Holt closed and locked the door behind him.

"Oh my God, did you just use your master key to get into my room?" Frey came flying into the living room from her bedroom with a napkin in her hand.

"No shit, Sherlock, I need to talk to you. Would you please stop screaming so everyone on this floor doesn't hear you?" Holt watched her pull her cell phone from her back pocket and type in the number on the napkin. *Was that the napkin with that guy's number? Oh, hell no!* "Who the hell are you calling? We need to talk. Please, put the phone down." Holt watched, waiting to see what she was doing.

Frey crumpled the napkin in one hand and threw it at him, aiming for his face while she held the phone up to her ear with her other hand. Holt caught the napkin before it hit him. Unraveling it, he saw a man's name and number scrawled on it. He saw red when he looked up at Frey. She was fighting dirty. He hadn't gone looking for Candy, but here Frey stood calling another man.

"Hang up the fucking phone," he growled.

"Hey, Ted, no I'm fine. It's my brother's best friend. Just ignore him. I called to let you know I would love to go out with you." Frey smirked at him.

Holt's eyes widened in shock as he watched Frey. He couldn't hear Ted's side of the conversation, but the part he could hear had blood surging to his face. Squeezing his hands into fists, he listened to Frey flirt with another man on the phone. Was she insane? Did she not see the steely glint in his eyes as he watched her? That look usually scared the piss out of people.

"Yes, I would love to go out with you on Saturday night." Frey stared at Holt with a snarky ass smirk.

Holt's nostrils flared, and he clenched his jaw. He was positive Frey could see the anger in his eyes.

"Frey, no," Holt snarled through clenched teeth. "Put down the damn phone." Holt pointed at the floor.

"Okay, great, I'll meet you downstairs. See you then, bye." Frey hung up the phone and glared at Holt.

"My woman will NOT be going out with another guy!" Holt yelled at her as soon as she clicked off.

"Well then, it's a good thing I'm not your woman. Friends with benefits, remember?" Frey spun around, but he was not letting her walk away.

Holt grabbed her wrist as she walked by him. "We are not friends with benefits. I just let you believe that because that's what you said you wanted. We will figure this out and tell your family when the time is right. You are mine and I'm yours. Call him back and cancel."

"No," Frey said, sounding disgusted. "You lied to me. Oh, and by the way, thank you for taking my virginity. Now I can fuck whoever I want without having to worry about telling them I'm a virgin. Now. Let. Me. Go." Frey enunciated every word and jerked her hand out of his grip. Barrett and Holt taught her well, enabling her to break free from a wrist hold, much to his chagrin. Frey angrily walked out of her room, leaving him standing in her foyer, absorbing the impact of her hurtful words.

Holt flinched. How had such a good morning gone so bad? He began the day with hopeful dreams, but it turned into a horrible nightmare. Except he wasn't asleep, and this was his new reality. Following her into the bedroom, he tried to explain what she saw.

"Look, by the way you're acting, you must have seen Candy in my room this morning, but you're blowing this all out of proportion. I haven't seen her in months. I didn't invite her. Barrett let her into my room. Fuck! I was with you all night when could I have possibly invited her?" Holt rubbed his face. "I got rid of her. Nothing happened. You're acting irrational." Holt placed his hands on his hips, facing Frey.

"I'm irrational!" Frey grabbed her pillow and threw it at him.

"Yes," Holt batted the pillow away. "Stop acting like a child. We need to talk about this like adults."

"Now I'm a child!" Frey threw her other pillow. "You fucking took my virginity. I'm obviously not a child, dickhead."

"Frey," Holt blocked the other pillow. "Stop. She means nothing to me."

"Well, you clearly mean something to her. She must love your dick because she came for more." Frey reached for another pillow and threw it.

"Frey, stop!" Holt caught it and threw it right back at her. *Shit,* he thought she would catch it like he did, but she looked so surprised when he threw it back that it smacked her in the face.

"I'm sorry." Holt stepped toward her. "Are you okay?"

"Get. Out." Frey growled through gritted teeth.

Maybe this wasn't the right time to talk about this. He would leave for now and talk to her later, after she had time to calm down.

"I'll go for now." Holt backed up. "But we will talk about this later and you will cancel that date."

Frey screamed, and Holt bolted out of the room. Holt knew he had to make this right, but he didn't know how or who to talk to. His family and friends were all part of Frey's family, leaving him with no one to confide in about this situation. He didn't have any siblings and hadn't spoken to his mom since high school, not that he would approach Betty after so many years for anything. The other security officers that he worked with were more acquaintances than friends. Although they spent time together, he needed to keep his situation with Frey a secret from them, because if they slipped up, Barrett would find out.

Going into his room, he gave Frey time to calm down. He'd discuss it with her tomorrow. By then, maybe they could talk like calm, rational adults instead of hurling insults and objects at each other. He had to talk some sense into her and stop her from going out with Ted. *How could she go out with a stranger when she still had a chair wedged under the doorknob?* He hated that she wouldn't listen to him and ran into Ted's arms. Frey would cancel that date if he had anything to say about it—she was his now and he didn't share.

Chapter 12

Time with Tori

Frey

Last night, Frey evaded Holt while working. Now it was time to relax with Tori and watch movies in Alex's room.

"Hey, BFF!" Frey said before she saw it was Alex opening the door.

"Hey Frey." Alex hugged her.

"Hey bro, where's my bestie?"

"Hi Frey." Tori came from the bedroom and smiled at Frey.

"Ready for another Girl's Night In Movie Day?" Frey walked up to Tori and grabbed her arm, dragging her to the couch. "Look, I even brought us some popcorn. She's in expert hands now. Alex, you can go do your thang."

Alex shook his head at Frey.

"I'm gonna see if Holt or Barrett can work from up here." Alex said from the kitchen.

"Sounds good. What do you want to watch, Tori?" Frey asked, turning on the TV and hoping it would be Barrett with them and not Holt.

"You pick. I'm good with anything." Tori sat next to Frey on the couch so they could share the popcorn.

"Baby, Holt is coming up here to work in the family security room. I'll be back as soon as I can." Alex bent down and kissed Tori. "Frey be good."

"Always," Frey smiled with popcorn between her teeth.

"Ladies, I'm here," Holt announced from the adjoining door to Barrett's room shortly after Alex walked out. "Let me know if you need anything. All the doors will be open."

"Thank you, Holt," Tori smiled at him.

"Yeah, thank you Holtie," Frey snickered.

"You're in rare form, Frey," Holt mumbled and walked away.

"Are you mad at Holt?" Tori raised an eyebrow at her.

"No." Frey waved her off. "We had a disagreement. No big deal." Frey put on an action movie. She wasn't in the mood for anything with romance in it.

Frey wasn't paying attention to the movie. What she really wanted to do was get Tori's advice on what had happened with Holt, but she wasn't sure how to start the conversation. How could she start the conversation? *"I was a virgin and Holt popped my cherry"*. *"Holt's an asshole because he screwed me and then cheated on me with his blow job slut."* *"Holt's a man whore and now I'm just another notch on his bedpost"*. *Ugh...what to say?*

Finally, the movie ended, and it was time to decide if Frey wanted Tori's advice. But first, she would make sure Tori was doing okay. Nothing like delaying her issues with Holt for a few more minutes.

"How are you doing? I heard Winston was outside the center today?"

"Yeah, the shelter boys saw him," Tori sighed. "I just want him to get caught so I can relax. No one is safe until he's caught."

"I agree. Not gonna lie. I've been feeling scared at night, even though I know our floor is secure," Frey whispered.

"I'm sorry, Frey." Tori sat up, facing her. "This is all my fault."

"No, it is not. It's that asshole's fault." Frey got up and sat next to Tori. "You did nothing wrong. I started it with that stupid bet."

"Aren't we a pair?" Tori smiled at Frey. "Here we are, both blaming ourselves when neither one of us did anything wrong. If any of this would have happened with a sane man, we wouldn't be in this situation."

"True," Frey sighed. "But then we wouldn't have been able to hang out as much as we have. I have truly loved every minute of our time together."

"Me too," Tori hugged Frey. "Now, what will we watch next?"

"Something funny, please." Frey handed the remote to Tori. She chickened out and decided it wasn't a good time to talk to Tori about Holt.

Tori selected a film that depicted the extreme measures a girl would take to make a guy break up with her in under two weeks. It was just what Frey needed. Maybe she would try some of those things to piss off Holt. So much for not wanting to watch a romance. Oh well, at least she got to watch a girl drive a guy crazy.

They stayed Holt-free until Alex came back home and snuggled on the couch with Tori to watch the next movie.

"Hey guys," Holt said from Barrett's doorway. "I'm not gonna be switching with Barrett. He's gonna keep walking the casino floor, and I'll stay up here. Frey, are you working tonight?"

"Nope," Frey hit pause on the movie. "Mom gave me the night off."

"Okay," Holt nodded. "If you guys need anything, come get me. Frey, can you come here for a minute?"

"Sure," Frey stood up and started the movie back up, placing the remote by Tori. "Just tell me what I miss."

Holt waited until Frey came to him. He stayed by the door, probably thinking if Alex and Tori could see them, he had a better chance of Frey staying calm for this conversation and not throw pillows at him.

"Frey," Holt whispered. "Please cancel your date tomorrow night. You don't even know that guy."

"Nope, I will not," Frey stood her ground. He wouldn't charm her and ruin her fun night. She was mad at Holt and her mind was all twisted between hating and loving him. They say it's a fine line between the two and at this moment a part of her felt vindictive and wanted to hurt him, like he hurt her. Maybe her date with Ted would turn out to be nothing and she could let him down easy. Only time would tell.

She knew she was being childish and immature, but she didn't give a damn. Holt shouldn't have asked her to keep their relationship a secret before he made out with Candy in his room. She understood Barrett let her in, but she was having a hard time getting over it.

"Then at least stay here. Don't go anywhere with him." Holt begged.

"I'm not stupid, Holt. Barrett is already running a background check on Ted. I'll be careful, especially after what happened to Tori. But I am going on a date with him, and I expect you to be civil to him. If you can't, then just ignore us. I'm fine with that."

"Dammit, Frey," Holt pleaded with his eyes. "I don't care about Candy. I told her to stay away from me. I also told Barrett not to let any other girls into my room. Please be reasonable. What we have is special." Holt placed his hands palms together in prayer form. "I'm begging you to please cancel your date so we can talk."

"Sorry, no can do." Frey crossed her arms and shook her head.

"Okay, I can see I'm not getting through to you," Holt sighed, hands on hips. His shoulders deflated in defeat. "Please be careful and don't go anywhere with him."

"Of course." Frey turned around and waved goodbye, going back into Alex's room. "See you later. I have a movie to finish."

She knew Holt wouldn't follow her and cause a scene in front of Alex because then he would have to explain himself and their relationship—something he seemed determined not to do.

"Okay," Frey said when she came back in and got under the cover on her couch. "What did I miss?"

"Uh, let's just rewind," Tori raised herself up, leaning on Alex's chest and rewound the movie. "I think it's best you see it." After Tori hit play, she laid back down on Alex.

Frey wished she could be lying on the couch with Holt, but he'd ruined that. Thinking about how to explain her situation to Ted while still enjoying their dinner at Savor, she realized she wasn't paying any attention to the movie. Frey glanced at Tori and noticed she was stroking Alex's chest. It was time to leave them alone for the night.

"I think I'm gonna turn in." Frey smirked at Tori. "I'll finish watching the movie another time. Have a good night."

"Okay," Tori said from behind her, "I'll talk to you tomorrow."

"Yup, I'm gonna close this door since Alex is home, but I'll leave Barrett's door open," Frey said as she gently pulled Alex's adjoining door closed. She snuck out of Barrett's room. The last thing she needed was another run in with Holt. If she was quiet, he wouldn't hear her from the security office next to Barrett's room, even with the door open.

Despite having the night off, she went downstairs to work because Alex was with Tori and Holt was upstairs. Being away from Holt was her primary goal at the moment. Plus, she loved her job. It'd be fun to surprise a coworker with a night off and see the joy on their face. They'd totally appreciate it.

Chapter 13

Horrible Parents

Holt

Holt enjoyed walking through the casino instead of watching the monitors upstairs. The nightlife at the casino energized him. Yet, being in the security room reminded him of his childhood when he, Barrett, and Frey were too young to be on the casino floor. They had spent hours watching the monitors and acting like they were interrogating the suspects. Every time they played, Frey would always pretend to be the dealer while one of them played the role of cop or robber in the casino. It's no surprise that Frey became a dealer while they became security officers.

Playing every day helped them become skilled at reading people's tells and catching cheaters. The security staff had trusted their tips to watch certain individuals even then, as they were often accurate. Those were the good old days, except for when he had to leave at night and go back to his mom's trailer.

Betty wasn't fond of her job and hardly earned sufficient income at the restaurant attached to the truck stop gas station. She only worked a couple of days, so she could still cash her welfare check. Despite working as a waitress at a restaurant, she never brought a full meal home for him—only her leftovers—and she expected him to be grateful.

On rare occasions, she would stock their kitchen with Ramen noodles, peanut butter, and bread, because those items were cheap. It helped that Holt could eat the free lunch at school. Along with her leftovers, she brought home various men. Many of whom were truckers coming in for a pit stop that wanted to do drugs, drink, and fuck her—not caring if her son was in the room.

Desperate to find someone to take care of her, Betty settled for a string of losers. The different men were a revolving door several times a week. Most of which would leave after she helped satisfy them, especially if they saw Holt. Holt had heard one of them say they didn't want to be saddled with a kid. To his horror, his mom replied that the kid helped her get government money.

Holt wondered if she met someone willing to take care of her, if she would run away with them and leave him behind. Working and taking care of him wasn't her first priority.

The night Betty took Holt away from his dad in New York, Holt had overheard his mom and dad yelling in the living room. He'd snuck out of his room and tiptoed to listen to what they were saying. Until then, he thought they were one happy family. He didn't know what caused them to fight a lot that week, but that last night was the worst.

"I don't give a shit about you or your bastard son," Holt's father, Jack, hollered at Betty before storming into the kitchen. "How many times do I need to tell you that?"

"He's your son," Betty screamed at Jack, grabbing his arm to stop him from leaving. "You need to take care of us."

"I don't need to do shit. I don't even know if he is my son." Jack ripped his arm out of her grip. "You spread your legs while you are married to me for the last time. I forgave you the first time, but never again. You're a whore, and I never want to see you again. Get the fuck out of my house and take your bastard son with you. Now!" Jack screamed in her face and pointed toward the front door.

Holt didn't know what a bastard was, but it sounded like a bad thing. Why was his dad yelling at his mom? What did he mean by spreading her legs? Was she doing a split? Was she in a gymnastics class? Whatever it was, he didn't want to leave his dad. When would he see him if they weren't living together?

"Daddy." Holt ran to his father. "Please, I don't want to go. I want to stay with you." Holt tried to latch onto his father's legs. His father always made time for him, helped with homework, taught him how to fish, and played games with him. Holt treasured those times. Jack pried his fingers off and shoved him back.

"I'm not your father. Your mother is a whoring piece of trash, making you bastard trash. I want you both out of my house." The words were bad enough, but seeing the hatred in his father's eyes cut deep and froze him to that spot in the living room. His life came crashing down around him.

"You'll regret this, Jack," Betty snarled before she took hold of Holt's arm and pulled him with her into her room to pack.

She pulled out two suitcases, giving one to Holt. "Don't be selfish and pack all your clothes and toys. You only need a couple of outfits and one toy. I need your suitcase to pack any items I can sell so we can eat once we get to Florida."

That night was the end of his peaceful childhood and the beginning of his horrible nightmare. Holt never saw his father again. After the divorce, Jack moved on, got remarried and started another family—totally forgetting about Holt.

When they lived in New York, Betty always gave him attention in front of his dad. However, when he wasn't home, she ignored him. Her favorite game to play was to leave him with a babysitter and tell him it was their little secret. He hated secrets, which was why he wanted just a little time to organize his thoughts and then talk to Barrett. He didn't want their relationship to be a dirty little secret.

After he and Betty moved to the trailer in Florida, Betty stopped pretending to be a mom because she didn't have to hide anything from Holt's dad anymore. She got the job at the truck stop but only worked minimal hours so she could still get welfare checks and meet men. Now not only was she high, drunk, or passed out on the couch, she was usually there with a scary man.

The men never stuck around for long, and some of them enjoyed using Holt as their punching bag. His mother never defended him. She only informed the men to not punch him in the face, while she continued with her drugs and alcohol. Their hits packed a solid punch and left bruises all over his body. If Holt screamed out in pain, begged his mom for help, or asked the men to stop, she would laugh at him. Holt remembered the punches hurting, but not as much as his mom's indifference to him getting a beating. That pain went straight to his heart and tore him up inside. *How could a mother let that happen to her only child? Did his dad know his mom was letting other men hit him?* One time, he tried to call his dad, but the recording said it had either been disconnected or was no longer in service. The only reason he knew his dad remarried was because his mom threw it in his face one day when she was high.

Holt heard Betty tell a man once not to hit him in the face because a neighbor or someone at school could turn her into the police and they would take him away. The last thing Betty wanted was the Department of Children and Families coming to the house. Holt later learned that Betty needed to keep him at home to get more money from the government. If the DCF put him in foster care, her welfare check amount would decrease.

Afraid of being alone, Holt always wore jeans and a long sleeve shirt or a hoodie over his t-shirt. If a teacher questioned him at school about his clothing or any bruises, he would shut down and refuse to talk about it.

He learned to avoid his mom and any of her current boyfriends. Catching his mom using drugs while scantily clad on the couch was not a situation he liked. Initially, he attempted to convince her to stop. After a few slaps and punches to his body at a young age, he realized he was better off just going to his room and leaving her alone to her vices. Holt felt lost and alone, not having someone he could trust. Going to school was his escape from his hellish home life. There he felt safe from angry men, drugs, alcohol, and even got a healthy meal to eat.

While talking to Barrett once, Holt slipped up and told Barrett that he normally went to bed hungry. He wasn't trying to complain, he just wanted Barrett to know how lucky he was to eat in a restaurant every night. The next day, Barrett gave Holt a loaf of bread and a jar of peanut butter. Holt was shocked and grateful. He wasn't looking for pity or handouts, but it was hard to turn down Barrett's gift. He'd never had a friend like Barrett. When Holt got home, he hid the items in his room away from his mom and her boyfriends.

Once Holt reached middle school, he stayed away from his house after school and got a ride with Barrett's mom to the resort. Frey, Barrett, and Holt would do their homework upstairs and then, if there was time, they would swim in the pool and eat dinner at RUSH, the casual dining restaurant in the resort. The Panther family ate for free since they ran the place and since Barrett's mom always said Holt was her fourth child, he also ate for free. Holt never went to bed hungry again.

Holt also asked Barrett if he could use their gym on the family floor to bulk up. He figured if he could get bigger and learn how to fight, he could protect himself from Betty's men. Barrett was okay with it because he and Alex always used it, and Holt was like a brother to them.

It's a good thing the casino was quiet because he'd spent almost an hour reminiscing about his childhood. He was barely paying attention to the monitors and tuned out the other security officer's conversations in his ear from the earpiece they all wore.

Chapter 14

The Night His Life Took a Turn for the Better

Holt

Leaning back in his chair, feet propped on the desk, and hands clasped behind his head, he continued going down memory lane.

When Mrs. Panther drove Holt home in the evenings, he always asked her to park a few trailers away so he could sneak in and avoid any confrontations. It didn't matter how far away Mrs. Panther parked, he always turned around before entering and watched her drive away. If he noticed an unfamiliar car or motorcycle in front of the trailer, he would make up an excuse about having to buy something at the gas station near his house and ask Mrs. Panther to drop him off there. As soon as he saw her car pull away, he'd walk home and crawl in through his bedroom window, avoiding the drug activity happening in his living room. Ignoring his mom and her men was his number one priority. Holt assumed Mrs. Panther knew about his mom and their situation, but she never mentioned it.

The less he saw his mom, the better his life was. Avoiding his mom wasn't too difficult because she was predictable. She either went to other men's houses for sex and drugs or passed out on the couch from the drugs she snorted or the alcohol she drank. The harder part was staying hidden from the fuckers her mom dated.

He often went to bed wishing he was part of Barrett's family and could live with them at the resort. The love and care that Barrett's family displayed were completely unfamiliar to him, but heartwarming.

The best day of his life had been when Sehoy and Osceola took him to his mom's and let her know they were taking custody of him. Not in the court system, but in every other way. He'd been suspended from school for fighting and was afraid to go home and spend his three-day suspension with Betty and her lovers, but Sehoy and Osceola saved him.

Whatever Sehoy had over Betty, he didn't know, but it worked. That was almost eight years ago and the last day he saw Betty. The Panthers not only provided him with shelter, but he never had to worry about being abused again. Holt stayed with Barrett in his room until they cleaned out the playroom and made it a bedroom for Holt like Barrett, Alex, and Frey's. He also got to enjoy complimentary meals, and had full use of all the amenities, except the casino, because of his age.

Holt remembered that first night when he crashed in Barrett's room.

"Are you going to be okay on the couch?" Barrett asked Holt when he got back from Betty's trailer with his things.

"Yeah." Holt laid down and put his hands behind his head. "Believe it or not, this couch is a hundred times more comfortable than the nasty mattress on my bedroom floor."

"Do you want to talk about it?" Barrett moved closer to Holt and sat on the edge of the couch. "Will you miss your mom?"

"No." Holt sighed and closed his eyes. "That makes me sound like an asshole. But she hasn't acted like a mom to me in a very long time."

"I'm sorry, man." Barrett looked down at his hands hanging between his parted legs. "That sucks."

"It does." Holt rubbed his eyes and stared at the ceiling. He wanted to tell someone about life with Betty, but he didn't need anyone's pity. Although Barrett never treated him any differently, even after he found out Holt lived in a trailer on the wrong side of the tracks. Not to mention all the times Barrett gave him food to take home. They were silent for a few minutes until Holt blurted out his childhood to Barrett, summarizing his life with Betty before and after the divorce.

"Wow." Barrett listened to everything Holt said without interruption. "I don't know what to say. I mean, I knew something was wrong, but I didn't know how horrible it was for you at home. I always wondered why you wore the same long sleeves and pants to school. Shitty friend that I am, it never occurred to me it was to cover up your bruises. I'm sorry. I wish you would have said something. Maybe me or my parents could've helped sooner."

"I don't think there's anything you could have done. Betty would never have let me go if I was younger." Holt smirked and looked at Barrett's confused look. "Less welfare money. Now she doesn't care since I'll be eighteen in a couple months."

"What a crappy mom." Holt pulled his legs up so Barrett could sit back on the couch.

"Yeah." Holt nodded. "You're lucky to have a great mom. I never had someone who cared about me before."

"Well, you do now." Barrett turned and faced him on the couch. "We're family. Brothers." Barrett put his fist out and Holt fist bumped him.

"Thanks, Barrett." Holt's eyes watered at Barrett's words. To hear Barrett tell him they were brothers got him all choked up. A sense of belonging he hadn't felt since he was a young boy playing with his father travelled throughout his body. He was finally home. Sometimes the family that chose you was better than the family that gave birth to you.

Holt never shared his story with anyone else in the Panther family. It was hard enough talking about it with Barrett since most of it was really upsetting and made him embarrassed.

He believed a foster home would be worse than his own house. Betty was always talking about kids getting sexually abused in foster homes and how he should be grateful to live with her. In Holt's mind, being physically abused was bad enough. Fear of being moved to a faraway foster home that was zoned for another school made him keep his mouth shut. He didn't want to lose his friendship with Barrett, Alex, and Frey, and their parents. It would have been unbearable to not be able to escape to the Panther's resort and hang out with them. It was his safe place. The Panthers had treated him like family since the first day he started hanging out at the resort after school to do homework with Barrett and Frey. It was the only place he felt like safe.

Holt owed so much to Sehoy and Osceola. They didn't technically adopt him, but that was how they made him feel. They always included him in family meetings and decisions as an equal participant—another one of their children. That was another reason he wanted to make sure when he dated Frey, it would be serious and not a one-night stand. He would be devastated if he did anything to let them down. Their disappointment in him would be a hundred times worse than Betty's behavior as a mom.

But shit, Frey was turning this into a one-night stand, and that's not what he wanted.

Chapter 15

Incident at Frey's Table

Holt

S peak of the devil. Holt froze when he saw Frey at her blackjack table on the monitors. Why the hell was she on the floor at her table? Frey had told him she wasn't working. Damn, he was really fucking this up if she was lying to him now.

Holt analyzed everyone around her, looking for threats, when he realized their old schoolyard bully, Dave, was at her table. Wow, he hadn't seen Dave since they graduated high school. As much as he hated Dave and Tami, his old girlfriend, for making Frey's high school years a living hell, the suspension Holt got from punching Dave had led to a better life for him with the Panthers. In a weird way, he was grateful to the bastard.

To make it worse for Frey, Dave was at the table gambling, and Candy was standing behind him. His body jolted when Candy rubbed her tits on his back. *Did they know each other? Was this a setup to hurt Frey? How did she figure out about them?*

Holt and all the security officers wore earpieces to talk to each other. It was easier than two-way radios where the guests could hear their conversations. Sometimes they bullshitted with each other, but once someone spoke something important, they all sprang into action. He'd been tuning out the joking in his ear, but now he had to alert the guys to watch over Frey.

"Hey Barrett, stop checking out that girl's ass. Unless you're going to tap it, she's mine tonight." Jake, one of our security officers, spoke.

"I'd like to see you try. I'm hotter than you, buddy. Once I approach her, you'll never get a chance with her," Barrett laughed.

"Not when I tell them I served this great country in special forces," Jake chuckled.

"Hey, fuckers," Holt found Barrett and Jake on the monitors before interrupting them. "Can one of you stop fucking around and check on Frey? Her old bully from school is at her table, and I don't want any trouble."

"Shit," Barrett grunted. "You mean that fucker, Dave?"

"Yup, that's the one. And to make it a double whammy, Candy is also at Frey's table." Holt turned back to the monitor and pointed to Frey's table.

"Why is that a double whammy?" Barrett asked.

Oh Shit. He just stuck his foot in his mouth.

"I just mean that Candy can be a bitch when she isn't happy," Holt sputtered. "She might be a problem for Frey."

"Does she know Frey? Is she playing? It looks like she's just standing behind Dave," Barrett whispered as he strode to Frey's table. "How could you hit that? She is a wack-a-doodle."

"I didn't hit that. She gave me a blow job, and I kicked her out." Holt watched Barrett moving closer to Frey's table.

"Shit, man, was she good?" Jake's voice came over the intercom, reminding Holt that it wasn't just him and Barrett on comms.

"I got off, but I don't want a repeat performance," Holt answered. "If you want to do a test drive with her, feel free."

"Thanks man, I just might," Jake responded. "I don't give a shit if she is a wack-a doodle as long as I can wack her."

"Nice. Do you kiss your mom with that mouth?" Holt grinned and continued to watch Frey's table while he gave Jake shit.

"Every fucking Sunday when she invites me to her house for a home-cooked meal," Jake responded.

Holt loved working with Jake. He was a good worker and funny as hell. Jake was a former military sniper. Not only was he well versed in many types of firearms, but he also trained all the security officers in hand-to-hand combat. All the officers on the property carried a gun, but it was mostly a deterrent. Usually, they detained their offenders for the police with a taser when necessary, but it didn't hurt to have an excellent marksman like Jake in case they ever had a situation with an active shooter. Hiring him was the best decision they ever made.

Dave threw down his cards and began yelling at Frey. Frey's fear was clear to Holt as her trembling hand clung desperately to the edge of the table. All their cell phones went off with an alert to go to her table. Dave was being an asshole, but Frey kept her cool as she spoke to him. Holt was proud of her. Had he not seen her hand tremble, he wouldn't have known how scared she was. *What the hell was he saying to her?* Holt watched Barrett step in and place his hand on Dave's chest while Dave gestured violently at Frey.

"Barrett, shut that shit down," Holt growled. As soon as Barrett got close enough to Dave, Holt could hear the conversation clearer through his earpiece.

"That bitch cheated!" Dave was screaming.

"Dave, remember me?" Barrett was saying. Holt knew he was trying to divert Dave's attention from Frey. "Let's step outside and cool off."

Holt watched Barrett put his hand around Dave's arm and pull him away from Frey toward the casino exit. The security officers always tried to take the irate guests out quietly and cause the least amount of commotion as possible. If the situation got too heated, they would detain the guest and call the police.

Holt breathed easier when Dave was gone. He watched Frey wave down Abigail to take over her table. He knew she was going to the dealer's lounge for a minute to get herself together. She looked startled and upset. Holt wished he could go to her, but he knew Barrett would check on her as soon as he finished escorting Dave out. Luckily, Candy walked to the slot machines. Thank fuck, they weren't there together. Otherwise, Frey might have lost it. Maybe Jake would go hit on Candy and she would finally leave him alone.

After a few minutes, he saw he was right. Frey was walking back to her table when Barrett caught up to her and gave her a hug.

"Are you okay?" Holt heard Barrett ask her.

"I'm fine, thanks, bro."

"Don't thank me," Barrett taped his earpiece. "Thank Holt. He saw what was happening on the monitors."

"Great," Holt heard Frey murmur. "Thank him for me."

That's all she had to say? *Well shit, he must really be in the doghouse.* Normally, when he saved her ass, she would fall all over herself to thank him.

Holt told himself he would talk to her when she finished her shift, but then he got busy watching other guests trying to cheat a dealer at the poker table and lost track of time. By the time he went back to check on Frey's table, Abigail was the dealer. Holt checked his watch and saw it was close to three in the morning. Frey's shift usually ended sometime between one and two in the morning. She was probably asleep by now. It was late, and he knew he should go to bed. The downstairs security officers would take over.

"I'm signing off, boys," Holt spoke to the security crew. "All's quiet up here. See you all in the morning."

"Night, Holt," several officers said.

"See ya in the morning," Barrett called out.

Holt took out his earpieces and walked to Frey and his adjoining door. Lightly, he knocked on the door, not wanting to wake her up if she was already asleep.

"Frey?"

Holt heard nothing. He would have opened the door if she hadn't put that damn lock on it. He'd just have to talk to her tomorrow.

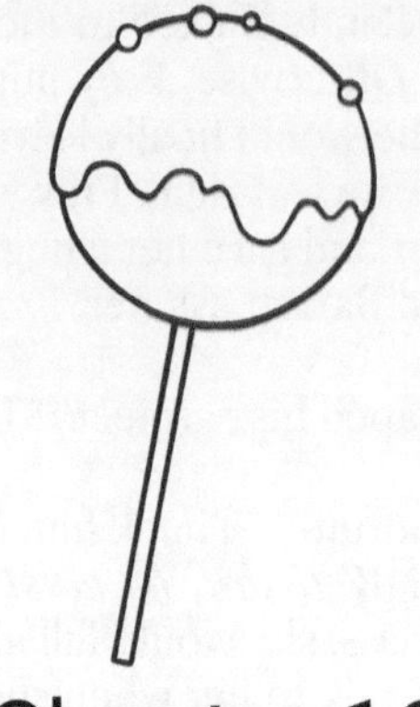

Chapter 16

Trolling for Holt

Candy

C andy glanced at the picture on her phone and compared the girl in the picture to the dealer in front of her. The dealer's name tag told Candy the name matched the person she was looking for and 'Freya' was a unique enough name that Candy decided she was at the right table. She wondered if this was the woman dating Holt.

Candy stopped at a slot machine near the entrance and pretended to play until Barrett came back. She wanted to find Holt, and since Barrett had let her into his room before, she figured he was her best shot. Out of the corner of her eye, she saw Barrett pass behind her on his way back to Frey's table and she followed him from a safe distance, stopping along the way at different tables. After Barrett had a conversation with Frey, she decided it was time to approach him.

Despite being rejected by Holt, she still wanted to fuck his thick, long cock. She'd heard about his reputation for being good in bed. Maybe he would fall for her, and they could both live in the lap of luxury at the resort. She would love to not have to pay rent, cook, clean, or work, for that matter. With no bills to pay, she could spend his money on anything she wanted. Lounging by the pool and being able to go shopping sounded like a great life.

Candy hoped he didn't catch on to her scheme before she had a chance to enjoy some of the resort's perks. But if Holt got suspicious, she would dump him before he could dump her. No man had ever dumped Candy before. They usually saw her and bent over backwards for her curvy body and beautiful face. *Momma always said to use your assets if you want to get what you want.* And right now, she wanted Holt in her bed.

"Hey handsome," Candy approached Barrett from behind.

"Hey," Barrett turned around and pointed at her, "Candy, right?"

"You remember," Candy purred, as she grabbed Barrett's arm and rubbed her tits on his arm. "I just wanted to thank you for letting me surprise Holt."

"Yeah, sure. No problem."

"Any chance you'll let me into his room again? I have another surprise for him." Candy batted her eyelashes at Barrett.

"I'm sorry, babe, but I can't do that." Barrett pulled his arm out of Candy's hold.

"Why not?" Candy gave Barrett her best pouty look.

"He asked me not to let any girls into his room. You'll just have to talk to him down here."

"Is he here?" Candy perked up.

"Not tonight." Barrett shook his head.

"Tomorrow?"

"I don't really know his schedule. Sorry, babe, but I gotta run." Barrett turned around and bolted away from her before she could stop him.

"Dammit!" Candy crossed her arms and stomped her foot.

"Hey, why is a pretty girl like you looking so angry?" Candy looked up and saw another sexy security guard looking at her.

"Well, hello there, handsome." Not one to miss out on an opportunity, Candy slowly eye fucked him from his feet to his head. Placing one hand on her hip and twirling her hair around the fingers of her other hand. "What's your name?"

"Jake. What's yours?"

"I'm Candy."

"Yes, you are." Jake winked at her.

"Do you work here?" Candy winced internally. Of course he worked here. He was wearing their security officer uniform. Time to act like an airhead and get him to help her.

"I do." Jake nodded. "I'm on a break. Can I buy you a drink?"

"Sure. Do you know where Holt is?" Although this guy was hot, and she would like to have a go at him, she still needed to find Holt.

"Damn Candy, you're breaking my heart, asking me about another man when I want to get to know you." Jake placed his hand over his heart. Candy giggled and played coy. "Holt's working remotely tonight, but I can help you with anything you need."

"Oooh, sounds good." Candy leaned into him and wrapped her arm around his, pulling him toward the bar. Well, a girl had to have some fun. Jake could take the edge off until she could find Holt, or he could tell her where Holt was working remotely from. Jake escorted her to the upstairs bar while Candy held onto his every word.

"What would you like? Carl can make anything." Jake looked at the bartender. "Right Carl?"

"Yup." Carl placed a napkin in front of Candy.

"I'll take a Sex on the Beach." Candy smiled at Jake.

Jake smiled wickedly at her, then looked at Carl and said, "Put it on my tab."

"Got it," Carl responded and walked away to mix her drink.

"Is that what you want?" Jake got closer to Candy. "Sex on the beach?"

"Maybe." Candy batted her eyelashes at him.

"Babe, that's a yes or no question." Jake sat on the stool and pulled her between his legs.

"Brought you a water, Jake, since you're working." Carl placed both drinks in front of them and walked away.

"Thanks, man," Jake said, not breaking eye contact with Candy. Reaching his hand back, he grabbed his water and whispered, "I'm parched. I bet you'd taste better than this water."

Candy ran her tongue seductively over her lips while she watched his Adam's apple bob as he tipped his head back and drank half the bottle of water. His eyes never leaving hers. *Oh, my goodness, he was hot and making her hotter by the second.* Feeling thirsty, Candy grabbed her drink and took a sip. Jake placed a hand on her hip, holding her in place.

"So, sex on the beach?" Jake asked again.

"Yes," Candy answered, before latching onto his lips.

Jake kissed her back. Breaking the kiss, he leaned back and stared at her. "I get off at one. Will you still be here?"

"Yes," Candy whispered, mesmerized by his beautiful green eyes.

"Okay. I gotta go back to work. Meet me in the lobby and we'll go to the beach to watch me and the sunrise." Jake smirked at her. "Deal?"

"Deal. Let's shake on it," Candy lifted her hand, but Jake batted it away.

"Fuck a handshake. I want another kiss." Jake went in for his kiss, releasing her lips only after he had fully explored her mouth and left her breathless. Candy was still panting when she opened her eyes and saw him standing in front of her, grinning from ear to ear. "See you at one."

"Okay." Candy stepped back and sank onto her bar stool as she watched him walk away. *Fuck, he was hot!* Once she lost sight of him, she finished her drink.

"Do you want another?" Carl asked.

"Yes, please. But I need to use the little girl's room. Can you keep it behind the bar until I get back?" Candy grabbed her purse and stood, looking at Carl.

"I'll make it when you get back," Carl nodded.

"Thanks, Carl."

Once Candy entered the restroom, she made sure it was empty before pulling out her phone.

"Hey," Candy whispered, when the person on the other line answered.

"Did you see her?"

"I did."

"Have you seen Holt?"

"No, he's working remotely. What does he see in her, anyway?"

"I told you I think he's been in love with her since they were in school. But she doesn't matter. Use your body and charm to get him back and get rid of her."

"I'm working on it," Candy grimaced before reapplying her lipstick.

"Well, work harder and faster." The voice on the other line seemed upset. Candy was tired of dealing with them. For now, she wanted to get her drink and wait until she got to go to the beach with Jake for some fun. Putting Holt on the back burner for a night.

"Fine. I gotta go." She knew her date wasn't until later, but she wanted to get off the phone and end this conversation. She hated having to check in with them every night. They needed to trust her. She knew what she was doing. "I got a drink and a date waiting for me."

"I thought you said you didn't see Holt?"

"I didn't. It's another sexy man." Candy fluffed up her hair.

"Don't fuck this up, Candy! Holt might not want to share."

"That's what I'm counting on. A little jealousy goes a long way." Candy pulled her shirt down and hiked her skirt up. Spinning around while looking in the mirror. She wanted to make sure her assets were on full display for Jake. He was now working the upstairs where she would sit drinking her sex on the beach and flirt with him as he walked by or when he glanced her way.

"Whatever, just keep your eye on the prize and don't screw this up for us. I need our plan to work."

"Got it." Candy rolled her eyes. "I'll talk to you later."

"Later."

Chapter 17

Where's Frey?

Holt

In the early morning hours, Frey was nowhere to be found on Holt's monitors. It seemed she'd left the casino, and he didn't know where she went. Holt stormed to the gym to relieve his pent-up frustration.

Heading to the treadmill, he put on his earphones and began his run. After an hour, he had completed a ten-mile run. He decreased his speed to a leisurely walk and let his mind unwind. Running always helped him settle down. As a boy, he used to open his bedroom window, climb out, and run for miles to clear his mind and escape the shithole that was his home.

"Hey man," Barrett stepped up to the treadmill next to Holt.

When Holt saw Barrett, he removed his earphones. Barrett had walked in unnoticed amidst his loud music and daydreaming about Frey.

"Hey." Holt nodded. "How late did you work last night?"

"I went off duty after you."

"Did Dave ever show up again?" Holt tried to be calm as he asked about Dave.

"No, I think he got the message." Barrett did a couple of leg stretches on the treadmill before turning it on.

"What was your message?" Holt wanted to hear exactly what Barrett said, in case he missed something.

"I told him he had to leave and cool off. If he ever wanted to gamble here again, he better not harass the dealers, specifically Frey." Barrett set up the treadmill settings.

"That was very reasonable of you." Holt said between gritted teeth.

"Yeah." Barrett sighed. "All I really wanted to do was kick his ass. Bottom line, though, he was just another irate customer."

"I haven't seen him here before. Have you?"

"A few times, but this was the first time I've seen him at Frey's table. He usually keeps to himself and plays roulette." Barrett started walking before he ramped it up to a full out run.

"I can't believe I haven't seen him," Holt pondered. What kind of security officer was he that he hadn't seen him before?

"You might not have been working the casino floor on those days. He doesn't come often. I remember walking around with Jake both times I saw Dave. I pointed him out to Jake as Frey's bully in school."

"I'll have to keep an eye out for him." Holt walked until his heart rate went down.

"Yeah, we all will. By the way, your blow job girl asked me to let her into your room again. I don't think she got the message if you told her to leave you alone."

"Candy? Shit. She's not my girl." Holt stopped the treadmill and scowled at Barrett. "What did you tell her?"

"I told her you didn't want me letting anyone into your room." Barrett began his run. "She got upset and started pouting—I walked away. I don't like that drama shit. I think Jake hit on her after I left."

"Idiot. He always falls for big tits. I wish him luck." Holt chuckled. "Did Dave say anything to you on the way out?"

"He kept saying Frey was cheating because she didn't want him to win. I set him straight. Frey doesn't cheat, she's just a good dealer."

"Yeah, Frey is fantastic." Holt grabbed a towel and dried the sweat on his face.

"So, what are you going to do today?"

"I was going to chill by the pool. What about you?" Holt held the towel around his neck, waiting for Barrett's response.

"I was gonna work in the family security room, but last night Alex said he was taking Tori to work. Damn, chilling by the pool sounds great. We could pick up some babes and get a little afternoon delight. I can get a workout from a good fuck if I find the right girl."

"Now who's the horn dog?" Holt raised his eyebrow at him, not that Barrett could see him. "I'll go shower and meet you down there. But I'm gonna pass on the afternoon delight." Holt walked to the door, ready to leave this conversation.

"Since when?" Barrett hollered at Holt.

Holt stopped and turned around. "You know I'm looking for something more serious than a hookup, right? I've told you that already." Holt needed to figure out a way to change Barrett's opinion about him being a man whore.

"Yeah, so you keep saying," Barrett answered. "But I'm not sure I believe you."

"I'm serious, man." Holt placed his hand on the doorknob. *Why wouldn't Barrett believe him?*

"Sure, I'll believe it when I see it. I know you'll want to get your dick wet soon. Your sex drive is like mine and we both know you can't stay celibate for long. I'll do half my run and meet you at the pool in an hour." Barrett inserted his earphones and continued his run.

"I'm gonna prove you wrong!" Holt yelled on his way out. Not sure why he yelled, Barrett probably didn't hear him with the heavy metal music blaring in his ears.

After showering and getting dressed, Holt heard noise coming from the laundry room. When he walked in, he saw Frey standing on her tippy toes, trying to grab a game out of the cabinets.

*** **Frey** ***

"Hey," Holt said from the doorway. "Can we talk?"

"Shit, you scared me." Frey jumped. "I can't talk right now. I'm getting a game for Tori and me to play. We're hanging out in her room while Alex works." Frey was on her toes, but still couldn't reach the game she wanted. *Damn, why did she have to be so short? Or better yet, who put the games inside the top cabinet?* She just wanted to get the game and leave before she ran into Holt.

"Sorry, I didn't mean to scare you." Holt walked up behind her. "Let me get that for you." Holt whispered in her ear, ruffling her hair. "I thought Alex was taking her to work?" Holt wrapped one arm around her, holding her against him while he reached up to grab a game. "Which one do you want?"

Frey froze for a minute. She couldn't think clearly with his body rubbing along her back.

"Frey?"

"Um...Monopoly." She had to grab the game and go before her brain and body short circuited again. "Alex had an emergency and had to go in for a while."

"He didn't ask me or Barrett to work from up here. I'll talk to Barrett." Holt easily pulled the game out and handed it to her.

"He's only going to be gone for a few hours. I can always lock the adjoining door." Frey grabbed the game moving away from Holt, ready to leave.

"I'll call Alex." Holt ran his hand down his face. "Can we talk later? Before you go to work?"

"I took tonight off so I can go on my date, remember?"

"How could I forget?" Holt crossed his arms. "I thought maybe you cancelled since your name is still on the schedule."

"Nope." Frey shook her head. "Anastasia is taking my shift. I haven't told mom yet, but she won't care as long as someone is at the table."

"Why are you doing this to us, Frey?"

"I'm not doing anything to us, Holt. There is no us." The last thing Frey wanted was to get used by Holt. She needed to make sure she could trust him with her heart, and that would take some time. Alone time.

"Yes, you are," Holt sighed, threw his arms up in the air in frustration, and glared at her. "There is an us. We had a great night and now you're blowing me off. I already explained what happened with Candy. It was not my doing. She means nothing to me."

"Well, how convenient for you to keep me in one room and have your wingman place another girl in yours."

"Dammit, I told you I had nothing to do with that." Holt prowled toward her. She took a step back every time he took a step forward until he'd backed her up against the door. "I kicked her out as soon as I saw her in my room."

"Yeah, after you kissed her!"

"She came onto me, sweetheart." Holt grumbled while he pushed his body up against her. "I threw her out and came back to you, but you weren't in your room."

"You looked like you were busy. So, I bought myself a lock to keep you and your lies away from me." Frey could feel her body softening and thrusting into Holt. Damn her traitorous body.

"Frey," Holt murmured right before he licked her bottom lip. "Let me in."

Holt's seductive tactics charmed Frey out of her anger. She had loved him and wanted him for so long. Her heart still yearned for his attention, even though her mind was yelling at her to stop. She opened her mouth and allowed his tongue to sweep in. Holt tilted her head to the side, granting better access for their kiss. Holding the game against her chest, Frey could not push him away. Holt crushed the game as he pushed his pelvis against her.

"Sweetheart, I'm sorry. I swear nothing happened with Candy," Holt spoke between kisses to her mouth and neck. "You are the only woman I want."

"Holt, stop. I don't know if I can trust you."

"What?" Holt's head shot up and stared at her with pain-filled eyes. Frey couldn't stand to see the hurt, so she glanced down at the game in her hands.

"Look at me." When Frey didn't raise her head, Holt cupped her face with his hands and bent down to her eye level. "What do you mean, you can't trust me? I've never lied to you."

"I don't know that I believe you," Frey mumbled. She wanted to trust him. To believe that Candy being in his room was not his doing. But she couldn't get the vision of Candy on her knees in front of him out of her head. Holt released her face and straightened to his full height. He took a couple of steps back, spinning around and placing his hands on his head. Blowing out a deep breath, he spun back around to face her while he dragged his hands down his face to his hips.

"What do you want me to do?" Holt's voice sounded tormented. "I don't know how to fix this."

"I don't know." Frey shrugged. "I just need some time for us to be a couple without anyone knowing. Because what if it doesn't work out? What if I'm not enough for you?"

"How can you say that?" Holt's jaw became slack. "You are enough. You are everything to me."

"Then why did you sleep around with so many women? Why have you not asked me out before? You know what? I don't have time for this right now." Frey pushed him aside, ready to leave the room.

"Woman, you drive me crazy." Holt grabbed her arm, spun her around, and pushed her up against the wall before he attacked her mouth.

"Holt, stop," Frey gasped. "We can't get caught. Barrett might be in his room and the doors are open."

"Barrett's in the gym. Now, who's the dirty little secret?" Holt gazed up into her eyes. "Promise me you'll cancel your date, and we can sort all this out."

"It's too late to cancel, but I'll talk to Ted tonight and let him down easy." Frey's pulse raced. Crossing her legs, she tightened her thighs, trying to relieve the ache in her lady bits and realizing her panties were soaked. *Just from his damn kiss. How was he always doing this to her?*

"What time are you meeting him downstairs?" Holt stroked her cheek.

"Six in the lobby."

"Okay." Holt tucked a strand of her hair behind her ear. "I'll be nearby in case you need me."

"I'll be fine. I'll break up with him and come find you." Frey's body shivered with his every touch. "Are you working tonight?"

"It makes me so happy to hear you say that." Holt kissed her all over her face. "No, I'm off tonight."

Holt's kisses always had a way of melting her heart. Dread overwhelmed Frey as she faced the repercussions of her actions. It might have been a mistake to let Holt know she planned to break up with Ted at the hotel tonight. *What if Ted got confrontational? What if Holt stepped in?* Obviously, she would defend Holt, but Ted was a nice guy, and she didn't want him to get hurt. Holt packed quite a punch, as she had seen in high school and several times in the casino with irate customers. But...what if all this finally worked out, and she got Holt all to herself like she dreamed about all these years? *Could they finally be together?*

"I need to go," Frey whispered. "I have to take a shower and go back to Tori."

"You want some company? I just took a shower, but I'm more than happy to wash you." Holt brushed his hand through her hair and down her back to her ass. Cupping it and pulling her into him as he kissed her.

"No." Frey released one hand from the game and placed it on his chest, gently pushing him away. She needed to gather her wits about her and leave before they ended up fucking in the laundry room. "I'm on Tori duty and I have to get back as quick as possible, so Alex doesn't kill me."

"Okay, but please unlock the closet door so I can come see you tonight." Holt cupped her face. His eyes deepened to a smokey dark blue.

"Okay." Holt kissed Frey one more time and stepped back.

Chapter 18

Shower Later...Talk to Bestie Now!

Frey

Having wasted time with Holt, Frey skipped the shower and rushed back to Tori's room. She could shower before her date. It was time to talk to Tori about everything happening with Holt. Her feelings were all over the place. *Should she trust Holt?* Maybe Tori could give her some advice.

"Hey," Tori said when Frey walked in. "What took you so long? I was beginning to get worried."

"I need to talk to you." Frey burst into the room.

"Okaayy, is everything all right?"

Frey put the game on the kitchen table and headed toward the doors connecting Alex and Barrett's rooms. She peeked inside and didn't see Barrett. Frey left Barrett's door open but closed Alex's.

"Frey, what's going on?" Tori looked worried.

"Let's talk in your bedroom." Frey grabbed Tori's hand on her way there.

"Okay, fess up. You're scaring me," Tori said as soon as they entered the room.

Frey dragged Tori onto the bed. They sat side by side, their gazes locked.

"I think I'm dating Holt," Frey burst out.

"What? That's great! Wait" –Tori raised her eyebrow with a puzzled look on her face– "what do you mean, you think?"

"Well, we slept together a few days ago, and I thought everything was great until I saw him with Candy. So, I decided to go on a date tonight with Ted to make him jealous."

"Okay, who's Candy? I'm so confused. Start from the beginning and leave nothing out."

Frey's story began from when she met Holt in elementary school. Frey explained about her unrequited crush on Holt during middle and high school. She had outright flirted with him and attempted to get his attention, but he never flirted back and continued to think of her as a sister. Despite being heartbroken, she still cherished their friendship, so eventually she stopped pursuing him. Then, a few days ago, she slept with him and lost her virginity to him and found Candy in his room. She may have gone overboard, but she wanted Tori to understand her dilemma. When she finally finished, Tori was smiling.

"This is so freaking fantastic! I knew he liked you." Tori grinned at her like the Cheshire cat. "I even asked Alex if you guys were into each other."

"You did what? When?" Frey gasped, wondering if Alex would talk to Barrett and ask him if he noticed anything. Frey didn't want anyone to know they had slept together, especially Barrett. Even though she would hate Holt if he used her, she also knew he was Barrett's best friend and Barrett was very protective of her. Their friendship would be ruined, and Holt didn't have anyone else. Frey knew others wouldn't understand why she would want Holt to be okay if he hurt her, but she would always love him. It would hurt her if he lost his best friend because of her.

"The night we were watching a movie and Holt came to the door and asked to talk to you." Tori shrugged.

"Did Alex freak out?" Frey's heart raced out of control as her breathing sped up. She could not have a panic attack over this. She took some deep breaths and waited for Tori to answer her.

"Frey, calm down. It's okay. Alex was okay with the idea. He said you couldn't pick a nicer guy to date. Although, I'm pretty sure if Holt was fucking you with no commitment, Alex would go ballistic."

"Yeah, I get that. My brothers have always been very protective of me." Frey dropped her head into her hands. "I've made such a mess out of this. Holt said our lovemaking was not a onetime thing. I'm asking him to keep it a secret because I can't get Candy out of my head long enough to trust him. Like a bitch, I decide to go out with another man to make him jealous. I've never been that vindictive. What's wrong with me? I don't know why I'm acting like this. I don't know what to do?"

"It will be okay. Just go down tonight and let Ted know you are in love with someone else. Talk to Holt and let him know how you feel. Then you can both talk to Barrett." Tori smiled, proud of herself for coming up with a solution.

"No!!!" Frey hoisted herself off the bed and began pacing. "I mean, I am going to tell Ted that I'm in love with Holt, but I can't tell Barrett that I'm dating Holt because I don't even know if we are dating."

"Frey, if what you said about your conversation with Holt is true, then you are dating." Tori stared at her like a deer caught in headlights. "You gotta tell Barrett. If you keep it from him and he finds out, he'll be furious with both of you. You guys are his best friends."

"I can't." Frey massaged her temples. "What if I tell him and Holt isn't as serious about me as I am about him? What if I can't trust him? What if it doesn't work out? Then I could ruin Barrett's relationship with Holt." Frey frowned.

"Okay, I hear what you're saying." Tori chewed on her bottom lip. "But I think it will be better if your relationship is out in the open. I'm sure Alex will help you guys with Barrett. Barrett looks up to his big brother. If Alex tells him to accept your relationship, he will."

"I don't know." Frey stopped pacing and hugged her body. "What if Barrett hates Holt for taking my virginity and dumping me? Then Holt will lose his best friend and his family, and it will all be my fault!"

"Whoa, stop." Tori stood and squeezed her shoulder. "You can't play the what if game? It never ends well. Let's take this one problem at a time. You have to look at the glass half full instead of half empty or you're going to drive yourself nuts."

"I'm already in crazy land." Frey dropped her head down and sighed in defeat. "I'll talk to Holt and see what he wants to do, but I'm leaning towards a secret relationship. At least for a little while." Frey didn't know what to do, she was losing her mind.

"I don't agree, but I'll support any decision you make. Just talk to Alex before Barrett. That way, Alex can go with you whenever you tell Barrett, since you're worried about his reaction."

"I don't think so." Frey shook her head no. "I know my twin and he'd be furious with me if I talked to Alex before him. Been there, done that, and I'm not going there again." Frey remembered one time in middle school, when she asked Alex to teach her some self-defense moves. When Barrett came back from the movies with Holt and saw them in the gym, he lost it.

"What's going on?" Barrett swung the door of the gym open.

"Frey wanted to learn some self-defense, so I'm teaching her." Alex draped his arm around her shoulder.

"Why didn't you ask me?" Barrett glared at her. "I'm in Tae Kwon Do and Jiu Jitsu like Alex. I could've taught you."

"You weren't here." Frey shrugged her shoulders.

"What? She can't ask her big brother for help? Only you?" Frey knew Alex was joking, busting Barrett's chops. "You know, you're not connected at the hip. I can help her, too." But when she stopped laughing and looked at Barrett, she saw the hurt in his eyes.

"Barrett, I would have asked you if you had been here." Frey tried to console Barrett.

"Yeah, whatever. Come on Holt. Let's go somewhere and not bother their brother and sister bonding." Barrett turned and left. Holt mouthed 'sorry' and followed Barrett.

"Barrett, really?" Alex sounded dumbfounded by Barrett's reaction.

Barrett had been so hurt and angry with her, he didn't speak to her for a week. That was the loneliest week of her life because not only did Barrett not talk to her, but he made sure Holt stayed away from her too.

"I hadn't thought of that." Tori's voice brought Frey back to the present. Frey hated Barrett had acted that way. That day, she realized how much it meant to Barrett for her to confide in him first.

"Well." Tori tapped her lips with her pointer finger. "You're kinda stuck between a rock and a hard place."

"I know!" Frey dropped back down on the bed in a sitting position, staring at the floor while her hands rubbed her thighs. "That's why I think we should just keep it to ourselves."

"I'm so sorry." Tori sat next to her. "Let me know if I can do anything to help you." Tori rubbed her back. "Even if all you need is a shoulder to cry on or an ear to listen."

"Thank you." Frey turned and hugged Tori. "I'm glad I have you. Talking it out with you has helped." Frey thought Tori's suggestion was a good idea and felt better talking it out. Releasing Tori, Frey said, "I'll talk to Ted first, then Holt. Now, let's play a game so I can distract myself from the shitshow I created."

Frey felt more relaxed than she'd felt in days. Now she wanted to take her mind off what she needed to do tonight. She had a few hours to enjoy her time with Tori and think of anything but her problems.

"You got it." Tori grabbed her hand and pulled her up. "Which one are you going to teach me?"

"Monopoly because it lasts longer and if we need a break, we can leave it on the table to finish later." Frey walked with Tori to the living room table.

"Okey dokey. We never owned a Monopoly game, so I don't know how to play. We only played cards, cup and pin, archery, and stickball." Tori's comment shocked Frey. She'd never met anyone who hadn't played Monopoly.

"We played some of those games too when we had a yard. But once we moved into the resort it's hard to play some of them here, so we ended up playing board and pool games." Frey set up the game and explained the rules to Tori as she passed out the money.

Chapter 19

Is the Promise Null and Void?

Holt

Their talk in the laundry room left Holt energized about moving forward with Frey. Now he had to convince her to give them a real shot and trust him. Shit, was that all? The trust issue seemed like an uphill battle that might take some time.

He should probably explain his feelings for Frey to Barrett and her family before he grew their romance. If he told them he was dating Frey and that she was special to him, then surely Frey would know he was serious about her and trust him again. Sehoy and Osceola liked him. Although he did take her virginity before marriage—they wouldn't be happy about that. Might have to keep that part a secret.

Alex and Barrett were protective of her, but he didn't think Alex would get upset. Barrett was another story, and Holt had no intention of harming his relationship with Barrett.

It was important for him and Frey to approach this situation carefully to prevent any hurt feelings. First, he had to have a conversation with Barrett. The pool would be a perfectly relaxed atmosphere.

Holt called Alex to check if he needed someone in the upstairs security room.

"Holt," Alex answered, "what's up, man?"

"Hey, Frey told me you had to work?"

"Just a few hours."

"Did you need Barrett or me to stay up here? I was going to chill with him at the pool. But I can stay with the girls if you need me?" Holt grabbed his key from the foyer table.

"No, I'm only going to be down here for another hour at most. Just lock the adjoining door and tell the girls not to answer the door."

"Are you sure?"

"Yup. We have eyes and ears everywhere. As long as they don't open the door, they'll be good."

"Okay. I'll go talk to them and make sure Tori is okay before I head to the pool." Holt walked through the laundry room into Barrett's room.

"Sounds good. Thanks."

Holt hung up and noticed Alex's adjoining door was closed.

"Hey ladies," Holt knocked on the door to get their attention before he pushed it open. They were so focused on their Monopoly game—they didn't hear him. "Ladies," Holt spoke louder.

Tori jerked her head up. "Oh, hey Holt."

"Sorry, I didn't mean to scare you. Just wanted to let you know Alex should be back in about an hour. I was going to join Barrett at the pool. Will you ladies be okay?"

"We'll be okay," Tori answered first, since Frey kept staring at his chest. He'd put on his board shorts but no shirt. He was glad to see her attention was focused on his body. That meant she still wanted him, even though she continued to push him away. Tonight, he would change all that.

"Okay, but please lock this door. I'll leave this side open. Also, lock your front door."

Tori stood up and gave him a salute. "Yes, sir."

"Smartass. You've been hanging out with her too long." Holt smiled and pointed at Frey. Walking to their front door, he checked the lock and slid the metal bracket in place to prevent anyone from getting in if the door opened from outside. The last thing he needed was for someone like Winston to get into their room and hurt them. He would never forgive himself. Then he walked back to Barrett's room. "Okay, lock this one behind me. You'll have to let Alex in because I flipped the metal bracket on your door so no one can get in unless you let them in."

Holt closed the door and listened for the lock to click. "Hey ladies! Lock the door!" Finally, he heard the click. "Thank you!"

"Bye Holt!" Tori shouted loud enough for him to hear.

Holt headed for the pool. Finding Barrett, he grabbed a towel and sat down on the lounger next to him.

"Hey princess. What took you so long?" Barrett squinted up at Holt.

Holt gave him the middle finger and said, "Fucker." Barrett chuckled.

"I got held up." Holt laid back on the lounger and closed his eyes. "I heard someone in the laundry room and went to check it out. It was Frey getting a board game to play with Tori."

"Oh Shit." Barrett bolted upright. "I thought Tori was going with Alex to the cultural center. Do we need to run up and monitor from the security room?"

"No. I talked to Alex. He said he'd be up there within the hour. I made the girls lock both doors before I left. You know Frey has a date tonight, right?" Holt wanted to feel out Barrett's reaction if he told him he was dating Frey.

"What?" Barrett stared at Holt. "With whom? Is it that guy Ted she told me to check out?"

"No, it's me," Holt responded sarcastically, getting a feel for Barrett's response.

"Yeah, right, asshole." Barrett laid back down. "You know you can't date your sister."

"She's not really my sister." Holt turned his head and opened one eye, watching Barrett.

"Technically, no." Barrett closed his eyes. "But unless you want me to kick your ass and leave you eating out of a feeding tube, you'll leave Frey alone."

"Got it." Well, Holt thought, that answered that question.

"You are joking, right?" Barrett turned his head and stared daggers at Holt.

"Yeah, just kidding." Holt laughed nervously. *Why was Barrett so against him dating Frey? Was he not good enough for her?* Holt had stopped sleeping around and, he'd told Barrett, he was ready to settle down. Why didn't Barrett believe him? Barrett's comment gutted Holt. He'd thought maybe now that they were older that the high school promise had expired. Guess not.

"Is Frey really going out on a date?" Barrett pivoted his head back to survey all the women at the pool.

"Yes, and it is the guy you're running a background check on," Holt answered. Hoping like hell that Frey never saw that guy again. "He's an insurance agent. They're meeting tonight in the lobby at six. Did you find out anything suspicious about him?"

"Nope, he's clean as a whistle. I guess I'll just have to stop by and meet this dude." Barrett sat up and licked his lips. "I see a young woman in need of some Barrett lovin'."

"Gotcha." Holt glanced toward the girls Barrett was checking out and forced a grin. He was glad Barrett was distracted and this conversation was over. "See you later."

"Yup, later." Barrett left Holt and strutted over to a young lady in a teeny tiny yellow bikini laying on a lounger on the other side of the pool.

Holt noticed a girl walking toward him and immediately got up and exited the pool area. He wasn't in the mood to get hit on. Pool time was over.

Chapter 20

My Girl's on a Date...and it's not with me!

Holt

After talking to Barrett by the pool, Holt went to his room to take a shower. While the water was heating, he stripped out of his clothes. That conversation with Barrett sucked and got him nowhere toward his goal of dating Frey. Holt stepped in and let the hot water over his body. Barrett still didn't want him dating Frey. Shit! Holt grabbed the soap and threw it against the tile wall. The soap bounced off and dropped to the floor.

What the hell was he going to do? Holt leaned with both hands against the wall and lowered his head, praying for an answer to come to him. He couldn't bear to be apart from her now that he'd had her. He'd hoped that over the years Barrett had changed his mind. *Why couldn't Barrett see that he'd be good for her? He'd always looked out for her and wouldn't let anyone hurt her. He was a protector, just like her brothers.*

He had to talk to Frey. Finishing his shower, he got dressed and laid in bed until it was time for Frey to meet her date in the lobby. He didn't want to see her as she was getting ready. If she got mad at him again, she might change her mind and dump him to date Ted. *Fuck! Fuck! Fuck!* Holt screamed in his head and slammed his hands on the bed repeatedly.

Looking at the clock, each minute felt like an hour. He would never survive this night if he kept staring at the time. Deciding to save his sanity, he set an alarm on his phone for when he wanted to go downstairs. He would not look at the clock again. He grabbed the remote and put on a home improvement show, hoping to distract himself.

It didn't work. His mind kept racing with different scenarios about tonight. *Would she dump him as soon as she saw him? Would he leave? Would they eat dinner and then she would dump him? Would he try to change her mind? Fuck!* He was driving himself crazy. But he wasn't checking the time, so that was a plus.

Finally, his alarm went off. He bolted from the bed and headed downstairs. Instead of watching out for her from the monitors, he wanted to stay close to her in case Ted became angry and did something unpredictable. She had only met him once at her table. They didn't know how he would respond to being rejected. Which was the reason he was sitting in RUSH with a perfect view inside Savor. After Winston, he wasn't trusting any man with his woman.

The sight of Ted kissing her cheek when he saw her made Holt tense. Another man's lips should not touch any part of her body. Barrett interrupted them, bringing Holt some relief. He wondered what Barrett said that made Frey slap his arm and glare at him. Barrett just smiled at them and left. But Ted continued to stare after Barrett until Frey snapped her fingers in front of his face to get his attention. Ted shook his head and led her to Savor, placing his hand on her lower back. *Fuck! He needed to stop touching her or Holt would touch him, and it wouldn't be in a friendly way.* Just as Holt was prepared to spring into action, Tiffany, a waitress at RUSH, approached to take his order.

"Hey, Holt." Tiffany said. "Are you working tonight?"

"Hey, Tiff." Holt looked up at her. "No, just wanted to grab a quick bite to eat and then I'm going to sleep."

"Too many on call days, huh?"

"Yep, I'm beat." Holt handed her the menu, already knowing he was ordering his usual.

"What do you want to eat?"

"Can I get a burger and fries, please?" After watching them enter Savor, Holt figured Frey and her date would eat and chat for a bit. Shit. He wished Frey would have ended the date before it even began. Luckily, he'd picked the best seat to watch them during their so called 'date'.

Tiffany brought him out of his thoughts. "Sure. What do you want to drink?"

"Water, please." Holt smiled at her, feeling guilty for forgetting her existence. "You got it."

"Thanks, Tiff." Holt retrieved his phone and checked his work emails for any necessary responses. Tiffany brought his food when it was ready, and he ate while watching Ted and Frey. Stalkerish behavior, but that was his girl, and he wanted to keep her safe.

*** Frey ***

"Hey, Frey," Ted met Frey in the lobby and kissed her cheek. "I'm glad you called." Frey was nervous and wanted to get this date over with. She felt awful about leading him on. Especially when he looked so handsome in another suit and tie and smelled so good.

"Hi, Frey." Barrett came up behind her. "Who's your friend?"

"Barrett, this is Ted. Ted, this is my younger twin brother Barrett." Frey motioned toward them as she introduced them. *What the hell was Barrett doing here? She doesn't remember telling him she had a date.* She'd only asked him for a background check, which now that she thought about it, he never told her if he found anything.

"By only a minute." Barrett shoulder bumped her. Frey agonizes over the situation with Holt. *Would Barrett understand she wanted to date Holt, or should she just date Ted? No, she couldn't date Ted if she wanted to be with Holt.*

Ted stuck out his hand for a handshake. "Hi, Barrett. It's nice to meet you."

Ted's voice brought Frey back to the present. *How was she going to tell Ted about Holt?*

"You, too." Barrett shook his hand. "Where are you guys going tonight?" Now Frey knew she didn't tell Barrett about this date. He wasn't one to pretend to act stupid, and now she really wanted to know how he found out.

"Wait," Frey turned to her brother. "How did you know I was going on a date?"

"Holt told me." Barrett smiled at them both.

"Of course he did," Frey sighed and rolled her eyes. This is typical Holt behavior inserting himself into her personal life, like she couldn't handle breaking up with a guy on her own. Or maybe he thought she would chicken out. Though deep inside, she knew he was probably just being overprotective and sweet in his own way. She would bet money that if she looked around, she would find him somewhere watching them to make sure she was okay.

"Who's Holt?" Ted looked confused.

"He's my best friend and like a brother to Frey," Barrett stood braced with his arms crossed. Staring directly at Ted, he said, "We are all extremely protective of her. You fuck with her—we fuck with you."

Ted's eyes dart around the room as if he's looking for trouble.

"Nice Bare, thanks for that." Frey glared at Barrett like he was a lunatic and slapped him on the arm. "Ted, don't listen to him. He's an overprotective caveman. Bye, Barrett." Frey shoves Barrett to get him moving away from Ted.

"See ya later." Barrett chucked Ted under the chin, turned around, and headed to the casino.

"Your brother is intense." Ted rubbed his chin and stared after him.

Frey was well aware of Barrett's overprotective tendencies since high school when any boy tried to ask her out. He'd always tell the ones brave enough to ask her they could take her on a date with one condition. When they asked about the condition, Barrett told them they also had to take him, Holt, and Alex as chaperones. Her brothers found that funny. So, she didn't date much in high school and later on, she never let them know when she was seeing someone.

Ted looked nervous, so Frey tried to downplay Barrett's comments.

"He's a big teddy bear. Are you okay with eating at Savor or do you prefer a more casual atmosphere like RUSH?"

"I'd like a more private restaurant, like Savor, so we can get to know each other in a quieter environment."

Ted massaged the back of his neck and continued to watch Barrett as he entered the casino.

"Okay," Frey moved toward Savor. "Ted?" Frey turned and called out when she realized Ted wasn't beside her. He remained frozen in his spot, looking between Savor and the casino. "Ted, are you okay?" He was obviously terrified of Barrett. Well, this would help when she broke it off with him. Hell, Ted might be relieved. Little did Barrett know—he'd just helped her cause.

"Yeah, sure," Ted shook his head.

Frey waited until he caught up to her. "Normally you need a reservation, but I asked them to save a table in case you wanted to eat there."

"Sounds good." Ted placed his hand on Frey's lower back.

Frey wasn't sure if Holt was watching, but she would bet her future paychecks that he was. Holt wouldn't like Ted touching her, so she walked quickly into Savor. Now that they had agreed on a truce, she didn't want to do anything to piss him off.

"Hi, Mandy," Frey spoke to the hostess. "Can we have the table I requested?"

"Hi, Frey." Mandy smiled. "Absolutely. It's ready for you. Follow me."

They followed Mandy to the first table by the entrance. Frey chose that table in case things got dicey with Ted. Sitting close to the exit would make it easier for him to leave or for her to get help. Ted seemed like a nice guy, but she really didn't know him.

"I'm glad you called, Frey," Ted pulled out the chair for her.

His gentlemanly gesture took her so off guard she bumped into the table before she sat in the chair. Her nerves were on the edge. "Thank you, Ted."

"Hey, Frey." Their waitress came to the table. "What do you want to drink?"

"Hi Amy, I'll have water."

"Water for me also," Ted answered. "Frey, would you like a glass of wine?" Ted asked before Amy walked away.

"No, just water." Frey wanted to keep a rational mind when she spoke to Ted. "Ted, we need to talk."

"Already? We haven't even started our meal," Ted teased her. "Is this because of your brother?"

Frey forced a panicked laugh. "No, I needed to talk to you before Barrett got all caveman on you. I know I called you for a date..." Frey started.

"But there is someone else," Ted finished her sentence. His comment surprised Frey. Then Ted gave her a knowing look.

"Yes, I'm so sorry," Frey sighed, but continued before he could say anything. "This meal is on me since I dragged you out here."

"I had a feeling this was too good to be true. If I'm being honest, when you called me, I heard a man say, 'Frey, no, put down the damn phone.' I took up your offer because I wanted to make sure you were okay. I have two younger sisters, one of which was in an abusive relationship."

Frey took a sip of water right before Ted asked. "Is the man I heard abusing you? I can help you."

She was so stunned by Ted's comment that the water went down the wrong way and she couldn't stop coughing.

"Are you okay?" Ted looked worried and was about to get up when Frey waved him away.

"I'm fine." She croaked and continued to cough to clear her air way. "Holt would never hurt me."

"Okay. But if he ever goes too far. You know how to reach me." Ted didn't look convinced as he leaned back in his chair.

"Thanks." Frey's watery eyes cleared up and she could finally take a deep breath.

"For the record, it's not every day I get to have a meal with a beautiful woman so, I'm paying." Ted picked up the menu.

"If you pay, you are only paying for yourself, because since I work and live here, I always eat for free."

"Wow, okay. I'm sorry..." Ted sounded flustered. "I didn't realize that. I would have taken you somewhere else. You're the cheapest date I've ever had." Ted winked at her. "Now tell me what's really going on with this Holt guy?"

"Holt and I have been best friends since we were kids. I always had a crush on him, but he never reciprocated until recently. Yesterday he made me mad, and I wanted to hurt him, so I called you while he was in the room. I'm so sorry. I never should have done that to you. It was childish and inconsiderate of me." Frey fidgeted with the napkin in her hands.

"It's okay," Ted chuckled, reached across the table, and placed his hand over hers. "I get it, but I don't expect your brother will."

"Why do you say that?" Frey slid her hand out from under his as Mandy set their glasses of water down on the table and took their order.

"Uh, he is extremely protective of you, and he specifically said Holt was like a brother. Somehow, I don't believe his mind can shift from viewing Holt as a brother to your boyfriend."

"Hmm," Frey sighed, "that's what I'm afraid of. If Holt is serious about our relationship, I'm not sure how to tell Barrett. Which is why I want to keep it a secret for a little while."

"Personally, I think the faster you tell your brother, the better. If one of my sisters was dating my best friend, I'd want to know." Ted took a drink of his water. "However–" Ted wiggled his eyebrows "–if you need to buy yourself some time, I'd make a good fake boyfriend."

"Yeah. I don't think Holt would like that." I chuckled. "Besides, why would you do that for me knowing I'm with someone else?" Frey squinted at Ted. "You don't even know me. I mean, we only met a few days ago."

"Because you seem like a genuinely nice person and if this thing with Holt fades, I want a shot to truly date you." Ted's intense stare made her uncomfortable. She should not have accepted this date. It was not nice to play with someone's feelings. There was no way in hell she would use him as a fake boyfriend. She either gave Holt a shot or she walked away, ready to date Ted as a real boyfriend.

"I don't know what to say." She had been mooning over Holt for so long, she hadn't given any other men a chance. Even though she told Holt she had written him off, deep down, she hadn't because of her trust issues.

"Say nothing. Just know that I will help you if you need me." Ted looked sincere in his offer.

"You're not mad?" Frey winced.

"Nope," Ted shook his head. "I mean, I would have liked to date you, but I guess I'm too late."

"Thank you for understanding." Frey smiled at Ted as Mandy delivered their food. Frey wanted to talk to Holt and see if they had a chance before she said anything to Ted. As far as Ted was concerned, Frey and Holt were dating.

"It's done. Let's have an enjoyable night, eat this delicious meal and get to know each other as friends," Ted nodded.

"You're a really nice guy." Frey meant every word. Ted was easy to talk to as opposed to Holt, who knew how to push her buttons and drive her crazy. Her emotions would go from zero to sixty in seconds with Holt.

"Ugh." Ted grabbed at his heart. "The curse of the nice guy. We always seem to finish last."

Frey laughed at his dramatics. While they ate, Ted told her about some of the weirdest insurance reports he'd filed. Frey didn't realize the insurance business had so much fraud, but she guessed cheaters and liars were everywhere. Their conversation flowed easily as they tried to outdo each other with who had the weirdest story and who had the funniest. Frey felt comfortable with Ted, but there was no romantic chemistry there. She didn't feel that tingling in her belly like when she was with Holt, but she did like Ted as a friend.

After finishing their dinner, Ted walked her to the lobby.

"Thank you for the meal and company," Frey reached out and grabbed his hands.

"I should thank you," Ted laughed. "I can't believe you grabbed the bill before me. If you ever finish with Holt or want to make him jealous, call me. Or heck, call me if you need a friend or someone to talk to."

"Thanks again, Ted. I'm hoping it works out with Holt, but I could always use another friend." Frey leaned in and kissed his cheek. "I'll see you around?"

"Absolutely." Ted squeezed her hand. "I would love to be your friend. Goodnight, Frey."

"Goodnight."

Frey waited until he left the lobby, turned, and walked toward the elevators.

"*Chackshosti!*" Frey heard her mom's voice.

Crap. Rushing to get to Holt, she didn't notice her mom behind the lobby desk. Now she had to explain her date to her mom. Wait a second...this could be exactly what she was looking for. If everyone assumed she was dating Ted, they wouldn't question her if they saw her with Holt. It was a perfect cover until she was certain Holt was serious about a relationship with her. She wanted forever with Holt.

"Hi, *chatski.*" Frey turned and walked to her mom.

"Who was that cute young man you were just with?" Sehoy raised an eyebrow at her. "Were you on a date?"

"His name is Ted. He's an Insurance Agent and yes, I was on a date."

"How long have you been dating him?" Sehoy always got straight to the point. "Is it serious? I'm not getting any younger for grandchildren."

"*Chatski*, I literally just met him." Frey rolled her eyes. "That was our first date."

"Well, it's always a good time to consider your future. Your dad and I already had Alex by your age."

"I know, I know. Not that story again," Frey sighed. "You were lucky to meet dad when you were young. He's a catch."

"He sure is," Sehoy smiled brightly, "but there are other nice young men out there for you if you would just give them a chance."

"Okay, *chatski.*"

"When are you seeing him again, and when do we get to meet him?" Sehoy was relentless.

"Slow down, *chatski*. Soon." Frey started panicking. Now she would have to call Ted and take him up on his offer to be her pretend boyfriend while she hid her real boyfriend from her parents. What a tangled web she was weaving.

"How about Sunday dinner tomorrow?" Sehoy pressed.

"Ah, he's busy, but I'll ask him about next week." Frey wondered how long she could play this game with her mom until she caught on to her deception.

"Mrs. Panther," one of the hospitality employees interrupted, "I'm sorry to bother you, but I need your help with a reservation."

"Okay, Cami." Sehoy nodded. "I'll be right there."

"*Chackshosti*, enjoy the rest of your evening. I'll talk to you tomorrow." Sehoy turned around and followed Cami to the lobby front desk.

"Goodnight, *chatski*."

Cami could not have come at a better time. Whew. Time to leave and find Holt before her mom solved the problem and came back to talk to her. Hurrying to the elevator, she proceeded to her room. So much adrenaline was coursing through her body that she was fumbling with the lock on the connecting closet door. She couldn't wait to tell Holt how understanding Ted was about their situation. And that he'd even volunteered to help them.

Frey slid the door open and sprinted in, bubbling with excitement.

"Holt. Guess what?" Frey froze when she entered his bedroom. Her excitement faded to worry when she saw Holt running his hands through his hair while he paced like a caged tiger. Rolling her eyes, she walked up to him.

Chapter 21

Time to Pacify the Beast

Frey

"**F**inally! I've been waiting for you ever since your date left." Holt closed the space between them, anger blazing in his eyes. "Where have you been?"

"Mom stopped to talk to me." Frey smiled wryly. *Why was he acting so mad? I came up as soon as I could,* Frey thought. "She asked me about my date." Frey bounced on her toes and clapped her hands, ready to give him the good news. "Ted offered to be my fake boyfriend and help us with our cover up if we need more time before we talk to everyone. Wasn't that nice of him?"

"What the hell are you talking about?" Holt stopped and braced his hands on his hips.

"If everyone assumes I'm dating Ted, they won't suspect that we're dating. It's perfect really." Frey grinned at her plan.

"Frey." Holt walked up to her and pulled her into his arms. "It's not perfect. I was going to beat that guy up if he touched or kissed you again. How am I supposed to keep my cool if you date him again and he touches you?"

"Were you watching us?" Frey smirked and pinched his waist, feeling some satisfaction at hearing the green-eyed monster in Holt's voice.

"Hell yes." Holt stepped back and glared at her. "I was sitting in RUSH until he kissed your cheek. Then I had to walk away before I stormed over there and kicked his ass." Holt rubbed his eyes and ran his hand down his face.

"So." Frey stroked his chest with her hands and licked her lips. "You were jealous?"

"Yes," Holt said through gritted teeth, his eyes fixated on her mouth.

"How jealous?" Frey whispered as she licked his neck and grabbed his cock through his pants. Holt hardened and grew in her hands while she stroked him. She couldn't wait to submit to him again in the bedroom.

"Go to your room and strip. Wait for me on your bed. Now." Holt pushed her away from him and stared into her eyes.

Frey smiled and sashayed her way into her room, stripping on her way. She left her clothes on his floor for him to retrieve on his way to her. This was going to be fun. She loved when he took charge in the bedroom.

Frey never made it to her bed. Holt swooped in and picked her up, tossing her onto it. She bounced once before he landed on top of her, trapping her with his body and a heated kiss. Frey wore only her bra and thong. Meanwhile, Holt was over dressed.

"You have too many clothes on." Frey tugged his shirt out of his pants.

"So do you." Holt sat up on his knees and took off his shirt.

Frey would never tire of seeing the heat in his eyes as he looked at her. Running her hands down his chiseled chest, feeling every one of his defined abs to his waist.

"I'm in my underwear. You still have pants on." Frey reached out to undo his pants, but Holt pushed her hands away.

"And they are staying on until I satisfy my woman and she only thinks of me. Now lie still and enjoy the ride, sweetheart." Holt stated as he reached down and unsnapped the front clasp of her bra.

Catching the lacy material of her bra before it fell away, he cupped her breasts and slowly, but thoroughly, rubbed the abrasive material against her nipples until they hardened. Her sensitive nipples responded as he rubbed and tweaked them. An overwhelming sensation of pleasure traveled through her entire body like lightning, causing a forest fire. She could feel the wetness between her legs. She was dying for him to put his mouth and tongue on her tingling breasts.

"Holt, suck them," Frey moaned.

"I'll suck them when I'm damn good and ready," Holt murmured. "You are so fucking beautiful."

When her nipples were harder than a rock from his massage, Holt peeled away her bra, leaned down, and flicked her nipple with his tongue.

"Dammit, Holt," Frey groaned. "Suck them!"

"Yes ma'am," Holt chuckled. Holding her breast to his mouth, he dragged his tongue slowly, licking around her areola before engulfing her breast into his mouth and vigorously sucked it. Frey arched her back, and he used his thumb and index finger from his other hand to roll her nipple back and forth.

"Oh, shit! That feels so good." Frey writhed on the bed.

Holt switched his mouth to her other breast and ran his hand down her body, slipping a finger between her legs. All his attention to her breasts left her drenched. His fingers slid into her with ease. She was ready for him.

"Fuck, sweetheart, you are so fucking perfect." Holt said before sitting up and cupping her breasts for a quick massage before running both hands down her body to just above her pussy. He grabbed her thong with both hands and ripped them in half.

"I liked those," Frey mumbled as she squirmed on the bed. Fuck, it was so hot to see him rip her underwear.

"I like those too. Lace is so much easier to tear." Holt's gaze held a glint of mischief. "I'll buy you a new one." Holt crawled down the bed, pulling her with him until her ass was on the edge and he was kneeling on the floor. Holt draped her legs over his shoulders, pushed her legs wide, and dove into her pussy.

"Oh, my ever-loving God," Frey screamed out, and Holt groaned while he alternated between licking and sucking her clit. Frey was undulating her hips to get away. It was too much. Her clit, along with her breasts, were extremely sensitive. Holt wasn't putting up with her attempts to push away from him. He placed one hand on her belly to keep her in place and used the other to finger fuck her while he continued to suck her clit. When her breathing raced out of control, he bit her clit with just enough pressure to coax her to come.

"Holt!"

"Let go, sweetheart, I got you," Holt said into her pussy.

Those were the right words. As soon as they left Holt's lips, Frey exploded in his mouth.

"Yum." Frey heard Holt hum as he licked her up. "You taste so sweet and tangy. My favorite flavors." Holt lowered her legs as he stood and took off his pants. "Scoot up the bed."

"I can't. I don't feel my limbs and I don't have the energy to move."

"Okay. I can work with this position, no worries." Holt grabbed her ankles and pulled them up. Creating a 'v' shape, he rested them on his chest, grabbed her hips and rammed himself into her. Crap, it's a good thing she was limber because having her legs up to her shoulders would otherwise really hurt. Not that she held that idea for long before her second orgasm ripped through her body.

"Fuck, Frey! You feel so damn good," Holt grunted and thrust into her. "Jesus Fuck!" Holt screamed before he came inside her.

It occurred to Frey that she felt all of him and his come. He hadn't worn a condom. Come to think of it, he hadn't worn a condom when he took her virginity either.

"Um, Holt?"

"Sorry sweetheart. I'm too heavy to lay on you like this." Holt released her legs, pulled out, and scooted them up in the bed. Rolling over he pulled her into his arms.

"Holt." Frey laid on top of him and braced herself on his chest staring into his eyes. "Did you wear a condom?"

"Uh" –Holt lifted his head off the bed and stared down at her– "no. I'm so sorry. But I promise you I'm clean. I've always gloved up with everyone else and I haven't slept with anyone in over a year."

Chapter 22

Assumptions and Insecurities

Frey

"What?" Frey drew her eyebrows together. Holt was always with a girl.

Holt dropped his head back and stated, "I've been celibate for about a year."

"How? I've seen you with a different girl almost every night." Frey made a fist on his chest and rested her chin where her pointer finger and thumb met.

"Frey, that's not true. About a year ago, I got tired of one-night stands and wanted something better. I stopped sleeping with every girl that came onto me."

"Really?" Frey's eyes widened in innocent confusion. "So, sex is a no, but blow jobs are a go?"

"Can we please forget about that?" Holt pulled her up over his body, cupped her face, and begged her with his eyes. "I had a weak moment. If I'm being honest, I was getting ready to stop her, but then I saw you in my doorway. You looked so fucking hot in that sexy outfit. I got hard watching you, not what she was doing." Holt held up his hand. "Not that what I was doing was right, but you should know I was going to push her away. I'm so sorry I hurt you."

Frey's emotions were all over the place as she gazed into his sorrow filled eyes. She was shocked and excited to hear that she had caused Holt to explode, but she wished it hadn't been in Candy's mouth. Holt seemed sincere in his apology and if they wanted to make this work, she had to accept it and move on.

"While I'm on a roll with apologies, I need you to know that I didn't tell Barrett to let Candy into my room the morning after we made love. I told her after the blow job fiasco that I never wanted to see her again because I was in a relationship. She jumped on me. I was trying to get her off me, but I didn't want to hurt her. I'm not an abusive asshole to women. I'm sorry for hurting you then, too."

"Please don't ever do that to me again." Frey swallowed the lump in her throat as she waited for Holt to agree. "It's hard to forget what I saw and trust you again."

Holt nodded. "I understand. It will never happen again."

Frey looked down at his neck, embarrassed by her assumptions of his dating habits. "I didn't realize you weren't sleeping around anymore."

"I hide it well, because I don't want anyone in my business. I'm sure Barrett assumes I'm still fucking around, but I'm not." Holt leaned up, giving her a quick kiss.

Frey slid down his body and rested her cheek on his chest, feeling better now that they got that out in the open. If they were serious about each other, they had a future.

"Well, I was a virgin, so I'm clean" –Frey mumbled– "and I haven't been with anyone in the last few days."

"Thank fuck," Holt sighed and kissed the top of her head.

"Uhm, Holt?" Frey whispered. "What if I'm pregnant?"

Holt's body tensed. His head snapped up and Frey saw a flash of alarm on his face. "What do you mean? What if you're pregnant?"

"Well, you've now fucked me without a condom, twice." Frey might be a virgin, but she knew how babies were made, and her period was not regular.

"True." Holt rolled them over and braced himself on his forearms next to her head to continue their conversation. "Are you not on the pill?"

"No," Frey felt her heart racing. "I didn't need to be because I was a virgin."

"I'll glove up from now on." Holt cupped her cheek. "Don't panic, it'll be okay. I'm sorry, I didn't think about it. Will you let me know if you miss your period and we'll tackle it together?"

"Okay." Frey squinted at him. "You sure are handling this well. What's going on?"

"Nothing," Holt's eyes widened. "I care about you, and I don't take my responsibilities lightly. I thought you were on the pill. Now that I know you're not, I'll protect us. If you are pregnant, I'll have your back with whatever you decide to do with our baby."

"Whatever I decide to do?" Frey pushed at his chest. "Do you think I would get rid of our child? Get off me!"

"Frey, sweetheart. Stop." Holt grabbed her hands and put them above her head and kissed her. "First, we don't even know if there is a baby. Second, if we made a baby, I wouldn't want you to get rid of our child. I just said that because it's your body and I would support you in your decision."

Holt's words sunk in, and she relaxed when she realized they would both want their baby. He was just being considerate. "I'm sorry." Frey took a few deep breaths. "I sounded crazy, huh?"

"Sweetheart, it's all good. I'm gonna clean us up. Then I'll come back so I can hold you while we sleep."

"Okay."

Frey stayed where Holt left her until he cleaned her up. He was so gentle with her. Surely, he loved her. Or is that how he treated all his girlfriends after sex? She had to stop thinking about other girls. He was with her now, and that's what mattered. Once Holt came back, he crawled into her bed, and she laid on his chest. She didn't want to ruin the moment by talking about other girls, so she relaxed into his warm arms and listened to the steady beat of his heart.

"I'll go see the doctor and get on the pill, but you'll have to wear protection for a few weeks." Frey murmured between kisses to his chest.

"Okay." Holt kissed her head. "Not a problem."

"Did you close your door to the laundry room?" Frey stroked his chest.

"I did. Why?" Holt placed one hand behind his head while the other massaged long, soothing strokes down her back.

"So, I don't have to get up and lock our closet door. I don't want Barrett catching us." Frey draped one leg between his.

"Frey, I've been thinking about it, and maybe it would be best if we talked to Barrett about us dating instead of keeping it from him. I feel guilty keeping something this important from him."

"No," Frey bolted up. They hadn't even said the "L" word to each other. Telling her family might not be such a good idea. If things didn't work out, not only would Holt lose her, but her entire family. Frey didn't think Barrett and Alex would forgive Holt if they broke up. She couldn't be the reason Holt lost everything.

"Let's think about this for a few more days." Frey dropped back onto the bed. "Uh, do all men think alike? That's what Ted said."

"Wait, what?" Holt was the one who bolted up this time and leaned over Frey. "You told Ted about us?"

"Yes. I had to say something." Frey shrugged. "I was breaking up with him before we even started dating. Plus, when I met him in the lobby, Barrett came over and puffed out his chest. All protective caveman-like to scare him. How did he even become aware I was meeting a man?" Frey pointed an accusatory look at Holt.

"Sorry" –Holt winced– "that's my fault. I told him to have another set of eyes on you. I didn't expect him to say anything mean to the guy."

Frey huffs and thinks about how crazy protective he can be. Even though Holt's meddling frustrates her, she understands his need to protect her after what happened to Tori.

"Well, he freaked Ted out. While doing so, he also mentioned your name, so then I explained who you were and gave Ted the four-one-one."

"Okay." Holt nodded. "Now that you've told Ted, shouldn't we tell Barrett? If we keep telling everyone but Barrett, he's liable to find out, and that would be bad."

"Are you crazy?" Frey closed her eyes and took a deep breath. "Ted won't say anything. He knows we're keeping it a secret. Besides, I don't plan on seeing him again."

"Sweetheart," Holt ran his thumb over her cheeks. "I'm thinking it's better to rip off the Band-Aid. I know I promised Barrett I wouldn't date you, but things have changed."

"You promised Barrett what? When?" Frey's eyes widened.

"In high school. I told him I wanted to ask you out on a date. He told me not to touch you and made me promise not to date you."

"Oh shit! That makes this worse. I thought he would only have to get over being overprotective of me and your friendship, but I also have to worry about you breaking a promise. Fuck!" Frey closed her eyes and slammed her hands palm down onto the bed.

"Look at me." Holt held her chin. "If we just tell him. I'll deal with the repercussions. I'll make sure he knows I started all this, not you." Holt gave her a quick peck on the lips. "I'll take all the blame, but I think it's best we don't drag this out."

"Please, just give me a few days to think about this?" Frey looked at Holt with pleading eyes.

"Okay," Holt laid down and pulled her onto his chest and rubbed her back. "I don't agree, but I'll keep quiet for now."

"Promise me, Holt." Frey was on edge, hoping he would go along with her decision. Waiting for him to say something.

"You Panther's sure do like your promises." Holt grumbled.

"Please?" Frey peppered his neck with kisses.

"Yeah," Holt kissed her forehead. "I promise."

"Thank you," Frey relaxed her body against Holt even though she was more worried now about Barrett's reaction than ever. She didn't want to come between their friendship. If Barrett had been so adamant enough to make Holt promise to stay away from her, their relationship was going to be trickier than she thought and possibly doomed even before it blossomed into a future. Maybe she could enlist Alex and Tori's help since by now Frey was sure Tori had told Alex all about their conversation.

*** Holt ***

Holt wished he could have fallen asleep as quickly as Frey. Unfortunately, his mind would not stop thinking about how to tell Barrett. Holt thought he was pretty clear when he told Frey how he felt about keeping their relationship a secret. He hated lying to his best friend and truly believed it would be worse if he found out on his own. They never kept secrets from each other. Eventually, Barrett would find out and the shit would hit the fan. Not that he was in any hurry to get an ass whooping from Barrett, but the quicker it happened, the faster they could move on.

Holt intended to date Frey with or without Barrett's consent. Over time, he believed Barrett would come to his senses and accept him as Frey's boyfriend, then fiancée, and finally, husband. Because Holt had plans to marry Frey and have a family with her one day. He knew he couldn't fight his attraction to her any longer. Every time he made love to her, he lost a little more of his heart and soul to her.

The sight of her with another man pierced his heart like a dagger and served as a powerful wake-up call. No man would ever touch what belonged to him. He would be Frey's first and last if he had anything to say about it. Frey had entrusted him with a special piece of herself, a treasured gift, and his commitment to protect that would remain unwavering until his dying breath.

He had a sinking sensation that hiding this from Barrett was going to bite him in the ass. It would ruin Barrett's trust in him, but breaking his promise to Frey would ruin their trust. He found himself trapped between a rock and a hard place. For now, he would follow Frey's lead and hope he could change her mind soon. When the time came, he would beg Barrett for forgiveness because he didn't want to lose his best friend.

Chapter 23

Sexy Time

Frey

Frey woke up the same way she went to sleep—wrapped up in Holt's arms. As she explored her way down his powerful chest, she felt his manhood stir by her thigh. With a smile on her face, she kissed her way down, sensing him harden the closer she got.

"Holt," Frey murmured against his cock.

"Hmm."

"Are you awake?" Frey licked the bulbous head.

"Mmhmm."

"Are you going to our Sunday Brunch today?" Frey licked the sides.

"Planning on it." Holt groaned and pushed his pelvis toward her face.

"You're not saying anything to my family about us, right?" Frey cupped his balls with her hand.

"Sweetheart," Holt held the back of her head. "Please don't talk about your family while your sweet mouth is on my cock and your hand is on my balls."

"Sorry," Frey chuckled and kissed him.

"You can make it up to me by sucking it and making it feel better." Holt pushed his cock toward her mouth.

"Okay," Frey opened wide and sank her mouth down until she felt him at her throat.

"Oh, shit," Holt's body jolted, and his hand tightened in Frey's hair.

Frey looked up as she slowly pulled back before she took him all the way down her throat again. He was gazing down at her with a glazed expression. His body moved slowly into her mouth.

"Fuck, sweetheart," Holt sat upright, grabbed her waist and turned her around, pulling her pussy towards his mouth as he laid down. Frey had only gone to first base with previous dates. Her sexual experience was limited because she never wanted to go any further with any boy who wasn't Holt. She knew what to do from reading romance novels, friend's conversations, and movies. Once she even watched a porn flick to see what all the fuss was about. She was aware of sexual techniques but had never experienced them. She'd seen this position before and loved the fact that they could pleasure each other at the same time. Although it also made her feel exposed. Yet he had already seen her pussy and tasted her. This was just a different angle.

He opened her legs wide and fit his mouth on her clit. While sucking her clit, he inserted a finger into her pussy. Frey's concerns disappeared as warm tingling sensations flowed through her body, causing her to buck her hips into his face, chasing her orgasm while she continued to suck his cock. It didn't take long for Frey's body to tremble against his lips as she lost control, releasing him from her mouth.

"That's it, sweetheart," Holt mumbled against her clit and inserted another finger. "Fuck my face."

"Ahh!" Frey screamed when he found her special spot in her pussy and rubbed it with his fingers. Between his hands, tongue, and dirty talk, her orgasm was so intense, she fell on top of him like dead weight. Holt gave her a few seconds to catch her breath before he grabbed her hips pushing her down his chest and onto his cock—reverse cowboy style.

"Holt!" Frey sat upright, placing her hands on his powerful thighs to brace herself as he pumped his hips into her.

"Ride me, sweetheart," Holt grunted as he held her hips and pushed up into her.

"Holt, I want to see you," Frey moaned as she slammed down onto Holt.

"We can arrange that." Holt held her hips. "Turn around slowly and keep me inside."

Frey put her feet on the bed and, between each rotation of her body, she pushed herself onto him until she was facing him.

"Oh fuck, you feel so damn tight." Holt was panting.

Frey was now facing Holt. With her hands on his chest, she slowly lifted herself up and down on his cock. Holt held her hips and ground into her in every downward motion.

"I need you to come with me," Holt groaned and sped up his thrusts. "Lean back and put your hands on my thighs."

Frey felt exposed in this position, but she trusted Holt. Holt gripped her hip with his left hand and rubbed her clit with his right hand as she rotated her hips on his cock.

"Oh...my...Holt!" Frey threw her head back as her body trembled with her orgasm and her pussy clenched down on Holt's cock.

"Fuck, Frey!" Holt held her tightly until he released himself into her.

Frey dropped onto his chest, completely depleted but content. Holt wrapped his arms around her and kissed the top of her head.

"I like the way you say good morning, sweetheart," Holt chuckled. "I could wake up like that for the rest of my life."

"Mmm, me too," Frey reached up and ran her hands through his hair. Shifting closer to his body, she peered into his eyes. "Holt, we really need to keep condoms by our beds."

"Yeah," Holt sighed. "We seem to keep forgetting that. When can you get on the pill?"

"I'll go to the doctor tomorrow, but it usually takes two weeks for the pill to work."

"Okay." Holt pushed her hair back from her face. "Let's shower and change before brunch."

Holt pulled her legs around his waist, sat up, turned on the bed, and stood holding her.

"Holt," Frey laughed and wrapped her legs around his waist tightly. Holt put his hands on her ass to hold her up and kissed her. "How did you do that?"

"You don't weigh much, Frey." Holt quirked his eyebrow at her. "Besides, these muscles aren't just for show."

"You mean they're not just for me to drool over?" Frey wiggled her eyebrows at him.

"Well, you can drool all over them, but they will also kick anyone's ass that comes near you." Holt squeezed her ass.

"Ah, there's the caveman I love." Frey tightened her hold when she realized what she'd said.

Holt froze in place and whispered. "Do you love me, Frey?"

"I could say I'm joking with you," Frey saw Holt's face fall, "but I'd be lying. It seems like I've loved you since the day I met you."

"I love you too, sweetheart," Holt murmured right before he placed her on the bathroom counter and cupped her face, gazing into her eyes. "I've loved you since you saved me from those bullies," Holt grinned. "But I was too young to recognize what those feelings meant. Then I was afraid to admit it for fear of you not loving me back. Once I moved into the resort, I figured out you might like me back, but by then, I had already promised Barrett not to date you. Afraid of losing the best family and friends I ever had, I chickened out from telling you. I thought if I ignored my feelings, they would go away. I was wrong." Holt leaned his forehead against hers. "We gotta tell them. If we love each other, they will understand. This isn't a one-night stand, this is forever. At least for me it is. Is this forever for you?"

"Yes, Holt. I want forever with you." Frey's eyes fluttered closed when Holt's lips nipped and licked her bottom lip, prodding her to open her mouth to let him in. Parting her lips, his tongue entwined with hers in an enchanting dance. Her pulse accelerated as her body tingled with arousal. Holt's hands on her face turned her head gently to control their kiss. She loved him, she had no doubts.

Bringing the kiss to a close, Holt moved back and planted kisses on her forehead, nose, and cheek. Holt helped her off the counter, turned on the hot water, and got the temperature just right for them. "Ladies first."

"Okay, but I think you need to go to your room and get a condom," Frey winked at him and got in the shower.

"Oh, sweetheart, you will be the death of me."

Frey heard Holt mutter before he walked out of the bathroom. Smiling, she stepped under the spray and washed her hair. Life was good. She had Holt after so many years of dreaming about being with him. Everything was looking up. They would tell Barrett, just not today. She wanted some time to just enjoy being with him before all hell broke loose.

Frey smelled Holt's musky scent before he turned her around to face him. Her nipples hardened as they brushed against his chest. His hands ran through her hair, helping her rinse out the shampoo. Her body was becoming accustomed to his touch, craved it even. Wanting to tease Holt and make him jealous, she said something to unleash the animal within.

"Mmm, Ted, that feels so good." Frey licked his neck and ran her hands down his sides.

One of his hands tightened in her hair while the other turned her around and pressed her up against the tile wall. Without a word, Holt's cock slammed into her pussy from behind.

"I never want to hear you call me another man's name again," Holt said while he fucked her hard.

Frey didn't expect such a powerful reaction, but she was glad she had said what she did. Experiencing Holt out of control was exhilarating.

Holt grabbed her hands and placed them against the wall. "Leave them there." He ran his hands over her back, nuzzling her against the wall. Pressing her aching nipples against the cold tile of the wall created a mind-numbing friction that sent tingles from her breasts directly to her pussy. His fingers swirled against her clit while his cock continued his assault. Warmth flooded Frey's body. Her heart beating hard and fast like it was going to fly out of her chest. Euphoria burst through her body, and she went limp as she climaxed.

Holt placed his hands over hers on the wall, holding her up while he pumped into her until he reached his orgasm.

"I'd like to say I'll never say that to you again" –Frey gasped– "but that...was...incredible." Holt turned her around and held her face up to him.

"I will do that and so much more for you, but sweetheart, please don't call me another man's name again. No other man will touch what is mine."

Frey saw the severity in his eyes as he pleaded with her. She never intended to hurt his feelings. If the roles were reversed, she wouldn't have wanted Holt to mention Candy like she did Ted when they were having an intimate moment. She would never make that mistake again. They needed to trust each other if this relationship was going to last. A stupid attempt to make Holt jealous had not been a good idea.

"I'm sorry. I was just kidding, but I will never do that again. You are the only one I want." Frey stroked his cheeks with her hands.

"Thank you. I accept your apology." Holt's gaze softened, and his lips lifted on the side in a slight smirk. "You are the only one for me, too. Let's finish our shower or we'll be late."

After Frey got dressed, she grabbed her phone and noticed she had two missed calls and four texts from her mom.

"Oh Shit!" Frey swore.

"What's wrong?" Holt ran out of his closet.

Chapter 24

Anger and Frustration

Frey

"**M**y mom called several times and left texts while we were in the shower. I need to call her." Frey motioned for him to stay quiet with a finger to her lips. "*Chatski*, what's going on?" Frey held her phone out in front of her and placed it on speakerphone so Holt could also listen.

"*Chackshosti*, where have you been? I've been calling and texting you for the past hour. I need you to come down and start the lasagna," Sehoy sounded out of breath on the phone. "Alex won't be here because he's taking Tori to Sarah's house. He left food for us to eat, but we need to cook it. Bernie is trying to help, but he is still busy with the breakfast crowd."

"Okay *chatski*, I'm so sorry. I didn't know Alex would not be here. I'm on my way." Frey finished getting dressed and sat on the bed to put on her shoes.

"What took you so long to answer me?"

"I...," Frey stared at Holt like a deer caught in headlights. Holt rubbed her back and mouthed 'tell her'. "I was sleeping in. I must have left my phone on silent." Frey shook her head at Holt.

"*Chackshosti*, I've told you not to do that when you are not working. What if I need to reach you for an emergency or to know you're okay?"

"I know. I'm sorry. Let me finish getting dressed and I'll be right there." Ever since Tori's incident, Frey noticed her mom wanting to know exactly where she was if she wasn't working in the casino. Didn't her mom realize if she was in trouble, she might not be able to use her phone, anyway? Not that she would tell her mom that, it would probably put her over the edge with worry. Frey finished getting ready, but she wanted to talk to Holt before she left the room.

"Okay, see you soon," Sehoy said and hung up the phone.

"Why didn't you just tell her?" Holt raised his arms in exasperation toward her.

"I can't just tell her over the phone!" Frey threw her phone on the bed.

"Okay. We'll tell everyone at brunch."

"No." Frey whirled around to face Holt. "We've got to talk to Barrett first. When I talked to Tori about it, she said Alex could help us, but I think that would make it worse."

"Are you serious? You talked to Tori?"

"I had to talk to someone. You were acting like an asshole with Candy!" Frey was fuming. "Talking to Tori helped me calm down and be open to your perspective."

"Okay. Fine." Holt ran his hand over his head in frustration. "Now, two people know before Barrett. There isn't a snowball's chance in hell that Tori didn't tell Alex. This is going to get ugly really quick. I don't want to lie to my best friend. You and I love each other. This isn't a passing fling. When we tell Barrett that we're serious about each other, he'll understand."

"Why can't you give me a couple of days?" Frey stood and grabbed his arm. She wanted him to stay quiet a little while longer. She was terrified she'd lose Holt or her family. What if no one understood their love? If everyone thought like Barrett, then their dating would be incest. Don't be stupid, Frey, she told herself. That was the dumbest thing she'd ever thought. She was not related by blood to Holt.

Frey was glad they'd said they loved each other, but maybe it would be best if they got married before telling everyone. Then no one could break them apart. That was a crazy thought. Her mom would kill her if she married Holt without her family. What was she thinking? Obviously, she wasn't thinking she was spiraling and just needed time to think.

"I'm scared. Okay." Frey shook his arm. "I know it doesn't sound rational, but what if everyone thinks it's a bad idea and tries to break us apart?"

"You don't think I'm good enough to date you?" Holt moved away from Frey.

"No!" Frey yelled. "That's not what I meant. I love you, but if they don't take our dating well, then what happens to us?"

"I don't think you're making any sense. I don't understand why you would think that. I would love to have your family's approval, but I'm not leaving you if any of them get mad. Over time, they'll understand how much we mean to each other."

"Please. Just a few days." Frey pleaded.

"Fine, Frey." Holt held her. "I don't want to argue with you, and we need to get downstairs. We'll continue this later."

"Okay," Frey leaned up and kissed him. "I gotta help *chatski*. I'll see you later at brunch." Frey tried to leave the room fast before he changed his mind.

"Yeah." Holt rubbed his hand over his face. "Call me if you need me to help you. Or I can come with you now."

"No!" Frey jolted. "You can't come now. How will I explain you were with me when I called my mom?" Frey could see the frustration written all over his face.

"Frey, we've been friends forever. I've shown up with you to brunch many Sundays. I think you're panicking and overthinking this. If we keep lying, the lies are going to catch up with us." Holt sat on the edge of the bed, head down, shoulders slumped, and his hands dangling between his knees. "Eventually, we're going to fuck up."

"I know, you're right." Frey placed her hand on his shoulder. He looked defeated. "It's just my guilty conscience because I do feel guilty about keeping secrets from my family."

"Well, if you're feeling that guilty about lying, we can fix that." Holt raised his hands again in frustration.

"Gotta go." Frey kissed his cheek and reached for her phone on the bed. "How about you give me a five-minute head start?"

"Frey." Holt grabbed her hand. "Seriously. We need to sort this out."

"We already have. You promised to give me some time to figure out how to tell Barrett." Frey pulled her hand away. "I gotta go, talk later."

"Fine," Holt mumbled as she raced out of her room.

Holt

Sunday Brunch held a special place in Holt's heart ever since he moved in with the Panthers, but this specific one was going to be one to remember. How on earth was he supposed to resist touching Frey and not gaze at her as if she meant everything to him?

Holt stood in the middle of Frey's bedroom, placed his hands on his hips, dropped his head, and sighed. *Fuck! Fuck! Fuck! He screamed internally.* He could talk to Tori since Frey involved her in their secret. Tori might have better luck convincing Frey, they should tell Barrett.

Hell, if Tori had already told Alex, then Barrett would truly feel fucked. This was turning into a real shitshow. Because the Panthers always treated him like family, Holt felt certain they would approve of him dating and marrying Frey. The only exception was Barrett. Holt always thought Barrett would go ring shopping with him as his best friend and it would be an exciting time. But under these circumstances, he would have to pick something out himself. With a ring, everyone would know he meant business.

Holt worried they wouldn't take him seriously since he had played the field for so long. They would never believe that he'd always loved Frey. An engagement would serve as proof of his seriousness. However, he wanted to ask Mr. Panther for permission to marry Frey, and he couldn't do that if he proposed to Frey before revealing his intentions.

Fuck! He needed a different perspective and Frey just kept bolting instead of talking this out. Talking to Tori seemed like his best idea. He would wait until tomorrow and try to catch her alone, which would be a challenge all on its own since Alex or Frey were always with her.

Deep breath, Holt, he told himself. For now, he would head down to Savor and see if he could help. He'd been standing there for at least twenty minutes pondering his problem. Plenty of time had passed where no one would be suspicious.

Holt pulled himself together and left from his room in case Barrett was by the elevator. All was clear as he took the elevator downstairs and headed toward Savor.

Chapter 25

Sunday Family Brunch

Holt

"Hello everyone." Holt watched Sehoy, Frey, Amy, and Bernie scurrying around in the kitchen. It appeared as if all the guests had already left, and they were tidying up after the breakfast crowd. "How can I help?"

Sehoy put Holt to work, drying dishes and setting the table for seven. Bernie, Savor's Head Chef, and Amy, one of their waitresses, would join them instead of Alex and Tori. Holt stayed away from Frey in case his body language gave him away. It was hard not to brush up against her and want to touch her.

"*Chakpootsi.*" Sehoy tapped his back. "Let Barrett and Osceola know to get down here so we can eat."

"Got it."

It warmed Holt's heart every time Sehoy or Osceola called him son. They never pushed him to call them mom and dad, but they were the only parents who cared about him. It had been an honor when they told him it was okay for him to refer to them as his parents. Holt used his cell phone to text Osceola and Barrett.

"*Chatski*, they're on their way," Holt told her after they texted him back. "What can I carry out for you?"

"Everything on this table needs to go out there." Sehoy pointed toward the kitchen island. "Everyone, grab a dish and let's go eat."

Osceola and Sehoy each sat at the heads of the table across from each other. Holt and Barrett sat on either side of Osceola. They all wanted to keep watch on the lobby. Frey sat with Holt on one side and Amy on the other. Amy and Bernie sat on either side of Sehoy, with an empty seat next to Bernie and Barrett. Bernie and Sehoy both wanted to be closest to the kitchen.

The lasagna, salad, sliced bread, small dishes with olive oil, and meatballs occupied the center of the table. Once everyone sat down, they started helping themselves. Everyone passed around the red wine, white wine, and water pitcher.

"Where's Alex?" Osceola asked.

"He took Tori to Sarah's house for lunch," Frey answered first while passing the breadbasket to Holt.

"Well, that's nice, but I wish they were here. Sehoy, maybe next time we can invite them all over for brunch."

Holt would like that. He didn't really know any of them well.

"That would be nice." Sehoy nodded. "I'll talk to Tori and Alex about it."

"Tall Bear and Spirit-of-the-Eagle will come for the cultural center opening. They will arrive Wednesday night and stay with us until Saturday morning," Osceola informed them. "It is a surprise for Tori, so we can't let her know they are here until we head to the opening."

Holt grinned, knowing he would see Tall Bear in the casino at least once during his visit. He loved to gamble.

"She will be so happy to see her father," Frey said between bites. "She's told me she misses him."

"I think the feeling is mutual," Osceola mumbled. "If my daughter had gone through such a traumatic experience, I'd want to see her too."

"Have they found Winston yet?" Sehoy asked.

Holt glanced at Frey. He knew talking about Winston made her nervous. He'd suggested several times that she talk to her mom or a therapist to help her with her fears. Although...now that he thought about it, she seemed calmer when they slept in the same bed, but he noticed she still had a chair under the adjoining door to Tori's old room.

"No, they think he might be hiding with Lucifer's Renegades, the motorcycle club." Barrett took a drink of water. "They have some officers doing surveillance on the clubhouse, but haven't spotted him yet."

"I hope they find him soon," Frey spoke up. "I'll be happy when he's off the streets." Holt squeezed her thigh under the table. He knew Frey was freaking out about Tori's safety and her own.

"*Chackshosti*," Osceola looked at Frey and changed the subject. "I heard you had trouble at your table last week."

"It was nothing, chacteka. Barrett handled it." Frey continued to cut her lasagna. Holt saw she didn't look up.

"What happened?" Sehoy grimaced at Frey. "You didn't tell me."

"Remember that asshole bully Dave from school?" Barrett commented.

Holt placed his elbow on the table, leaned his mouth into his hand, holding the fork to hide his smile as he waited for Sehoy to reprimand Barrett for cussing at the table. She had drilled respect and manners into them since they were young. Cussing was not a behavior she accepted in her presence.

"Language *chakpootsi*," Sehoy corrected Barrett.

"Sorry, *chatski*. Remember that mean bully Dave from school?" Barrett smirked as he corrected his language.

"Yes," Osceola spoke up. "What about him?"

"He accused Frey of cheating. Holt watched his behavior at Frey's table escalate through the monitors. He let us know, and I went to supervise the situation since I was patrolling the floor. I remained calm and escorted him out of the casino."

"Did he make a scene?" Osceola asked, concerned as he looked between Holt, Barrett, and Frey.

"No." Barrett shook his head. "I got him out of there fast. Then Holt's girlfriend Candy came to find me when she couldn't find Holt. The night turned out to be quite fascinating."

Holt froze and gave Barrett his best evil eye. Barrett smiled at him. *Why the fuck did Barrett have to bring Candy into the conversation? Fucker.* "She is not my girlfriend." Holt said through gritted teeth. "I told you that."

Frey rubbed his thigh under the table and the tension drained from his shoulders. Knowing Frey wasn't mad calmed him down.

"You have a girlfriend?" Frey turned to Holt and smiled. "When can we meet her?"

What the fuck? Holt's head spun in her direction. He couldn't believe she would take part in this game with Barrett. So much for Frey's hand, calming him down. He knew she was attempting to mislead her family, but it was royally pissing him off.

"Like I told Barrett." Holt raised his eyebrow at her. "She is NOT my girlfriend."

"Okay, okay," Sehoy interrupted them. "Leave Holt alone. Clearly, he doesn't like this young lady."

"That's a nice way to describe her," Barrett mumbled under his breath.

Holt scowled at Barrett. Now the Panthers would think he only dated sluts. Shit, he had to change the subject quick.

"*Chackshosti* is dating someone and mentioned she would bring him to brunch next weekend," Sehoy beamed at her daughter.

"*Chatski*, I told you I'd ask Ted. I'll see if he is available, but I'm not promising anything." Frey patted Holt's thigh and ate a forkful of lasagna.

Frey better not invite Ted to their family brunch, or he was letting the cat out of the bag. *Fuck it!* He would rather tell everyone about their relationship than share a family brunch with Ted. No way was he going to sit and watch Ted flirt with her or vice versa. If she didn't stop talking about dating Ted, he was going to drag her up to their room and spank her ass for trying to make him jealous again. Diversion tactic or not, no one was her date for brunch but him. *Was she fucking serious?*

"Did you ask Ted to join us?" Holt turned to look at Frey, squeezing her thigh under the table.

"Not yet." Frey winked at him and rubbed his manhood through his pants.

Holt's body jolted. His cock hardening at the feel of her hand. He wasn't expecting her to touch him like that during their family brunch. Granted, he was so far under the table, no one could see what was going on. She was playing a dangerous game. Holt glanced at her and saw the smirk on her face. Two could play at this game.

Holt straightened in his seat and slid his hand up her thigh and pulled her leg closer to him. Creating a larger space between her legs for his hand to pleasure her under the table.

"He seemed nice, but I definitely put the fear of God in him." Barrett looked at his dad and Holt. Holt grinned and ran his finger back and forth over her panty covered pussy.

"As you should." Osceola stated as he cut into his food.

"*Chacteka*," Frey gasped, squeezing Holt's cock when he pulled her underwear aside and slid his finger into her pussy. "Barrett was rude. At least Holt refrained from threatening him." Frey glared at Barrett while her hand squeezed Holt harder.

Holt grunted and moved his other hand down to ease Frey's grip. Damn, if she squeezed any harder, she might break it off.

"Barrett was just protecting you. It's what brothers do." Osceola nodded.

"Boys," Sehoy sighed. "At some point, you are going to have to let your sister date."

Frey didn't realize in Holt's mind he'd beaten the shit out of him multiple times. Not wanting to continue the discussion on Frey's dating life, he shifted the conversation to something else. "So, who's working at the center on opening night?"

"Thunder wants Frey with Tori since Alex will be in the kitchen all night. I'm thinking he might want some of our security, but I'll have a better idea after I talk to him later this week. Barrett, clear your schedule." Osceola nodded. "If he needs extra security, I'm sending you since the exhibit is about our people and you can answer questions. Both you and Frey should prepare your pow wow outfits. Thunder likes for the American Indian workers to be in their pow wow regalia."

"Okay, chacteka," Barrett got serious and nodded.

"Holt, if Thunder needs extra help, I'll send you," –Osceola continued– "but for now, I want you to stay here and be in charge of the security team."

"Yes, sir," Holt said. He always felt honored when Osceola trusted him with responsibility. Osceola was a father figure to him, and he cherished the chance to step up and make him proud.

Holt slid another finger inside Frey. Frey slid lower in her chair and spread her legs wider, releasing a low moan.

"What's going on over there?" Barrett pointed between Frey and Holt. "Something you guys want to talk about?"

"Uh, no?" Holt withdrew his hand, his eyes darting between Barrett and Frey.

"Is that a question or a statement?" Barrett raised an eyebrow and stared at them.

Frey busted out with a forced laugh and placed her hand on his shoulder, shoving him playfully.

"I met Candy and gave him a hard time. He can do better." Frey turned to face Holt and gave him a warning look.

"Uh," Holt's eyes widened. He cleared his throat. "Yeah, Frey didn't like Candy." It was the truth. Frey didn't like Candy, but the way she said it suggested that Holt was planning on seeing Candy again. Holt knew that look. She was mad at him, but he didn't know why. She was the one that started the under the table game.

"You're seeing Candy again?" Barrett smirked at Holt.

"No." Holt held up his hands and shook his head vehemently. Holt glared at Frey. *Thanks a lot sweetheart for bringing Candy up again to deflect any questions directed at you. Fuck me.* "Frey was just bringing it up to tease me. She knows I don't like Candy."

"Holt, who is this, Candy?" Osceola asked. "Is this the girl we were discussing earlier?"

"Um, yes, it is. She's a girl I met at the casino. No one important, which is why I've never introduced you to her."

Osceola nodded. "You've never introduced us to any of your girlfriends."

"That's because he's a horn dog, *chackteka*," Barrett slammed his hand down on the table and threw his head back to laugh.

"I am not a horn dog." Holt frowned at Barrett. "As a matter of fact, I'm seeing someone." *Take that fucker.*

"Shit." Barrett stopped laughing and shouted. "Frey! Were you aware Holt was seeing someone?"

Holt held his breath and turned to Frey, hoping she would help him out and not be mad at him.

Frey had been talking to Amy next to her. "What? What did you say, Barrett?"

"I asked if you knew Holt was dating someone?" Barrett's head ping ponged back and forth between Holt and Frey.

"No, why would I? I thought he was with Candy," Frey said, giving Holt and Barrett a look.

There was a small part of Holt that thought, *Dammit Frey, that was our chance!* Holt knew they had talked about keeping their relationship a secret, but Barrett had given them the perfect chance to tell everyone. Holt was getting more and more frustrated with this conversation. If the Candy stuff didn't stop, he was excusing himself and leaving.

"For the last time, I am not dating Candy!" Holt took a drink of water, trying to calm down. "Can we please stop talking about her?"

Barrett rubbed his hands together, savoring this juicy gossip. "Okay, Candy's out. This new girl is in. Who is she?"

"Yes, *chakpootsi*, who is this young lady?" Osceola chimed in. "You should've invited her to brunch."

"She had to work today." Holt gripped his fork and speared a piece of lasagna, quickly placing it in his mouth. With food in his mouth, he didn't have to answer questions. He kicked Frey under the table hoping she would help him out, but Frey smiled at him and kicked him back.

"Where does she work?" Barrett asked.

"Um, the mall." Holt wiped his mouth with his napkin and stood up. "I'm sorry to cut this short, but I need to make a phone call." Clearly, eating would not shut Barrett up and Frey was no help. He needed to leave while he could.

"Calling the little missus?" Barrett laughed.

"Yeah." Holt picked up his dishes and took them to the kitchen. He'd had enough of lying to his family. "Thank you all for brunch. I'll see you later."

Everyone said goodbye to Holt before he walked up to his room. Holt opened their adjoining closet door so he could hear Frey when she got to her room. Turning on his TV, Holt laid down on his bed and closed his eyes, taking deep breaths to calm down. He didn't have to wait long until Frey stormed into his bedroom.

* * * **Frey** ***

"What the hell, Holt?" Frey exclaimed when she entered his room.

"Why are you so mad?" Holt leaned back against the headboard and raised his hands in frustration. "You kept throwing me under the bus about Candy and you told them you were going to invite Ted!"

"I'm seeing someone." Frey mimicked Holt's voice. "What was that?"

"I was trying to show them I'm not a horn dog fucking every girl I see." Holt was beyond pissed.

"Yeah, but now they want to know who you're dating." Frey stood with her hands crossed and her hip cocked.

"Then let's tell them!" Holt sat up in bed. "Sweetheart, I love you and I want the world to see how much we care about each other."

"No, Holt. It's too soon." Frey glared at him.

"How is it too soon? We've known each other forever and we both love each other?" Holt threw his hands up in the air. He seemed to be doing that with her a lot lately. Her argument was frustrating the shit out of him.

Frey sat on Holt's lap. "You said you would give me some time to think about how to tell Barrett." Frey showered him with kisses all over his face and neck. After pulling his shirt off, she pushed him down and trailed kisses down his chest to his lower abs, stopping at his jeans.

"Frey, stop." Holt placed his hands over the button on his jeans. "I need you to tell me why you're so scared to tell Barrett." Holt sat up, grabbed Frey, and pulled her up to straddle him.

"Do you remember Barrett's friend Jeremy? We were all in the same home-room freshman year." Frey traced his abs while she talked.

"Yes. What about him?" Holt scooted them back and leaned on the head-board.

"Do you not remember that day he came over to hang out with Barrett, but followed Jenny into my room and stayed in there with us?"

"No." Holt gripped her wandering hand. "Did something happen?" His voice sounded low and dangerous. His body was taut, like he was ready to find Jeremy and kick his ass.

Frey jerked her head up. "Not what you're thinking."

"Thank fuck." Holt released his breath and his body relaxed.

"Anyway, Jeremy came into my room and was hanging out with me and Jenny on the couch when my mom came in to ask if we wanted a snack. Mom was pissed because boys weren't allowed in my room. We were just talking, but Jeremy had his arm around my back on the couch with his thigh touching mine. Mom blew a gasket and yelled at Jeremy to leave my room and go hang out with Barrett. Jeremy apologized and hurried out. Thinking back, I guess it looked intimate. But it's not like we were alone or sitting on my bed."

"Hell. Even I knew not to go into your room." Holt muttered.

"Yeah. I talked to Barrett later that night after everyone left and he was mad at me for stealing his friend. Barrett said he felt hurt because Jeremy pretended to be his friend, but clearly, he just wanted to go out with me." Frey looked down and fidgeted with her fingers. "As far as I know, he never spoke to Jeremy again."

"I wondered why we never invited him again to hang out with us, but Barrett never said." Holt sighed and closed his eyes.

"I don't want him to do that to you," Frey whispered before cupping his cheek and giving him a soft kiss on the lips.

"Okay." Holt opened his eyes and frowned. "But that was so long ago. We were only what...fourteen?"

"Yes, but what if he shuts you out?" She would be devastated if Holt lost his best friend because of her. Barrett and Holt were like two peas in a pod. Anyone that saw them would think Holt was Barrett's twin instead of Frey. This scared the crap out of her. It wasn't Barrett or her family knowing that they were dating, it was Barrett's reaction to Holt, especially after that 'don't date my sister promise.'

"I think if we talk to him alone and explain everything–it will be okay. Barrett and I have been friends for over seventeen years. He only knew Jeremy for a few months. When we tell Barrett how much we love each other, I think it will all be okay."

Frey heard everything Holt said, but it still scared her shitless to tell Barrett.

"Just give me some time to think about this, please?" Frey's tongue followed her roaming hands down his body to the button on his jeans. The time for talking about this was over, as far as she was concerned. Now she wanted to show him how much she loved him.

"Okay." Holt sighed, watching her mouth travel down his body. "But I still think we should talk to Barrett. The sooner the better. You're not gonna change my mind about that."

"I bet I can." Frey grinned at Holt while her hands unbuttoned his jeans and pulled the zipper down. "Just lay back and relax while I get close and personal with little Holtie," Frey stated before dropping her mouth onto his cock.

"Shit, sweetheart." Holt cupped her head against his cock. "Don't call him little. There is nothing little about him." Holt lifted his hips when Frey slid her hands on either side of his hips and slid his jeans and boxer briefs down.

Frey cat crawled backwards until she reached the end of the bed. Standing up, she raised her arm up and dropped his clothes to the floor. Watching Holt lying on the bed naked, pupils dilated, and fully aroused, gave her the idea to strip slowly.

Frey had never done anything like this before, but his heated gaze empowered her to sway her hips seductively to an imaginary slow rhythm only she could hear. Her hands traveled up over her body, under her hair, and up to the sky while she threw her head back. Gyrating her hips in a slow sensuous circle, she spun around, facing away from him.

Undoing her pants, she slowly pushed them down past her hips, jutting her ass out as she bent down. Giving him a full view of her thong. Frey heard him groan. Smiling to herself, she stood neri stepped out of her pants. After she pulled her shirt off, she glanced at him over her shoulder. Holt licked his lips as he stared at her ass. Frey looked at his lap and saw his cock standing at attention. *Oh, yeah, Holt was enjoying the show.* Frey turned her face around and undid her bra, letting it fall in front of her.

Frey cupped her breasts and turned around to face Holt, her hips swaying again. Nostrils flared he gripped the comforter holding his body still as he watched her. His eyes darting all over her body as if they didn't know what part of her body to focus on. Frey was enjoying this power. She began massaging her breasts, using her thumbs to circle her nipples. Holt moaned and briefly closed his eyes.

Frey kept one hand on her breasts while the other made its way slowly down her belly into her panties. Frey closed her eyes and moaned when she slid her finger into her pussy.

"You're fucking killing me." Holt growled. "Come here."

Frey opened her eyes and smiled wickedly at the sight before her. Holt was panting. His eyes focused on her hand in her panties while he stroked his cock. Holt curled his finger, calling her over.

Frey crawled up the bed between his legs like a cat on the prowl for her next tasty morsel. Shoving his hands out of the way, she gripped them and placed them on either side of his body. Frey positioned her mouth close enough to Holt's cock that he could feel her breath. With half-lidded eyes, Frey glanced up to look at Holt.

His body stiffened, and she heard him take a deep breath. Frey grinned and flicked her tongue out to lick the liquid oozing out before sinking her mouth onto his cock until he reached the back of her throat. Frey could feel the vibrations of Holt's shudders.

"Fuck, sweetheart, come up here." Holt leaned forward, placed his hands under her arms, and tried to pull her up.

"I'm not done down here yet," Frey mumbled around his cock and applied suction. Holt dropped back onto his back, his hips jerking toward her mouth. She had to admit, it was a powerful feeling watching him lose control.

Chapter 26

Run Holt Run

Holt

The next few days flew by in a blissful blur. Going to bed and waking up with Frey was a dream come true. Slowly, Holt rolled over and grabbed a condom from his nightstand. He wanted to be ready when he woke Frey and slid inside her. Holding her close from behind, he felt her move in his arms.

Today was opening night at the American Indian Cultural Center featuring the Seminole Tribe of Florida exhibit. Because the exhibit was about her tribe, Frey and all the other Panthers were working tonight. He could not attend with her because he was on security duty at the casino. What he could do was fuck her silly and put a smile on her face before she left. Leaving her with some soreness between her legs would guarantee her thinking of him tonight. He knew that made him sound like a controlling boyfriend, but he wanted to remind her of what was waiting for her at home.

"Good morning." Holt cupped Frey's breasts and pulled her against his chest while gently kissing and nipping her neck.

"Morning," Frey moaned and trailed her hand to his ass. "I wish you were coming with me tonight."

"I wish I was too, but I'm not sure I'd be able to keep my hands off you all night. You feel so good." Holt used one hand to cup her breast while the other travelled down her body to her pussy. "Hmm," Holt groaned into her neck, "you are so wet for me. Were you dreaming about me?"

"Always."

Holt slid one finger into her as his thumb stroked her clit. Frey pushed back into him. She was so wet and ready for him—he glided into her from behind after sliding his hand out and pulling her leg over his thigh, opening her wide. As he bottomed out inside her, warmth filled his heart, creating a sense of coming home. "Fuck, Frey. I love you."

"I love you too."

Holt rolled them, exerting control over their lovemaking by keeping her in place face down on the mattress. Frey turned her head and grabbed the sheets, pushing herself back into him every time he thrust into her. He was so close to coming, but he wanted Frey to go first. As he played with her nipple, he reached under her with his other hand and plucked and squeezed her clit. He sensed her body clench around him, and they both climaxed simultaneously.

Holt rolled off Frey. "Let me clean up. I'll be right back."

Holt went to the bathroom and threw out the condom, grabbing a washcloth to clean Frey up. Returning to the bed, he smiled when he saw Frey was still in the same position she was in when he left.

"Sweetheart, did I wear you out?" Holt kissed down her spine while he cleaned her up and threw the washcloth onto the bathroom floor.

"Mmm," Frey mumbled.

"Come here." Holt rolled her over onto his chest. "Let's snuggle until you gotta leave me. I want to hold you."

BANG! BANG! BANG! "Frey, are you in there!" Holt and Frey sprung apart and stared out the bedroom door.

"Shit," Frey bolted out of bed, ran into the bathroom and grabbed her robe. "That's Barrett, go."

"Why? Let's tell him." Holt sat up and swung his legs to the floor, ready to stand up. "No time like the present. We have privacy."

"Really, Holt?" Frey whirled on him and smacked his chest. "You want to tell my overprotective twin brother that we are fucking while your cock is hanging out? You think that's a good idea? Hmm?"

"Well, when you put it that way, no." Holt got up and grabbed his clothes. "I was thinking more along the lines of you closing the bedroom door and buying me some time to get dressed before I step into the living room, and we all discuss this like adults."

"Frey?" Barrett called out again.

"I'm coming. Give me a second." Frey walked to her bedroom doorway and screamed, then turned back to Holt. "I'll come get you when the coast is clear."

"Fine." Holt didn't even bother getting dressed. He made sure he had all his clothes and stomped through the closet to his room. He realized they were almost caught, but they weren't doing anything wrong. They were two consenting adults who were in love with each other. So, why did he feel like a dirtbag running out of his girlfriend's room buck naked?

He would take a nice, long, hot shower and calm down. If Frey came to get him after Barrett left, they could talk. If not, he would take a nap before work. It was going to be a long night, and they were short staffed in every department without Osceola, Sehoy, Frey, and Barrett.

*** **Frey** ***

Frey closed her bedroom door and ran to open her front door to Barrett.

"Hey." Frey was out of breath. "What's up?" She opened the door and was leaning on it.

"Why are you out of breath?" Barrett's gaze darted up and down her body. "Are you running in your room before you shower?"

"How do you know I wasn't in the shower and hurried to get out to answer you banging?" Frey let Barrett in and closed the door.

"Duh." Barrett pointed at her head. "Your hair's not wet."

"Maybe I didn't want to wash it." Frey crossed her arms and glared at her brother.

"Why are we having this stupid conversation about your shower habits?" Barrett walked into the room holding a garment bag.

"You started it. What's in the bag?" Frey pointed toward it.

"My regalia." Barrett unzipped the bag. "My iron isn't working. I wanted to use yours to iron my shirt."

"Leave it here," Frey offered. "I'll iron it." Frey didn't want to iron Barrett's shirt, but she was ready for him to go so she could get back to Holt.

"Really?" Barrett looked shocked. "You're going to iron my shirt? You never iron my stuff. What's going on?"

"Nothing. I thought I would be nice to my younger brother." Frey stressed the word younger and shrugged one shoulder. "But if you want to do it yourself, I'll give you my iron." Frey stepped around Barrett, but he grabbed her arm before she could make it to her bedroom door. Thank goodness he stopped her because she wasn't sure Holt had left her room.

"Wait." Barrett turned and smiled at his sister while holding her arm. "I appreciate your offer and I accept. When do you want me to come back to get it?"

"Come back around five." Frey pulled the shirt out of the garment bag and zipped it back up. Handing it back to him. "You can take the rest of your stuff."

"Sounds good." Barrett grasped the hanger. "Thank you, sis." Barrett leaned over and kissed her cheek. "You are my favorite twin sister."

"Yeah, right...jerk." Frey wasn't mad. She loved her brother and their banter. Would this change between them once he found out Holt had slept with her, and they were dating?

"Barrett..." Frey grabbed his arm and hesitated. *Should she tell him? Should Holt be with them when she told him? Was she being selfish, keeping Holt all to herself? Wouldn't Barrett be okay if someday Holt truly became his brother by marriage?* All these thoughts raced through her head, but in the end, she said nothing.

"Yeah?" Barrett stared at her with a furrowed brow. "Are you okay?"

"Yeah, sorry." Frey let go of his arm and shook her head, wanting to ignore the thoughts that could ruin their relationship. "Just daydreaming. I'll have your shirt ready."

"Okaayy, but if you need to talk" –Barrett hugged her– "just know I'm always here for you. I love you."

"I love you, too. Thanks, Bare." Frey walked him to the door, firmly closing it as soon as he stepped through. Leaning against it, she took a deep breath to calm her racing heart. She almost told Barrett, but she held back because she didn't know if Holt would want to be there. Shit, maybe she should also have Alex with her. Barrett listened to Alex. *How mad would Barrett be?*

Frey pushed off the door and headed to Holt's room to check on him.

"I'm sorry," Frey said from the closet doorway. Holt was lying on his bed watching TV.

Holt reached over, grabbed the remote, and muted the sound.

"I'm sorry, too." Holt reached his hand out to her. "Come, lay down with me. I just want to hold you."

Frey walked into his arms and laid her head on his chest. "I gotta get up around three so I can shower and iron Barrett's shirt."

"Is that why he was here?" Holt stroked her back.

"Yes."

"If you want to relax longer, I'll iron it." Holt kissed her forehead.

"That's really sweet, but I think I'll have enough time." Frey kissed his chest. "I almost told Barrett about us. I came so close."

"Why did you stop?" Holt tilted his head down to see her face.

"Part of it was because I thought you might like to be with me when I told him." Frey shifted so she could see his face. "But the bigger part was that I was scared. I didn't want my twin to hate me or my boyfriend."

"Oh, sweetheart." Holt cupped her face. "I don't think your brother could ever hate you. He might hate me for a while and kick my ass, but he would never hate you."

"I don't want him to hate you either," Frey whispered.

"I love you, Frey. There is nothing in this world that would keep me from you. If your brother steps between us, I will try my hardest to win him over. Together, we can convince him that what we have is special and will last a lifetime." Holt pulled her up for a kiss. "We need to tell him and stop obsessing over his reaction."

"Okay." Frey laid back down, snuggling her face on his neck. "Let's get past the opening tonight."

"Sounds good. I love you." Holt squeezed her tight and raised the volume on the TV.

"I love you, too." Frey got comfy as they watched a home improvement show. They ate lunch in bed, filling their bellies and their sexual appetite one more time before taking a nap. Holt set the alarm for her to wake up in time to shower and iron.

Chapter 27

Crazy Night

Holt

O sceola left Holt at the casino as head of security. He felt honored to be left in charge. Wanting to catch a glimpse of Frey before she departed, he appeared in the lobby, dressed for work to see everyone off. Frey looked stunning in her pow-wow regalia. He'd seen her dress before, but now she was his woman and she looked sexy as hell.

Holt stood back while Osceola gave them instructions. Suddenly, Alex professed his love for Tori in front of both their families. It wasn't a proposal. Alex didn't have a ring, but it was a beautiful moment. One he wished he could have with Frey. Even though he was happy for Alex and Tori, he felt the sting of jealousy over their open and accepted relationship.

"Hey." Holt grabbed Frey's hand when everyone walked off. "You look beautiful. Be careful."

"Thanks. I'll be fine," Frey smiled and hurried to catch up.

Holt wanted to hold her and kiss her so badly it hurt as he watched her walk out the front door. Working in the casino would be a great distraction from not being with Frey.

He spotted Dave standing at one of the roulette tables as soon as he stepped into the casino. Holt was glad Frey wasn't working tonight. Seeing Dave might have upset her. Dave needed to know that if he pulled a stunt like last time, he would be blackballed from this casino.

"Dave." Holt placed his hand on his shoulder and squeezed. "How are you?"

Dave turned around. "I swear I'm not here to cause trouble, Holt." Dave was shifting his weight and placed his hands in his pockets. "I wanted to let off some steam and apologize to Frey for the way I acted. Is she here?"

"No, she's off tonight. Why the change of heart?" Holt showed no reaction on his face, but inside he wasn't buying what Dave was selling. It was difficult for Holt to believe that Dave was a nice guy after so many years of bullying her. He would need to keep an eye on him.

"Adulting," Dave sighed. "Therapy has been a part of my journey. I'm happily married now with a newborn. I realized I would hate for my child to go through what I put Frey through during school. I really am sorry."

"I'm happy to hear you say that, but I'm not gonna lie, man—I'm shocked as shit."

"Yeah, I get that," Dave nodded.

"I'll talk to Frey when I see her." Holt decided it would be best for him to talk to Frey about Dave before he blindsided her.

"Sounds good. Thanks, man. I'll apologize personally next time I play at her table as well."

Holt believed in that, saying, 'Keep your friends close and your enemies closer'. Dave had always been the enemy and Holt didn't trust a word that came out of his mouth. For Dave's sake, he better be telling the truth or else he was going to find himself on the floor again, with more than a fucking bloody nose this time. "Great. Enjoy your evening." Holt slapped him on the back and continued to walk to the floor, looking for issues.

Holt never expected to get an apology from Dave in this lifetime. Only time would tell if he meant it.

"Hey, handsome."

Shit! Holt recognized that voice before he turned around. It was like nails on a chalkboard. He hated hearing it. He winced before he turned around to face her. "Candy, how are you?"

"I'm good." Candy rubbed her breasts against his arm. "I'm seeing Jake, but I'd be happier with you."

"I'm glad you're with Jake. He's a good guy." Damn, he really needed to warn Jake about Candy. Jake didn't need this kind of trouble in his life.

"What time do you get off tonight?" Candy tried to grab his arm, but he stepped out of her grasp.

"Candy, I'm not interested, and you just said you were with Jake." Holt continued to scan the casino, not giving Candy his full attention.

"Holt, we're not in an exclusive relationship. We just fucked one night."

"Sorry to hear that, but my relationship is exclusive." Holt stared at her.

"She doesn't need to know." Candy pulled his belt loop toward her.

He couldn't believe the words coming out of her mouth. *Shit, she's persistent.*

"Sorry, but I would know." Holt pulled her hand off his pants. "I gotta go. Have fun tonight." Holt strode away and tapped his headpiece. "Jake, were you able to catch all of that?"

"Yup." Jake's raspy voice answered.

"You gotta stay away from that. She's not stable." Holt hoped Jake listened to him, because Candy was a piece of work.

"No worries. I already tapped that and I'm not tapping it again."

"And they call me a horn dog," Holt laughed. "Where are you stationed tonight?"

"I'm roaming upstairs right now. Did you need something?"

"Nope, just wondering who was on the floor with me since Barrett left." Holt looked around, making sure everyone was behaving themselves while they indulged in their fun.

"It's Travis and you on the first floor. I'm on top, just the way I like it. We can rotate whenever you want," Jake answered.

"I'm by the gambling tables." Holt heard Travis chuckle and say, "All is quiet here."

"Cool." Holt shook his head at Jake's comment. "Let's hope it stays that way. Not only is Candy in the house, but bully Dave is here, too. Keep your eyes open for any trouble. Especially from those two. I'll rotate out with you, Jake, in about an hour."

"Got it," Jake murmured.

"Ditto man, ditto." Travis confirmed.

Everything was smooth sailing at the casino. Holt's phone buzzed in his pocket. Pulling it out, he saw Frey's name. Holt smiled and turned off his earpiece before he answered the phone. He didn't want anyone to overhear their conversation. Checking the time, he was surprised to hear from her since the opening didn't close for another hour.

"Hey sweetheart, miss me already?" Holt grinned, even though she couldn't see him. "How is it going?"

"Holt! Tori's been kidnapped." Frey blurted out.

"Shit! Are you okay? What the hell happened?" Holt barked into the phone. To say Holt was shocked was an understatement. *How could she be kidnapped with so many people around?*

"I don't have all the details, but I think Winston took her." Frey sounded frazzled. "Barrett, Grayhorse, and Alex bolted out of here trying to catch them. Thunder called George and told us to close, then head over to the resort to wait for them. I'm scared Holt." Holt wished like hell he was with her right now.

"I'm so sorry. I wish I was there with you." Holt pinched the top of his nose and closed his eyes. *Fuck!* As if Tori hadn't been through enough. Frey must feel so helpless with her best friend missing.

"I wish you were too." Frey's voice was quivering. *Shit! Frey was crying.*

"I'll give Sam a head's up to make some coffee. Please be careful and text me when you get here." Holt's heart was racing, filled with adrenaline. The cultural center was only a fifteen-minute drive, but Osceola left him in charge so he couldn't leave.

"Okay." Holt could barely hear her voice. "I love you, sweetheart. They'll find her. Alex won't let anything happen to her."

"I know. I just want this nightmare to be over. I love you too," Frey mumbled. Holt heard loud voices in the background.

"Holt, we're leaving now and heading over to you. Isa is calling me over so we can lock up and set the alarm."

"Okay. I'll see you in a few." Holt hung up and turned his earpiece back on.

"Guys, something is going down at the cultural center. Someone has kidnapped Tori. We need to keep our eyes and ears open in case we see or hear anything."

"Oh crap," Jake buzzed in, "we'll be on the lookout. Do you need to head over there?"

"No, they're locking up and heading over here. I'll keep you all informed if I receive any updates."

Holt was normally calm, but tonight he was jumpy and scanning the room incessantly. He would not relax until he saw Frey. Holt jogged into the kitchen and told Sam what was going on.

"Let's make a big carafe of coffee. They might need it."

"Will do, boss."

Holt went back to the casino to wait for Frey's text. He was storming through the casino watching everyone carefully. He would feel better when Frey and Tori were back home. His phone buzzed again.

"Holt." Travis' voice through the earpiece jolted him from his thoughts. "Frey's back. She's in the lobby."

"On my way." Holt reached into his pocket, saw it was Frey's text, hurried out of the casino while he spoke into the earpiece. "Can one of you in the security office come out and monitor the floor?"

"Copy that. On my way," one of them replied.

"Frey!" Holt hollered across the lobby. Freya huddled with her parents and all the center volunteers. Holt didn't see Thunder, Grayhorse, Alex, Barrett, Tall Bear, or Spirit-of-the-Eagle.

"Holt." Freya turned and met him halfway.

Holt hugged her when she reached him and whispered in her ear. "I was so worried about you, sweetheart." Holt looked up and saw the puzzled look on Sehoy's face. Releasing Frey, he stepped back and cleared his throat.

"Do you have an update?" Holt draped his arm over her shoulders in a side hug. He wanted to keep her close.

"Thunder told us to close and meet them all back here. He took off with Tall Bear and Spirit-of-the-Eagle when he got a text from Alex. I'm assuming he's going after Tori. We don't have any updates. I'm worried, Holt. There were so many of us there. How could he get to Tori?"

"Sshh, sweetheart," Holt squeezed her shoulder. "Thunder will figure it out. Let's get everyone seated in RUSH. Sam is making some coffee. Why don't you check and see if anyone wants tea?"

"Okay." Frey looked so lost.

Holt didn't want to leave her, but he couldn't keep holding her. He lightly rubbed her back before turning around and heading for the kitchen.

"Sam, is it ready?"

"Yup." Sam pointed to the counter. "It's hot. Fill up cups instead of carrying it over there."

"Good idea. I'll get a head count and check to see if anyone wants tea. I'll be right back." Holt left the kitchen and approached Frey while she seated everyone.

"Frey, how many coffees? Does anyone want tea?"

"Everyone wants coffee except Isa. She wants water." Frey was hugging herself, her body swaying from side to side as she stared toward the lobby.

"Got it." Holt pulled a chair out for Frey. "Why don't you sit down? I'll get the coffees. Is anyone hungry?"

"No, we had leftover food from the center that Aurora wrapped up and brought with her." Freya pointed to where Aurora and Sehoy were unwrapping the tin foil pans before she dropped into the chair.

"Any news yet?"

"Not yet," Freya was fidgeting with her hands and biting her lip. "I'm scared Holt. What if he hurts her?"

"He won't. Alex, Thunder, Grayhorse, and Barrett will help her." Holt bent down and whispered in her ear. "I wish I could hold you right now."

"I want you to hold me, too," Frey's watery eyes gazed at him. "Tonight, okay?"

"You can bet on it," Holt nodded. "Let me go get the coffee. I'll be right back."

Holt walked into the kitchen. Sam had already poured several cups and placed them on a serving tray for Holt to carry out.

Holt ran back and forth, getting everyone a cup and cream, sugar, or anything else they needed. He also placed several plates by the food Sehoy and Aurora set out. Everyone got some food and were talking about everything that happened. No one had the whole story, but as they were saying what they saw, Holt figured out that it was Winston who kidnapped Tori and they had gone to the Sunshine Marina. They would have to wait for the rest of the story. Holt sat at a table with Frey and her parents when Sarah suddenly stood and screamed.

"Grayhorse!" Sarah ran to her husband.

"*Wíŋyaŋ mitáwa*." Grayhorse caught his wife and spun her around. "I'm fine."

"Thunder!" not one to be outdone, Isa ran toward him.

"Honey." Thunder placed his hands on his hips and shook his head at his wife. "Please do not run. What if you trip and fall?"

"Then I know you will catch me." Isa kissed her husband.

Holt, along with everyone else, left RUSH and headed toward the lobby. Barrett explained everything that had happened while Alex took Tori upstairs. Holt was relieved to see Tori. He'd feel even better once he had Frey curled up with him in bed.

Chapter 28

Holt to the Rescue

Frey

After Tori came home safely, she confided in Frey that she was tired of hiding. She wanted to hang out with the girls. So, a few days after the opening, Sarah, Thunder's sister and a childhood friend of Tori set up their Girls' Night Out. Everyone thought it was too soon, but Tori said she didn't want to be the victim anymore. No one wanted to argue with her, so Freya worked the daytime shift on Saturday and took the night off.

Running into her room after her shift, she found Holt lying on her bed.

"Hey, sweetheart." Holt was already dressed for work.

"Hi." Frey ran in and dove on top of him.

"Oof." Holt grabbed her and they laughed while their bodies bounced on the bed.

"Did you have a good day? I missed you." Holt kissed her.

"I missed you too." Frey ran her hands through his hair. "I promise to come visit you naked when I get home."

"I can't wait." Holt grabbed her ass, pushing her into him. "I can't wait until I get an invite to hang with the guys."

"I know." Frey sighed. "I'm sorry. Soon. Okay?" Whenever the girls had a night out, their significant others hung out together. Holt couldn't come because only Tori knew they were dating, and she was sworn to secrecy. Holt wasn't happy about not coming with her. He'd told her about it several times over the past few days, but she would make it up to him tonight.

"Is Alex driving you guys?" Holt rubbed Frey's back while she lay on top of him. She loved using him as a body pillow. Her soft edges fit just right with his hard body.

"Yes." Frey groaned. "I gotta get up and shower. And no, you can't join me, or I won't be ready in time." She felt Holt's chest rise and fall as he chuckled.

"You know me so well." Holt kissed the top of her head. "Go on, get up. You don't want to keep Tori waiting." Holt smacked her ass.

"Hey!" Frey rolled off him and stood. Rubbing her backside, she gave him a little pout. "That hurt."

"As if," Holt grumbled and got up. "You want me to kiss it and make it better?" He wiggled his eyebrow as he reached for Frey.

"No." Frey yelled, laughing as she ran into the bathroom. "Don't touch me or I'll never be ready in time."

Holt crashed into her back, wrapping his arms around her. He walked her into the bathroom and pressed her against the sink, watching her in the mirror. Frey held her arms over his. She loved being in his arms.

"Have a good time tonight. I love you." Holt kissed the back of her head.

"I love you too." Frey smiled and spun in his arms, initiating a nice, long kiss that would tide her over until tonight. After a couple of quick kisses, Holt groaned, gave her a hug, and left.

*** Holt ***

Holt was hoping Frey had a good time with her friends. It would be nice for the girls to have a fun night at Sarah's with no worries. While he was making one of his many rounds in the casino, his phone rang. Wondering if it was Frey, he took his phone out of his pocket and looked at the caller ID.

Betty? Why the fuck was she calling him? He hadn't spoken to her in a long time. He didn't have anything to say to her, so he let it roll over to voicemail. A few minutes later, it rang again, and it was her.

"Hey guys. I need to make a phone call." Holt spoke into his earpiece. "I'm gonna take a quick break."

"Copy." Jake's voice rang out. "I'll head down and cover you."

"Thanks." Holt turned off his earpiece and answered the phone as he stepped outside the casino into the lobby.

"Hello."

"I need money." Betty uttered.

Betty's comment did not surprise Holt, she was always after money. What did surprise him was her calling him after having radio silence for almost eight years. *Why now?* She could've at least pretended to miss him and ask him how he was doing.

"Hello to you too, Betty." Holt sighed and rubbed his forehead. "I'm not giving you money for drugs or alcohol. Don't you have a job?"

"My job and welfare don't pay enough now that I don't have a kid living with me."

"You haven't had a kid living with you in eight years. Why now? What's changed?" Holt walked outside the resort. The last thing he needed was anyone overhearing his conversation.

"I'm late paying my mortgage. If I don't pay, they're going to kick me out of our trailer." Betty was crying.

Betty never cried. *Fuck! What game was she playing now? She was probably high as a kite.*

"How much do you owe?" Holt knew he was going to hate this question. She would probably lie to him to get more money like she used to lie to the men she let use her.

"$40,000." Betty was sniffling into the phone. Holt wasn't buying her crying act. The last time he saw Betty cry was when his father kicked her out. Even then, he didn't remember seeing tears.

"There is no fucking way. That was a used trailer when we moved into it and it didn't cost $40,000 when you moved in." Holt closed his eyes and took a deep breath to calm down. He needed to keep his wits about him when dealing with Betty. "Tell you what. I'll call the bank tomorrow and find out your exact balance. If I can afford it, I'll pay it off."

Holt knew the name of her bank because several times while he was growing up, Betty got eviction notices taped to the door. As a teen, Holt hated Betty. She'd been a horrible mother who put her loser men, drugs, and alcohol before him. Now, as an adult, he didn't think about her enough to care. Out of sight, out of mind. But Sehoy and Osceola had taught him to help others if they needed it and he couldn't find it in his heart to leave anyone homeless.

"Of course you can afford it. Don't you eat and live there for free? I'm your mother. The least you can do is help me out in my time of need," Betty cried harder.

Fuck me! Holt knew she was playing him, but until he spoke to the bank, there was nothing he could do. She was right that he didn't have any expenses other than his car payment and insurance. The Panthers treated him just like they treated their kids and wouldn't let him pay for anything. But there was no way he was handing over $40,000 when he was sure she owed less than that, and he was not giving her money for her vices.

"How would you know what I pay here? I haven't talked to you in over eight years." Holt was rubbing the back of his neck while he paced in the parking lot.

"I know things. So, are you going to help me?" Betty's fake cry now sounded like she was coughing.

"I told you I'll call the bank tomorrow." Holt checked his watch and realized he'd been out there for almost ten minutes. He had to get back inside. This conversation was going nowhere. "Betty, I gotta go. I'll talk to you tomorrow."

"You'd better. Would it hurt you to call me mom?" Betty's voice now sounded angry, no crying or sniffling. Holt snorted. *Figures. Did she really believe he bought her crying act?*

"I'll call you tomorrow after I talk to the bank." Holt hung up before he threw the phone across the parking lot. He couldn't believe she asked him to call her mom. *Fuck No!* The last thing he would call her was mom. That was a title she didn't deserve. Not now, not ever. Not from him.

Holt couldn't wait to tell Frey about this conversation. It would shock her as much as it had shocked him. Going back inside, he ran into Osceola.

"*Chakpootsi.* Is everything alright?" Osceola wasn't his birth father, but he always knew when Holt was upset.

"*Enca, chacteka.*" Holt didn't want to get Osceola involved with Betty's bullshit. Betty was his mom and his problem. He'd take care of it.

"Okay. But if you need to talk to someone, you know I'm always here for you." Osceola put his arm around him and walked with him back into the casino.

"Thank you, *chacteka.* I appreciate it."

"Have a good night, *chakpootsi.*" Osceola patted his back and walked away.

Holt was blessed to have found Osceola and Sehoy. Best parents ever.

"I'm back." Holt turned his earpiece back on. "Where do you want me?"

"I'm going back upstairs. Barrett is still in the family security office. You stay down here with Travis." Jake answered.

"Copy that." Holt smiled. He knew Jake preferred working the upstairs slots and bar. Having been a sniper in the military, he preferred the overhead view of the casino tables.

"I knew eventually you civvy's would learn my military lingo." Jake chuckled.

Holt heard Barrett honk like a seal over the earpiece. He knew it was Barrett because he loved to make that noise at Jake.

"Yeah, well, you're a civvy now, too." Holt teased him back.

"So true, my friend, so true."

Holt continued to banter with Jake, Barrett, and Travis while he scanned the casino. Every so often, he and Travis would cross paths and do a low fist bump. Sometime later, Barrett's voice interrupted Jake's joke.

"Hey, Holt. Alex just called me. Apparently, the girls tied one on and Alex needs help getting Frey to her room. Can you get her? I'm busy watching a couple of tables. I think someone is counting cards."

"Will do. Are they here?" Holt pivoted and headed to the exit.

"ETA is five minutes. He called from his car." Barrett chuckled. "They sounded wasted."

"Barrett, let me know which tables. Travis and I will take care of it until Holt gets back." Jake said.

"Copy that."

Holt smiled and logged onto the tracking app on his phone. After what happened to Tori, Holt asked Frey to download the same app so they could find each other in case of an emergency. The app showed her turning into the resort parking lot. Dropping his phone back into his pocket, Holt decided to make Jake smile.

"I'm bugging out." Holt heard Jake laugh right before he turned off his earpiece and walked to the parking lot just as Alex pulled in.

"Barrett told me you needed help." Holt opened the door by Freya. "He had something he had to deal with in the casino and asked me to come get her."

"Thanks man." Alex got Tori out of the car on the other side. "I appreciate it."

"Hi Holtie," Freya fell into his arms. "How you doin'?"

"Apparently" –Holt bent down, put his arm under her legs, and picked her up– "better than you. Put your arms around my neck, Frey." Well, she had tied one on if she was calling him Holtie. Somebody needed some pills, water, and sleep.

"Okey dokey," Freya sighed and placed her head on his chest, clinging to his neck.

"Are they okay?" Sehoy asked when they walked by the Lobby Desk.

"Yup," Alex replied. "Just had a little too much fun at Sarah's with the ladies."

Frey and Tori waved at Sehoy, giggling while they carried them into the elevator.

"What's up with the nails?" Holt commented when he looked at Tori's hand.

"They did manicures while drunk," Alex smirked.

"I hope they have nail polish remover," Holt laughed. "I think they'll need it tomorrow after they wake up."

"What do you mean, Holtie?" Freya pulled her arms from around Holt's neck and looked at her hands. "I think they look great, right Tori?" Frey and Tori giggled and high five'd each other.

"Holtie?" Alex raised an inquisitive eyebrow at Holt.

Holt grunted. "Please don't call me that, Frey. I will never live that down now."

"I think our nails look wonderful!" Tori exclaimed while she looked at hers. "Don't you think our nails look wonderful, Alex?" Tori shoved her nails in front of his face.

"They look beautiful, baby," Alex kissed her fingers and grinned at Holt. Good one, Alex. Clearly, he was getting laid while Holt had to go back to work.

"See you tomorrow, Alex." Holt said as he walked out of the elevator and headed to Frey's door.

"Yup." Alex stepped outside the elevator and looked at Holt. "Thank you again, Holtie, for coming to get Frey." Alex laughed while Holt gave him the middle finger.

"No problem." Holt used his master key to open Frey's door. "I'll get her to her room and go back down to work. Have a good night." Holt announced unnecessarily because Alex wasn't going to check up on him. He had a very drunk woman to focus on.

"Have fun at work, Holtie." Alex opened his door, laughing as he walked in.

"Fucker." Holt grumbled.

"Do you have to go back to work?" Freya asked while her fingers crawled up his chest. "Can't you stay with me and play?"

"Sweetheart, did you really tie one on? You know when I fuck you, I need you to be an active participant."

"I'm not that drunk." Frey rolled her eyes.

Holt released her legs, helping her to stand upright. Freya wobbled, laughed, and stumbled into him.

"Right," Holt chuckled. "Let's get you in bed. And yes, I've got to go back to work, but I'll check on you when I get off."

"No, Holtie." Freya whined and grabbed his cock through his pants.

"Frey, stop." Holt chuckled. "We're short-handed downstairs. I have to get back to help Barrett." Holt removed her hands and stepped back so he could undress her.

"Fine, but look at what you're missing." Freya stripped out of her clothes, dropping them on the floor as she sashayed her sexy little ass to the bedroom.

Fuck me! She was so hot as she shimmied out of her clothes. She loved leaving a clothes trail for him. Holt picked up each item as he followed her. Making his way into the bedroom just as she got under the covers, buck naked. *Shit!*

"Sweetheart, I'll come back and check on you later."

"Mmhmm," Freya mumbled.

Holt put her clothes in her hamper and tucked her in. Walking into the kitchen, he grabbed a bottle of water for her and two ibuprofen pills. He wanted her to take them before she was fully asleep.

"Sweetheart, sit up for a minute." Holt stood beside the bed.

"Noo."

"Come on. I'll help you." Holt placed the water and pills on the nightstand. Pulling her up, he sat behind her and grabbed the pills and water. Frey leaned against him. "Take these." Holt placed the pills in her hand and lifted her hand to her mouth. "Now, drink this, please." He handed her the water, helping her hold it while she took several gulps.

"Holtieeee." Frey tried to push the water glass away from her mouth. "I don't want to drink anymore." Frey turned her head against his chest.

"Come on, sweetheart." Holt tilted the water toward her lips again. "Do this and I'll leave you alone."

"Fine." Freya turned her head, held the glass, and finished the entire glass. "Happy?"

"Yes." Holt kissed the top of her head. "Now go to bed." Holt got up and tucked her in. Frey was out before he even left the room. He couldn't wait to come back and cuddle with her, but he figured she'd still be out of it until morning.

Chapter 29

I'm Never Gonna do that Again!

Frey

"**G**ood morning. How are you feeling?" Frey felt the bed dip and a kiss on her forehead. She drank too much last night at their Girls' Night Out. They were having so much fun talking, telling stories, and watching a dating show that she lost track of how many drinks she had.

"Why are you talking so loud?" Frey mumbled into the pillow, her head throbbing.

"Sweetheart, I'm whispering." Holt chuckled.

Frey turned her head and opened one eye. Squinting at Holt, she saw the grin on his face. "This isn't funny. I haven't been drunk for a long time. I swear I'll never do this again."

Saying that only made Holt laugh harder and shake the bed. Frey slapped him in the chest. "Stop laughing at me and shaking the bed. You're making me nauseous."

"Sorry, you're cute when you're hung over." Holt leaned down and kissed her temple.

"Let's see how cute I am when I throw up on you." Frey heard Holt chuckle. "I had plans to wait for you naked in bed," Frey whined. "Why didn't you wake me up when you got home from work?"

"I crawled into bed with you. You were naked but passed out. You were sound asleep all night, and I didn't want to disturb you. It looked like you needed your sleep. You can wait for me naked tonight. Come on, it's shower time. You slept in and we need to be downstairs for brunch in thirty minutes."

"What time is it?" Frey yawned and tried to sit up. Holt helped her up off the bed.

"It's almost noon. If you don't get up now, we'll be late."

"Oh Shit!" Frey swiped her hair back and stared at him. "Why didn't you wake me up sooner?" Picking up her phone, she saw several texts from her mom. "Mom tried to text and call me. I can't believe I didn't hear my phone."

"That's why I'm waking you up now. I wanted to let you sleep, but after she called me because she couldn't reach you, I realized your sleeping in was over. So, let's go, Sleeping Beauty."

"Uh, Holt." Frey stood up, ran to the toilet and threw up. Holt held her hair back until she finished all her dry heaving.

"Okay, let's get you in the shower and clean you up." Frey felt him tying her hair in a ponytail. She glanced under her arm and saw his clothes drop to the floor. Well, I guess he's going in the shower with me. She was still naked on the floor praising the golden throne when she felt Holt's hands under her legs and behind her back as he lifted her up and walked into the shower.

The water was hot. He must have turned it on while she was holding her head over the toilet. Frey wrapped her arms around Holt's waist when he set her down. He gently took her hair out of the ponytail and tilted her head back to shampoo and condition it. When he finished with her hair, he washed her body. She was feeling much better, body wise, but her head was still throbbing. Frey reached down to grab his cock when he stood up.

"Sweetheart, there's no time for that." Holt kissed the top of her head. "Let's get you rinsed and dried off. We'll play later."

"Okay," Frey sighed and placed her hand on her forehead, rubbing her temples.

"Is your head still hurting?" Holt stepped out of the shower to get her a towel.

"Yeah." Frey hadn't felt like this in a long time. She wished the jackhammer in her head would stop pounding.

"Okay. Dry off and I'll get you some ibuprofen." Holt handed her the towel, got dressed, and left the bathroom.

Frey was on slow-mo, but if she didn't finish soon, her mother would pound on her door, making her headache much worse. She was shocked her mother hadn't come looking for her yet. Holt probably told her she got drunk last night. Wait a minute. She had seen her mom when she got home last night as Holt carried her through the lobby. She was going to have some explaining to do. Frey hung up her towel and sighed. Shit. She walked into her closet and got dressed.

"Here take these." Holt held out two ibuprofen pills in one hand and a glass of water in his other. "You need to drink the entire glass of water."

"Thank you." Frey handed back the glass when she finished. Grabbing a dress, she dropped it over her head, put on some sandals, and stared at Holt with her hands on her hips. "Which one of us is going to dry their hair? We can't both walk in there with wet hair since mom sent you in here to get me."

"Well, if you'd let me tell them I love you and we're together, this wouldn't be an issue." Holt stated with a raised eyebrow.

"I don't want to argue right now." Frey's body deflated, and she rubbed her forehead.

"I don't either," Holt sighed. "I'll dry my hair. It'll be quicker. I made you some toast and left it on the kitchen counter. Why don't you nibble on that while I finish here?"

Frey watched Holt grab her blow-dryer and within a few minutes, his hair was dry. It must be nice to be a man. Getting ready to go out was so much quicker.

"Sweetheart, stop staring at me and go eat your toast. It will settle your stomach."

"But staring at you is so much more fun." Frey heard Holt chuckle as she walked out of the room. True to his word, there were two slices of toast, lightly buttered on a plate with another glass of water. He was so good to her. Frey grabbed the plate and sat at the table, picking up her phone as she called her mom.

"Where have you been?" Frey heard her mom's frantic voice. "Did you talk to Holt? Are you hungover? You know it's Sunday, and this is the second Sunday in a row that I've had to call you to get you down here. What's going on with you?"

"Hi *chatski*. I slept in. Holt woke me up and left." Frey looked up and saw Holt walking up to her. She placed her finger up to her mouth, telling him to stay quiet. "I'm so sorry, and yes, I am hungover, but feeling better now that I ate."

"Well, get down here. You and Tori can sit together and wallow in your poor decisions."

"Okay, *chatski*," Frey rolled her eyes at Holt. This was going to be a long brunch. "I'll be there in a few minutes." Frey finished her conversation and dropped her head in her hands.

"I see you and Tori are being placed in the kids' section of our table." Holt smiled.

"Ha, ha. Wait until you get drunk sometime and let's see if I take care of you," Frey harrumphed. "And stop laughing. That's not nice."

"Come here." Frey walked into his arms. "I love you even when you are pouty, bossy, and hungover."

"Yeah, yeah, yeah, let's go before someone comes up and catches us. I'll go down first." Frey stepped back, got up on her tippy toes, and kissed him on his cheek. "See you down there."

Chapter 30

Sunday Brunch Hangover

Frey

A few minutes later, Frey entered Savor and made a beeline for Tori. There was strength in numbers and Tori was going to be her wing woman today.

"Hey." Frey sat down and hugged Tori.

"How are you feeling?" Tori mumbled in her ear.

"Not great. How about you?" Frey noticed Tori was talking softly, which she was grateful for. Unfortunately, everyone else was screaming, and the ibuprofen hadn't kicked in yet.

"I've been better. But it was so much fun." Tori smiled. "Best Girls' Night Out ever!"

"That's not what you were saying over the toilet last night, baby." Alex leaned down and kissed both their cheeks, then placed a coffee cup in front of them.

"Thanks, bro." Frey grinned.

"Thanks, honey." Tori took a sip.

"No problem. I'll be right back. I need to help mom get all the dishes out. You ladies want to help?" Alex placed his hands on their shoulders and shook them a little.

Frey was sure he shook her more than Tori. She slapped his arm. "Funny guy...not. Just go away."

"Okay, ladies, relax while I do all the heavy lifting." Alex laughed on his way back to the kitchen. His loud laughter sounded like nails on a chalkboard to Frey.

Frey and Tori both ignored Alex's parting comment and enjoyed their coffee in silence. Frey hoped to feel better before everyone came to the table to eat. She saw her mother heading her way and braced for the incoming accusations about her poor judgement.

"I hope you ladies had fun last night?" Sehoy immediately asked as soon as everything was ready, and everyone sat.

"I think they had a great time," Alex teased Frey and Tori.

"I don't think you should talk unless you want us to show your new hairstyle." Frey threatened. Not one to hold back, she told her parents about Lucy's

Fashion Show. "Lucy got a hold of him and went to town. Let's just say Alex is creepy as Princess Leia."

"What are you talking about?" Osceola wrinkled his brow.

"Thanks, Frey," Alex mumbled under his breath. "Just remember, karma's a bitch."

Frey squirmed in her seat and smiled at her father. "Alex went with the guys to the park and let Isa's niece braid his hair. He was very sweet with her. Apparently, she likes to do Thunder and Grayhorse's hair whenever they get together."

"Alex, that was very sweet of you to allow Lucy to braid your hair." Sehoy beamed at her eldest son with so much pride in her eyes.

"We've raised such good kids. A toast to my wonderful kids and beautiful wife," Osceola raised his glass.

Everyone raised their wine or beer except Tori and Frey, who drank water for lunch.

"Well, I'm glad I have short hair," Barrett interjected. "No way they can braid mine."

"Oh, ye of little faith," Alex said between bites. "I've seen that little girl's work and I guaran-damn-tee you, she can braid your hair."

"Language," Sehoy raised her voice across the table.

"Yeah, language," Barrett repeated.

"Sorry *chatski*." Alex looked down, grabbed a pea, and waited until Sehoy looked away to throw it at Barrett.

"I saw that." Sehoy glared at Alex.

"Remember, your mother has eyes all over her head, not just the back," Osceola laughed. "Alex, what's been happening with Winston?"

"They charged Winston with burglary, theft, rape, kidnapping, attempted murder, possession, distribution, and trafficking of illegal substances. They didn't award him bail and placed him in jail," Alex explained. "The district attorney wants to make sure he gets life without the possibility of parole."

Frey took a deep breath, feeling relieved that Winston was finally in jail where he belonged. Holt reached out under the table and squeezed her thigh. Frey placed her hand over his and, with a quick glance his way, she smiled at him. She was still going to keep a chair under the doorknob of her adjoining door, just in case. Although thinking back, she realized she was sleeping better now that she shared a bed with Holt.

"Good." Osceola nodded. "What about the others?"

"Bull faces charges of attempted murder because he picked up the gun and shot at Tori as she jumped overboard. They didn't set bail, and he's being imprisoned until his trial. The district attorney wants to make sure he gets at least twenty-five years in prison. But he will probably be able to have parole."

"He can get parole, even though he shot at Tori?" Sehoy was stunned.

"It's possible. And Reaper, I think got off easy. They charged him with burglary, theft, accessory to kidnapping, and possession of an illegal substance. But he never threatened Tori with the gun, and they caught him buying drugs, but not selling it. They set bail for him, and the motorcycle club paid for it. The district attorney wants him to at least serve ten years in jail with the possibility of parole in five years. But the MC has a talented lawyer, so we'll see."

"Winston always gave me the creeps, but I didn't realize he was involved with a motorcycle club and selling drugs." Frey tensed when she heard Winston was connected to Reaper. *Shit!* Frey knew some of the members because they gambled at her table. They were always making inappropriate sexual comments and propositioning her. She never told anyone because when she ignored them, they left and went to another table. Reaper was the worst. She supposed she had peace of mind for at least five years, unless he got out early for good behavior.

"Especially in our casino." Holt drank his beer. Squeezing her thigh, he whispered to her. "Are you okay?"

"What did you say about our casino?" Frey whispered back because she had zoned out. *Were they coming to the casino?*

"Winston was dealing in our casino." Holt's gaze flickered to Frey, and he squeezed her thigh again. "It was mostly outside, but we have it under control with more cameras and surveillance. You're safe. I won't let anything happen to you. I promise."

Alex continued, "The police decided Winston was the mastermind of the entire operation, and that lightened the sentences for the other two."

"Tori, are you feeling a little better?" Osceola asked, concerned.

"I was always terrified of Winston, but I don't think Bull or Reaper will come after me, especially since they are on law enforcement's radar and now have a record." Tori lifted the side of her mouth in a half smile.

Frey listened to the conversation, glad that she wasn't the main topic today like last Sunday, when they questioned her and Holt about their significant others. It seemed like her mom had forgotten about Ted. And it was great to get an update on Winston and his cronies.

"Frey, where is that young man you were going to introduce us to?" Sehoy pointed her fork at her.

Shit, not only could she see everything, she could read minds.

"Um," Frey felt Holt kick her under the table. "Ow!" Frey leaned down and rubbed her calf.

"What's wrong?" Sehoy frowned.

"Nothing, I got a leg cramp." Frey said before kicking Holt back.

"Did you just kick me?" Barrett scowled at her while Holt used the napkin to cover his laugh.

"Leg. Cramp." Frey annunciated each word between gritted teeth while she glared at Holt.

"What about the boy, chatski? Why is he not here?" Sehoy asked again.

"He had to work." Frey smiled at her mom.

"On a Sunday?" Sehoy sounded surprised.

"I guess being an insurance agent is a twenty-four-hour job." Frey shrugged her shoulders and took a drink of water, then moved the food on her plate around with her fork.

"Or maybe he doesn't want to see you." Barrett kicked her back.

"Barrett, that is not nice. Your father just toasted to his wonderful kids and look at how you are acting toward your twin sister." Sehoy stood to get another pitcher of water.

"Yeah, Barrett, be nice to your older twin sister." Frey smirked.

"By one fucking minute." Barrett mumbled and glared at Frey.

"Language!" Sehoy smacked Barrett on the back of the head on her way to the kitchen.

Frey laughed and pointed at Barrett while everyone else chuckled except Osceola.

"Don't make me come to your side on the way back and smack your head too, *chackshosti*." Everyone heard Sehoy's parting words.

Frey loved her family. They might give each other a hard time, but when it came down to it, they all had each other's backs. They all continued to joke and eat until they finished brunch. Holt had been quiet throughout most of the meal. He answered questions when asked, but didn't offer any extra information.

Suddenly, Holt stood and placed his hand on Frey's shoulder. "Frey and I have something to tell everyone." Holt announced and looked down at her.

Chapter 31

Don't You Dare Tell Them

Frey

"**W**hat do you need to tell us?" Osceola washed down the food in his mouth with a drink of water and all eyes turned to them.

Holt opened his mouth to speak, then snapped it shut when Frey stood and slapped his back, causing him to waver forward.

"We just wanted you guys to know that I...well, I." Frey fidgeted with her hands and tilted her head down, shifting her eyes to watch Holt as she semi-lied. She was telling the truth, just not the truth about their relationship. "I haven't been sleeping well, and I mentioned it to Holt. But now that Winston is in jail, I feel much better." Frey looked up, facing everyone but ignoring Holt. She could see him out of the corner of her eye. He gave her his best evil eye and looked livid. If looks could kill... *Shit!* She was going to have to make it up to him.

"Why didn't you tell us?" Sehoy got up and walked to Frey for a hug. "I thought something was going on, but I wasn't sure."

"I'm sorry, *chatski*." Frey rubbed her mother's back during their hug. "I'm doing better now. No need to worry about me." Frey made the mistake of glancing at Holt. *Yup, still mad.* Frey knew he hated keeping things from her family. *But a few more days couldn't hurt, right?*

Frey released her mom and looked at Tori, who was staring down at her food. Alex was whispering to Tori and Barrett raised his eyebrow at her. Either he didn't believe her, or he didn't understand why she hadn't told him. They were very close. Some would blame the twin thing. They didn't feel each other's pain, but they always told each other their problems and knew when the other was lying. She knew if she had talked to Barrett about her fears, he would have camped out on her couch until she fell asleep, making it harder for her to be with Holt.

"We'll talk later," Barrett grumbled.

"Sure, later." Frey lifted the corner of her lip in a partial smile. "*Chatski*, let me help you clear the table." Frey moved quickly from the table to the kitchen, avoiding anyone else's questions. Each time she went back to the table, someone else had left. When she finished, she hugged her mom and headed upstairs. She had some making up to do.

Entering her room, she locked her door and strolled through to Holt's closet door. She slid the door open and walked into his bedroom. Holt was lying in bed with one hand on his stomach and the other arm over his face.

"Are you okay?" Frey sauntered to the bed and sat next to him, holding his hand on his belly.

"No." Other than gripping her hand, he didn't move.

"Are you mad at me?" Frey leaned into him and laid her head on his chest.

"We agreed we were going to tell everyone." Holt moved his arm off his face and glared at her. "What the hell happened? Why did you change your mind? That was the perfect time to tell everyone. They were all there!"

"I know." Frey moved her leg over him and sat on his hips while she still held his hand. "I'm sorry. Please don't be mad at me. I panicked and couldn't do it. Maybe we can just tell Barrett when it's just us? That way, we don't have an audience and we can calm him down. I just wasn't ready for him to be mad at you or me."

"We don't even know if he'll react to us like he did to Jeremy years ago." Holt pushed her off him and sat on the edge of the bed, ready to stand up. "I know you're scared, Frey, but this secret is killing me. Every time I see him, I want to tell him, but I don't want to hurt you." Holt rubbed the back of his neck. "Let's go tell him now. He won't stay mad forever. Besides, he knew you were lying. Didn't you see the questioning look on his face?"

"Technically, I wasn't lying?" Frey moved to hug him from behind, but he pivoted too fast and stood.

"Really?" Holt crossed his arms, facing her with a steely gaze and a tight-lipped smile. "That's the hill you want to die on?"

Frey scooted to the edge of the bed and stood in front of him, running her finger down the zipper of his pants. "Come on, Holt." Frey smiled seductively at him. If she could distract him, they could keep quiet a little longer. "Let's not fight. I just bought us a little time. Besides," Frey gripped his cock through his pants. "This is the hill I'd prefer to die on."

"That's not funny, Frey." Holt removed her hand and paced his bedroom like a trapped animal. "This lie has to end."

"I know." Frey stepped in front of him to stop his pacing. "I just need a little more time."

"Why? I think more time is making it worse. I hate lying to my best friend. It's eating me up inside." Holt ran his hand over his hair to the back of his neck and sighed.

Frey tried to make light of the conversation. "I thought I was your best friend." That was the wrong thing to say. Now he was glaring at her again.

"You know what I mean." Holt braced his legs and placed his hands on his hips. He looked at her like she was a child throwing a temper tantrum. She could see the disappointment in his eyes. Somehow, that was worse than his anger. Maybe he was right. They were all adults now. *How mad could Barrett get?*

"I do." Frey wrapped her arms around him, trying to diffuse the situation with an apology instead of seduction. "Soon. I promise. I'm sorry I chickened out. I love you."

Frey could feel him take a deep breath before he wrapped his arms around her. "I love you too, sweetheart."

"Can we snuggle on the bed before we go to work? Maybe watch TV?" Frey mumbled into his chest.

"Yeah, sure." Holt released her, getting under the covers and holding them up for her. He grabbed the remote and wrapped his arms around her. Frey stayed quiet and gave him time to calm down. She could feel his breaths slowing down and hear his heartbeat return to normal.

"I love you." Frey looked up and kissed his chin.

Holt rolled them over and peppered her face with sweet kisses on her forehead, nose, cheeks, and lips. Frey opened her mouth, giving Holt the entrance he needed to devour her with his tongue. Her senses on overdrive between his taste and his manly smell.

After chasing and sucking her tongue in his mouth, he trailed kisses down her neck to her collarbone. Frey tilted her neck for him to have better access. When his lips skimmed over her neck on their way down her body, she moaned. Her aching nipples hardened, begging for his attention. He hadn't shaved this morning and his newly grown whiskers felt raspy, sending shivers down her spine. She wondered how his face would feel between her legs.

Holt pressed his hips into her, pinning her onto the bed.

"Sweetheart, the next time you wear a dress, can you make sure it has buttons so I can open it to suck on your tits on my way down?" Frey hadn't thought of that when she chose this dress. Not that it stopped Holt. He sucked her breasts through her bra and dress, giving her nipples a quick bite before moving lower.

"Noted." Frey smiled, glad that Holt was no longer mad at her. All was right with the world if he was thinking about her tits and not their lies.

Holt slid down her body to her thighs. Slowly licking and kissing each one while he raised her dress up. Once at waist level, he hooked his fingers around the sides of her panties and pulled them off. Frey smiled when he gave her his best smolder and threw her panties over his shoulder. Frey laughed, but it didn't last long because he spread her legs and dove in.

"You are the best dessert ever," Holt murmured into her pussy. Between his tongue and verbal vibrations, she was close to the edge. Frey undulated into his mouth. His rough beard was abrasive and added another sensation that was turning her on.

"Holt, please." Frey needed him to increase his intensity so she could release the fire burning through her body. Holt slid two fingers inside while his tongue continued his assault on her clit. *Yes!* Holt gripped her dress above her waist and pulled her toward his face. Oh fuck! That felt so good. His dominance turned her on. He gently bit her clit and off she went into the stratosphere. By the time she came back to earth, he was entering her and sucking on her neck.

"Harder, Holt!"

Frey knew all she had to do was ask and he would satisfy all her demands. Just because he was dominant in bed didn't mean he didn't listen to her needs.

Holt slid his arms under her back up to her shoulders. Turning his hands, he gripped her shoulders and pushed her toward him while he fucked her hard.

"Oh, my...yes...yes...HOLT!" Frey screamed as they came together, and he dropped his weight onto her for a couple minutes before rolling over and taking her with him.

"I love you." Holt held her tightly against his body.

"I love you too," Frey ran her hand through his hair.

"I gotta get up and get rid of the condom." Holt rose, tucking Frey under the sheet. "I'll be right back."

"Can I stay here with you and take a nap until work?" Frey yawned.

"Yes, ma'am."

Frey felt when Holt came back and cleaned her up before he snuggled up to her back.

"What time do you work tonight so I can set an alarm?" Holt asked as he slipped into bed.

"I start at six. Can you set it for five?" Frey rolled to her side. Her back to Holt. She loved when he spooned her.

"Done." Frey felt Holt roll over and come back to her.

Chapter 32

Lying and Hiding is Getting Old

Holt

For the past few days, Holt and Frey continued to hide their relationship. Holt's frustration level was off the charts. It didn't matter how much he begged and pleaded with Frey to tell Barrett. She ignored it.

Holt was pretty sure Sehoy and Osceola had noticed his attitude toward Frey shifting into a more loving relationship. They would have to be blind not to. But neither of them said anything to him.

One day at work, Barrett asked him if he was okay because he seemed distracted. Holt told him about Betty's phone call and asked him not to tell his parents. Holt would handle it. Barrett didn't agree with Holt paying off the trailer, but said he'd help any way he could. Now, when Holt looked concerned, Barrett thought it was about Betty.

Every day, Holt felt worse and worse. Not having a mom and dad who loved him, he truly treasured his newfound family and didn't like keeping secrets from them. Now he was keeping two secrets from Osceola and Sehoy.

Keeping their relationship away from Barrett was harder than they thought. There had been too many close calls when either Frey or Holt had to run into their rooms because Barrett was at their door. He was sick and tired of playing this game.

On top of all that craziness, he went to the bank the day after Betty called him and found out that she only owed $10,000. He wrote the check while he stood there. He'd saved plenty of money to cover that expense. When he left the bank, he called Betty and told her he'd paid off the trailer and never wanted to hear from her again.

Unfortunately, Betty didn't get the message and continued to call and text him at least once a week. He let the calls go to voicemail and didn't answer her texts. He was not going to be her cash cow. She could get her ass in gear and get a job.

Holt never got a chance to tell Frey about Betty because she had come home drunk that night. Then, after talking to Barrett and paying it off, he forgot. It seemed like every time Betty contacted him; he was busy and never got around to talking to Frey.

Tonight was Halloween. Frey went to Gaby's house to trick or treat with them. Lucy wanted to braid the guy's hair and have them dress up as her security guards. He wanted to be there too, but how the hell was he going to explain his presence? If his hair was long, he might've found an excuse, but he had short hair—shorter than Barrett's. So, he stayed behind to work while all his friends went out to have fun. It sucked balls!

The casino was busy, and some guests dressed up for Halloween while they gambled. Guests who wanted to dress up could not wear anything that covered their heads and face, but anything else was fair game. Most women wore slutty nurses, cops, or waitress costumes. He saw Candy walking around wearing a cat woman costume, and he spent most of his night avoiding her. Holt wished she would just go somewhere else—any other casino but his. But he couldn't ban her because she hadn't done anything wrong. His only option was to stay away from her so she wouldn't get any ideas about dating or fucking him.

"Hey, Holt," Candy whispered from behind as her hand reached around him and stroked his cock.

"What the fuck!" Holt grabbed her hand, pulled it away from his body, and turned around.

"I've missed you." Candy whined as she tried to push herself onto him. "Don't you want to stroke this pussy?"

"Nope, I do not. We need to talk." Holt grabbed her arm and led her to the back of the casino. He decided to have a face-to-face conversation with her like adults and be as blunt as possible. "Candy, I really don't want to make a scene, but you need to stop. Grabbing me while I'm at work is not acceptable. Either you behave or I'm banning you from the casino. Are we clear?"

"Holt, I just miss you. Why can't we be together?" Candy ran her fingers up his chest and played with his shirt buttons.

"Because I'm seeing someone." Holt grabbed her hands, stopping her from undoing his buttons.

"Who are you seeing? What's her name?" Candy stared at him. "I can guarantee you I'm better than her because I know how to satisfy my man."

"My girlfriend is none of your business," Holt exclaimed. "You and me will never happen, so please stop. Are we clear?"

"Crystal." Candy's demeanor changed, and she pulled her hand out of his grip. "You're gonna regret this," Candy hissed, before turning around.

Holt grabbed her arm and spun her around before she could walk away. "What the hell does that mean? Are you threatening me?"

"Take it however you want." Candy pulled her arm away and stormed off.

Holt had a sinking feeling in his stomach. Candy didn't know Frey was his girlfriend. He needed to talk to Frey when she got home, so she would be careful around Candy. If Candy got wind of their relationship, she would love to be the one to expose them. Holt watched Candy until she walked out of the casino later that night.

Candy

"Why are you calling me? Do you have an update? Did you get the money?"

"Nice way to greet someone," Candy grunted. "No update, except the bitch has to go. I can't get Holt if she's with him."

"I already told you she had to go. She's like a sister to him."

"I think it might be more. He told me tonight he's in a serious relationship and I'd bet it's with her." Candy got in her car and locked her door. "He's hanging around her table more than usual when she's working. It's got to be her. I don't see him with anyone else."

"I hope he's not dating her. That will not work out well for us. He's always been protective of her and her family."

"No Shit!" Candy started her car. She'd done enough for the night. She needed to rethink her approach to Holt now that he wasn't responding to her flirtatious attempts. "If he is dating her, I'll have to get close to her and find a way to get rid of her. Afterwards, I'll console him after his loss."

"How do you know it's her he's dating?"

"I can tell when a man is fucking a woman. They are both smitten with each other when they are working in the casino. But I'll befriend her and make sure. Let me think about it. I'll let you know what I come up with." Candy rubbed the back of her neck. The stress was making her tense. When she got Holt and his money, she'd schedule a massage.

"I don't care how you do it—simply get it done. I'm running out of cash. You said he lives there and eats for free, so stop fucking around. He's got to have a stash of money somewhere—find it!"

"Fuck! What do you think I'm trying to do? You come and try this if you think it's easy. I need to be careful. He's mad at me right now."

"Why did you make him mad? He's supposed to fall in love with you, not hate you."

"I'm aware! Do you think you can do better than me?" Candy got looks from pedestrians walking to their cars. She must appear insane screaming in the car at her phone. "I gotta go. I'll talk to you when I have an update."

"You'd better and work faster. I have bills…"

Candy got great satisfaction from pushing the end call button. She'd had enough of people yelling at her.

Candy had the perfect body and looks, except for her breasts, but that's what implants were for. She always got any guy she wanted. There was no way Holt was getting away from her. He was so hot and well endowed. From that one night of kissing and giving him a blow job, she knew he would be good in bed. His long, thick dick would stretch her open and reach her g-spot. Candy moaned at the thought. He would be hers, come hell or high water.

Candy started her car and drove home. She had to play nice and gather information every night she spent in the casino. Information was power when wielded correctly. For now, Candy needed some alone time to figure out how to get him to dump that bitch and run back into her waiting arms. In the comfort of her home, sipping a glass of wine and surrounded by tranquility, she would devise a plan.

Chapter 33

Stomach Flu?

Frey

A week after Halloween, Frey woke up and ran into the bathroom, hoping she made it to the toilet.

"Sweetheart." Holt ran in behind her and grabbed her hair back. "Are you okay?"

"Yeah." Frey sat down on the floor and held the toilet seat.

"Did you eat something last night that upset your stomach?"

"I don't think so." Frey leaned on the toilet seat and stood. She headed to the sink, rinsed her mouth, and brushed her teeth.

"Can I get you anything? Maybe you should call the doctor and make an appointment." Holt sounded worried.

"No. I just want to get back in bed and sleep."

Holt helped Frey get back in bed and tucked her in.

"If I don't feel better by the end of the day, I'll call."

"I told Barrett I'd run errands with him today. Are you going to be okay? I can see if Tori's here? She's off on Mondays." Holt ran his hand over her forehead, brushing back her hair.

"I'll be fine. But I would love to have a girl's day in with my bestie. Can you see if she's available?" Frey laid down and snuggled in.

"Sure." Holt grabbed his cell phone from the nightstand and dialed. "Hey Alex. Is Tori around? Frey's not feeling well, and she wanted to spend the day curled up watching movies. Uh, since I'm next door, she called me asking for ibuprofen. When I came over, she mentioned she wanted a day with her bestie." Holt grimaced and stared at Frey. Oh shit, she hadn't thought about how suspicious it would seem having Holt call Alex for her. The web of lies was getting hard to keep track of.

"Yeah, I'm still here. I'll let her know. Thanks." Holt hung up the phone. "That was close. I'm so sick of this shit. Can we please come clean with your family?"

"I know." Frey shook her head. "Let me get better and we'll tell them all."

"This coming Sunday, Frey. We tell them and let the cards fall where they may. I love you and I'm done hiding it."

"Okay." To be honest, hiding their relationship was getting tiring for her too. "Is Tori coming over?"

"Yes, she'll be here in a few minutes. I'll stay and let her in when she knocks. Then I'll head out. Feel better sweetheart." Holt bent down and kissed her forehead. "Call me if you need me."

As soon as he straightened, Frey heard the knock on her front door. Holt left the room and Tori ran in.

"Hey bestie. What's going on?" Tori sat on the bed.

"I'm not sure, but I threw up this morning. I didn't eat anything strange last night. Maybe it's just a stomach bug." Frey rolled onto her back.

"Do you have a fever?" Tori felt her forehead.

"I haven't checked, but I don't feel warm." Frey only had a queasy stomach. Over the last few days, once she threw up and rested, she felt better.

"You're not warm. How about I make some tea and we watch a movie?"

"That sounds heavenly." Frey sat up and fluffed her pillows behind her. "I'll try to find something."

"Sounds perfect. I'll be back."

Frey found a romcom on TV and waited for Tori. "You are the best friend ever. Not only did you bring me tea, but popcorn. You rock!"

"Well, after you took care of me so many times, it's nice to return the favor." Tori handed her a cup of tea and the popcorn bucket. "Start the movie. I'll be right back. I couldn't carry everything, and I left my mug in the kitchen."

Frey loved hanging with Tori and watching movies. It had become their favorite pastime since Tori wasn't allowed to leave the resort until they found Winston.

By lunch time, Frey was hungry, and they called Alex and ordered two turkey sandwiches. Not only did Alex make their sandwiches, but he delivered them. He said he wanted to check on Frey, but she was pretty sure he wanted to see Tori. After lunch, Alex left, and they watched another movie. Frey's phone buzzed.

Holt: How are you feeling? I'm back. Are you alone?
Frey: I'm good. I just ate. Tori is still with me.
Holt: Are you working tonight?
Frey: Yes, I'm feeling much better.
Holt: Ok, I'll see you on the floor.

Tori stayed with Frey until she got ready for work. Frey was feeling much better by the time her shift started. She saw Holt and was heading his way when Candy bumped into her.

"Sorry," Frey automatically said, "I didn't see you." She was so focused on reaching Holt, she didn't realize who she bumped into until she looked at her. *Shit! Blow job girl.*

"No worries. That hunky security guard over there distracted me." Candy pointed toward Holt. Holt tilted his head as he stared at them.

"Yeah, he is pretty good looking," Frey agreed. She tried to keep a straight face. She didn't want Candy to know she'd seen her twice. The first time during the blow job and the second when Candy was sucking face with him while clinging onto him like a koala.

Frey watched Holt approach them.

"Well, he seems to be interested in you. I gotta go spend my few dollars for the night." Candy turned to Frey. "It was nice talking to you."

"Yeah, you too." Frey watched as Candy walked away.

"What was that about?" Holt asked when he approached her.

"Not sure, but she was nice to me. If she knew I saw her on her knees giving you head, she might not have been so nice." Frey grinned.

"Not funny. Plus, the last time you saw her was when Barrett escorted Dave out for harassing you. Not when she was in my room."

"True, I forgot about that." Frey nodded.

"Has Dave approached you again?" Frey watched Holt as he scanned the room for trouble.

"No. I've seen him, but he stays away from my table. Why?"

"I talked to him, and he was feeling guilty about that night, which was strange since he never felt guilty when we were young. Anyway, he gave me a song and dance about how he's happily married now and feels horrible about what he did. I don't buy it, so be careful around him." Holt placed his hand at the small of her back. "Come on. I'll walk you to your table."

"Okay. I'll be careful. What time are you working until tonight?" Frey looked around, trying to see if Dave was here tonight.

"I get off at one." Holt quickly rubbed her back and removed his hand.

"No, honey, you will get off at one-fifteen." Frey smirked, thinking about seducing him.

"No, sweetheart, it will be later than that. I need a hell of a lot more than fifteen minutes with you." Holt winked and walked away, turning his earpiece back on.

Damn, that man was dangerous to her heart. Frey watched him walk away for a few more seconds before turning and looking at Anastasia. It was time to relieve her.

"Hey Stacia, I'm here."

"You sure are. Not sure what Holt told you, but that was quite the blush." Stacia collected her cards and left.

Frey was glad she didn't have to carry on with that conversation. She opened a new deck in front of her players and got down to business.

Chapter 34

Strange Night

Holt

A couple of nights later, Holt watched Dave approach Frey's table.

"Heads up, gentlemen," Holt murmured into his earpiece, "Frey's bully at her nine o'clock, heading toward her table. I'm on my way."

"Got your back, bro," Barrett responded. "Heading downstairs now. Jake, I'll switch with you."

"Copy that. I'll take overwatch duty," Jake replied.

"Dave, what's going on?" Holt approached Frey's table from behind Dave.

"Not much. Just came by to say hi to Frey and apologize for the last time." Dave grabbed some chips and placed his bet.

Holt went around Frey's table until he stood next to her. "Frey, you, okay?"

"I'm good. All is well. Everyone place your bets," Frey continued, watching her players. Once all the bets were down, she flipped her cards. "House wins."

Frey collected the chips, and Holt watched Dave's reaction closely. Losing a hand was the perfect time to see if he got angry at Frey. Dave sighed and played with his chips, probably debating how much to bet on the next hand. He only had a few chips left. Holt stayed and watched a couple more hands while Barrett strolled past them several times. Dave won once but lost three more times, never losing his temper.

"I'm done. Thank you, Frey, for taking most of my money. I should've known better than to sit at your table." Dave smiled wryly. "I'm sorry for the last time. Have a good night."

"Apology accepted. Goodnight." Frey nodded and continued to hand out the cards for the next game.

"You good man?" Holt followed Dave.

"Yeah, just wanted to play a few games. I'm heading home to the wife. Have a good night."

Holt slapped him on the back. "Have a good night." Holt watched Dave walk to the cashier's window and cash out. He stayed nearby and made sure Dave left the casino without incident. Keeping Frey safe was his number one priority.

"Incoming at your six, Holt," Jake's voice said with a chuckle.

What now? Holt turned around and saw Candy sauntering toward him.

"Candy, how are you?" Holt stood with his legs a hips length apart and his hands clasped low in front of him. He was tired of her blatantly grabbing his crotch. In this position, he could stop her hands from reaching for him.

"I'm good now. How are you doing tonight?" Candy's smile was actually nice. *What was she up to?*

"Everything going alright?" Holt asked, searching her face for any signs of deception.

"Yes, just wanted to come in and play some slots." Candy held the cup with coins in her hands. "It's always nice to see you, though."

"Well. Have a good night." Holt stepped around her and kept scanning the room. That was weird and the only time he'd seen her where she didn't hit on him. She didn't grab him or try to stop him when he walked around her. Something was going on.

"Well, that was short and sweet," Jake mumbled.

"Yep, something's up." Holt felt like he was in the twilight zone between Dave's calm attitude and Candy's indifference.

*** **Frey** ***

Frey saw Holt talking to Candy out of the corner of her eye. This had been a strange night between Dave at her table and now Candy talking to him, without plastering her body all over him. She wanted the night to end. But that wasn't gonna happen for a few more hours.

On her next game, Candy sat at her table. She didn't realize Candy knew how to play blackjack. Frey watched her closely when she lost.

"I guess I was bound to lose at least one hand," Candy joked with the gentleman next to her.

"That's alright babe, you win some, you lose some. Can I buy you a drink? Name's Kent." Kent stuck out his hand for her to shake. Frey was used to the players at her table getting to know each other. She was glad Candy had another man in her sights.

"Thank you, Kent. I would like a gin and tonic, please. I'm Candy."

Kent signaled to the waitress and ordered her drink.

As the games progressed, Kent got a little more handsy with Candy. Frey was on the lookout for any problems. She didn't like Candy, but that didn't mean she wanted her to be assaulted at her table, either. Girls had to stick together.

"You want to get out of here, babe? I'll lick you like a delicate piece of candy." Kent grabbed Candy and licked her cheek.

Ew, Frey thought as she watched Candy's face. Frey pressed the red button under her table when she saw Candy trying to push him away. This could get ugly quick. The other players at her table stopped playing and placed their hands over their chips. Holt came to their table in a few seconds.

"Is there a problem here?" Holt looked between Frey, Candy, and Kent.

"No, just flirting with my new piece of candy." Kent leaned into Candy, but she leaned back, trying to escape his reach.

"Sir, please leave her alone. I don't think she wants your company." Holt laid his hand on Kent's shoulder.

"Hey man, we're good. She's leaving with me." Kent smirked and grabbed Candy's arm, pulling her from her chair. Candy tried to pull herself out of his grip with no luck.

"Let go of the lady. It doesn't seem like she wants to go with you," Holt spoke calmly to Kent. Frey noticed Barrett coming up to them in case there was serious trouble.

Kent held Candy's arm and pulled her ahead of him before grabbing her ass and pushing her forward.

"Hey, don't touch me. Leave me alone. I don't want to go with you." Candy anxiously glanced back. "Can someone please help me?"

Candy's plea shot Holt into action. He grabbed the man's hand on her ass and twisted it behind his back, lifting it high in the middle of his back to apply pressure to his shoulder. "I said release her. Now!"

"Fine!" Kent let go of Candy. "She's a cock tease, anyway. You stupid whore."

"Sir, please stop the name calling. Let's go." Holt was pushing him away from Frey's table. Barrett followed Holt as they escorted Kent toward the casino exit. Candy looked shaken. She was trembling, rubbing her arm with her hand.

"Are you okay?" Frey asked. No one deserved to be treated that way.

"I'll be okay, but can you go with me to the ladies' room? You know, safety in numbers." Candy looked scared as she looked around the casino.

"Sure. Give me just a minute to get a replacement." Frey pressed the blue button under her table. Abigail came immediately. "Abi, can you take over for a few minutes, please?"

"Sure." Abi cleared the cards from the table and opened a new deck.

Frey looked at Candy. "Let's go."

"Thank you. We bumped into each other earlier. My name's Candy. I know you're Frey from your nametag. I've also been to your table before."

Frey opened the bathroom door for Candy and followed her in.

"I have seen you, but until today, you've never played at my table. Was this your first-time playing blackjack?" Frey walked into a stall. This was weird. Never in a thousand years would she have thought she would have a civil conversation with the blow job girl. She may as well use this as her bathroom break.

"I usually play the slots, but I wanted to try something different today. In hindsight, maybe I should have stayed with the slots," Candy said from a neighboring stall. "That man Kent really scared me."

"I'm sorry that happened to you." Frey was at the sink washing her hands. "Is there anything I can do for you?" Her parents always drilled into her that customer service always came before personal relationships at work.

"No, I'll be okay now that he's gone. You seem really nice. Maybe we should hang out sometime. Maybe go somewhere and pick up real men, not assholes like that guy," Candy winced when she looked at her arm. A bruise had already formed. "Unless you have a boyfriend?" Candy watched Frey through the mirror.

"I am dating someone. Are you sure you're, okay? That bruise looks nasty. I need to get back to my table, but I can have one of our security officers bring you a bag of ice." Frey needed this conversation to end—like now.

"I'm good, but I would feel better with a bag of ice. Do you think that hunky security guard that saved me would bring me a bag? I'd like to thank him properly." Candy winked at her. "Oh." Candy covered her mouth with her hand. "Unless that's your boyfriend?"

Frey froze and felt heat rise into her cheeks. Looking up at Candy through the mirror, she tried to smile, but it came out forced. *By not denying Candy's comment, had she given away her secret? Was Candy fishing to find out if she was Holt's girlfriend?* Needing to calm her racing heart, she looked down and stepped away from the mirror to grab a paper towel.

"I'm sure he would appreciate you thanking him." Frey hoped Candy hadn't noticed her reaction to the boyfriend question. After drying her hands, Frey cleared her panicked facial expression, so she appeared to be calm, cool, and collected before facing Candy. But on the inside, she wanted to claw her eyes out and let her know that the hunky security officer was her boyfriend and was not available.

"He can definitely bring you a bag of ice." But being the professional she was, she smiled and left the bathroom.

"Are you okay?" Speak of the devil. Holt was waiting outside the bathroom door.

"Yep, I'm fine," Frey told him as she exited the bathroom. "But Candy would like a bag of ice for her bruised arm."

"Oh, my goodness, Holt, thank you so much for saving me from that horrible man." Candy threw herself at Holt and shed a tear. What the fuck! She hadn't cried when they were in the bathroom. "I could not have gotten through this without Freya's help." Holt gently peeled Candy off his body and looked at Frey, stunned by Candy's burst of emotion. Candy turned to face Frey and said, "She is a great dealer and friend. We are friends now, right, Freya?" Candy reached out and grabbed Frey's hand.

"Ah, sure." Frey pulled her hand back.

"I love having girlfriends. Are you working tomorrow night? Maybe I'll come back and hang out at your table again."

"Yes, I'm working tomorrow night." Frey's brows furrowed.

"I'm so excited!" Candy squealed and hugged Frey.

Frey stood frozen while Candy wrapped her arms around her. Not knowing what to do, she took one arm and patted her back. Frey jerked back when Candy screamed and touched her bruised arm. "Ouch, that hurt." *Shit, had she hurt her when she placed her arm around her?* Frey's arm had barely touched her arm when she patted her back. *What was Candy playing at?*

"Is that man gone? Holt, can you please get me some ice and escort me to my car?" Candy stepped closer to Holt. Frey looked at her arm and barely saw a bruise, but she knew Holt had to help a guest if they asked for help.

"Yes, he's gone," Holt looked at Frey over Candy's head and mouthed 'sorry'. "Let's get you some ice and then I'll walk you out." Holt waited for Candy.

"Bye, friend. I'll see you tomorrow." Candy held her arm and walked away.

"Bye, Candy." Frey lifted her hand in a slight wave. *What the hell just happened?*

Holt turned to Frey and raised his eyebrow questioningly. Frey shrugged.

"Come on Holt, my arm really hurts. I really need that ice," Candy whined.

"Right behind you," Holt murmured as he followed Candy.

Frey was ready for this night to be over between Dave, Kent, and now Candy she wondered if it was a full moon.

Chapter 35

Bartering Sucked

Candy

C andy made her nightly call to her accomplice.

"How did tonight go?" Her accomplice answered on the first ring.

"It went just as I expected. Getting Kent to come in and manhandle me worked like a charm. Now, you've got to pay him." Candy started her car, ready to pull out and go home.

"You pay him. It was your idea to bring him in for your plan to woe Holt. You know my money is tight. I don't give a shit about you getting Holt. I just want my money. Spread your legs and barter your body for payment."

Candy could feel her face heating in anger. She couldn't wait until this charade was over. Once she got her share, she was gone, ready to start over somewhere new. At first, she had wanted Holt, but now she just wanted the money for a new beginning and to get away from her crazy partner.

"Fine. I'll pay him, but you will reimburse me when we get the money from Holt. For your information, I don't want Holt anymore. I changed my mind. I just want the money. But we need him in order to get the money."

"Yeah, right? You want to fuck him, don't lie to me. Did you find out if he's dating that slut, Frey?"

"Pretty positive. But I'll break them up. I just need more time." Candy pulled into her apartment parking lot and saw Kent sitting in his car. Shit! She never should have asked one of her neighbors for a favor. Especially one that was always hitting on her. It had been so easy to convince him to do her that favor, but now she had to pay the piper.

"I don't have that much time. My bills are due."

"You mean you have to pay your drug dealer?" Candy waved to Kent and turned off her car.

"Whatever! Just get me my money!"

"I gotta go. Talk to you later." Candy hung up and got ready to face Kent.

"Hey, sweet Candy. How was my performance?" Kent walked up to her car, smiling with his arms spread wide.

"You did a great job. Thank you." Candy hoped a thank you would be enough.

"Yeah, a thank you won't cut it. You owe me. I did what you wanted."

She'd offer him a blow job, but the idea of his cock in her mouth repulsed her. At least if they fucked, he'd wear a condom. She could fake orgasms with the best of them.

"Well then, let's go to your apartment and I'll give you my best performance." Candy winked and grabbed his hand. It would be better in his apartment because when he finished, she could leave.

"Best idea you've had yet. I can't wait to see your 'best performance'," Kent grinned wickedly, pulling her behind him.

This was so not going to be fun, but she wanted to end on a pleasant note in case she needed Kent again. Of course, Candy would tell her contact that she paid him a thousand dollars. Easiest thousand bucks she ever made. Now to put on the best orgasmic performance of her life.

Chapter 36

Pillow Talk

Holt

The weirdest shift ever! Holt was glad when he finished his shift for the night. Frey left about an hour ago. Holt couldn't wait to see her. He got to his room, took a shower, dried off, and walked naked into Frey's room. Frey was already curled up in bed and Barrett was tucking her in.

Oh shit! Holt came to an abrupt stop so fast he held onto the closet door frame to stop himself from falling into her bedroom. He covered his junk with his hands and quietly, but swiftly, retreated into his closet. He nearly tripped trying to avoid being seen by Barrett.

Taking a few deep breaths while looking into Frey's closet, he slowly closed the adjoining door. Holy fuck! That was close. *Thank fuck, it was dark in her room and her closet light was off or else Barrett would have caught him.* Leaning back against the closed closet door, he closed his eyes and took some deep breaths to calm his racing heart.

Now he was wide awake after that adrenaline rush. *Why the hell was Barrett in there? Did Frey call him? Was she okay? Did she tell Barrett?* Fuck, all he wanted to do was wrap himself around her and go to bed, but he needed answers. Holt put on a pair of sweatpants and sat on his bed. He would wait a few minutes and go check on her. But what if Barrett was in her living room or bathroom? *Fuck!*

Holt made a quick decision to go into the security office. If Barrett's door was open, which it usually was when he wasn't with a girl, he could knock and see if he had returned to his room. Yeah, that sounded like a good plan.

Holt walked into the security room and messed with a computer for a couple of minutes before knocking on Barrett's open door.

"Hey, Barrett?" Holt called out.

"Yeah," Barrett came out of the bathroom with a towel around his waist. He must've been about to take a shower. "What's up?"

"Uh, nothing." Holt slipped his hands into his sweatpants. "Just wanted to let you know everything was quiet downstairs. I did a quick check on the monitors up here."

"Okay. You didn't have to do that after shift" –Barrett tilted his head– "but thanks for letting me know."

"Uh, yeah. Sure. No problem." Holt should walk away. He was acting weird, still standing there, staring at Barrett.

"You good?" Barrett pointed at him.

"Oh, yeah." Holt jolted out of his thoughts, smiled, and waved at Barrett. "See ya tomorrow. Sleep tight, don't let the bedbugs bite." Holt pivoted and left Barrett's room, wincing and covering his mouth with his hand. *What the fuck! He sounded like a preschooler. Where did that stupid comment come from?* Before he closed the door, he heard Barrett say, "Okay. That was fucking weird."

Holt headed straight for his room, locking the adjoining door, and continuing into Frey's room. This had been a long, shitty night.

Holt dropped his pants and quietly slid into bed behind Frey.

"Hey," Frey whispered.

"Hey." Holt wrapped his arms around her and nipped her neck. "Are you okay? Did I wake you?"

"Yes, but it's a great way to wake up." Frey grabbed his hand and placed it on her breast. Now this was what he wanted after a long night. Holding her against his chest was the closest thing to heaven he'd ever experienced. She made him feel like he was home.

"Mmm. Someone missed me." Holt sucked her neck.

"The ladies always miss your mouth and hands," Frey chuckled.

"Do they now?" Holt rolled her onto her back and gave the ladies the attention they deserved with his mouth. Pushing both breasts together with his hands, he alternated between licking each nipple.

"Stop playing around and suck them already." Frey squirmed beneath him.

"Yes ma'am. I aim to please." Holt ran his thumbs slowly around her areolas.

"Holt!" He chuckled and took one beautiful breast into his mouth while tweaking and pulling her other nipple. Holt enjoyed sucking her breast and planned on staying there for a while until he felt her hand sliding up and down his cock. He should have told her to keep her hands above her head. Once she stroked him, he would not last.

Despite Holt's efforts to escape by pulling his hips back, it only encouraged her grasp to grow stronger and stroke him harder.

"Where's the condom, Holt?"

"Impatient much, sweetheart?" Holt licked his way down to her pussy, which forced her to release him.

"Holt, I'm serious. I need you now. We can play later." Frey sat up to reach for the nightstand.

Holt was not having it. He placed his hand on her belly, pushing her back down onto the bed. Immediately sliding his fingers into her. He wanted one orgasm before he fucked her.

"I'm sorry, sweetheart, what were you saying?" Holt smiled while he drove Frey crazy until she came all over his hand. While she was coming down from her high, he reached into the nightstand, grabbed a condom, and put it on.

"Holt, please," Frey murmured.

"Okay. Since you asked so nicely."

Holt smoothly thrust into her, instantly overcome by his deep affection for her. He was determined to take his time during their lovemaking, wanting to express how much she meant to him. Tonight, he wanted to make love to her instead of fucking her. She deserved to feel special. Holt grasped her ass and rolled his body slowly, thrusting in and out of her.

"Harder, faster," Frey groaned.

"Not this time, sweetheart. You feel so good. I want to take my time."

"Holt, please." Frey tightened her legs around his hips, pushing him into her.

"Nope, not this time. Open your eyes and look at me. I want to watch you when you explode all over my cock." Holt thrust into her with more intensity and depth the moment she locked eyes with him.

"That's it, sweetheart. Come for me." Holt kissed her, his tongue mimicking his thrusts. Moving one of his hands toward her clit, he rolled and rubbed it until Frey began panting. He released her mouth and gazed into her dilated eyes. His hips and fingers increased speed until she clamped her nails onto his shoulders and came with her eyes wide open. It was a beautiful sight to see all her feelings reflected in her eyes, causing Holt to explode with his most powerful orgasm.

"Shit, sweetheart. You are incredible." Holt rained kisses on her face and neck. "I loved watching you give yourself to me. I love you so much."

"I love you too." Frey smiled. "I think I left claw marks on you," she giggled.

"You can mark me all you want." Holt kissed her again before getting off the bed and looking at his shoulders. "I will wear them with pride. I'll be right back." Holt headed to the bathroom for a washcloth and to dispose of the condom.

"Why was Barrett tucking you in?" Holt asked while he cleaned her up.

"His shift ended at the same time as mine, and he followed me while I told him about my night. He was worried about me and thought it would be funny to tuck me in." Frey sighed. "I was hoping you weren't going to come in while he was here. Good timing."

"Not really." Holt finished and sat on the bed facing her. "I came in after my shower–naked–saw him, and damn near tripped in the closet trying to backpedal back into my room."

"Oh shit, I'm sorry." Frey sat up and covered her mouth, laughing. "Wish I had seen that."

"I'm sure you do. Let's do something together tomorrow that does not involve staying in this room." Holt grinned at her.

"What do you want to do?" Frey leaned back onto her elbows.

"How about a movie so we can make out when the lights are out?" Holt wiggled his eyebrows, threw the washcloth over his shoulder, and dove onto Frey, rocking the bed.

"You are so naughty. But I love it." Frey laughed while he pulled her down onto her back. "You are the best boyfriend ever."

"I try." Holt curled his fingers towards his palm, brought them close to his mouth and blew on his nails before wiping them on his chest.

"You're so modest." Frey rolled her eyes. "A movie sounds great. Surprise me." Frey pecked his lips.

"So, whatever I pick, you'll watch?" Holt grinned.

"Yup. Man's choice."

"Really?" Holt quirked an eyebrow. "I need to fuck you missionary style more often. You are so amenable."

Frey slapped his shoulder. "Stop it. I let you have your way with some things."

"Yes, you do." Holt laughed at her attempt to smack him. "But tomorrow, remember, you let me pick the movie. So don't be mad at me when you don't like it." Holt kissed her check and rolled onto his back, pulling her on top.

"I won't be mad if we can spend the day together. Pinky promise?" Frey held out her pinky. Holt wrapped his pinky around hers, sealing their vow.

"I like a kiss promise better." Holt used his pinkie's hold on her hand to pull her up to his lips.

"Mmm, I like that better, too." With a smile, Frey planted another kiss on him, and rested her head on his chest.

"Hey." Holt stroked her hair. "What did Candy talk to you about?"

"It was so weird." Frey lifted her weight onto her elbow and stared down at Holt. "She was being nice. It was so hard to be cordial when all I wanted to do was pull her hair out and tell her to stay away from my man."

"Easy tiger," Holt smiled. "Your man, huh?"

"Yes!" Frey slapped his chest. "Don't look so smug. How would you like it if I had some guy chasing after me?"

"Sweetheart, that's easy. I'd kill him." Holt squinted at her. "Especially if he hurt you."

"I love you too." Frey laid back down on his chest. "Hopefully, Candy doesn't think we're best buds now. I don't think I could spend time with her and pretend to be her friend."

"I'm sorry." Holt kissed the top of her head. "At least you won the prize—you got me. Ow!" Holt's body jerked when Frey pinched his ass.

Frey laughed and settled into Holt. Holt held her tight and fell asleep, breathing in her sweet scent that was strictly Frey.

Chapter 37

Finally! A Date with my Sexy Boyfriend

Frey

"Holt, wake up," Frey planted kisses all over his face. Holt had promised her a movie date today, and she was on cloud nine. She wanted him to wake up so they could go and have fun. She knew they had to be careful since her family was well known, and she didn't want any rumors reaching them. But if they didn't hold hands in public, people would just think they were two friends hanging out. Hopefully, the movie theater would be really dark and they could snuggle there.

"What time is it?" Holt rolled over and grumbled into the pillow.

"It's already ten and I want to go to a movie like you promised me last night." Frey was on her knees, jumping on the bed.

She thought Holt was asleep, but he couldn't have been because suddenly he sat up and tackled her to the bed. "You're in a good mood."

"I am. I'm so excited to go on a date with you. To feel like a real couple, if only for a little while." Frey beamed at him.

"Really? You're excited. I couldn't tell." Holt looked at her wide-eyed.

"Funny guy." Frey shoved him. "Get up. Let's go."

"Bossy much." Holt said before Frey shoved him again.

"Okay. Okay, I'm going. Let me take a shower and I'll look up a movie and plan our date." Holt crawled over her and left the bed after a quick kiss.

"I'll be ready in twenty minutes," Frey shouted at his back. A jolt of adrenaline shot through her as she jumped out of bed. Whoa. Feeling sick, she leaned on the nightstand and barely made it to the toilet before puking. Standing up too fast made her queasy. Damn. She wasn't going to tell Holt because he would turn all alpha on her and make her stay in bed. And nothing was going to interrupt her date. Besides, she felt fine after emptying her stomach. Frey brushed her teeth in the sink as the water heated in the shower.

Frey was ready, as promised, by the time Holt came back into her room dressed in well-worn jeans and a tight t-shirt. She loved when his t-shirts showcased his muscular physique—so drool worthy.

"Stop looking at me like that or we'll never leave," Holt grumbled and gave her a kiss on the cheek. "So, how about a picnic and a movie?"

"A picnic? Really?" Frey hugged him. "That sounds fun. Thank you."

"Yep, let's get some sandwiches from the grocery store and eat outside. I don't want to get food from here, too many prying eyes. The movie doesn't start until two and I'll have you back by five."

"Yay! Let's go." Frey grabbed Holt's hand and pulled him out of his room. In her excitement, she didn't consider if someone could be in the family sitting area in front of the elevator. Too late.

Holt froze in place and dropped her hand, causing her to swing around and bump into him. "Why did you stop?" Frey looked up into his face. Holt lifted his chin, motioning toward the elevator.

"Hey, where are you guys going?" Barrett was standing in front of the elevator.

"Uh...," Frey's head was going back and forth between Holt and Barrett like a tennis match.

"Where are you going?" Holt replied, pushing Frey toward the elevator.

"Doctor's appointment." Barrett pushed the button.

"Ah, we're going to the grocery store and then the mall." Holt put his hands in his pocket and walked behind Frey.

"Since when do you go to the mall?" Barrett looked at Holt and asked sarcastically. Then Barrett snapped his fingers. "Wait, that's right. You're dating a girl that works in the mall."

"Uh, yeah, about that. We broke up."

Frey looked at Holt. He looked like a deer caught in headlights. Why was the elevator taking so damn long?

"When?" Barrett asked.

"Uh, a few days after I told you guys about her." Holt rubbed his forehead.

"Sorry, man." Barrett slapped his back.

"Thanks."

Was Holt sweating? Frey needed to end this conversation quick.

"Holt is going to the mall with me because I asked him. After what happened with Kent last night, I wanted someone to accompany me." Frey finally got her mind working.

"Why didn't you ask me?" Barrett asked, with a confused look on his face.

"You have a doctor's appointment."

"Yeah, but you didn't know that." Barrett pointed at her. Frey turned to Holt, not knowing what to say.

"She mentioned last night in the casino that she was going, and I volunteered to go. I gotta buy a new pair of sneakers." Holt interrupted, saving her from answering. Point for Holt.

"Oh, okay. Do you want me to reschedule my appointment and go with you guys?" Barrett sounded concerned.

Finally, the elevator doors open. Thank the lord. Holt walked in and held the doors for them.

"No, it's okay. Holt can suffer through it this time, and you can owe me a raincheck." Frey hugged her brother. "I'm sorry I didn't ask you last night, but it all worked out. Thank you anyway. What are you going to the doctor for?"

Frey wanted to change the subject. Their answers were getting convoluted the longer they talked.

"Just my annual checkup, no worries."

"Great. Next time I go to the mall, I'll come get you." Frey playfully punched Barrett on the arm.

"No problem, sis. Let me know if you need anything." Barrett stepped out of the elevator. "Thanks, man, for going with her."

"Of course."

Chapter 38

Picnic and a Movie

Frey

They all left the resort and went to their own cars. Once inside the car, Frey took a deep breath. "Well, that was close," Frey sighed.

"Yeah, we got lucky he didn't see us holding hands coming out of my room."

"I know, right?" Frey buckled up.

"You know," Holt hedged, staring at her after starting his car. "If we told him, we wouldn't need to sneak around. It's getting harder to keep track of all the lies."

"Let's not argue about this today. This is our first date and I want to enjoy every minute, please," Frey pleaded with him.

"Okay." Holt ran his hand over his hair before backing out of the parking spot and heading to the grocery store.

Once inside, they ordered two subs from the deli and walked around getting chips, cookies, and drinks. Holt drove them to the neighborhood park that was near the movie theater. They didn't have to stress about too many kids, since most were in school.

Holt spread out a blanket, and they sat down with their feast.

"I'm going to the American Indian Cultural Center tomorrow. Alex and I are going to teach Thunder, Tori, and their shelter kids how to do our traditional Stomp Dance." Frey mentioned after swallowing her first bite of her sandwich. "I'm so excited to go and meet the shelter kids that Tori can't stop talking about."

"Yeah, Barrett told me you guys were going. We both wished we were going with you, but we're having our monthly meeting with your dad." Holt sat crisscross applesauce in front of Frey. Frey thinks about what the monthly meeting is.

"Why are you guys meeting on a Friday? Don't you usually meet on Monday?" Frey takes a sip of her drink.

"Your dad's meeting with the tribal council on Monday and had to reschedule our meeting." Holt shrugs and takes a bite of his sandwich.

Frey was disappointed that Holt couldn't go with her.

"Alex is an excellent dancer, but it would have been great to have you and Barrett, too. For a non-native, you sure know how to do our dances well." Frey smiled before taking another bite.

"I learned from the best." Holt winked at her. Osceola and Sehoy wanted to make sure their kids learned their traditional dances. Since Holt was always with them, he learned right beside Alex, Barrett, and Frey. Frey remembered Holt being surprised when Osceola asked him to join them as they danced as a family around a burning fire pit at his first pow-wow. He followed Barrett and picked up the steps quickly. Smiling, the entire time.

"You know mom and dad have always thought of you as family, even before you moved in with us." Frey gazed into his eyes.

Holt's lips curve into a slow smile, his eyes softening. With one finger, he leaned forward and tucked a strand of hair behind her ear. "I love your mom and dad. They have always been kind to me. Which is why lying has been so hard for me."

"For me too." Frey sighed and took a sip of her water. "How about we tell them at Thanksgiving? It's a holiday about being thankful. Maybe everyone will take the news well."

Holt, ready to take a drink, stopped with the cup halfway to his mouth and stared at her. "If that's what you want to do, but it might ruin Thanksgiving if Barrett gets mad because we didn't tell him first." Holt took a sip and then opened the bag of chips, sprinkling them onto her napkin.

Frey knew Holt had a point. Hell, that's what she'd been saying from the beginning. But her family could be the buffer they needed.

"Let's talk about something else. What movie are we going to see?" Frey reached over and grabbed a chip.

Holt released a heavy sigh and shook his head, but didn't argue with Frey. "Since you loved those books about the kids that have to fight to survive and beat the district, I wanted to take you to watch the prequel." Holt smirked.

"Are you serious? I've been dying to see that." Frey leaned forward, grabbed Holt's face, and kissed him. "Thank you. I did like those books, and I saw the movies."

"I remember. You dragged Barrett and me to every one of them and made us read the books so we could discuss them with you." Holt gathered his trash.

Frey was so excited. She loved those books. She used to follow them around and quiz them. They had been such good sports about it because they knew it was important to her. *Shit!* Would Barrett get mad they didn't invite him to this movie? Another fucking lie. Frey ignored those thoughts and decided to worry about them later. Today was about her and Holt spending time together.

"Okay." Frey chewed quickly, devouring her sub as fast as she could.

"Sweetheart, you don't have to eat that fast. We have time." Holt leaned back on his elbows, lengthened his legs, and crossed them at the ankles.

"Do you remember the stories?"

"Most of it. I'm sure you'll fill me in if I ask." Holt looked her way.

"Let me know if you get confused. I've been watching trailers and listening to podcasts about this movie." Frey finished and put her trash in the paper bag.

"Of course you have," Holt smirked.

"Okay, I'm ready." She got up and ran to a trashcan to dispose of her trash. When she got back, Holt was smiling. He had already folded up the blanket.

"Come on Sparky, let's do this." Holt held out his hand.

"Sparky?" Frey took his hand, raising her eyebrows at her new nickname.

Holt shrugged. "Yeah, you're bursting with electrical energy like a spark plug."

Frey laughed. "What do you know about spark plugs?"

Holt pretended offense, clutching a hand to his heart. "Enough to know what a spark plug is and what it does. One of Betty's nicer boyfriends used to work on cars in front of our trailer, and I used to watch. I wish she had stayed with him. At least he didn't hit me." He added the last bit as an afterthought.

Frey overheard Holt telling Barrett once about a beating he got from one of Betty's men. It broke her heart that he had to go through that.

"I'm so sorry," Frey lifted onto her tippy toes and kissed his cheek.

Holt hugged Frey. "It's all good. That was a long time ago."

Frey always wondered how Holt really felt about his childhood because he never talked about it with her. Stepping out of his embrace, Frey grabbed his hand, throwing caution to the wind, they intertwined their fingers and swung their arms between them. They only needed to keep their secret for another couple of weeks. After Thanksgiving, they could date openly.

"I bought our tickets online so we can walk right in," Holt mentioned when they arrived at the movie theater.

When they walked in, the smell of popcorn immediately assaulted Frey.

"Can we get popcorn?" Frey placed her hand on his bicep.

Holt stopped mid-stride and blinked, puzzled by Frey's question. "You're still hungry?"

"I'm always hungry for popcorn at the movies." Frey pulled Holt to the concession line. They ordered a medium size popcorn with no butter and a bottle of water. After sitting in their seats, Holt moved the tray table and put his arm around Frey. They both reclined and got comfy. Frey was enjoying her popcorn watching the show before the previews when she saw Holt's hand reach in and grab a handful.

"Are you eating my popcorn?" Frey opened her mouth, pretending to be shocked.

"I never said I didn't want any. Just wanted to know if you were still hungry. I'm always hungry. I'm a growing boy." Holt popped another kernel in his mouth.

"Oh, I can get you growing." Frey cupped his cock through his jeans.

"Frey," Holt growled, "don't touch it unless you mean to satisfy it."

"You're right." Frey handed him the popcorn and dropped her head onto his lap just as the lights went down to run the previews. Frey knew she had ten to twenty minutes before the movie started. They were the only ones in the theater, and they were sitting in the back row. Perfect place for sexy time.

Frey unzipped his pants, stroked his cock, and licked it from top to bottom. "Shit Frey!"

Frey laughed and went down until she felt his head against her throat. Lifting her head up and down, she continued to suck and stroke him until he couldn't stop pushing up into her mouth. Frey slipped one hand under his cock and massaged his balls.

"Frey," Holt sucked in his stomach. Panting, he tapped her head. "Sweetheart, I'm gonna come."

"Mmm hmm," Frey doubled down and took him as deep as she could down her throat. Holt's body trembled until he grunted and released himself into her mouth. She guessed the fear of being caught sped up his orgasm because he'd never come so fast.

"Fuck, baby." Holt massaged the back of her head while his breathing slowed down. "Come up here. I love you. My naughty girl."

Frey smiled and kissed him while he straightened his jeans. The movie was just as good as Frey thought it would be, but the best part was sharing it with Holt.

Chapter 39

Stomp Dance

Frey

"**H**ave fun today, sweetheart." Holt said before he kissed her forehead.

"What time is it?" Frey grumbled.

"Too early for you to have to get up."

Frey reached out and grabbed his hand. "Come back to bed."

"No can do. I gotta go to my meeting. I don't think your dad would appreciate me getting there late." Holt raised her hand and kissed it. "I'll see you later."

If there was something Frey liked about her mornings lately, it was waking up in Holt's arms. Ugh! Today would not be one of those days. She was going to miss him today after their perfect date yesterday. Frey slept for another hour before her alarm went off and she had to get ready to go to the cultural center to teach the shelter kids the Seminole Stomp Dance.

Her excitement was bubbling over as she drove to the American Indian Cultural Center. She'd been looking forward to this day for a while now. It would be good to get to know the boys. Tori had told her that Thunder mentored them. Frey wondered if that was something Holt could do since he had also grown up in a broken home, but she wanted to meet them first before she brought it up with Holt.

"Hi, Mark. How's the security officer training going?" Frey walked to the lobby desk. Mark was very handsome with dark brown hair, longer in the front than the sides and back. He was well over six feet with a lean yet muscular build. His beautiful light brown eyes lit up when he smiled, which was often because he loved to joke around. His fun personality was part of his charm. Frey thought he was sexy, but she only had eyes for Holt.

Mark had been working with Thunder at the cultural center as a tour guide and receptionist since it opened. But after so many incidents, he'd asked Thunder if he could oversee the center's security. Thunder had agreed and Mark took as many classes as he could to become a certified security officer licensed to carry a weapon. Frey knew about his training because he often trained with Holt and Barrett. She'd heard Officer George and Officer Sean also helped him.

"It's good. I'm almost done with my training. I couldn't have done it without Barrett and Holt's help." Mark walked around the desk to give Frey a hug. He was also a hugger. She could only imagine how crazy the female guests would be once they saw him in a uniform. They already propositioned him all the time. Mark was not lacking for dates.

"I'm sure they were happy to help you. Are the kids here yet?" Frey looked around and thought how nice it was that they did this for the shelter kids.

"No, but they should be here soon." Mark went back to his chair.

"Where is everyone?" Frey asked.

As if on cue, Thunder came out of his office and smiled at her. "Hey, Frey, I thought I heard your voice. Thanks for coming in to help us."

Thunder was an Oglala Lakota who moved down from South Dakota to manage the American Indian Cultural Center in South Florida. The purpose of setting up the cultural center was to teach non-native people about the native cultures. The Lakota Tribal Council had spoken to the Seminole Tribe of Florida Tribal Council before they chose the location of their cultural center.

Osceola had helped Thunder when he moved down and needed to find reliable contractors. Which made Osceola a great mentor for Thunder since he'd already gone through that experience when his tribe built the Rock 'n' Roll Resort & Casino. Frey had met Thunder when Osceola gave him a tour, but she got to know him better during their Girls' Night Out events because the boys always showed up at the end. Tori was also from Thunder's tribe. She worked at the cultural center as the assistant curator, and Alex was their chef.

Thunder needed her help because the current exhibit was about her people, The Seminole Tribe of Florida. She was honored to come in with Alex to teach Thunder, Tori, and the shelter kids about one of their dances.

Frey hugged Thunder when he approached her. "No problem. The stomp dance is easy, and important to our culture. I'm happy to help."

"Tori's in the kitchen with Alex, 'helping him with the fry bread'." Thunder said, using air quotes. "Pfft, like he really needs help."

Mark rolled his eyes. "Those two can't keep their hands off each other."

"But they sure are cute," Frey winked. "I'm gonna go say hello."

"I would announce yourself before you enter." Thunder motioned with his head toward the restaurant and leaned against the lobby desk.

"Noted." Frey walked into the restaurant and could hear Tori's giggles coming out of the kitchen doorway. She didn't think they would fool around at work, but just in case, she knocked on the outer wall and announced herself.

"Hellloooo?" Frey rounded the corner, peeking through her fingers.

"Hi." Tori ran toward her. "I'm so glad you're here," she said before slamming into her for a hug. Frey hugged her back, laughing at her enthusiasm. It was exciting to see Tori outside of the Casino. She loved it there, but sometimes it felt like being trapped in a different dimension where the outside world ceased to exist. It was nice to get out occasionally.

"Hey sis," Alex chuckled and continued to roll out the dough.

"Hey bro." Frey walked over and hugged him from behind. "Are you making all the dough now for the frybread?" Frey thought about how much she and, undoubtedly, the shelter kids loved Alex's various frybread recipes.

"Yep." Alex turned and kissed her forehead before going back to work. "I'll drop it into the fryer after we finish dancing, so it doesn't get cold."

"Sounds like a plan." Frey turned to Tori. "Are we teaching you and Thunder before the kids or with them?"

"Thunder and I thought it would be best if we all learned together," Tori smiled at her.

"Our boys are here." Thunder slid into the kitchen in his moccasins. "Time to move and groove. Hokahey!"

Frey cracked up as Thunder danced his way out of the kitchen, shouting the Lakota battle cry that means "Let's do it!" She had never seen this carefree side of him.

Frey looked at Tori and pointed toward the door. "Is he always like that?"

"On the days that the boys are here, yes." Tori draped her arm over Frey's shoulders, leading her out.

"You guys go, I'll catch up. I gotta wash my hands." Alex went to the sink.

"Hey gorgeous." Tim, the oldest shelter boy, approached Tori for a hug, but got distracted by Frey standing beside her. He looked her up and down with wide eyes. "Man, Thunder, you got another hot chick at your place."

Frey laughed at Tim. He was way too young for her, but it was nice to be called a hot chick.

"Hey, watch it, Romeo," Alex said from behind them. "That's my sister you're talking about."

Frey was relieved not to have to respond to Tim.

"Hey, Chef Alex." Tim gave him a hug. "How's it going, man? Did you make us extra fry bread again?"

"Of course." Alex put his arm around Tim and turned him to face Frey. "This is my little sister, Frey."

"Hey, hey, Frey." Tim wiggled his eyebrows at her. "I'm Tim, the oldest of this crew."

Tim was a thin, blonde-haired, blue-eyed charmer. Frey was enjoying his theatrics. This was going to be a fun day. "Nice to meet you, Tim." Frey went in for a hug.

Tim gave her a quick hug and then held up his arms. "You saw that, right? She hugged me," he said to Alex.

"You're such a little shit. Come on, let's go learn the stomp dance." Alex grabbed Tim around the neck and pulled him to the center of the room while everyone else laughed.

Thunder looked around. "Tim, introduce everyone you brought today since Frey doesn't know you guys."

"Gotcha." Tim pointed to each boy as he announced their name. "That's Luke, Kenny, Jimmy, and Bryce."

Frey thought there would be more. Tori told her some boys didn't trust adults, and they never came. Thunder visited them at least once a week at the shelter to ease them into getting to know him.

"Hi guys, it's nice to meet you." Frey went down the line, shaking their hands.

"Let's all make a circle around the tree." Thunder pointed to the tree in the center of the room, guiding them in that direction. Once there, Thunder called out to Mark, who was still sitting at the lobby desk. "Mark, are you coming?"

"Sure, boss." Mark hurried over and found a spot between two of the boys.

Frey wished Holt was there. Seeing the boys standing there nervous waiting for the instructions reminded her of when Holt started learning the dances with her family. Back then, Holt seemed unsure and anxious until Barrett and Frey taught him the dances. He would practice with Barrett every day for a week before the annual pow-wow. Anyone who saw him dance would never know he wasn't from their tribe; he was so good at it. Holt would love this. She would talk to him about mentoring these kids because she felt like he could relate to them on so many levels.

"Who wants to explain the dance you'll be teaching us?" Thunder looked between Alex and Frey.

"Frey, do you want to do the honors?" Alex had never enjoyed talking in front of people. He was more of a behind-the-scenes person. Frey figured she'd let him off the hook. Focusing away from Holt's past and back on the present, Frey launched into an explanation.

"Sure." Frey stood where everyone could see her. "Historically, our stomp dance has its roots in the Green Corn Ceremony. The Green Corn Ceremony is a four-day gathering held each year to mark the renewal of seasons and express our gratitude to the Creator for providing food and life. Our men sing the stomp dance songs in a call-and-answer format following a male song leader, who often sets the dance rhythm using a handheld turtle shell rattle. Different tribes do this stomp dance. You can do it coupled with your partner or single file. Alex, come up over here with me and let's show them how to move their feet."

Alex stood next to Frey and held her hand. Frey turned to the right and took stomping steps as if they were marching while Alex followed her.

"This is what you guys will do. We will do this in a circle around the tree." Frey stopped and turned so she and Alex were side by side again. "Tori, come take Alex's hand and then everyone else follows suit. Make sure your right hand is holding onto the left hand of the person in front of you." Frey looked around to make sure everyone was in place.

"Okay, I'm gonna move to the back so Alex can call out the song. Alex, here is the rattle." Frey moved to the back of the line, but instead of being the last person she got between the last two boys. They were the youngest boys there. Frey reached for their hands. The youngest, Bryce, flinched, and Frey stopped. "It's okay, I just want to hold your hand to help lead you, but if you don't want me to, then just watch me."

Bryce glanced up and slowly gave her his hand. Frey smiled and nodded, then raised her head and looked at Alex. He had noticed the delay and was waiting for her to say she was ready. "Alex, you can begin whenever you're ready."

Alex nodded and began chanting while shaking the rattle, leading the group around the tree. They circled the tree until Alex finished his songs about five minutes later. When they finished, all the boys were still stomping in place and asking to do it again.

"I killed that, man!" Tim shouted when they finished. "Can we do that again?"

Frey was glad they were enjoying themselves. With kids, you never knew if they would like to participate or hate it. She'd kept an eye on Bryce, since he was the youngest, to make sure he was keeping up. Not only was he keeping up, but he was grinning from ear to ear.

"I have to get to the kitchen to fry up your bread" Alex let go of Tim's hand. "Thunder, I know you don't know our words, but you can use your own prayer with the rattle to keep the pace. Is that okay?"

"Absolutely, I'll say some of our gratitude songs for a great harvest." Thunder jogged to the front and accepted the rattle. Alex left and headed to the kitchen.

"Thunder, give me a second." Frey broke out of the circle toward Tori. "Tori, come here. I'll show you the fancy double step that some ladies in the tribe do, in case you want to teach the girls a cool move. We can practice it on this go round."

Frey showed her the step, and they moved back into the line between the boys. Thunder started his chant and off they went.

After they finished several songs, they stopped. The boys were red faced and giggling, talking over each other in their excitement. The adults were a little out of breath and glad for a break.

"Boys, why don't you go wash your hands and meet us back in the restaurant?" Tori instructed them. "I'll go get the fry bread Alex has ready so far."

Frey watched the boys doing the stomp dance toward the bathroom. They were so darn cute and funny. Frey used the restroom herself before entering the restaurant, thinking about last year's pow-wow and how Holt jumped right in and danced his heart out. Such a difference than that first pow-wow.

She heard the boys coming out of the restroom and wondered if they would like to attend their pow-wow next year. *Would they dance?* They would have several months to practice. She would talk to Tori and Thunder about it.

Alex had set up a taco bar for them to add the toppings to their fry bread. They let the kids go through the line first. They'd certainly worked up an appetite.

Chapter 40

My Heart Hurts

Frey

"Wow, this smells terrific." Tim placed a piece of fry bread on his plate.

Frey stood behind Tori in line. "Tori, that was a lot of fun. If you ever need help during a field trip, let me know. I rarely work during the day." Frey had loved teaching the boys the dance. She'd always wanted to volunteer for something worthwhile, but nothing had sounded fun. This was fun.

Tori blinked in surprise as she added cheese to her taco fry bread. "I would love that, but are you sure? Won't you be tired?"

Frey thought about her schedule. She was usually up by ten, so coming here wouldn't be a problem. "I'll be fine. What time are your field trips?"

Tori waited for Frey to add her cheese before going to sit down. "Kids usually arrive anywhere between ten and eleven if it's a morning field trip. Afternoon field trips sometimes can end around four. The shelter kids always come on Fridays."

Frey worked nights, so those hours were perfect. Just thinking about coming in and volunteering with kids sounded rewarding and exciting. She was going to tell Holt all about it and hope it was something they could do together. Maybe Holt would even become a mentor for the boys?

"I can do any of those times. I'm usually in bed by one thirty and I rarely sleep for over eight hours at night. So let me know when you schedule a field trip."

Tori side hugs Frey, "Thank you."

"You're welcome. I can't wait." Frey finished piling her fry bread with toppings and looked around for a seat. The two youngest boys were sitting alone in the corner. They were the most introverted of the group. She knew Thunder, Alex, or Mark would join them, but she wanted to be the one to sit with them since those were the boys' hands she held during the stomp dance.

"Tori, I'm gonna go sit with Jimmy and Bryce." Frey glanced at Tori.

"Sounds good." Tori winked at Frey before she turned and headed toward Tim's table.

"Hey guys." Frey smiled at them. "Mind if I join you?"

"No, ma'am," Jimmy, the older of the two, answered.

"Jimmy and Bryce, right?" Frey sat down across from them. "Have you had Alex's fry bread before?"

"Yes, ma'am," Jimmy answered while Bryce shook his head.

"Do you like it?" Frey tried to get them to open up, but it was like pulling teeth.

"I do. I especially like the toppings." Jimmy picked up his taco and started eating it.

Frey noticed Bryce was just looking at his plate, not eating. "Bryce, do you not like it?"

Bryce's eyes widened, and he shook his head. "I'm sorry. I'll eat it." He quickly grabbed the bread with meat and shoved a piece into his mouth. His eyes watered as he chewed.

Frey noticed Jimmy tap Bryce's elbow with his.

"Bryce." Frey placed her hand gently over his. "If you don't like it, you don't have to eat it. It's okay. Can I get you something else? It won't hurt Alex's feelings. He's used to me telling him when I don't like his cooking." Frey tried to make a joke.

Bryce seemed frozen with fear. His head bouncing between Jimmy and Frey. When Frey lifted her hand to rub his back, he flinched again. That was the second time she lifted her hand toward him and he flinched before pulling back. *Had someone hit him?* She had seen in the movies how abused women and children moved like that when their abuser lifted their hand, afraid they were going to get hit.

It broke her heart to watch him chew with tears in his eyes. *Had someone made him eat something he didn't like?* From the way he was forcing himself to eat, it seemed like someone had forced this poor boy to eat food he didn't like and beaten him if he refused. He looked to be somewhere around Lucy or Emmy's age. How could some parents be so cruel? It reminded her of what Holt went through in his childhood with a horrible mother.

Frey got up and knelt beside Bryce. She pushed the plate away and gently turned him while she held his hands. Bryce looked down as a tear rolled down his face.

"Oh, Bryce. Look at me, sweetie." Frey pulled him into her arms. She noticed everyone looking at her. Frey pulled back, held his face in her hands, and wiped his tears. "What can I get you?"

"Hey, big man." Alex crouched down next to them. "You don't have to eat that. How about you and I go into the kitchen, and I make you something else? Anything you want."

"Really?" Bryce squinted at Alex.

"Really. Come with me and Frey and we'll get you something good. Frey's not wrong. I'm always making her something special because she doesn't always like my gourmet cooking."

Bryce looked from Alex to Frey. "You're not mad?"

"Nope," Alex stood up. "Customers may not always enjoy a chef's food and we have to adjust. So, let's go adjust."

Frey grabbed Bryce's hand. "Let's go make Alex work for his paycheck."

Alex placed his hands on his hips and rolled his eyes. "Little sisters, you gotta love 'em."

Bryce cracked a smile and went with Frey and Alex into the kitchen.

"Okay, big man." Alex picked him up and sat him on the counter. "What do you like to eat? Sweet, salty, fruity, give me a hint."

"I like fry bread but not with taco meat."

"Okay, do you want it like a pizza or with honey?" Alex grabbed a fresh piece of dough from the pile he still needed to fry for the boys to take home.

"Does honey make it sweet?" Bryce scrunched up his nose.

"It can. Depending on how much honey you put on it." Alex dropped the dough in the fryer.

"Do you have chocolate?" Bryce asked, looking around.

"I have chocolate chips. Do you want it to be sweet like a dessert?" Alex dropped another one in the fryer.

"Yes, I like desserts. I never got to eat them at home." Bryce dropped his head and picked at his nails.

This little boy was breaking Frey's heart. He was so sweet and polite—how could someone hurt him?

"I have an idea. How about you help me try out some desserts? You can be my taste tester." Alex took out the first fry bread.

"Okay." Bryce sat up straight.

"Frey, take out the chocolate chips, Nutella, and bananas from the pantry. Then get the ice cream, cool whip, and strawberries from the fridge." Alex took out the last two fry breads.

He ended up making several concoctions for Bryce to try. On the cutting board he cut the frybread like slices of a pizza.

"Okay, big man. Let's try these." Alex picked up Bryce and set him down in front of his cooking counter.

"I can try all of them?" Bryce stared at all the different options, licking his lips.

"Sure, why not? I'll cut a piece off all of them and you can pick your favorite." Alex cut the tip off each one and Bryce ate them just as fast as Alex could cut. Frey's heart swelled to see the joyous expressions on his face.

"This one! This one!" Bryce was jumping up and down, announcing his favorite. "Can I finish it?"

"So, you like the one with chocolate chips, bananas, and strawberries? Good choice." Alex moved that one onto a plate for him. "We can take it out there and you can take your time eating it."

Frey grabbed his plate. Bryce followed her out to the restaurant to join the others.

"Hey, Bryce. What you got there?" Kenny shouted from his table.

"I have a special fry bread dessert." Bryce beamed, puffing out his chest. "I'm Alex's taste tester!"

"Lucky!" they all yelled at him.

"Alex, can they try the other ones, so they don't go to waste?" Bryce looked at Alex with big puppy dog eyes.

"Sure. I'll go get the other desserts." Alex brought them to a table, laying it out for everyone to try. He also cut the slices into pieces. "Alright, let me know what you all think. I'm gonna go fry the rest of your to-go fry bread."

"Wow." Tim walked over and grabbed a bite. "These all look great. Thanks for sharing, Bryce."

"Yeah, Bryce, thank you." All the boys took turns thanking Bryce and patting him on the back.

Thunder and Tori came over to Frey. "Frey, I can't thank you and Alex enough," Thunder placed his arm around her and kissed her forehead. "This is the first time I've seen Bryce smile and open up to anyone. He's always been quiet and keeps to himself."

"He is such a sweet boy. He flinched before the dance when I reached for his hand. I don't think he trusts a lot of adults." It reminded Frey of when Holt was a little boy and a strange man got too close to him. He would watch them warily and flinch if they made any sudden moves toward him. After that conversation she overheard between Holt and Barrett, Holt's childhood behavior made sense. Frey glanced at Bryce. He looked so happy now, talking to the boys. "Do you know what happened to him?"

"He's never said anything to me, and the boys are very tight-lipped when it comes to telling each other's secrets about their family life. But from what Tori and I have observed, we suspect physical abuse." Thunder lowered his arm and sighed. "But neither Tim, Tori, nor I could reach him. I'm glad you and Alex could help him. It's incredible how comfortable you both have made him feel in just a few hours."

Frey was glad she and Alex could help Bryce. Alex began to pick up plates and carry them into the kitchen.

"Yeah, thanks Frey. I'm gonna help Alex finish frying the bread and package it up for the boys," Tori squeezed Frey's forearm and scurried behind Alex into the kitchen.

"Sure, she will." Frey laughed and elbowed Thunder on their way to the boys.

"The Nutella one is the bomb." Mark was arguing with Tim when they walked up.

"Nah, man, it's the plain one with honey." Tim shook his head.

"You're both wrong. It's mine." Bryce put the last bite in his mouth.

Frey gave Bryce a thumbs up and winked, letting him know she agreed with him.

"Well, we wouldn't know 'cause you hogged that one." Tim shoulder bumped Bryce. Bryce grinned with a mouthful of food, his teeth coated in chocolate, and his cheeks puffed out like a chipmunk.

Frey was so impressed with the way the boys treated each other. It was obvious they had created their own family. For some kids and adults, the family you chose was better than the one you were born into. For her family, choosing Holt and making him a part of their family was the best decision her parents ever made. They all continued to joke with each other until they finished all the fry bread.

"So, which one is the favorite?" Alex walked into the restaurant carrying a fully loaded tin pan covered with aluminum foil.

They all shouted their favorites. There was a lot of variation going on. Alex laughed.

"Okay, big man. You know what this means?" Alex raised an eyebrow at him. Bryce shook his head no. "It means now I have to add desserts to my menu."

The boys erupted in cheers, and Thunder slapped Alex on the back. "Good job. I love dessert."

They all pitched in to help Alex with cleanup. Then the boys grabbed their food and headed out.

Frey felt a pull on her hand before all the boys left. Bending down, Frey got on eye level with Bryce.

"Frey, thank you." Bryce hugged her.

Frey's eyes watered. "Anytime, Bryce."

"Will I see you again?" Bryce looked down, scuffing his toe against the floor.

"Yes." Frey lifted his chin and made sure he was looking at her, "I'll find out from Tori when you're coming, and I will come see you." Frey wanted to invite him to the resort. The boys could go swimming, but she needed to clear it with her parents and Thunder before she mentioned it to him.

"Thanks, Frey." Bryce threw himself into her arms, knocking her over onto her ass. They both laughed.

"Come on, Bryce, we gotta go." Tim came over to help him up. Alex helped Frey stand up.

"Bye, Chef Alex." Bryce waved on his way out with Tim.

They all waved back, and Frey felt her heart swell.

Chapter 41

You've Got to Meet the Shelter Kids

Frey

"What an unbelievable day," Frey mumbled. Tori must've heard her because she responded. "Yup, that's why I love those boys. They always make me smile. We feel blessed to be a part of their lives."

"I couldn't agree more." Frey turned to Tori. "Please let me know when they come again. I am definitely coming over to hang out with them."

"You better be careful, or pretty soon you'll be here more than at the casino," Tori teased.

"Yeah, my dad would love that." Frey rolled her eyes. Frey loved the casino, but she definitely had room in her life for these boys. And if Holt came with her, then she could still see him, too.

Alex came up behind Tori and wrapped his arms around her. "That went really well." Tori turned in his arms and cupped his face.

"It was all because of you and Frey." Tori glanced between them. "Bryce has never been this animated. Thank you both."

"Yes, thank you both." Thunder and Mark approached them.

"Alex, you outdid yourself with those desserts." Mark placed his hand on his mouth for a chef's kiss and said, "Magnifico!"

"Why don't you all go home? Mark and I will stay and close." Thunder placed his hands in his pockets.

"Are you sure?" Tori asked Thunder.

"Yup. Frey, thanks for coming and helping us. Alex, thanks for the dancing and the food." Thunder nodded.

"Thunder, is it okay if I come back again and help with field trips and the shelter kids?" Frey asked, grabbing her purse as they headed toward the door.

"Absolutely. You're always welcome here. Come by whenever you want." Thunder walked over and gave her another hug. "Now, all of you...scoot."

Frey was bubbling with excitement. She couldn't wait to tell Holt all about her time at the center. She texted him as soon as she parked at the resort, before she got out of the car.

Frey: Hey are you free?
Holt: Yes
Frey: Where are you?
Holt: In my room
Frey: I'm coming up.
Holt: See you in a few

Frey went through their connecting door when she reached her room. Jumping on the bed with Holt, she snuggled on his chest and recounted her entire day while he held her.

"All the children were wonderful, but the youngest one, Bryce, seemed reserved and introverted when I first met him. He jerked back and was fearful of admitting his dislike for the taco fry bread. Pretty sure he was a victim of abuse. I know you don't like to talk about what happened to you with Betty and her men, but you could relate to him and maybe help him."

"That's quite an assumption you're making." Holt raised an eyebrow at her.

"You're right," Frey sighed. "That was wrong of me to say. I just want to do something to help, especially after Bryce opened up to me when Alex made him a special dessert and the other kids joined in. He broke my heart. I just wanted to wrap him up in my arms and protect him from anyone hurting him. I'd like to get to know him better and be there for him. Maybe you could both help each other?"

"Sweetheart, I know you want to help them, and you mean well. But don't assume this will make my childhood memories or theirs better. I'm not good at talking about my past. I'll try to talk to them, but to be honest, no one knows everything that Betty put me through. Barrett is the only one that I talked to about it and even he doesn't know everything."

"Can you please come with me sometime and meet them? I know you could really help them, since you can relate to them. And the little boy, Bryce, is so darn cute and sweet. I can't wait for you to meet him."

"He sounds like a great kid." Holt squeezed her. "I would love to get to know them. Let me know when you're going again. I'll see if I can go with you."

"Thank you, honey." Frey kissed his chest. "I love you. Let's put on a movie before we have to go to work."

"You pick one."

Frey put on a romantic comedy and snuggled into Holt.

Holt

Too many things were going through Holt's head. Between the shelter boys, their dating lie, Betty's money issues, and Candy's weird attitude, he was having a hard time focusing on the movie.

Frey came back with some interesting stories about the kids she met today. Hearing them, he wished he could have been there with her. He told Frey he'd try to go with her next time, but she needed to let him do it in his own time. If she pushed him, he knew he would shut down just like he did when teachers and counselors at school wanted to know all the details about his home life.

Holt wanted her to understand he had probably experienced similar situations while growing up, but he'd compartmentalized his childhood and hadn't spoken about it much. Frey was right in asking for his help. He understood it was coming from her heart. He hated talking about it because it made him feel embarrassed and angry to remember every beating he received from one of Betty's men. The sole difference between him and the shelter boys was the fact that Osceola and Sehoy looked after him and welcomed him into their home. He'd gotten lucky.

He wasn't eager to relive his story in front of strangers, but if he could do anything to help even one of those boys—he knew he would do it. They needed to know they weren't alone. Sometimes when you met someone who survived that hell, it made you stronger. This would be a good way to help others that were going through what he went through. They could see there was a light at the end of that scary, dark tunnel. Because, for him, the Panthers were that light.

The boys made quite the impression on Frey, especially Bryce. He'd pulled at her heartstrings. Frey told him she thought Bryce had been abused and, from the sounds of it, he would agree. He would help Frey with Bryce, but he would not leave the other boys out.

Once he had a plan for the shelter boys, his thoughts switched to their lie. He was glad they had an end date to it. Thanksgiving. Although Holt was going to convince Frey to tell Barrett before then.

Then there was Betty. *Shit!* He still hadn't told Frey. Glancing down to see her face, she was laughing and enjoying the movie. He didn't want to worry her after she'd had such a good day. Bringing up Betty would be one hell of a downer. He decided against telling her before she had to go to work.

Speaking of work, last night Holt saw Candy sitting at Frey's table, but everything appeared fine. Early this morning when they went to bed, Frey told him that Candy was being friendly. Candy, wanting to be friends with Frey, concerned him. He didn't want Frey to have to deal with Candy any more than he wanted to deal with her. Candy was a constant reminder of one of his mistakes, which he wished he had never made. *Why hadn't he pushed Candy away when he saw Frey's sexy body in that teddy standing in his closet?* He'd fucked up and wished he could go back in time and make a different decision, but that wasn't possible.

When he saw Candy again, he'd pull her aside and figure out what she was up to. The way Candy was behaving gave Holt a sinking feeling in the pit of his stomach. Something didn't seem right.

Why the hell was he letting all these thoughts take over in his head when he had the most beautiful girl in his arms? This moment was about him and Frey creating intimacy with nothing or anyone intruding on his thoughts.

Unfortunately, he made this resolution as the movie was ending. Holt hoped Frey didn't want to talk about it, because he'd missed most of it. Lucky for him, when the credits rolled, and he checked his phone, it was time to get ready for work.

"What did you think?" Frey lifted her head off his chest and looked at him.

Holt should have known, she would ask. She always wanted to talk about whatever they watched, whether it was a movie, series, or documentary.

"I think we have to get ready for work." Holt kissed her forehead. "It was good," he said, before extricating himself from her and getting off the bed. "I'm gonna go shower. Come get me when you finish, since you take longer than me."

"Jerk." Frey threw a pillow at him. Holt dodged it and left the room laughing.

When Holt finished, he waited in bed for Frey.

"Holt, will you really come with me to the cultural center at some point when the shelter boys are there and meet Bryce?" Frey stepped into his room, ready for work.

"I told you I'd try, and I will." Holt nodded.

"You know, you can always talk to me." Frey grabbed his hand from the bed. "I promise to just listen and not judge you or your mom. I can be your sounding board if you need to get something off your chest."

"Thank you. I appreciate you wanting to help me. For now, I'm good." Holt stood and held Frey in his arms. Someday, he would tell Frey everything about his childhood. But for now, he wasn't ready to see the pity in her eyes when she looked at him. "I'll go with you and meet the boys so I can get to know them, especially Bryce, who has already taken up a special place in your heart. You are so kindhearted and caring. You will make a great mom one day."

Frey reached up and pulled his head down for a kiss. "Thank you."

Everything happens for a reason and maybe this was the time to make peace with his childhood and use this opportunity to become a mentor to one or all of those boys. Meeting them and getting to know them was the key to helping them feel wanted and empowered to make goals they could achieve.

He wasn't a therapist, but those boys might feel more comfortable talking to someone with similar experiences that understood what they went through than a professional who learned things from reading a book. Not to bash therapists, they just weren't for everyone. But if one of the kids needed any type of support he couldn't provide, he would absolutely reach out to a therapist. Being a ward of the state must have some medical perks when it came to costs.

He was getting ahead of himself. Baby steps. First, he needed to meet them and allow them to become acquainted with him. The first one on his list was Bryce, since his impact on Frey was profound. Holt was eager to meet him. Maybe now it was his turn to pay it forward and help someone else.

Chapter 42

What the Hell Happened?

Frey

While they were enjoying their embrace, both Frey's and Holt's phones buzzed at the same time.

Barrett: Let's get dinner at RUSH before our shift
Holt: Sounds good to me
Frey: See you there, boys

"You go down first, and I'll be right behind you. I'll give you a few minutes' start." Frey looked up from her phone.

"Okay," Holt sighed.

Frey knew he was frustrated with their situation, but she was glad he didn't argue. He gave her a quick peck on the lips and left. It wasn't unusual for them to meet in RUSH. Many nights before work, if they shared the same shift, they would all get together and eat. A few minutes later, Frey found the boys at RUSH.

"Hey, boys," Frey sat next to Holt. "I notice you guys have already placed our orders."

"Barrett texted Alex our usual order." Holt pointed toward the plates. Their usual orders were burgers for the boys and a turkey and swiss sandwich for Frey.

"How was the Stomp Dance?" Barrett asked between bites of his burger.

"It was so much fun." Frey took a sip of soda. "Those kids are sweet. You guys will have to come with me next time. I told Thunder I wanted to volunteer during their field trips and when the shelter boys come."

"She connected with a little boy that never talks to anyone," Holt praised her. "Alex prepared a special dessert for him, and Frey helped make him at ease."

"I would expect nothing less of my siblings." Barrett threw a French fry at Frey. "They're the nice ones."

"Jerk," Frey grabbed a fry from Holt's plate and threw it at Barrett, aiming for his head.

"Hey, you're the nice one, remember?" Barrett ducked.

"Hey, not my fries." Holt pulled his plate away from her.

"Frick and frack. No food fights in my restaurant." Alex crossed his arms and gave them the evil eye.

"Stop sneaking up on us." Frey grabbed another fry from Holt's plate and threw it at Alex. He caught it before it landed on the floor. Frey couldn't help but be impressed, even if he'd done it a million times when they were young. "You should've been a ninja," she told him.

"I wasn't sneaking anywhere." Alex put the fry on the table. "I came from the kitchen at a usual pace. You just didn't see me because you were too busy throwing food at Barrett."

"I was just telling Barrett how impressive you guys were earlier today at the cultural center. Frey told me all about it." Holt spoke up.

Frey watched Holt slide his chair away from her and push his plate out of her reach.

"Kiss ass," Barrett coughed into his hand.

Frey watched Holt throw one of his fries at Barrett. She knew it was only a matter of time before Holt threw a fry at Barrett. The three of them were always pelting each other with food, and Alex was always yelling at them.

Alex planted his hands on the table and growled at them. "Stop fucking throwing food in my restaurant or I'm kicking you all out."

They all grumbled apologies.

"Well, this has been fun." Frey got up and left to go to work, leaving the boys to clean up the mess.

"Have you guys noticed she always leaves before cleanup?" Barrett spoke loudly enough for her to hear him. Frey didn't stop. Instead, she gave them the finger behind her back and sauntered into the casino to her table.

Her blackjack table was good most of the night. Then Candy showed up with an older woman who looked very familiar to Frey, but she couldn't place her.

"Betty, let's sit here at Freya's table." Candy pulled a chair out for her.

Did she say Betty? Shit, was this Holt's mom? Last time Frey saw her was years ago. She had brown hair back then, but now it was all bleached out. She looked rough, the embodiment of the expression 'rode hard and hung up wet'. What was she doing in the casino? Frey had never seen her here before. How did Candy know her? Was it a coincidence that Holt's mom and blow job buddy were here together? Highly unlikely.

"Freya, this is my friend, Betty Adams." Candy waved her hand at Betty. "Betty, this is Frey, my new best friend."

Best friend? Hardly. Shit! This was not good. Frey looked for Holt but didn't see him nearby. *How would he feel seeing his mom looking like this at his place of employment?* She feigned ignorance and didn't acknowledge Betty as Holt's mom. Maybe Betty wouldn't remember her.

"Hi, Mrs. Adams. It's nice to meet you," Frey said professionally and respectfully.

"We've met before, Freya. Holt is my son." Betty squinted at her. "Don't pretend like you don't know me."

Busted...Betty remembered her. What was she supposed to do now? She felt totally uncomfortable and royally screwed. She put on a poker face, smiled, and carried on.

"Of course. Let's place our bets, ladies." Frey moved the game along, since there were three other players at her table. Frey dealt everyone their first card.

"Is Holt working tonight?" Betty placed her bet before she got her second card and stared at Frey. "I've been calling and texting him, but he isn't answering me."

"I think so, but I haven't seen him." Frey dealt the second set of cards and waited for all bets to be placed. She didn't want to engage in a conversation with Betty. She wondered if Betty was telling her the truth because Holt hadn't said anything to her about Betty's calls.

"I'm surprised you haven't seen him since you stole him from me, and I'm sure you're fucking him. Do you have a golden pussy or something to keep him from coming home and taking care of his mom?" Betty's remark was loud enough for the other players to hear.

"Betty," Candy placed her hand on Betty's arm, "be nice. Frey's not Holt's girlfriend, right Frey?"

"Uh...," Frey's eyes ping-ponged between the two women. What should she say? If she said yes, then maybe Candy would leave Holt alone, but their secret would be out. Barrett would find out before she could tell him. She couldn't do that to Barrett. If she said no, would they believe her or keep pestering her? Frey could feel the heat rising in her cheeks. She would not engage. Sometimes it was best to avoid a confrontation.

All the other players were trying not to stare and continued to play the game as if nothing was happening. Some players wanted to hold, and others wanted another card. Frey ignored the comment and continued to act professionally. "Let's keep this game professional, please."

"See, she is dating him. Hell, she's been living with him in sin since they were seventeen years old. Of course they've fucked. Well, bitch, is your pussy golden?" Betty slammed her hands on the table and screamed at Frey.

"Betty, I'm sorry Holt hasn't contacted you. I'll talk to him when I see him," Frey said softly, backing up as she tried to smooth things over like Holt and Barrett did with angry customers.

Betty bolted out of her seat, leaned over the table, and pointed a finger in Frey's face. "You're sorry? Well, sorry don't cut it, bitch! You and your uppity family stole my child. He needs to come back home and take care of his mother! So, stop sinking your ugly ass claws into him."

Everyone at her table had remained calm—until now. Betty's aggressive behavior made the other guests uncomfortable. They began whispering to each other and looking around. Probably trying to figure out what to do. Frey's shaking hand placed the last card on the table and finished the game. Bile rose in her throat as beads of sweat trickled down her brow.

"Betty, if you can please sit down, I'll try to get Holt." Frey wiped her brow and lifted her arms up, trying to placate Betty.

"Betty, please sit. I didn't know you knew, Frey?" Candy placed a hand over her mouth.

Frey looked between the two women and didn't believe a word Candy was saying. *Did Candy think she was stupid?* Obviously, Candy and Betty knew who Frey was. Candy was not that good of an actress. Frey began feeling queasy and lightheaded.

"I'm not gonna sit down until this bitch answers my questions and tells me where my son is!" Betty was becoming angrier by the minute, causing Frey to press the red button. She hated pressing that button because she didn't want to start a fight between Holt and his mom, but Betty's anger was scaring her.

Frey hoped Barrett or Jake would answer her call. Holt didn't need to see his mother like this. She calmly collected the cards and the chips from the losing players. When her hand reached for Betty's chips, Betty pounded downward on Frey's hand with a fist, trapping Frey's hand on the table until she made her point. All the other players collected their chips and stepped away from the table.

Frey let out a loud cry as tears filled her eyes, then quickly lowered her voice. "Mrs. Adams, please, I don't want to make a scene. Let me get another dealer and we can talk away from my table." Frey noticed the other players looking around for help.

"Please." Frey faced the other guests and lifted her hand toward them to stop. "You all can stay here." Frey pressed the blue button. "Someone will be here in just a moment so you can continue to play. I'm so sorry for the inconvenience."

"Bitch, are you calling me an inconvenience? I'm not going anywhere with you." Betty took advantage of Frey leaning over her table to reach out to the other players and slapped her hard in the face. Frey wasn't expecting the hit, and her head snapped to the side.

Frey heard Anastasia scream. "Oh my God! Frey, are you okay?"

Frey's hand covered her cheek. Her mouth dropped open in shock as tears streamed down her face. She heard a commotion and turned her head. Holt and Barrett ran toward her. She stepped around the blackjack table to reach Holt. The terrifying look of pure hatred on Holt's face told her he saw Betty slap her. She didn't want Holt to do anything he would later regret. After all, Betty was his mother, even if he hadn't spoken to her in years. Then everything happened in slow motion.

She heard Holt scream, "Betty, no!", while he raced to get to her. *Was he coming for Betty or her? Why was he yelling?*

Candy jumped in front of Holt and tried to stop him from coming over. Barrett's eyes widened in horror as he looked between Holt, Betty, and Frey. Frey saw Betty out of the corner of her eye and turned to face her. That's when Frey felt an intense pain in her stomach.

Betty got in Frey's face and screamed– "DIE BITCH!" –glaring at her with malice shining from her beady eyes.

"Betty?" Frey glanced down at the bloody knife in Betty's hand. She stared at Betty and whispered, "Why?" I never did anything to you."

"You stole my son, bitch," Betty sneered, and all hell broke loose as guests screamed and ran away from them.

Frey placed her hands over her stomach to ease the piercing pain shooting through her body. *Why was her hand wet and sticky?* Looking down, she pulled her hands away from her body. Her hands and shirt were covered in blood. *Shit, Betty had stabbed her.* Looking up at Holt with her mouth open in shock, she saw he was trying to get to her. Taking a step toward him, her body swayed before she grabbed her blackjack table. She thought he was screaming her name, but all she heard was the pounding of her heart and muted voices. Her vision blurred, and she felt like she was being pulled out of a tunnel, the light from the opening getting smaller and smaller the deeper she went. Her body began to tremble and sway. She couldn't reach Holt. She felt her legs buckling. While staring at him, tears running down her face, she said– "I love you" –before everything went dark and she fell into the tunnel.

*** Holt ***

"Holt, you don't need her. Come with me," Candy begged, grabbing his arm, trying to pull him away from Frey.

"Somebody, call 911! We need a fucking ambulance!" Holt screamed into the earpiece. "Frey got stabbed in the stomach." Holt pulled his arm away from Candy and pushed her away. "Get your fucking hands off me." He watched Frey's trembling body sway, barely holding her up. Ripping his suit coat off, he ran to her.

"Barrett get Betty. I'll get Frey," Holt yelled after pushing Candy away and bolting toward Frey. He watched Frey struggle to get to him, but losing blood made her weak. Seconds before she passed out, she told him she loved him, then collapsed to the ground. *Shit!* He dove to catch her before her head hit the floor. Cradling her in his arms, he rocked her.

"Frey, sweetheart, wake up. Please." Holt stroked her face, pain ripping through his body while tears ran down his face. Bunching up his coat, he used it to apply pressure to her wound to stop the blood that was pouring from her stomach onto the floor. She'd lost so much blood; her skin became pale. He couldn't lose her now when they finally found each other. Life could not be so cruel.

"How could you do this to her?" Holt turned to Betty, his voice filled with rage. "If I lose her, I will make you pay for what you did."

Holt watched Barrett grab Betty's hand and twist it behind her back until she dropped the knife. Barrett kicked the knife away and secured her hands with the heavy-duty zip ties they always carried in case of trouble.

"No one touch that fucking knife." Barrett looked at all the guests that were fixated on the scene before them. "It's evidence. Please, everyone, step back until the police get here."

"Jake," Barrett spoke into his earpiece. "We need help here. Call the police and get an ambulance."

"Copy that. Already on my way," Jake replied. "I talked to George. The police are on their way."

Holt heard their conversation from his earpiece and thanked God they were good friends with Officer George Smith. George would get here as fast as he could with his partner, Officer Sean O'Reilly.

"Ahh!" Betty would not stay still. She kept trying to kick her leg back and hurt Barrett. "You're hurting me! What kind of son lets his friend hurt his mother?"

"You are not my mother. You've never been a mother to me. Barrett, take her away from me, please. I have no patience for that piece of shit." Holt pleaded with Barrett before turning his attention back on Frey.

"Stop fucking trying to kick me or I'll fucking zip tie your damn ankles together!" Barrett held her away from his body.

Holt heard the commotion behind him but ignored it, staring at Frey and holding her against his chest.

"Sweetheart, can you hear me?" Holt whispered. "Stay with me, please. I don't know what to do without you. I love you. Please hang on. Don't leave me. Help is on the way."

Holt frantically scanned the casino for the paramedics. Jake was securing Candy's arms behind her back like Betty's. *Where the fuck was the ambulance?*

Holt bent down and gave her a quick kiss. "Frey, can you hear me? Sweetheart, I need you to look at me. Show me your beautiful eyes, please." He moved one hand to her neck to feel for a pulse.

Holt heard a commotion behind him and turned, hoping it was the paramedics, but it was George and Sean escorting Betty and Candy out of the casino.

"Holt," Frey groaned, "it hurts."

"Sweet Jesus." Holt pivoted his head back to Frey. He thanked every deity he could think of that she was awake. "Stay with me, sweetheart. It's gonna be okay. I promise. Please hold on."

"Holt." Barrett laid a hand on his shoulder. "The paramedics are here."

Holt moved aside while they checked her pulse and put her on the gurney. "Sir, are you family?"

"I'm her boyfriend." Those three words burst out of his mouth because he was terrified and didn't want to leave Frey. If the paramedics thought they were just friends, he wouldn't be able to ride in the ambulance with her. Unfortunately, he forgot Barrett was right next to him.

"Oh, Fuck No!" Barrett pushed Holt out of the way. "I'm her brother. He's her friend."

"No! I'm her boyfriend." Holt pointed at Barrett. "He didn't know. Can I please go with her in the ambulance?" Holt looked at the paramedic, panicked.

"Fucker, let go of her hand," Barrett growled at Holt.

"Holt," Frey whispered, "I'm scared."

"I'm right here, sweetheart. I'm going with you."

"No, you're fucking not, asshole." Barrett waited until Holt turned to face him and punched him in the face, causing Holt to release her hand and drop to the ground.

"Fucker! God Damn, that hurts!" Holt's nose started gushing blood. Pinching the top, he tried to stop the bleeding. He didn't have time for this. It was all about Frey right now, not Barrett's fucking feelings. "You fucking broke my nose!"

"That's not all I'm gonna fucking break!" Barrett started toward Holt again.

"Gentlemen, get your shit together. We need to go and now we need to take you, sir, to stop your bleeding." The paramedic began wheeling the gurney out of the casino with Holt in tow.

"Oh, my Goodness! Is that Frey? Why is Holt bleeding?" Holt heard Sehoy but kept after the paramedic. Then he heard his best friend.

"That fucker's mom just stabbed Frey, and he's an asshole. I never want to see or talk to him again. Did you know he and Frey were together?"

Holt felt like he'd been sucker punched in the stomach. Barrett had been his best friend for nearly two decades. How could he hate him so quickly? He knew he should have talked to Barrett about their relationship. Then again, who knew their secret was going to come out like this? He couldn't believe Betty stabbed Frey.

On their way to the hospital, one paramedic faced Holt. "Sir, let me look at your nose while my partner helps her." Holt turned his face toward the paramedic but continued to look at Frey out of the corner of his eye. "Well, good news is...it's not broken, but you will have at least one black eye to go with that nosebleed. Pinch your nose at the bridge and look down." The paramedic handed Holt some tissues.

"Thank you." Holt followed directions, but kept glancing at Frey.

When they arrived at the hospital, they rushed the gurney into surgery. They had called ahead, so the nurses were waiting for them. Another nurse guided Holt to the waiting room.

"Sir, you can wait here. Someone will come and talk to you in a few minutes. We need you to fill out some forms for her. I'll bring you some ice. They took her into surgery. The doctor will come talk to you as soon as she comes out of surgery."

Holt sat down and prepared himself for the storm that was coming. He didn't have to wait long before he heard Barrett's voice.

"Where is my sister? Someone stabbed her. How is she?"

"Sir, we don't know anything yet, but you can wait in the waiting room. Since you are her brother, please take these forms and fill them out."

"Sir, here is your bag of ice." The nurse tapped Holt on the shoulder.

"There you are...you fucker! You have a lot of explaining to do!" Barrett barreled into the waiting room, pointing the clipboard at Holt.

"Sir, stop right there." The nurse said, putting her hand out to stop Barrett. "You need to calm down. This gentleman is hurt."

"He isn't hurt enough!" Barrett attempted to go around the nurse to get to Holt.

"Stop or I'll call the police!" The nurse actually stood in front of Holt to keep Barrett away.

"Barrett, stop it!" Alex ran into the room and pulled Barrett away from the nurse. "What the fuck is wrong with you?" Alex looked at the nurse. "I'm so sorry. I'll take care of this. No need for the police. But thank you."

"Okay, but if he keeps carrying on like that, I will have him escorted out." The nurse glared at Barrett as she walked off.

"What the hell is wrong with you? What happened?" Alex shoved his shoulder.

"Chakpootsi, oh my goodness, are you okay?" Sehoy hurried to the chair next to Holt and hugged him. "What happened? We heard your mom stabbed Frey, but what happened to you? Barrett left the casino so fast, and we were waiting for Alex and Tori."

"Don't fucking call him that!" Barrett hollered. "He is not your son. He is a liar and a cheat and I'm gonna fucking kill him!"

Holt removed the tissues and realized his nose was no longer bleeding. He turned and held Sehoy's hands.

"Barrett, stop bro," Alex continued to hold Barrett back.

"*Chatski*, my mom stabbed Frey before I could stop her. I'm so sorry." Holt had tears in his eyes. "I'm so sorry."

"Don't call her that. You should be sorry. You fucking promised me, you fucker! Why would you do this to me?" Barrett was trying to get to Holt again while Alex held him back.

"Calm the fuck down. Do you want to get kicked out?" Alex turned to Barrett and shoved him back. Then turned to face Holt. "Holt, what the fuck is he talking about?"

Osceola had moved to stand next to Sehoy's chair. "*Chakpootsi*, is there something you need to tell us?"

Holt gazed into Sehoy's eyes and blurted out everything. "Frey and I have been dating for the past month."

"Motherfucker!" Barrett growled, interrupting Holt.

"I love your daughter, chatski. We wanted to tell you all, but we weren't sure how. We were going to tell everyone on Thanksgiving because we are so thankful for each other." Holt stood and turned to Barrett. "I'm sorry. I know I broke my promise to you to never date your sister, but I fell in love with her. How could I not? She's smart, beautiful, kind, funny, caring, and just wonderful."

"You promised," Barrett whispered, as his body deflated. "You were my best friend and you've been lying to me." Barrett ran his hand over his hair.

"I'm sorry, Barrett. I swear I wanted to tell you. Please, let's put this behind us and focus on Frey."

"I'll focus on Frey, because you mean nothing to me." Barrett directed the coldest stare Holt had ever seen at him. Barrett turned and walked to the other side of the room.

"Man, you should have told him, but I get it." Alex nodded and walked to Barrett to talk to him.

"I really screwed that up." Holt ran his hand down his face.

"He'll be okay. Focus on Frey and then you can fix this." Tori hugged Holt. "Alex and I will help you."

"Thank you." Holt released her and faced Osceola. "*Chacteka*, I'm so sorry we lied to you and kept our relationship a secret. Deep down, I was afraid I wasn't good enough for her. And I didn't want to lose my family if you all turned against me. I was a coward."

"*Chakpootsi*, I know why you did it. You've been through so much in your life. I'm not gonna lie to you. I wish you had come to us. But we love you. Nothing will ever change that. If you and Frey love each other, then we give you our blessing." Osceola hugged Holt.

Holt released his breath and finally felt like a great weight lift off his shoulders. He was relieved that he didn't have to carry this secret any longer. But he wasn't sure if Frey was going to be mad at him for telling everyone. No going back now. Looking up, he cringed when he saw the hatred burning in Barrett's eyes. *Shit! This is what he'd been afraid of.*

"Who is here for Freya Panther?" A nurse announced as soon as she walked into the waiting room.

"We are." Everyone answered and crowded around her.

"She received a stab wound on her upper right side, piercing her liver and bowel. The doctor asked me to come out and say it's going well so far. He will come speak to you as soon as he finishes."

"I'm her mother. How much longer will it take?" Sehoy asked.

"I'm not sure, but I wanted to give you an update." The nurse squeezed Sehoy's hand and walked away.

"Well, at least she's hanging on." Sehoy's voice quivered, and she broke down while Osceola held her.

"Frey is a fighter. She will not give up," Tori spoke to no one in particular as Alex pulled her into his arms.

Holt attempted to walk to Barrett, but he glared at him and shook his head no. Holt stopped and sat in a chair, waiting for Frey to come out of surgery.

"Tori and I are going to get some coffee." Alex looked around. "Anyone else want some?"

"I'll go with you. I need to leave this room," Barrett followed them out.

Holt leaned his head against the wall and closed his eyes. Fuck! He knew something was wrong, but he never would have guessed that Betty and Candy would work together to kill Frey to hurt him. He should have kept Frey in bed with him, and they should have both called in sick. Although that might have just delayed the inevitable, considering Betty and Candy were unstable.

"Here." Holt felt a tap on his shoulder and heard Tori's voice. Holt opened his eyes and tilted his head toward her. "I brought you some coffee."

"Thanks. I appreciate it." Holt took the coffee and took a sip. "Where's Barrett?"

"Alex took him outside for a few minutes. It'll be okay." Tori and Holt drank their coffee in silence. A few minutes later, Alex walked back in with Barrett and he seemed calmer. At least he wasn't staring daggers at Holt.

A doctor appeared in the doorway, and they all stood and rushed over to him.

"Hello, I'm Dr. Wallace. I just finished the surgery on her liver and bowel. We have sewn them both up and we expect her to have a full recovery...'Thank God' echoed from everyone in the room. "She should be able to get up and walk around within the next 24 hours. Barring any infections, she can go home within three to seven days. She's getting settled into a private room. The nurse will come and get you as soon as possible. She is a very lucky young lady, but ..."

Chapter 43

Confessions and Lies and Arrests, Oh My

Candy

"**S**tupid bitch! Why did you fuck this up?" Betty screamed at Candy as the officer led her to the police cruiser. "Do not cuff me. She's the one to blame. I'm innocent. It's all her fault. Who the fuck do you think you are?"

"Ma'am, please calm down. I'm Deputy Smith and that's my partner, Deputy O'Reilly. Please settle down." Candy heard Deputy Smith speaking to Betty as he led her to the police cruiser.

"Me! You fucking stabbed her. Why couldn't you just wait a few more days, and I would have handled the situation? But nooo, you had to come in and ruin everything!" Candy hollered back and could barely hear Deputy O'Reilly reading her rights. When he finished, he put his hand on her head and guided her into the same cruiser as Betty. Great, now she had to put up with her on their ride to the police station. Just Fucking Fantastic!

"Well, I had to do something since you were just fucking around." Betty shoved her with her shoulder when she got in the back. Candy was sure she would have hit her if they both didn't have their hands handcuffed behind their backs.

"What are you doing?" Candy yelled at Deputy O'Reilly, kicking him as he grabbed her legs and pulled a noose-like strap over her legs and tightened it at her ankles.

"Tying your legs down so you don't kick her" –Deputy O'Reilly pointed at Betty– "or me."

"What about her?" Candy screamed.

"Don't worry, Deputy Smith will constrain her." Deputy O'Reilly tossed the other end of the strap out the door.

"You are such an idiot throwing that strap out the door."

"Ma'am, calling your arresting officer an idiot is not a smart idea. As far as the strap, I will control it and you from the front seat." Deputy O'Reilly spoke calmly before shutting the door and walking away.

"Look what you've caused them to do. Now I can't even move my legs!" Betty screamed at her after he shut her door and reached into his front seat for something.

"Hey, Deputy Smith," Candy hollered when he reached into his seat. "Don't leave me in here with this crazy bitch. If you gotta take me in, take me in—in another fucking car!"

Candy watched the officer smirk at her, get out, and slam the door. Great, now she was alone with the crazy bitch. "Why the fuck did you have to stab her?" Candy stared at Betty.

"Because if she's dead, then he would come home." Betty glared at Candy like she was an idiot.

"How stupid are you? Didn't you realize if you killed her, he would hate you forever?" Candy asked, stunned by Betty's response.

"I'm not stupid, so stop yelling at me. I needed money for a hit, and you were taking your sweet time. Now I just want a fucking cigarette. Do you think they would give me a cigarette?" Betty was looking all around her. As if a cigarette was about to magically appear.

"Are you insane? You just stabbed someone, you crazy bitch. We're arrested in the back of a fucking cop car heading off to jail and you're worried about a fucking cigarette? I should have never listened to my brother. He's another stupid ass druggie like you. Look at you, shaking from withdrawal. Fucking losers. I just wanted something better for myself, boy was I stupid to go along with your half-assed plan."

"Listen, little girl, you are just as greedy as me. Your brother and I might have wanted the money for drugs, but you still went along with it. You wanted the money too. So don't act so damn innocent." Betty snarled.

"Fine, I wanted the money. Okay, I admit it. Getting Holt would have been a nice bonus. But after your little stunt, I'm gonna have to leave town without him. He's never gonna look at me again. Because he knows we were working together. Jesus, fuck, I can't believe I followed your plan and had to fuck my neighbor." Candy sighed and leaned back in her seat.

"Once a whore, always a whore. I never told you to fuck him. I told you to pay him. But since you love to spread your legs, that's what you chose. That's on you. Don't be putting that on me," Betty harrumphed.

"Whatever. You stabbed that girl. I didn't hurt her. After we get put in jail, I'll get my brother to bail me out." Candy closed her eyes, thinking her brother would bail her out instead of Betty. At least she hoped Betty's pussy wouldn't be a deciding factor. Her brother wasn't exactly a stellar human being, but she prayed he loved her more than he loved having sex and doing drugs with Betty.

"You're delusional. He'll bail me out before you. What the hell have you done for him lately? We should have never brought you into our plan. A decision I will forever regret." Betty glared at Candy.

Candy wiggled on the plastic back seat, trying to get comfortable. "Like you could have gotten any money from Holt. He hates you, from what I hear. I don't know how you thought this was going to play out, but I just needed more time."

"If he hates me so much, why did he pay off the mortgage on my trailer?" Betty huffed.

Candy stared at Betty wide eyed. "Are you fucking kidding me?"

"Okay ladies, time to go for a ride," Deputy Smith said from the front seat. Both officers got in and they drove to the station.

"These handcuffs are too tight. Could you loosen them?" Candy asked from the back seat.

"Can I have a cigarette?" Betty interjected.

"How the hell are you going to smoke a cigarette with your hands tied behind your back, Betty?" Candy asked through gritted teeth. Could this bitch shut up about a cigarette?

"Fuck you, bitch," Betty tried to kick Candy, but the strap tightened. "Fuck, officer, that hurt!"

"Ma'am, please settle down and I won't have to pull the strap," Deputy Smith said from the driver's side. "It's gonna be a long fucking drive," Candy heard him mutter under his breath.

"Copy that, bro," Deputy O'Reilly muttered back.

"Officers" –Candy scooted close to the dividing window between the front and back seat– "I'm innocent. She is the one that stabbed that woman. I had nothing to do with it. I just happened to be at the wrong place at the wrong time."

"Shut up, bitch!" Betty snapped at her. "You are not innocent. You were part of the plan all along. Your brother and I had it all figured out, but you wanted in so you could get Holt and live the high life at that resort and casino. It's your fault we got caught."

"Fuck you, Betty. You're delirious. You never would have gotten any money from Holt without my help. We had a good plan. It would have worked if you hadn't gotten so fucking impatient. What the hell was that with the knife?" Candy's pulse was speeding up with every word Betty spewed out of her mouth. "I never, and I mean never, agreed to stab anyone."

Deputy Smith snickered from the front seat.

"See" –Betty smiled, showing her rotted teeth from too many drugs and cigarettes– "even he doesn't believe you."

Candy tried to kick Betty, but Deputy O'Reilly pulled her strap on her legs when he felt a tug. "Settle down! We're almost there."

"I want my phone call as soon as we get there," Candy was quick to ask. She wanted to call her brother before Betty.

"I want a fucking cigarette." Betty's legs were bouncing more than before. Her withdrawal becoming worse.

"Shut up with the damn fucking cigarettes!" Candy yelled at her. "You are in fucking serious trouble and you're worried about a damn cigarette. You are such a loser."

"Bitch..." Betty never finished her statement because they arrived at the corrections facility.

"Ladies, please be quiet." Deputy Smith interrupted their ramblings before he pushed an intercom.

"I have two whiskey foxtrots, cooperative, but combative toward each other," Deputy Smith spoke to the voice that greeted him.

"Pull in."

Candy had never experienced being arrested before. Her heart was racing out of control, waiting for her impending doom. Two female officers and two nurses stood waiting for them, and her gut clenched. *Were they going to sedate her?* They should sedate Betty. She was the one with withdrawals. Candy didn't do drugs. Watching her brother struggling with drug addiction since high school was enough to deter her from even trying the stuff. Fear rippled through her body, and she shivered as Deputy O'Reilly pulled her out of the car to face the oncoming pair. Glancing at Betty, she saw Deputy Smith getting her out and walking her to the other pair.

The nurse asked her questions that she barely remembered answering while the officer watched her with a stoic expression on her face. She could hear Betty still hooting and hollering at the officers with her, but she tuned her out. This was real, and she did not want to piss these people off. She should not be here. She wasn't a bad person. Apparently just stupid and greedy. If she ever got out of this, she was going to leave town and start over.

"Ma'am. I'm Corrections Deputy Archavette Word. Please take off your shoes and put these on." Candy looked up to see a kind, but stern African American woman in uniform handing her a pair of black crocs. Candy immediately took off her heels and replaced them with the crocs. Corrections Deputy Word took them and stood by a table ledge. "Please put all your personal items on this table."

"I...I don't have anything on me," Candy patted down her body and looked at Ms. Word with tears in her eyes. "I left everything at the casino."

"Okay, ma'am. Please step over here, I need to pat you down." Corrections Deputy Word pointed to an outlined square painted on the floor in front of a set of sliding doors. Candy stepped into the square and received her first of several body checks. Upon entering the building, she received another pat down and was told to step into another painted square on the floor with a number one painted inside. A deputy stepped out from behind a desk to asking her questions about substance abuse, previous arrests, etc.

Candy watched everything going on around her. It felt so surreal. This couldn't possibly be happening to her. Corrections Deputy Word placed her shoes in a plastic bag. The nurse and officer that met them by the car escorted Betty, who was still yelling and screaming for a cigarette, into an office. Another prisoner arrived and stood in painted square number two.

After Candy answered the officer's questions, she followed Corrections Deputy Word to a body scan machine, fingerprinting, and got her mug shot. The gravity of what she had done finally sunk in when Corrections Deputy Word took her to a room and told her to strip. Candy was strip searched before they gave her three blue prison outfits, one bed sheet, one blanket, and a hygiene pouch. She was going to jail. *How had she gotten here?* Well, she knew, but how could she have been so stupid?

Corrections Deputy Word escorted her to a room where she could make a phone call—which she did. She called her brother, informed him of her arrest, and assured him she would notify him once they set bail so he could come and get her.

"You'll have your first appearance before a judge tomorrow at 8:00am. I'll come get you," Corrections Deputy Word told her as she escorted her to her cell. Candy was in a daze as she walked into a cell block and entered her new home. Dropping her bedding, she spun around when the clunk sound of the cell door slamming shut registered in her mind. Her cold reality sunk in. On autopilot, she made her cot and looked around, seeing her sink and toilet combo and a small desk. Nausea churned in her stomach as she heard another prisoner using the toilet in the cell next to her. Her privacy was gone. She was a criminal that had to depend on her deadbeat brother. She was so screwed.

Chapter 44

Shattered Hearts

Holt

"Who is her boyfriend or husband?" Dr. Wallace looked between Barrett, Alex, and Holt.

"I'm her boyfriend, sir." Holt stepped up to the doctor. He could hear Barrett grumbling behind him.

"I'm so sorry I couldn't save the baby." Dr. Wallace reached out and placed his hand on Holt's shoulder.

"Baby?" Holt mumbled. He felt the blood drain from his face, hands trembling. The relief he felt after hearing about Frey's recovery soured, twisting into a growing horror that stole his breath. She would live, but...life was full of twists and turns...and their baby...They'd made a baby that he would never meet...the life they created was gone forever. Heart pounding in his chest, pain shooting through his body, Holt fell to his knees, covering his face with his hands. He didn't think he had any more tears to shed after seeing Frey bleeding on the floor, but he was wrong. An intense pain pierced through him from his heart down to his very soul. A quiet scream resonated in his head and painful tears streamed down his face. *Frey was pregnant with his baby? Their baby died? His mother killed her grandchild. How fucked up was that?*

"Fuck!" Barrett screamed. "What did you do to my sister?"

"Barrett, stop." Holt heard Alex yell to Barrett, but he wasn't paying attention to Barrett's comments. His world narrowed to an empty void full of sadness and hopelessness. They had never talked about having kids. Despite his childhood fears, Holt had so much love to give. Frey would have been a wonderful mom. He had to get himself together and be strong for Frey.

"I'm so sorry." Dr. Wallace tried to comfort the family with his soothing voice. "I assumed that all of you were aware of her pregnancy. She was about five weeks along."

"Holt." Tori bent down and brushed his hair back. "The nurse is here to escort the first visitor. Do you want a few minutes with Frey?"

"Yeah." Holt stood up and wiped his face. "Yes, please." Holt turned to Dr. Wallace. "Doctor, is she aware that she was pregnant and had a miscarriage?" Holt needed to know before he entered her room and turned her world upside down.

"I do not know, but I haven't shared it with her. She wasn't fully awake from the anesthesia when I left her." Dr. Wallace shook his head. "Would you like me to go in with you and tell her?"

"No." Holt straightened his spine, preparing to face Frey. "I'll tell her."

"Follow me, sir," the nurse turned around and led him to Frey's room.

Holt ran through all the ways to tell Frey and they all sounded horrible. How do you tell the love of your life that we lost our baby? He hoped when he entered the room, he would gain insight from above and find the right words.

"She's in here." The nurse waved her hand for him to enter.

Frey looked so fragile lying in the hospital bed. Holt walked up to the bed and kissed her forehead. "Hey, sweetheart. How are you feeling? You scared us."

Frey blinked her eyes open and smiled. "I'm sorry."

"It's not your fault. You didn't do anything wrong." Holt grabbed one of her hands and kissed it. He didn't want to touch her other hand because it had her IV. "I need to talk to you about something."

"What's wrong? Well, other than the obvious." Frey smiled. Holt loved her. She always tried to make light of tough situations. Holt sensed moisture gathering in his eyes. "What is it?" she asked again, her smile fading.

"Sweetheart, I'm at a loss for how to tell you this, so I'll simply say it." Holt took a deep breath. "You were pregnant with our child." Holt held her hand to his lips and placed a kiss.

"I'm pregnant? Wait, what do you mean, 'were'?" Frey's hand moved to her abdomen as realization dawned.

Holt nodded as tears slid down his face.

"Yeah, there was no permanent damage to your liver or bowels, but they could not save our baby." Holt choked out the last word.

"Our baby," Frey whispered before pulling her hand away from Holt and embracing her belly with both hands. She rolled to her side into a fetal position away from Holt and cried so hard her entire body shook.

Holt bent down and held her as tightly as he could, saying, "I'm so sorry."

"Holt, I didn't know. I swear, had I known I would have told you and taken care of our baby. I had an appointment with the doctor next week." Frey was hysterical, her words garbled as she gasped them out between sobs.

"Frey, shh, sweetheart." Holt ran his hands through her hair, pulling it back away from her face.

Frey suddenly turned and faced him. "You believe me, right?"

"Of course. How could you have known my crazy bitch of a mother was going to stab you? I know you would protect our baby and tell me if you were pregnant. You would be a wonderful, caring mom." Frey settled into the bed with a shaky exhale. Holt flinched. How could she think he would blame her for this? Was he that much of a bastard that she would think he would hold her accountable for his mother's actions? If this was anyone's fault, it was his. No matter how much he despised her, Betty was still his mother—his responsibility. If he'd answered her calls or text after he paid off the trailer, maybe she wouldn't have resorted to this. But now wasn't the time to consider what ifs. Frey needed him, and there was one last thing she needed to know. One more thing he'd fucked up.

"Before your family comes in, there's something else I need to tell you." Holt kissed her forehead.

"There's more?" Frey's voice broke as she released something between a laugh and a sob.

Holt winced. "Sweetheart, I told everyone we've been dating for the past month." Holt braced himself for her reaction.

"What? Why?" Frey's eyes widened, her breath coming in great gasps like she couldn't get enough air.

Holt squeezed her hand, keeping his voice calm and his breathing even. He hoped she would subconsciously match his energy—the last thing her stab wound needed was her hyperventilating. "It just came out when you were being hauled into the ambulance and I wanted to ride with you. They wouldn't let me if I wasn't your boyfriend. And if I hadn't told them, I'm sure they would have figured it out when the doctor came out and told us you lost the baby. I broke down. It would've been obvious at that point that we were together."

"Oh Shit," Frey leaned forward, wincing. "How's Barrett?"

Holt couldn't believe Frey tried to get up.

"Sweetheart, be careful." Holt helped her lay on her back. "Barrett's not good. He punched me and won't speak to me."

"Oh my God, how did I not notice your face?" Frey grabbed his chin and rotated his head from side to side.

Holt grabbed her hand and gently removed it from his face. "You had other things on your mind. I'll be fine. It's you and Barrett I'm worried about." It was so like her to be concerned for his bruises when she was lying in a hospital bed with a stab wound. Barrett was right. He didn't deserve her, but she had chosen him, even if she kept it from her family.

"I'm sorry he hit you," Frey whispered as tears continued to steam down her face. "I'll talk to him and explain I was the one that wanted to keep the secret."

Barrett wouldn't believe that, and it would only make things worse for Frey. Holt shook his head. "No, Frey. We both made that decision. Do not say it was your fault. I can take care of myself. We'll handle this together."

He wasn't sure she really processed his words. Her expression was stuck in a mask of shock, but she nodded. "Okay. Can you please get my mom? Is she here?"

"Sweetheart, everyone is here." Holt smiled. "I'll go get her."

"Thank you."

Chapter 45

Not Leaving Her Side

Holt

When Holt entered the waiting room, he proceeded directly to Sehoy, ignoring everyone staring at him for an update.

"*Chatski*, she wants to see you. I just told her about the baby. She did not know about the pregnancy. I also told her everyone knows we were dating. Please go easy on her."

"Don't tell my mother how to speak to her daughter," Barrett barked at Holt.

"Okay, Barrett, I think it's best if you come back later to see Frey. She doesn't need your shitty attitude right now. Tori, do you want to go home with us?" Alex pulled Barrett away.

"You can come home with us." Osceola draped his arm around Tori's shoulders. "Alex, take Barrett home now. I'll take Tori home after we've seen Frey."

"You got it." Alex pushed a struggling Barrett out the door.

"Holt, I'm assuming you're staying the night?" Tori placed her hand on his back. "Alex and I can bring you a change of clothes."

"Tori, you and Alex stay with Barrett. I'll bring Holt some clothes after I take you home." Osceola saw his wife waving to him.

"Tori, go with Osceola. I'm sure Frey would love to see her best friend. I'll go back in after you all leave." Holt gave Tori a gentle shove.

Holt sat leaning his elbows on his knees, head hung in defeat as he wrung his hands. He understood he had to give Barrett some time to cool off, but eventually, they would have to talk about what happened. Holt didn't want Barrett to take out his frustration on Frey. She didn't need anyone else upsetting her. At some point, he also needed to go talk to Betty. Despite not wanting to see her, he needed to understand the motive behind her attack on Frey—just how responsible was he for this shitshow?

Frey hadn't done anything to Betty, ever. Hell, he couldn't remember Frey ever saying a word to her. *What was Candy's connection?* Clearly, they were familiar with one another. How and when did they meet? He had too many questions and not enough answers. He wondered why the police hadn't appeared to question Frey yet. Holt appreciated it had been George and Sean on the scene. Frey was familiar with them, so it wouldn't be as challenging to provide her statement when they came to question her.

"Holt, we're gonna go now. Frey is asking for you." Tori gave him a hug when he stood. "I'll stop by tomorrow."

"Okay. Thank you," Holt returned her hug on autopilot. It was becoming harder and harder to hold himself together.

"*Chakpootsi*, I will take them home and come back with some clothes for you. Text Alex what you want so he can have it ready for me." Osceola put his arms around Sehoy and Tori, escorting them out.

Holt hurried into Frey's room. He didn't want to leave her alone.

"Hey, sweetheart." Holt sat in the chair next to her bed.

Frey gave him a wobbly smile. "Hi. You should go home. They gave me something for the pain and it's making me sleepy, so I might be out of it until tomorrow morning."

"That's fine. Don't worry about me. I'm not leaving you alone." Holt wasn't sure of much, but that was one thing he felt in his bones. His place would forever and always be by her side. Holt looked at the couch in the room. "I can sleep on that couch."

"Holt, you're too tall to sleep on that," Frey mumbled, already fading.

Holt smiled. She would be out soon. "I'll be fine. Just rest, sweetheart." Holt grazed her lips with a kiss and headed over to the couch. It was going to be a long and uncomfortable night. Frey's eyes fluttered closed. Holt watched her breathing even out. Her tear-stained face broke his heart all over again. His gaze strayed to her abdomen where her hands rested—cradling a child they would never get to meet. Holt sniffed and cleared his throat. He had to be strong. Clearing his throat again, Holt called Alex instead of texting him.

"Hey man, how's Frey?" Alex answered.

"She's asleep. They gave her something for the pain and it put her to sleep. Tori should be home soon. Osceola said he would bring me some clothes. Do you mind going into my dresser and getting a pair of sweatpants and some t-shirts? I have a duffle in my closet for you to put it all in." Holt rubbed his face.

"On it. I'll also grab a toothbrush and toiletries."

"How's Barrett?" Holt held his breath, waiting for Alex to answer.

"He's passed out. Chugged some tequila as soon as we got back. He's messed up. I'm sure he's going to be kissing the porcelain god in the morning. I'm sorry he was such an asshole to you tonight," Alex sighed.

Holt heard him opening and closing drawers. "Nah, no apology necessary. I deserved it. I should have told Barrett sooner."

"How's your face?" Alex chuckled.

That was the last thing on his mind right now. Holt's blank stare moved to the bag of melted water in his hand. His nose gave a dull throb. "It hurts and my ice melted, but I'll be fine." Holt replied.

"Maybe that nice nurse will give you some ibuprofen."

"Good idea. I'll ask her if she comes in again." Holt sat down on the couch. "Alex, thank you for your help."

"No problem. Just so you know, I am not opposed to you and Frey getting together as long as it's a mutual relationship and you don't hurt her. She couldn't ask for a better man. Just don't fuck up. I'd hate to have to kick your ass."

"Hang on a second Alex, the nurse is here, and I need to talk to her." Holt turned to the nurse that entered the room. "Excuse me, can you please bring me a pillow, blanket, and ibuprofen?"

"I can bring you the first two, but I can't give you any pills unless you are a patient." The nurse checked the IV. "But I can bring you another ice pack."

"Thank you. I appreciate that." Holt placed the phone back up to his ear.

"Sorry, I'm back. I just asked the nurse for ibuprofen, but she can't give it to me, so can you grab the bottle out of my medicine cabinet and toss it in my bag?"

"On it."

"Thanks. As far as dating your sister, I can't promise that I won't fuck up, but I do promise to I love her. She's, my soulmate. I can't imagine my life without her. I know we lost a child tonight, and that... that really hurts, but I hope we can get married in the future and have another. It will never replace this one, but I would be the happiest man alive if I got to grow old with her and our children."

Alex was quiet for a moment and Holt's insides twisted as he braced for a Barrett-level freak out. Maybe Alex was okay with them dating, but would he want her to be with someone like him long term—with all the baggage he brought?

Finally, Alex responded. "Thank you for that. Dad's here and I had you on speakerphone, so he heard everything you said. He seemed very pleased." Some of the tension leaked out of Holt's shoulders as Osceola's voice came over the phone.

"*Chatpootski*, there isn't a more suitable man for my daughter. I would be honored to have you as my son-in-law. Alex gave me your stuff. I will be there in about thirty minutes," Osceola said.

Holt nodded, though they couldn't see him. He didn't immediately trust his voice. "Thank you both. *Chacteka*, I promise you I'll do everything in my power to make Frey happy."

"I know you will *chatpootski*. How is my daughter?"

"She's asleep from the meds. The nurse said she would come back and check on her in a couple of hours. I don't know if she'll be awake when you get here."

"That's okay. She needs her rest. I will see you soon."

"Okay, see you soon." Holt hung up the phone and went back to sit next to Frey. Grabbing her hand, he held it in both of his. A few minutes later, the nurse came back in, carrying items for him.

"I brought you a pillow, blanket, and an icepack. I'm assuming you're staying the night?" The nurse placed the bedding on the couch at the end of the room and brought him the icepack. "I'm sorry I can't give you pain pills, but I hope this will help relieve some of your pain. It will definitely help with the swelling and black eye you're going to have."

"Thank you." Holt grinned, took the pack, and placed it between his eyes on the bridge of his nose. It was nice she brought him an icepack, but he really needed ibuprofen for the throbbing in his head. "Yes, I'm staying." He nodded and turned back to Frey. He'd almost lost her, and that thought was wreaking havoc with his heart. "I need to be near her." Holt answered the nurse.

"She's lucky to have someone who loves her so much. Here's the button for the nurse's station. Buzz me if either of you needs anything."

"Thank you." Holt murmured. He stayed next to Frey until Osceola returned with his stuff. Osceola sat with Frey for a few minutes while Holt made up his couch and took the pills.

"Thanks, *chacteka*," Holt whispered, checking if Frey was still asleep. "I'm aware this may not be the time or place, but I would like to request your daughter's hand in marriage. What happened tonight scared me to death. My life flashed before my eyes, and I realized I don't want to live it without her. I love her and can't wait to ask her to be my wife."

"Of course, *chakpootsi*. You have mine and her mom's blessing. We love you both." Osceola gave Holt a hug. They bid each other goodnight, and Holt got as comfy as possible on the couch.

Chapter 46

Police Visit

Frey

Frey was grateful for the prescription pain pills they gave her last night. She slept through the entire night with no pain or bad dreams. Betty stabbing her came completely out of left field. She'd only seen Betty twice when her mom would take Holt home. It was hard to come to terms with why Betty stabbed her. And...her baby. She'd lost their baby. How could she not have protected her baby? Why didn't she realize her throwing up was morning sickness?

Frey curled up and cried into her pillow, not wanting to wake up Holt, who sat in the chair next to her bed. The silent sobs wracking her body caused her stomach to hurt. But the physical pain paled in comparison to the devastation in her heart. She hadn't realized she was pregnant, but now she felt the loss like a sucker punch to the gut.

Missing her baby, she grieved like a person trying to sort through the rubble of their life after the earthquake of loss hits. Floundering under the onslaught of her thoughts, she didn't know what to do or what would happen with her relationship with Holt. Even though she tried to be quiet and muffle herself, Holt must have heard her because he crawled in bed behind her and wrapped his arms around her.

"Holt, you can't get into bed with me. We'll get in trouble," Frey hiccupped between sobs.

"I'll get up when someone comes. Right now, I just need to hold you," Holt said as he tightened his arms around her. "I'm so sorry for what Betty did to you. She will pay for taking our child away from us, I guarantee you. I love you so much."

Holt's love for her overwhelmed Frey. She'd thought he would be mad at her, instead he'd worried about her and their baby. Frey heard a knock on the door, and Holt eased off the bed.

"Hello, can we come in?" Deputy George Smith and Deputy Sean O'Reilly stood in the doorway.

Frey rolled over and watched Holt head over to them and shake their hands.

"Frey, we need to ask you some questions. Is that okay?" George walked to the bed and Sean opened his notebook.

"Yeah, that's fine," Frey held her hand out to Holt, and he took it.

"Tell me what happened last night?" George leaned against the bed.

Frey took a deep breath. "Everything was going well until Candy and Betty came to my table. At first, I didn't recognize Betty, but she recognized me. She kept calling me a bitch for taking her son away from her. I was trying to calm her down. We don't like to make a scene in the casino and interrupt our guests. But, as I circled my table to reach Holt because she was scaring me, she stabbed me. I was so stunned I fell, and everything became dark after that. Next thing I remember is waking up here with Holt." Holt squeezed her hand, his expression hard.

"We arrested Candy and Betty last night. It seems Betty needed money for drugs and couldn't find a man to barter services because her new man was Candy's brother and he's a poor druggie. She got it in her head that Holt must be rolling in dough since he lives at the resort and doesn't pay for anything."

"Wait, how did she know that?" Holt interrupted George. "I haven't seen her since I moved in with Barrett my junior year of high school."

"Candy told her. Apparently, Candy's brother has been staying with Betty. When they got to talking, Betty found out Candy was interested in dating you. They set out a plan to get rid of Frey so Candy could comfort you and convince you to help your mother financially."

"Wow." Frey's mouth dropped open. "That's quite a plan."

"They also told us how they got Kent, Candy's neighbor, to manhandle her at the casino so Holt would be nice to her, and she could get closer to Frey."

"Fuck! Kent was her neighbor?" Holt rubbed his face. "Un-fucking-believable."

"So, they confessed to you?" Frey was confused.

"Not knowingly. When we arrested them and put them in our squad car, we hit the record button and got their entire conversation. Then at the station, Betty yelled at Candy as they were being booked about who Candy's brother was going to bail out and confessed again in front of several witnesses." George beamed at them. "Not the brightest bulbs on the tree, if you know what I mean. We also sent officers to Betty's trailer and arrested Candy's brother. Now that we've talked to you and your story is the same, we can move forward. Do you want to press charges?"

Frey looked at Holt. After all, it was his mother.

"Hell yes," Holt told George before looking at Frey. "She almost killed you and she killed our baby. I want her arrested and locked up for a long time."

"You were pregnant?" Sean looked up from his pad.

"We were, but we didn't know. That was quite a shock to wake up to," Frey murmured with tears in her eyes.

"I'm so sorry. We will leave you both alone. If you think of anything, please call us." George and Sean shook hands with Holt and ran into Tori and Alex in the doorway on their way out.

"Hi guys." Tori hugged them both. George and Sean had been an enormous help to her when was dealing with Winston. Tori also saw them at the cultural center at least once a week since Thunder had been George's mentor when he was a shelter boy.

"Hey," they both answered, accepting Tori's hugs. "We came to talk to Frey, but we're done. Catch up with all of you later," Sean said as he left before George.

"Keep us informed if there are any changes," Holt shouted before George departed.

"You got it," came his reply through the open doorway.

"What are you guys doing here?" Frey groaned as she tried to sit up. Holt promptly rushed to her aid and helped her up, adjusting her pillow behind her.

"Can't a girl visit her bestie?" Tori grinned and gave her a kiss on her cheek.

"Absolutely. I'm glad you came." Frey smiled, happy to see her.

"Okay, lazy ass. Get better so we can gaze upon your lovely face at home." Alex bent down and kissed her forehead. "Holt, how about we leave these two ladies alone for the day? I'll drive you home so you can shower and change, then I'll bring you back later tonight."

Holt looked at Frey, and she nodded. "I would love some alone time with my bestie."

"Okay sweetheart." Holt bent down for what he thought would be a quick kiss until Frey slipped her tongue into his mouth.

"Oh, no! Big brother does not need to witness that." Alex covered his face with his hands, and Tori giggled.

"I love you," Holt whispered against her lips. "I'll be back later."

"I love you too."

"Okay Romeo, get your shit and let's go." Alex squeezed Tori's waist and kissed her cheek. "I'll see you later."

Once the boys left, Tori sat on the bed facing Frey and held her hand. "How are you feeling? Not only were you stabbed, but you lost a baby."

"I feel like a steamroller ran over my body and took something important away from me." Frey's eyes became teary. "Holt and I didn't wear a condom the first couple of times. In the heat of the moment—we weren't thinking. Once we realize it, he gloved up every time. But by then it must've been too late. I'd like to say I'm unhappy I got pregnant, but if I'm being honest...I would have loved to have his baby growing inside me. I missed out on seeing my belly grow, seeing beautiful sonogram photos of their progress. Was it a boy or a girl? Would they be sucking their thumb? Would you be able to see all their fingers and toes? I can never rub my belly to comfort them when I felt them kick. I've lost out on one of the best days of my life when I would get to see them come into this world. A beautiful gift of our love." Frey takes a quivering breath, tears streaming down her face.

"All of those moments to share with Holt would be a dream come true, but they were ripped away from me. Instead, I'm living with the nightmare of losing our child. I'm drowning in the loss of all those moments we'll never have. It's like I'm standing at the edge of a dark hole of emptiness and guilt, ready to drop into an unknown vortex. I don't even care how much pain I'm in. I just wish I hadn't lost our child." Frey drops her head in hands and breaks down. Deep sobs tremble through her body.

"Oh, honey," Tori gently leaned into Frey for a hug. "I am so sorry that happened to you both. There is no doubt in my mind, you both would've been great parents. I know you can never replace this baby or the way you feel. But time will dull your pain. You'll be able to think about your little angel in heaven and make another little angel to love and hold with Holt. You both love each other, and now that your relationship is public, you can look to the future. As far as feeling guilty, stop that. You did nothing to hurt your baby. This is all on Betty, not you. Besides, *Hesakitaemisi* works in mysterious ways. Maybe your baby was the perfect angel he needed."

"Thank you for saying that." Frey took a couple of deep breaths to calm down and thought about her baby in heaven, safe from Betty's hatred. "You're right. Holt and I will always think of this baby. Looking forward, I want to marry him and have a house full of little Holt's and Frey's running around."

"I have no doubt in my mind that you will." Tori grabbed Frey's hand and squeezed.

"Speaking of my not-so-secret relationship, how is Barrett?" Frey winced when she reached for her water cup.

"I'll get it." Tori gave the cup to Frey and put it back after she took a few sips. "Are you sure you want to talk about this now?"

"Yes, please." Frey sighed. "I need a change of topic. I'm sure when everyone leaves tonight and I'm left with my thoughts, I'll fall back into my black hole. But for now, I need a distraction, and I'm worried about Barrett."

"I haven't seen him much." Tori leaned back into a sitting position. "But I know Alex has been talking to him. I think he is getting through to him about being happy for you guys."

"I hope so. We really didn't want to hurt Barrett. It was all my idea to wait until Thanksgiving. Holt wanted to talk to Barrett sooner, but I kept putting it off."

"I think you guys should have told him, but we can't go back in time." Tori reached for the remote. "Let's chill today and worry about issues tomorrow. I'm off today and I would love to watch movies with you. So, let's find something." Tori sat in the chair, placed her feet up on the bed, and channel surfed.

"Pick whatever you want to watch because when the nurse comes and gives me another dose of pain meds, I'll be fast asleep." Frey relaxed into the bed. She was glad to be spending a day with her bestie. Tori's soothing personality was a balm to Frey's craziness. When Tori was working, she didn't get to spend much time with her because they worked different shifts. Plus, Alex took up most of her time. Which was fine, but Frey missed her. She was going to have to set up a regular day and time for their Girls' Day In.

Tori chose a home improvement show but like Frey thought, a few minutes in, the nurse brought her meds. Frey wasn't paying attention to the show. Her thoughts were on her little baby. What would they have named the baby? Would they have named the baby after their names? Definitely not, Holt's parent's names. Maybe Frey's parent's or grandparent's names? Those were her last thoughts before the meds kicked in and she drifted off to sleep.

In and out of sleep, she saw when Holt came back at night. Knowing he was with her helped her relax and feel safe.

Chapter 47

What did Barrett Say?

Holt

Holt went looking for Barrett when he left yesterday to shower and change, but he wasn't around. He knew at some point this morning Barrett would visit Frey. They were extremely close, and it wasn't because they were twins. The Panthers were a close-knit group. Suddenly, the door swung open, and Barrett stood in the doorway. *Speak of the devil.* He'd wanted to talk to Barrett alone before he came in to see Frey. Holt wanted to take the blame for the secret so he wouldn't be too upset with Frey. She didn't deserve any confrontations right now.

"How's my favorite, sis?" Barrett shouted when he stepped into the room.

"Hi, Bare." Frey's smile was hesitant. Neither of them knew how he was going to react.

Holt moved aside so Barrett could be near his sister.

"Can I have some privacy with my sister?" Barrett raised an eyebrow at Holt.

Holt looked to Frey. "Are you okay with this?"

"I'm not gonna hurt my sister, asshole." Barrett braced his hands on his hips and glared at Holt.

"Barrett, stop!" Frey yelled at him, then turned to Holt. "I'll be fine. Can you give us a few minutes? Please?"

Holt didn't want to leave, but when she threw in the please, he backed up.

"Of course. I'll go get some coffee." Holt nodded at Frey and glared at Barrett on the way out. This would not be good. Holt walked into the small cafe near the main entrance of the hospital, ordered his regular black coffee, paid, and sat down with his phone and wayward thoughts. Barrett hadn't said hello to him; and only acknowledged him by asking him to leave and call him an asshole. Which was just fucking great. He hoped like hell Barrett would not start bashing him to Frey. She was already feeling bad about the baby. She didn't need any more guilt. Sehoy and Osceola didn't seem upset with their relationship. Come to think of it, the only person mad at him was Barrett.

He would grant Frey and Barrett some alone time and then return. Osceola had given him and Frey a couple weeks off from work so they could focus on her recovery and their mental state. Experiencing the loss of a child was incredibly heartbreaking. Granted, they hadn't known they were pregnant, but he knew now, and his head was spiraling out of control with grief.

Holt didn't know if he would be a good father, but Frey would have helped him ensure their child experienced a sense of safety, love, and belonging. They would have married sooner rather than later to be ready for the birth.

Holt would have been delighted to watch her belly grow during her pregnancy. She would've glowed more than she already did. But it was not to be. His mother had killed their baby with her selfishness. Never in his wildest dreams had Holt imagined Betty could do such a horrible thing. Especially after he paid off her trailer. He'd hoped she would shack up with another loser guy and leave him alone. Now he realized his mistake. By not answering her calls and texts, he'd put her over the edge. But what was he supposed to do, give her money every week? Hell, before she asked for money, he hadn't seen her for years and assumed she was out of his life forever.

How wrong he'd been. He needed to go visit her and sever all connections with her. She would not be a part of his life ever again after what she did to Frey.

Shit, he should have told Frey about the money. Maybe then she would have been more careful of Betty. But Frey had done everything right that night. She called him quickly and tried to keep Betty calm. Holt knew because after he took his shower and couldn't find Barrett, he watched the view footage of the stabbing. Watching it again was just as painful as the first time, if not worse. Because now he knew the knife had not only hurt Frey, but it had pierced their baby's little body. Killing their unborn child.

Checking the time, he realized he had been in the cafe for over an hour. Maybe Barrett was gone by now. Holt grabbed his coffee cup and headed back to Frey. Barrett was sitting in the chair next to Frey when he opened the door. They were both smiling at each other. That was a good sign. Barrett wasn't mad at her for keeping their relationship a secret. There was hope for their friendship.

"Sorry." Holt stepped in. "If you need more time, I can come back later."

"No." Barrett stood. "We're done for now. I'll come back tomorrow." Barrett bent down and Holt heard him whisper, "Remember what we agreed on?"

Frey bit her lip and nodded. What the hell did they agree on? Barrett walked to the door without looking at Holt. He'd been wrong. Their friendship was still in shambles. Holt sat in the chair Barrett vacated and reached out to hold Frey's hand. She glanced at Barrett and swiftly withdrew her hand, evading his touch, and turned her head away from him. Shit! What the hell just happened?

"Frey, what's wrong?" *Why did she pull her hand away after exchanging a look with Barrett? Did Barrett tell her not to date him? Did he fill her head with his venom?*

"I think you should go home," Frey whispered.

Holt's face jerked to the side as if someone had slapped him, and he glared at Barrett. *What had they talked about?*

"I don't want to go home. I want to stay here with you." Holt's eyes darted between Frey and Barrett. "Yesterday when I went home, I packed enough clothes for a few days, and I don't want you to be alone." Holt focused back on Frey and rubbed her arm. Frey flinched and pulled further away from him, then looked at Barrett again. Holt's heart dropped to the pit of his stomach. *What was she doing? Why did she keep looking at Barrett? What about him and their love? What the fuck was going on?*

"I called my mom and I want her to spend the day with me. Just us girls." Frey wouldn't look at him.

"She needs time with her mom, not you," Barrett snarled from the door. Holt was trying hard to keep it together, which was hard to do because the love of his life just told him to piss off. *He had fucked this all up. He'd known having a future with Frey was too good to be true. He was sure Barrett had reminded her of the worthless piece of trash that he was. He had no family and didn't own anything other than his car. Hell, he was basically living off her family. He was a fucking loser, just like Betty.*

"Okay." Holt hung his head. "I'll do whatever you want," Holt murmured, his heart hurting that she didn't want to be with him during this time. He had to try one more time to tell her his feelings, even if it was in front of Barrett. "I love you."

Holt waited a few minutes for Frey's response, but it never came. It was like someone had stabbed a knife into his heart and twisted it to inflict the most amount of pain possible. Frey always responded with 'I love you too'. They both sat in awkward silence until Sehoy appeared at the door.

"Now that mom's here, I'll see you later, sis," Barrett said before leaving.

"*Estonko*, how are you both this morning?" Holt stood and hugged Sehoy before she moved around the bed to face her daughter and stroked her hair.

"I'm good, *chatski*," Frey replied softly.

Holt saw the smile that Frey gave her mom and longed for one himself.

"Holt, I think you should get all your clothes. Pack everything up and go so I can spend time with my mom," Frey said while looking at Sehoy. She still had not made eye contact with him. Holt's hands curled into fists as he looked from Frey to Sehoy.

"I was planning on coming back tonight." Holt held his breath.

"I don't think that's necessary," Frey said and turned onto her side, giving him her back. "The police have Candy, her brother, and Betty in custody, so I'll be fine. Besides, Barrett mentioned he plans to take the night off and stay with me."

"If that's what you want. I'll leave you alone," Holt murmured, staring at the back of her head, willing her to look at him. His heart broke with every moment she continued to ignore him. Finally, he stalked to the couch, folded up the blanket, and placed the pillow on top. Gathering all his clothes, he shoved them into the duffle and turned to leave.

"*Chakpootsi*, wait." Sehoy approached him. "Here, take my keys to the car. Someone can come get me later."

"Thank you." Holt took the keys and left the hospital. Holt slammed the car door as he got in, tears running down his face. He had just lost everything. His soulmate and his baby. She refused to be near him. Two days ago, he held everything in his hands and now it was all gone. It was all his fault. Betty was his mom, and he didn't protect Frey or his baby from her. If only he could turn back the clock. What could he have done differently? For one, he could've told Barrett about their relationship. He could've warned Frey about Betty. He wasn't sure if any of that would've worked. All he knew was that he felt gutted and alone.

No, Holt slammed his hands on the steering wheel. He wouldn't give up, dammit. They loved each other. He would talk to Barrett and find out what the hell happened. Frey was fine before their conversation. He had to change whatever was said. But first, he had to visit the jail and leave his past behind for good.

Armed with a plan, he felt a little better. The drive to the jail gave him time to think about what he would say to Betty. Once he arrived, an officer led him to the visiting area, which was a small room equipped with a table and two chairs. It looked like the interrogation rooms you see on TV, but without a two-way mirror. Holt pulled out a chair and took a few deep breaths. Another officer led Betty in with handcuffs.

Betty looked like shit. Holt assumed she must be experiencing withdrawals from lack of drugs. Holt guessed this was probably the longest she'd ever been clean. He knew he should feel bad for her, but all he felt was hate for what she did.

"I knew you'd come to bail me out." Betty smirked. Her body trembling and sweating.

"I didn't come to bail you out. I came to tell you I never want to see you again. I tried to help you, even though you never cared about me. Clearly, paying off your trailer wasn't good enough. You got greedy and wanted to live off me instead of the government or one of your loser boyfriends. That ends right now. Not only did you hurt the woman that I love, but you killed my baby. I will make sure they prosecute you to the fullest extent of the law. You deserve to be behind bars for the rest of your miserable life." Holt's jaw clenched, adrenaline running through his body like an electrical current. He gripped his hands on his lap, trying to keep himself from lashing out. Just looking at her made him want to jump over the table and strangle her ass. But the last thing he needed was to wind up in jail in a cell next to hers.

"I didn't know she was pregnant!" Betty fidgeted with the cuffs. "I didn't mean to stab her."

"You are so full of shit. You were a horrible mother, and you will never get the chance to be a grandmother to any future children we may have. Forget about me, because once I walk out that door, I am totally forgetting about you." Holt was fuming as he got up from his chair and pointed at Betty. "Don't you ever call, write, or contact me. My mother died when I was a little boy. She died the day you allowed men to beat on me."

"I gave you a roof over your head. Which, by the way, is yours now, since I'll probably be spending the rest of my life here! You ungrateful..." Betty yelled at him, but he interrupted her.

"I don't want your fucking trailer!" Holt screamed, interrupting her. Betty snapped her mouth shut and glared at him. Bracing his fists on the table, he leaned down close to Betty's face. "Listen to me and listen carefully, because

I'm not going to repeat myself. I don't want anything that would remind me of you. You no longer exist to me." Holt stood up and moved to the door, turning to face her before stepping out. "Bye Betty, and good riddance."

Even after he left the room, he could hear Betty yelling obscenities at him and the officer in charge of taking her back to her cell. With that ugly event behind him, he could focus on fixing things with Barrett and Frey.

Chapter 48

Mother Knows Best

Frey

"That was mean, *chackshosti*. I raised you better than that." Sehoy pursed her lips and glared at Frey. "That man loves you deeply, and you just ripped his heart out."

"I know, *chatski*," Frey rolled onto her back and stared at the ceiling while tears streamed down her face. "But it's for the best."

"How? You didn't see his face."

"*Chatski*, I don't want to talk about this now." Frey wiped her tears. She felt bad enough when she looked at Holt's face. She would fix this, but first, she had to calm Barrett down.

"Well, that's just too bad because we are going to talk about it now."

Frey's mother's voice brimmed with anger. Her mother never had to yell. Whenever she was angry or disappointed, her tone would alert her and her brothers. And if her tone was any sign of her anger, Frey was in for quite the lecture.

"Why are you hurting Holt and breaking his heart? I don't understand what you just did. That boy is grieving, and you both need each other right now."

"I had to choose, and family always comes first. Isn't that what you always taught us?" Frey glared at Sehoy.

"Don't you take that tone with me. I don't care how bad you are hurting. I'll roll your butt over and spank you. You both should be comforting each other after losing your baby."

"I can't, okay!" Frey screamed in frustration and slammed her hands on the bed.

"Why not? I don't understand. What did you mean by choosing? Holt is family." Sehoy lifted her arms up, pleading with her daughter. Then Sehoy placed her hands on Frey's hip and pretended to roll Frey over. "You better talk to me, or I'll spank your little tushy."

"*Chatski*, stop," Frey's eyes widened, and she slapped her mom's hand away. They playfully started slapping each other's hands while laughing, relieving the tension in the room until Frey suddenly stopped and grabbed her side. "Stop making me laugh *chatski*, that hurts."

"Talk." Sehoy crossed her arms.

"Barrett came in and made me promise I would choose him over Holt. Barrett is hurting and I can't hurt him anymore." When Frey said it out loud to her mom, it sounded stupid.

"Is that what this is about, Barrett not understanding your love?" Frey nodded. "Oh chackshosti, don't let Barrett dictate your love life just because he's hurting. And don't hurt Holt just to make Barrett feel better. Barrett is a big boy and in due time, he will see things differently. You can't just ignore and abandon Holt while you try to calm Barrett down. Barrett is feeling hurt and is lashing out, afraid of losing his closest friend. He doesn't get that you're turning his best friend into his brother-in-law, because all he sees right now is the lie. But, with time, he will understand."

"Like he understood when he stopped being friends with Jeremy in high school because he was jealous of him hanging out with me?" Frey crossed her arms.

"That was years ago. Jeremy was never as close to Barrett as Holt. If you had just been open and honest with your relationship, you might have saved yourself this dilemma you're in." Sehoy placed her hands on her hips. "Making that stupid promise to Barrett. What were you thinking?"

"I thought I was doing the right thing. I just needed more time to ease Barrett into seeing Holt as my boyfriend. I was afraid if Barrett cut Holt off like he did Jeremy, then I could have ruined their friendship forever. I panicked and made Holt keep the secret. But in hindsight, Holt was right. We should have told him as soon as we started dating. At least then, we wouldn't have lied and gone behind Barrett's back."

"Why didn't you tell us all? We love Holt. I'm over the moon that you chose him. He's grown into a fine young man."

"At first, I wasn't sure if Holt was really into me. Then Holt told me he made this dumb promise to Barrett in high school to never date me." Frey sighed. "I didn't want to tell you and dad before Barrett because I knew that would hurt him. Barrett and I have always shared everything. We always go to each other first."

"Okay. I understand what you were thinking, even though I don't agree with you. Still, the Jeremy thing and high school promise were so long ago. Barrett might have changed his mind. You're all adults now." Sehoy shook her head.

"That's what Holt thought, so as a joke, he brought it up with Barrett a few weeks ago and Barrett freaked out. Hence the secret relationship." Frey rolled her eyes.

"What is it with Barrett and promises? I need to talk to that boy."

"*Chatski*, no, I'll handle this. It's my problem to fix." Frey sat up and reached out for her mom's hand.

"Well, do it soon, or I will step in. In the meantime, let's hope Barrett comes to his senses. He's acting like a child."

"I hope so, because it will be difficult to stay away from Holt." Frey laid back down. Her side hurt when she sat up.

"Why do you need to stay away?" Sehoy sat on the edge of the bed.

"Because of my promise to Barrett." Frey threw her arms up in frustration. Was her mom not listening to her? That action caused her to wince. Bringing her arms back down, she fidgeted with her fingers, embarrassed about what she was about to say. "I kinda promised Barrett I'd stay away from Holt."

"That is a terrible promise, *chackshosti*." Sehoy paced back and forth a couple of times, muttering under her breath.

Frey knew her mom was frustrated with the way she had handled everything. Her mom always paced and mumbled when they were kids and did crazy things. They all thought it was her way of gathering her thoughts and calming down. Frey sat quietly, knowing when her mom was ready, she would continue with her comments.

Finally, Sehoy turned and pointed her finger toward Frey. "Be careful not to harm Holt while you console Barrett. Don't forget that Holt needs comfort as well. It's important to remember that both his mother and father abandoned him. Don't abandon him as well, there's no need. It's important that you apologize to him for your behavior today."

"I'll talk to Barrett and Holt tomorrow." Frey squeezed her mom's hands. She knew her mom was right. Shoot. She probably should have talked to her mom about Holt. Her mom would've helped her and Holt. "Thank you chatski. I love you. I know you're disappointed in me right now, but I really need my mom. I still can't believe I lost my baby. Can you please spend the day with me?"

"Oh *chackshosti*, there was nothing you could do about your little angel. I know it seems like you did something wrong, but everything happens for a reason and many times we don't know those reasons. Just know that *Hesakitaemisi* never gives you more than you can handle. At another time, you and Holt will have a baby that you can love and hold forever. I'm sure of it." Sehoy leaned down and stroked Frey's hair like when she was a little girl.

"Tori said almost the same thing." Frey whispered.

"That's because Tori is a smart girl. And so are you. I know you would've loved that baby with your whole heart. There is no doubt in my mind, you would be a loving mom. And in my heart, I truly believe you'll get that chance again with Holt." Sehoy kissed her forehead.

"Thank you *chatski*. I love you." Frey clung to her mom and let the tears come. Sehoy wrapped her arms around Frey, comforting her until the wave of pain subsided—for now. Then Sehoy leaned back and wiped Frey's tears.

"I love you too. And it's good you invited me to stay all day because I took the day off and was planning on spending time with my little girl." Sehoy beamed at her daughter. "Now, let's see what's on TV. Maybe we can watch something good. Scoot over."

Frey grinned and created room for her mom on the bed. Both Frey and her mom were petite, measuring just under five feet two and slim. Sehoy laid down and Frey wrapped her arm around her. Frey's head on her mom's chest,way, listening to the steady beat of her mom's heart. There was nothing more comforting for Frey than lying with her mom and feeling Sehoy's hand run through her hair like when she was a little girl. Her mom always knew what to do to make Frey feel better.

If she was lucky enough to have more kids, she wanted to comfort them like her mom taught her and let them know how much she loved them. Her mom was special. How many moms would take in an abused child and treat him like family? Fully including him in everything they did as a family. Showing him that not all moms were like his mother, who was mean and uncaring. Yeah, Frey thought, she won the lottery when she was born to a wonderful, caring, loving mom. *Hesakitaemisi* had most definitely blessed her with the best mom in the world.

When they delivered Frey's food tray at lunch, Sehoy got up and sat in the chair so Frey could eat comfortably on the bed. Her mom pulled out a sandwich and a water bottle from her purse.

"Well, you came prepared," Frey chuckled as she watched her mom pull food out of her bag.

"Alex made me a sandwich. I told you I was staying for the day." Sehoy grinned at Frey.

"Hello." Dr. Wallace knocked and stepped inside. "Freya, how are you feeling?"

"I'm feeling better, thank you," Frey said between bites.

"That's great. Remember, if you need to speak to a professional about the loss of your baby, we are happy to recommend a doctor. Before I leave for the day, I wanted to drop by and share the good news with you."

"What good news?" Frey stopped eating and sat up.

"We will keep a close eye on you for the next few nights. But if everything goes according to plan, you'll be able to go home by Thursday."

Sehoy jumped out of her chair and hugged the doctor. "Thank you so much, Dr. Wallace. That is good news."

Frey saw the surprise on Dr. Wallace's face when her mom gave him a big hug.

Dr. Wallace laughed. "That's the first time I've gotten a hug for giving good news. And believe me, I give a lot of good news."

"My mom's a hugger." Frey chuckled.

"I see that." Dr. Wallace smiled at Frey and Sehoy. "I will return tomorrow morning to see how you're doing."

"Thank you." Frey held her stomach and smiled at the doctor.

"Is your stomach hurting?" Dr. Wallace's smile quickly turning to concern.

"A little." Frey winced.

"Let me take a look." Dr. Wallace approached the bed, pulled back the sheet, and gently pulled off the dressing. "It looks good. No infection. I'll have the nurse come in and change your dressing. She can also bring you pain medicine. It will help you sleep after you eat." Dr. Wallace left the dressing off but pulled the sheet to cover her.

"Thank you, again." Frey smiled. "See you tomorrow."

"No problem. See you tomorrow." Dr. Wallace wrote on her chart and left.

"*Chackshosti*," Sehoy said after she sat in the chair to finish her lunch, "that is great news. We will make a plan to get you home."

Frey was indifferent about who came to get her to drive her home. She looked forward to sleeping in her own bed and having her family nearby.

Shortly after the doctor left, the nurse came in and applied the clean dressing on her incision. She left the pain pills in a tiny cup and told her to take them after she finished eating.

Chapter 49

How Could She Fix This?

Frey

B arrett relieved Sehoy yesterday and spent the night with Frey. Frey attempted to talk to him then, but he kept changing the subject. She was so woozy from the pain meds that it wasn't hard to distract her. This morning, she was clear-headed, at least until after breakfast, when she got the next dose. It was time to put her big girl panties on and have a heart to heart with Barrett.

"Barrett, you've forgiven me. Now you need to forgive Holt." Being direct was her best option.

"You're my sister. Of course I will forgive you." Barrett snorted.

"He's your best friend and brother." Barrett had to forgive Holt. *How was she supposed to live happily ever after with Holt if Barrett hated him?*

"Nope, he is not my best friend anymore because he broke his promise." Barrett shook his head. "And technically, he is not my brother."

"Barrett, please talk to him. You guys need to work this out. I don't enjoy being stuck in the middle."

"You're not stuck in the middle. You either choose me or him. It's a simple decision since I'm your brother." Barrett crossed his arms and smiled at Frey.

"Bare, please don't do this to me. It's not right to make me choose between two people that I love. Why are you doing this?" Frey pleaded. "I hate your fucking promises. They end up hurting people." How was she going to convince him to talk to Holt and forgive him like he had forgiven her if he wouldn't talk to her? He'd probably forgiven her because she lost a baby. His niece or nephew. But Holt had lost a baby too. She had to get rid of that stupid promise to ignore Holt. Right now, everyone was hurting.

"Yeah, well, you already chose, and you picked me, discussion closed." Barrett strolled to the side of the bed and sat down. "I don't want to talk about him or this anymore. What I want to know is how my sister is feeling this morning?"

Barrett was so stubborn when he got a crazy idea in his head. *Why were friendships black and white with him?* Everything in life has shades of gray. There's always a compromise that can be reached. Frey had to find a way to reach him.

"Better, but my side still hurts." Frey shifted on the bed, attempting to get comfortable.

"Do you want me to get the nurse?" Barrett's forehead wrinkled.

"No, I'm sure the nurse will be in soon with my pain relievers. I can wait. Right now, I want to talk to you about forgiving Holt and forgetting about that stupid ass promise." Frey folded her hands on her stomach, turning her head when she heard the door opening.

"Good morning, sweetheart," Holt said, walking into the room. "Special delivery of beautiful flowers for my beautiful gi...," Holt stopped dead in his tracks when he saw Barrett sitting on her bed. "Barrett, I've been looking for you."

"Well, you found me. Now you can leave." Barrett made a shooing motion with his hand.

Holt froze in place. Frey grabbed Barrett's hand tightly and glared into his eyes, wishing they possessed telepathy, like those twins in superhero movies.

"How are you feeling, sweetheart?" Holt placed the flowers on her bedside table.

"How the hell do you think she's feeling?" Barrett continued to spew venom at Holt. Frey squeezed his hand to the point of pain.

"Is there anything I can get you?" Holt gently placed her hair behind her ears and bent down to kiss her cheek.

"No." Frey's gaze shifted between the two of them. "I'm good. Thank you for the flowers." Frey locked eyes with Barrett, using her fingers to open the fist he made when Holt kissed her. She was not going to let Barrett punch Holt again.

"Where's your mom?" Holt looked around. "I thought she was spending yesterday and night with you?"

"No, *chacteka* came by in the afternoon to visit and take her home. They stayed until Barrett got here. He stayed with me last night." Frey held her breath, thinking Holt was going to fly off the handle.

"That's good." Holt looked at her and said, "I can spend the day with you."

"Unnecessary," Frey glanced at Holt. Barrett kept trying to make a fist with his hands, his leg bouncing up and down so fast he was making her nauseous. She had to separate them until she could calm Barrett down. She did not want them to fight in her hospital room. "My mom is coming over again today."

"Oh, okay." Holt's gaze slid away from her. Shoulders slumped, away, he turned to Barrett. "Can I talk to you for a second outside?"

"No, but once I'm back at the resort, I'll track you down," Barrett said, glaring at Holt.

"Okay." Holt leaned closer for a kiss, but Frey quickly pulled away because Barrett looked like he was about to swing at Holt's face. She needed Holt to leave—now.

"I'll text you later," Holt mumbled.

Her intention was to de-escalate the situation. She didn't want to cause either of them any more pain, but from the tone of Holt's voice and the concern in his eyes, she was failing. Hurting Holt was hurting her. She had to convince Barrett to let go of his hatred before she lost Holt forever.

Sehoy casually entered the room and said, "Good morning. Wow, those flowers are beautiful."

There was no response from anyone. Holt's eyes bore down on Frey, making her nervous. After a quick glance, she looked away, not wanting to see the hurt reflecting on them.

"Holt, did you bring flowers for Frey?" Sehoy finally inquired.

"Yes ma'am. I'll leave you all alone. I know Frey enjoys spending time with her family." Holt slipped around Sehoy and walked out.

"*Chakpootsi?*" Sehoy turned as she called out to him.

"Let him go," Barrett said harshly, and bolted up from the bed, pulling his hands away from Frey. "He's not wanted here."

"Barrett Panther, how dare you talk to your best friend like that? Stop acting like a toddler and get over yourself. Stop thinking like a child and think about your sister and Holt. They need your support right now. They're hurting over their lost child. Which would have been your niece or nephew. Have you thought about that during your temper tantrum?" Sehoy scolded Barrett, then pointed at Frey. "And you, just sitting in bed, not standing up for the love of your life. What has gotten into the both of you? This has gone on long enough, and it needs to stop."

Frey didn't know what to say. Her mom was right. Looking at Barrett, she saw his face drain of color and his body stiffen. Barrett was probably so wrapped up in losing his friend, he hadn't quite come to the realization of losing his niece or nephew.

"Bare?" Frey whispered.

"I gotta go. Stay strong, Frey." Barrett squeezed her hands and stormed toward the door.

"Barrett Panther!" Sehoy yelled out. "You stop right there. Do not leave when you are so upset."

"I can't talk about this right now," Barrett spoke through gritted teeth. "I don't want to say something that I will regret. I love you, *chatski*. And yes, I realize Frey's baby was going to be my niece or nephew. It kills me they didn't survive, but it's all his fault." Barrett's voice rose, and he pointed at the door.

"Bare, how can you say that?" Frey placed her hand on her forehead. This conversation was giving her a headache.

"How? So many fucking reasons." Barrett raised a finger for every reason he gave. "One: He never should have touched you—he promised. Two: Why the fuck didn't he wear a fucking condom?" Sehoy took a loud breath and covered her mouth, looking at Barrett like he had lost his mind. "Three: He lied to my face multiple times about your relationship. Four: If he hadn't called his fucking stupid ass mother back and paid off the trailer, my sister wouldn't be lying here grieving the loss of her baby! Do you need any more reasons? I'm sure I can come up with a few more." Barrett's chest was heaving after that speech.

Frey didn't know where to start, but the one thing that stuck out from his speech was what he said about Betty. "What do you mean, he talked to her and paid off her trailer?"

"He didn't fucking tell you?" Barrett smirked. "Of course he wouldn't. He's good at telling lies."

"Barrett, please stop cussing." Sehoy said calmly. "You know I don't like that."

Barrett grumbled, sorry.

"Bare, please tell me what happened with Betty." Frey needed to know what happened so she could find out from Holt later, why he didn't tell her.

"Holt told me she called him Halloween night crying and begging him to give her money. He didn't want to give her cash in case she used it for drugs or alcohol, so he paid off her trailer. Asshole probably thought it was over. Then she continued to leave messages and texts, saying she needed more money, but he ignored them. He never should've answered her first call to begin with." Barrett ran his hand over the back of his neck.

Frey didn't know what to say. Had Holt's kindness led to her being stabbed? Frey didn't think so. Betty seemed unhinged that night.

"Barrett, you don't know for sure that Holt paying for the trailer was what tipped Betty over the edge." Frey tried to reason with him.

"How can you say that?" Barrett spun around to face Frey.

"Because even if he hadn't paid, Betty had already made a plan with Candy and her brother to extort money from Holt. Deputy George told me about the plan when they came in to talk to me about what happened. Candy and Betty confessed when they were in the police car."

Frey watched Barrett's expression of shock turn to disbelief.

"Barrett, consider the fact that Holt probably didn't want to be the one responsible for leaving his mom homeless." Sehoy reached out and rubbed Barrett's back. "Holt is not like his mother. He's a good person."

"I gotta go. I need to be alone." Barrett hugged Sehoy and strode out of the room.

"Do you think he's going to be okay?" Frey asked Sehoy after the door shut.

"I do." Sehoy sighed. "I just think he needs to process everything we said. What happened, anyway? I thought you were going to talk to Holt?" Sehoy sat on the bed.

"Barrett was here, and I didn't want to do it in front of both of them." Frey ran her hands over her forehead.

"I never took you for a coward, *chackshosti*," Sehoy sighed.

"I know! I don't know why I didn't stand up for Holt, except I didn't want to hurt Barrett." Frey was so confused.

She'd messed up again. By trying to calm Barrett down, she had inadvertently taken his side. But she didn't mean to take Barrett's side. *Shit. Barrett's holier than thou attitude was really pissing her off.* She hoped that after their conversation, he would reconsider his behavior toward Holt. Then she had to talk to Holt about the money he gave Betty. These men were driving her crazy.

"So, you hurt Holt instead? Again?" Sehoy shook her head. "You need to fix this *chackshosti*."

"I know. I keep messing everything up. But I'm gonna fix it as soon as I get home. Can you help me go for a walk?" Frey moved her legs to the edge of the bed. "I have to show them by walking around multiple times today that I will be fine at home. If they give me the green light, you can pick me up tomorrow at lunchtime."

Frey was ready to go home and talk to Barrett and Holt. This craziness had to stop.

"Okay *chackshosti*, let's go."

Sehoy came well-prepared today. She not only assisted Frey in standing up and walking multiple times, but she also brought her travel bingo game in her bag. They agreed to avoid discussing Barrett or Holt and simply have quality time as mother and daughter.

Chapter 50

Taking the Trash Out

Holt

Yesterday, Holt attempted to locate Barrett after being essentially forced out of Frey's room. Now he knew Barrett had been with Frey in the hospital, feeding her shit. Barrett shutting him out, was royally pissing him off. Bringing her flowers this morning could have brightened her mood, but Barrett's presence changed everything.

Once more, Holt found himself alone, making his way back home. But was that really his home anymore? If Frey was truly abandoning him like garbage, he had to reconsider his living arrangement. Not being able to be with her, despite seeing her every day at work, would be soul-crushing for him.

Wanting to release some tension, he made his way to the gym on their floor. Going for a long run sounded like a great idea for clearing his mind. He put on a worn-out t-shirt and shorts, headed into the gym, and started the treadmill on his favorite running program. Inserting his earphones, he pressed play. The program began with a warmup, then alternated between running and sprinting, concluding with a cooldown.

Halfway through, he was so fixated on his breathing that he failed to notice someone hitting the stop button. "What the fuck?" Holt yelled, reaching for the sides of the treadmill and barely catching himself before he face planted.

"What the hell Barrett?" Holt got off the treadmill and shoved him. "That could have really hurt."

"No shit sherlock. I wanted it to hurt," Barrett yelled before he punched Holt in the stomach.

"Shit man. Fine, get your shots in." Holt raised his hands up in frustration. He didn't think Barrett would actually beat him up, but he did his best. Holt refused to retaliate. He defended against as many attacks as possible until Barrett became exhausted. It seemed to drag on forever. "Are you done?"

"Nope." Barrett swiped his feet out from under him. "Now, I'm done."

"Fuck Barrett!" Holt yelled as his body hit the floor. "You couldn't hurt me more than I already hurt."

"That's 'cause you let me beat the shit out of you," Barrett looked at his raw knuckles and shook out his hands. "You could have fought back."

"Why? I deserved it. I was actually referring to Frey and our baby, not the beating. I take responsibility for her getting hurt." Holt slowly stood up, eyeing Barrett in case he was going to punch him again.

"Yeah, it was. So maybe you should leave her alone. Leave all of us alone." Barret shook out his hand.

"Is that what you want? For me to leave?" Holt's eyes widened, taken aback by Barrett's unexpected demand. Barrett glanced at the ground and shrugged his shoulders.

Holt retreated towards the doorway. "What did you tell Frey yesterday?"

"I told her to choose between me or you. She can't have us both." Barrett stared at Holt with so much hatred in his eyes. "She chose me. You lose."

Holt rubbed his face with his hand and winced when he felt the tenderness around his eyes and cheeks. He felt something trickle down his chin and wiped it with the back of his hand. It came away red. His tongue licked his bottom lip, and he tasted the metallic tanginess of blood. *Fuck, he'd probably have a black eye, a swollen lip, and be homeless by tonight. He was really living up to the deadbeat stereotype he'd always feared he would become.*

Holt put his hands on his hips and glanced downward. Taking a deep breath, he nodded and headed to his room. He'd had a good run with a family. From now on, he must rely on himself. He wouldn't impose himself on anyone. Barrett's ultimatum clarified Frey didn't love him. It's not surprising that she would choose her relationship with Barrett over whatever she had with him. Barrett was her twin brother. They had a connection no one could come between.

There was no way Holt could even come close to competing with that. Sure, Frey said she loved him, but in the end, Holt just wasn't worth the trouble to keep around. There was always something more important. He was a fool to think anyone would put him first. That kind of love wasn't in the cards for people like him. Holt took a shower and emptied his closet and drawers. When he looked around, he noticed all he had was his duffle bag. Not a problem. He would gather the rest of his clothes and place them in a trash bag. That's how he became a part of this family. Exiting it in the same way just made sense.

Holt entered the security room next to the laundry room, composed a resignation letter, and printed a hard copy. Hopefully, Osceola would provide him with a favorable recommendation. As an employee, he'd done a good job.

With his duffle bag and trash bag in hand, he made his way down to the lobby. Sehoy was probably still with Frey because she was not at the front desk.

"Hey Ginny. Would you mind handing this to Mr. Panther?" Holt handed her his letter.

"Sure thing, Holt. Would you like me to contact him for you?" Ginny took the letter.

"No, just give it to him when you see him."

"Okay, are you taking out some trash?"

Holt smirked. "I suppose you could say that. Hope you have a good day."

"You, too."

Holt drove aimlessly for a few hours, unsure of his destination. Ultimately, he settled on driving to his mother's trailer. With Betty in jail, he hoped no one was there. And if what Betty said was true, it now belonged to him. If Candy's brother or any other men were there, he'd kick their ass out. He needed some place to think without interruptions. The trailer would become his home again until he found a place to live and looked for another job.

While en route, he bought a bottle of tequila, whiskey, and a case of beer. His stomach was grumbling. He hadn't eaten since yesterday. Pulling into a drive thru he ordered a burger and fries. With food and drinks taken care of, he was prepared for his pity party. As he approached the trailer, he realized he didn't have a key. A locked door wouldn't stop him, he could enter through a window. No one ever locked the windows. But luck was on his side tonight because the front door was unlocked. Even the heavens knew he belonged there.

Stepping into the trailer, the stale air was stifling. The air conditioning was not running, and the heat was unbearable. Placing the alcohol on the kitchenette, Holt walked to the AC unit in the window. As he turned all the switches, he realized it was broken. *Figures*.

Holt grabbed the beer and opened the fridge. *Holy Shit!* He immediately backed up and covered his nose and mouth as the putrid smell assaulted his senses. *Fuck!* There wasn't much in it, but the few containers of old food left were repulsive. There was no way he was putting his case of beer in there with that rotted food. Knowing he needed to throw out all the foul-smelling food, he picked up a garbage bag and disposed of all the containers. In addition, he disposed of the dirty dishes in the sink. He refused to wash that shit. How could Betty live like this?

He took the trash bags out and grabbed the rest of his shit from the truck. Grabbing a beer, he stored the rest in the fridge, and headed to the living room with his beer and alcohol to watch TV. After taking a few bites of the burger, it felt like lead sitting in his stomach. Wrapping the burger back up, he tossed it into the to go bag and threw the bag toward the kitchen. He'd get it later. Dropping onto the sofa, he flipped through several channels. He became engrossed in the storyline of a romantic film. Without realizing it, he absentmindedly reached for his phone and messaged Frey.

Holt: Can I come see you?

He sent another text a couple of minutes later.

Holt: Frey, I love you and I miss you. Please don't shut me out.

Frey didn't reply. The longer he contemplated why Frey was ignoring him, the more alcohol he consumed until eventually he passed out on the couch for the night.

Chapter 51

Homecoming

Frey

"What brings both of you here? Weren't you supposed to be at work at the cultural center?" Frey was surprised to see Alex and Tori at the hospital.

"Thunder told us to take the day off so we could be there for you on your first day home." Tori hugged her.

"Are you ready to go?" Alex pointed at the wheelchair in her room. "Your chariot awaits."

"Yes," Frey sighed. She didn't want to leave in a wheelchair. She could walk out on her own two feet. "I can't believe I have to be pushed out in a wheelchair. The nurse instructed me to notify her when my transportation arrived."

"Well, buzz away and get in here." Alex grabbed the wheelchair and wheeled it to Frey.

"Tori, can you grab my stuff?" Frey pointed to the bed.

"Is this all of it?" Tori picked up her stuff.

"Yep, that's it." Frey got comfortable in the chair.

"I see your ride is here." The nurse smiled from the doorway. "Let's head on out. I'll push her if you want to pull your car around and meet us at the front entrance."

"Sounds good." Alex jogged down the hallway and took the stairs.

"Are you glad to be going home?" the nurse asked.

"I sure am. You all have been so kind, but there's nothing quite like your own bed."

"I hear ya sister." The nurse smiled and pushed her to just outside the entrance. Once Alex arrived, she slowly got out of the wheelchair and strode toward the backseat. Tori stopped her and instructed her to sit in the front for added comfort.

"Are you hungry?" Alex asked, pulling out of the hospital.

"I am." Frey was tired of hospital food. She was craving Alex's turkey and swiss sandwich.

"Do you want me to go through a drive thru? Or I can fix you something when we get home." Alex turned to get on the highway.

"I'd rather just go home." Frey leaned her head back on the headrest and closed her eyes. "How are Barrett and Holt?"

"Holt tries to talk to him, but Barrett avoids him." Alex glanced at Frey.

"It's gonna be okay." Tori squeezed her shoulder from the back seat. "Alex and I will help you with anything you need."

"Yep," Alex confirmed as he pulled into the resort parking lot. "What can I make you ladies?" Alex asked as he helped the ladies out of the car.

"Turkey and Swiss," they both answered in unison.

"So predictable," Alex sighed and went to the kitchen to make their sandwiches.

"Hey ladies. Frey, how are you feeling?" Tiffany asked.

"I'm better. Can we get two glasses of water, please?" Frey and Tori found a table in RUSH.

"Of course. I'll be right back." Tiffany placed the silverware down and left.

"When are you going to talk to Holt?" Leave it to Tori to get right to the point.

Frey crossed her arms and leaned on the table. "I was hoping to knock on his door and talk to him this afternoon."

"Frey, he's not here. He's gone." Tori reached out and held her forearm.

"What do you mean, he's gone?" Frey assumed Tori meant he had left for the day. Maybe go to the beach or somewhere else to unwind.

"Alex told me he had a fight with Barrett and left." Tiffany dropped off their waters and Tori took a sip.

"I'm sure he'll be back." Frey fidgeted with her napkin.

Tori's eyes brimmed with sadness as she replied, "I don't think so. He also handed in his resignation letter to Osceola."

"No." Frey covered her mouth as her eyes got glassy. "Why would he do that?" *Holt had left her? She hadn't gotten to him quick enough to explain what was going on between her and Barrett.*

"Sehoy said because you told him to," Tori said slowly.

"My intention was to get him out of the room so I could talk to Barrett. I wanted to calm Barrett down before I spoke to Holt. I didn't mean for him to leave me forever." Frey dropped her head in her hands and sobbed. "What am I going to do?"

"I'm sorry. I'll help you any way I can."

"What's going on?" Alex put their plates in front of them. "You told her Holt left?"

"Why would he leave, Alex?" Frey looked up and wiped her eyes.

"You really should have told Barrett that you wanted to be with Holt." Alex rubbed his face. "You and Barrett would've fixed things. But turning your back on Holt, you really hurt him."

"I know!!!"

"Why didn't you pick Holt?" Alex sat next to her.

"Because I was stupid. I let Barrett's insecurities get in my head." Frey turned her head and stared out the window. "I knew this was going to be hard for Barrett, but I'd hoped he wouldn't turn on Holt. Then again, I never thought Holt would leave me."

"Honey," Alex gently massaged her back. "You and Barrett both told him to get the fuck out. Not in so many words, but that was the gist of it. Well, Barrett told him to get the fuck out and then beat the shit out of him. What did you think he would do?"

"I thought he would wait and let me explain." Frey's head swiveled to Alex. "Wait, what do you mean, Barrett beat the shit out of him?"

"I don't know the details, only that Barrett told me he beat him up yesterday in the gym. He said Holt has a black eye and swollen lip. Frey, I love you and I will always have your back, but I gotta tell you: You never gave Holt any sign to wait for you. Once you finished speaking with Barrett, you ignored him completely. At least that's what mom told me."

"You're right. I needed to put my big girl panties on and speak to both of them when they were in the room with me, but I told Holt to leave." Frey stared at Alex. "Now what do I do? I can't lose him."

"We talk some sense into Barrett and look for Holt." Alex stood up. "Finish your food. I'll text him and tell him to get his ass down here. Then we will talk like mature adults."

"Okay." Frey took a bite of her sandwich. Alex was always the peacekeeper when they all argued or fought. Having him on her side would be a great asset.

"Do you know where he might be? Any special place for him?" Tori asked.

"No." Frey opened her chips and ate one. "This was his special place, his safe haven, and I ruined that." Tears slipped down her face again. Who knew someone could cry so much in one day?

"Oh, honey." Tori came over and sat next to her, putting Frey's head on her shoulder while rubbing her back. "We'll find him."

Frey shook her head, wiped away her tears, and they silently finished their lunch. Concern for Holt weighed on Frey. Who would he turn to? Where would he go when he was feeling down?

"That's it!" Frey snapped her fingers.

"What's it?" Tori raised an eyebrow.

"I think he went to the trailer he shared with Betty. Since she's not there, he'll be by himself," Frey stated, standing up. "We have to tell Alex."

"Tell Alex what?" Barrett strolled up to their table.

"I know where Holt is." Frey grabbed Barrett's arm. "We need to go get him and bring him back."

"Why?" Barrett smirked.

"Barrett, sit down," Alex stormed to their table.

"Alex, I know where Holt is. Let's go get him," Frey was shifting her weight from foot to foot, ready to bolt.

"I suggest we all head to the security room to talk. This conversation requires privacy. We can't talk here with other people around. We need to have a plan to convince him to come home." Alex called Tiffany over. "Tiffany, we need to have a family meeting. Would you mind cleaning up our plates?"

"Of course." Tiffany stacked the plates while they headed to the office behind the lobby desk. Leaving RUSH, they found Sehoy behind the lobby desk. They asked her to call Osceola because they wanted to have a private family meeting in the security room. Once Osceola arrived, the door was closed, and they gathered around the conference table.

"Okay, everyone now knows that Holt left us. And we all want him back." Alex was the first to speak.

"Not everyone," Barrett grumbled while he sat with his arms crossed.

"Stop acting like you're five. Holt has been your best friend for years. You can't accept that he wants to marry your sister instead of just fooling around with her? I would think you'd be happy. He's already a brother to you. Your mom said she talked to you about it yesterday. Did you not pay attention to her words and hear what she said?" Osceola pointed at Barrett. "Stop your whining and look at what it's doing to your sister." Osceola waved his hand toward Frey.

Barrett pivoted to Frey. "Do you want him back?"

"Yes Barrett, I love him." Frey stared at Barrett, hoping he would see the truth in her eyes.

"Why didn't you say that?" Barrett threw his arms up in frustration. "I made him promise me not to date you when we were young because you are my baby sister and I had to protect you. Holt was a Romeo Joe, dating and sleeping around. I didn't want you to be another notch on his bedpost, and I feared losing my best friend." Barrett stared down at the ground and shook his head. "I know it sounds juvenile, but if he had used you, I wouldn't speak to him again." Barrett sighed and looked up at Frey. "Then you lost the baby. I just saw red, because if he loved you, he should've protected you from his evil mother. I beat him up yesterday thinking it would make me feel better because he lied to me, but he never hit back and that made me feel worse. So, if you both love each other and are going to get married, then I'm okay with it."

"What changed your mind?" Barrett's change of heart confused Frey. "You were so angry when you gave me that ultimatum at the hospital. I was going to wait a few days before trying to convince you to change your mind."

Barrett rubbed the back of his neck. "The talk we had with mom at the hospital made me think about how I was acting toward both of you."

Barrett, I shattered Holt's heart because of our pact. I'm sorry, but I change my mind and I choose him. I can't imagine my life without him. He's the love of my life and I am going to marry him. But first, I have to find him and hope he forgives me. You gotta believe we never meant to hurt you. Holt always wanted to tell you. It was me that stopped him. When we find him, please hear him out?"

"I will." Barrett opened his arms for Frey. "Do you forgive me?"

"Of course. I love you." Frey ran into Barrett's arms for a hug. Barrett had been through the ringer, just like her and Holt. If only he'd come to those conclusions before she kicked Holt out of the hospital room. Now her main priority was finding Holt and making him understand she had made a huge mistake in how she handled the situation. She could blame it on the pain meds and her grief, but that wasn't fair. Holt was also grieving. Frey needed to take accountability for the things she said and grovel. She saw lots of groveling and begging when she found him.

"I'm sorry. That bedside promise was stupid. I let jealousy get in the way and almost lost my best friends. Now that I know how serious you guys are, I'll hear him out. I know I've been an asshole." Barrett looked around the room. "I hate to admit I was afraid that now he would have you and wouldn't need my friendship anymore. Stupid, I know."

"You've all always been the best of friends. I don't see how Holt and Frey being together would change that," Alex interjected. "Well, except for the fact they would share the same room."

Frey punched one of Alex's arms at the same time Tori slapped the other.

"Ouch. What?" Alex shrugged. "It's the truth." Then he pointed to both of them. "You two need to stop hanging out together all the time. Frey, stop influencing Tori."

Frey laughed. Yeah, right, like that was happening anytime soon.

"Influencing me to do what?" Tori crossed her arms and glared at Alex. "Stand up for myself? Tell you when you're wrong? Share my opinion?"

Barrett coughed and said, "Someone's in the doghouse."

"Okay. We're getting off topic. Besides, Holt and I have already been sharing the same room," Frey chuckled.

"A mother and father do not need to know that *chakshosti*," Osceola growled.

"Sorry, *chacteka*," Frey cleared her throat. "But remember,Yes, I was pregnant."

Osceola gave her a stern look. "Can we not talk about this now?"

"Yes sir." Frey bowed her head in shame.

"Okay, moving on. Now that we're one big happy family, we need to find Holt and bring him home." Alex looked around the room. "Any suggestions?"

"I have a feeling he might be at his mom's trailer," Frey said, her gaze darting between everyone. "With Betty in jail, he would be alone."

"I think Frey is right." Barrett nodded. "Holt told me he paid it off. It's a good place to start."

"Okay, we'll try there first," Alex stood. "Who's coming with me?"

Frey, Barrett, and Tori said 'me'.

"All of you go." Sehoy wrapped her arms around Osceola. "We'll cover your shifts."

Frey was praying for Holt to be there, because if he wasn't, she wouldn't know where to find him. Holt never really left the resort. As far as she knew, he didn't have a special place.

Chapter 52

The Hunt for Holt

Frey

When they arrived at Holt's childhood trailer, they immediately recognized his truck in the gravel driveway.

"Let me go in first." Frey was already opening her door.

"Okay. I'll give you five minutes and then I'm coming in." Barrett got out and leaned against the car.

"Ten." Frey raised an eyebrow at him.

"Fine, ten." Barrett crossed his arms and nodded.

Frey climbed the trailer steps and tested the door. It was unlocked. She took a deep breath to calm her nerves before entering. Frey stepped inside and immediately covered her nose. She saw a fast-food bag with the contents spilling out littered across the floor, and the place wreaked of alcohol and rotted food. Following the path of empty beer bottles, she ended up in the living room. Holt lay passed out on the couch. He had one hand on his stomach and the other pressing an empty bottle of tequila to the floor.

"Holt." Frey went to her knees beside him. She gently caressed his face with her hands. "Holt."

Holt's eyes fluttered open. "Have you come to yell at me again?" Holt murmured. Frey recoiled from his foul-smelling alcoholic breath.

"Holt, I'm so sorry." *Had he been drinking since he got here? How much could he possibly drink in one day?*

"No need. I arrived as garbage and departed as garbage. Got the trash bags with my clothes to prove it." Holt closed his eyes and pointed to the bags by the end of the couch. "You don't belong here." Holt groaned. "Go. I did what you asked me to do. I can't afford to have my heart broken by you again."

Frey never thought of him as garbage. *What was he talking about? He wasn't making any sense.*

"Holt, please." Frey ran her fingers through his hair, brushing down his bed head. She missed being able to touch him. It seemed like forever since they shared an intimate moment.

"Go!" Holt pushed her arm away from him. "Get the fuck out of here!" Holt opened his eyes and sat up so fast Frey fell back on her ass.

Frey knew Holt was hurting, but she never expected this much anger being hurled toward her. He'd never raised his voice or hand at her. This Holt was scaring her. *Was he so far gone that he would hurt her?*

"Holt," Barrett said from the doorway as Frey crab crawled backwards. "Don't yell at her. We came to apologize and take you home."

"I am fucking home. Now get the fuck out!" Holt stood up, pointed to the door, swaying. "I don't need your pity."

Frey sensed arms under her armpits lifting her off the ground. "Frey, go outside with Tori." Alex whispered in her ear.

"No, please. Let me just talk to him." Frey mumbled.

She wanted to be there with Holt. He needed to know she would never leave him again. They could sit on the couch. She would talk to him—calm him down. *There was no way he could've fallen out of love with her in just a couple of days, right?* Then again, she told him to leave her alone. Unfortunately, Alex didn't agree, and he nudged her toward the door. Frey couldn't bring herself to open it and step outside. She had to see this through.

"Holt, come on, man. I'm sorry. I don't pity you. You're my best friend." Barrett approached Holt to hug him. Holt delivered a forceful punch to Barrett's face, knocking him to his ass.

"How does that feel, asshole?" Holt screamed at Barrett.

"Holt!" Frey screamed and covered her mouth with her hands as tears streamed down her face. She tried to get to Barrett, but Alex positioned himself in front of her, blocking her way.

"Will you both stop hitting each other? You want to wrestle it out, go ahead. But stop doing damage to one another." Alex held his hand out to help Barrett stand.

"All of you, get the fuck out!" Holt yelled at them again. "I did what you all wanted. I got the fuck out of your lives. Now get the fuck out of mine!"

"We're not leaving," Alex stood in front of him with his arms crossed. "You smell like shit and your breath wreaks like a fucking brewery. Go take a fucking shower and brush your teeth so we can all talk like adults." Alex shoved Holt. Holt stumbled back, then turned and went into another room.

Frey hoped it was the bathroom. She'd never been in the trailer.

"Frey, please go sit in the car with Tori," Alex pleaded with her. "I promise after he comes out and calms down, I will get you. Tori, take my keys so you can lock yourselves in and run the AC. Honk if you encounter any trouble." Alex handed her his keys and pushed them both out the door.

Tori and Frey sat in the locked car, staring at the trailer.

"What do you think is going on in there?" Frey mumbled.

"I think they will talk some sense into Holt and then let us in. Personally, I'm glad we're in the car and not the trailer. That trailer with no AC felt stifling, not to mention stinky." Tori squeezed her nose with her thumb and index finger.

"You're right. It was pretty nasty in there. But being out here in this neighborhood is scary." Frey turned her head on a swivel, making sure no one was near them. "How long has he been there? I hated seeing Holt like that." Frey winced and reclined the seat.

"Is your stomach hurting you?" Tori looked concerned.

"A little, but it's okay now that I'm lying back." Her stitches felt much better when she could rest in a reclined position. But she wanted to come and talk to Holt, so she ignored everyone telling her to stay at the resort. No way was she letting them come here without her. And there was no way she was leaving here without Holt.

"He submitted his resignation letter yesterday. So, my guess is he came after he did that."

"Wow" –Frey's eyes widened– "he drank that much in a twenty-four-hour period? At least he had enough sense to get some food. Even though most of it was on the floor. How could it smell so bad from one day of old food?"

Frey saw Tori pointing at something. Sitting up a little, she saw some trash bags leaning against the trailer. She would bet her next paycheck there was food in there and the smell in the trailer was lingering from what was in those bags. At least Holt had thought to clean some of it out before he got wasted.

"Yeah, it would have been nice if he'd thrown the leftovers out in the trash. It stunk in there, but I'm sure it smelled bad before yesterday's meal. That wretched smell has probably been there since Betty was living in it and with no AC it just festered in there." Tori kept staring at the trailer.

"Yeah, it was pretty rancid." Frey sighed. "I was thinking the same thing. Between the food, alcohol, and no AC, no wonder he stinks. Drinking that much alcohol in that sauna is bound to make you stinky and drunk. I just hope Alex and Barrett can talk some sense into him."

"Me too, sister," Frey noticed Tori scanning the area for any unwanted visitors while she laid back and tried to stop the pain in her stomach. She should have grabbed some ibuprofen. Frey didn't want the prescription meds anymore. The last thing she wanted was to get addicted to them.

Chapter 53

Why The Hell Are They Here?

Holt

Holt remained under the spitting spray of lukewarm water until it became cold. It didn't take long. Betty neglected to pay for the water heater to be fixed. That's okay. In order to face the Panther clan in his living room, he needed a jolt of cold water to sober up. Why the hell were they here? Seeing them was breaking his heart all over again. He couldn't go through that pain again. It hurt worse than when he was young, and his mother abandoned him for sex and drugs.

Holt heard what they said, but it was best for him to stay away. He was born trash and would always be trash, just like he told Frey. He proved he was just like his mom. As soon as his girl dumped him, he turned to alcohol. The apple doesn't fall far from the tree.

After taking a cold shower to wake up and help him deal with the shitshow waiting for him in his living room, he dried himself off and brushed his teeth. Placing his hands on the sink, he looked at himself in the mirror, disgusted with what he saw. Moving his head around, he looked at his injuries from Barrett's fists. His swollen, bloodshot eyes reflected both sadness and the marks of Barrett's punches on his face. The cut on his lip had scabbed over and he could see some bruising on his chest. Taking a few deep breaths, he didn't have pain in his ribs. Good, they were just bruised, but not broken. He'd let Barrett pound on him so he could get his anger out. Holt figured he deserved it. But now he wanted to be left alone. Beating Up Holt Day was yesterday, not today. Despite tidying up, he still felt nauseous, and his head throbbed like a jackhammer between his temples. Fuck! Time to go out there and get rid of them.

When he entered the living room, Alex and Barrett were the only ones waiting for him. They must have cleaned up because all the alcohol bottles were missing, along with the leftovers from last night.

"Where are the girls?" Holt asked before sitting down and holding his head.

"In the car. I didn't want Frey to see you when you're acting like a mean bastard." Alex glared at him.

"It's not safe in the car. This neighborhood is shit. Tell them to come in." Holt looked up and pleaded with Alex. "I promise not to lose my temper." The last thing he needed was for something to happen to Frey and Tori on his property. He would never forgive himself for that.

"Now, you care about them?" Alex crossed his arms and stared him down.

"I've always cared about them. It's you guys that didn't care about me," Holt protested.

"Stop being such a damn whiny baby wallowing in self-pity. We're here, aren't we?" Alex sighed and raised his arms, proving his point. They were there. "I'll get them. Barrett, say your piece. Holt, you better listen." Alex pointed at him with a no nonsense look on his face. "And no more fucking fighting!"

Alex always was their older brother and disciplinarian before they went to their parents. *Why the hell am I still thinking of them as my family?*

"I don't want to hear any yelling coming from this trailer or I'll knock both your asses out." Alex pointed to both of them before leaving.

"He sure is bossy when he's pissed," Holt grumbled.

"How could you forget all those times he yelled at us or smacked us upside the head when we were goofing off?" Barrett smirked.

"True. He yelled at us a lot." Holt sat on the couch and remembered Alex reprimanding them every time they got into mischief. He never told Osceola and Sehoy, although he threatened to.

"I think I have a permanent handprint on the back of my head from all his head smacks," Barrett chuckled.

"Yeah, me too," Holt laughed with Barrett before he realized they were getting along.

"Hey, man. I'm sorry." Barrett sat next to Holt. "I was out of line. Thinking back, jealousy got the best of me. You're my best friend and I didn't want to lose you to Frey. Hell, I didn't want to lose Frey to you either. Not only was I jealous, but I wanted to protect my sister from being one of your many women. That's why I had you make that promise. Now that I know you guys are serious and considering marriage, I'm good."

"I do love..." Holt's feelings were all over the place.

"Stop." Barrett raised his hand to stop Holt. "Let me finish."

Holt nodded and listened to Barrett, wondering where his relationship with Frey stood after she pushed him away. His feelings of abandonment weren't going away overnight. Holt felt like he was standing on a precipice and if he wasn't careful, he would fall again. But would Frey catch him?

"Then the shit with your mom pushed me over the edge" —Barrett sat back fidgeting with his hands and continued— "even though I know none of that was your fault. Anyway, I acted like a jackass—that wasn't cool. I'm sorry for everything."

"I felt horrible lying to you. You're not just my best friend, but my brother. I wanted to tell you from the beginning, but remember when we had that conversation about a month ago about Frey going on a date with me?"

"Yeah, I reminded you of your promise." Barrett stared at his hands, picking at his nails.

"I was trying to get a feel for your reaction. You were so adamant that I keep my promise. I couldn't find the courage to confess my desire to date her. Barrett, I genuinely didn't intend to hurt you. I'm head over heels in love with her. It was beyond my control, but I'll stay away if that's what you want."

After Barrett accepted their relationship, he didn't want to jinx it by saying he wasn't sure if there still was one. He needed some time to clear his head. Then he would talk to Frey.

"As far as Betty." Holt rubbed his neck. "If I even thought for one second she would hurt Frey, I would have stopped her. I didn't realize paying off her trailer would lead to her asking for more money."

"To be honest, I think she would've asked for money with or without the trailer payment. She wasn't stable. Probably too many drugs." Barrett shrugged.

"You're probably right. I just wish I could have protected Frey and saved our baby." Holt sighed and leaned back next to Barrett. He appreciated Barrett's apology. It was one less thing he had to worry about.

"I'm sorry about the baby." Barrett muttered.

"Yeah, me too." Holt tilted his head back and closed his eyes. "Not sure if I would've been a good dad, but I sure as hell wanted to try."

Every time Holt thought about their baby, his heart felt like a gaping wound. It was a never-ending sense of despair that overwhelmed him. Maybe God took the baby away because he wouldn't have been a good father. His own father disowned him. And yet, Osceola treated him like a son and showed him how a father should love their son.

"I think you would have been and will be an awesome dad." Barrett leaned forward and turned to face Holt. "You are not your parents. You are a good person who cares about others. Look at me." Barrett poked Holt in the chest.

Holt immediately opened his eyes. Was Barrett going to hit him again?

"They do not define you. I've grown up with you and seen your kindness toward others. Don't let your shitty parents mess with your head." Barrett now poked Holt's head with his finger. "Do you hear me?" Barrett closed his fist and held it out. "Don't leave me hanging, brother."

"Loud and clear." Holt fist bumped him. "Thanks, man." Holt hadn't had a lot of reasons to smile lately, but this was one of them.

Alex, Tori, and Frey entered as the door swung open. "Are we good?" Alex asked, entering before the girls.

"Yeah, we're good." Barrett stood and put his hand down for Holt.

Holt grabbed it, and Barrett pulled him up into a hug.

"I'm really sorry, man." Barrett muttered.

"Thanks," Holt nodded, "me too." Holt was glad he had worked things out with Barrett, but he never said one way or the other if Holt should stay away from Frey when he asked. *What the hell should he do?* Ask Barrett again? It didn't matter. He'd already decided to slow down the relationship with Frey. They had a lot to talk about and they both needed to be in the right head space.

"Great, now let's get out of here. This place is not safe. Pretty sure in the few minutes I was out there, I witnessed a drug deal going on in the trailer next door." Alex turned and grabbed Tori's hand.

"Is that your shit?" Barrett pointed toward the trash bag and duffle.

"Yeah." Holt rubbed his eyes with his hand. Barrett grabbed them both, handing the duffle to Alex, and they walked out to the car.

"Holt." Frey reached out and touched his shoulder.

"Not now, Frey." Frey flinched and released his shoulder. Holt gently turned her and placed his hand at the small of her back, leading her out.

He had no intention of arguing with Frey. After speaking with Barrett, he felt raw and exposed. One heart to heart a day was good enough for him. Besides, when he talked to her, he wanted to have a clear head. Currently, he needed pain relief for his throbbing head and sleep.

No one said a word during the drive home. Sehoy rushed toward him as soon as she spotted him in the lobby. "*Chakpootsi*, what happened to your face?"

"It's nothing." Holt hugged her. "I'm fine."

That last thing he wanted to do was get Barrett in trouble with his parents for hitting him. Especially now that they were in a good place.

"Please don't leave us again." Sehoy held his face in her hands and kissed his cheek. "We were so worried about you. We love you."

"I'm sorry to worry you, *chatski*," Holt hugged her tightly, feeling her arms wrap around him so tenderly and with so much warmth, he finally felt like he was home. Holt knew if he had seen Sehoy before he walked out yesterday, he wouldn't have been able to leave. She was the mom he'd never had in Betty. He saw Osceola coming out of the security room and immediately released Sehoy. He wasn't sure if Osceola was going to be angry with him and he wanted to take his punishment like a man. After all, he left like a coward, dropping off his resignation without waiting to speak with him in person.

"I can find a job somewhere else," Holt faced Osceola. He was ashamed of his behavior for not giving two weeks' notice and walking out.

"Nonsense. You were only gone a day or so. Besides, even if you were gone a year, you would always have a job here, chakpootsi." Osceola pulled him into his arms for a tight hug and whispered. "I ignored that letter. As soon as I read it, I tore it up and threw it away." Osceola leaned back and gripped his biceps. "As far as I'm concerned, I never saw that letter."

"Thank you both. I appreciate you welcoming me back." Holt's teary-eyed gaze bounced between Sehoy and Osceola.

"Come on." Barrett shoved Holt with his shoulder. "Your bag is heavy. Let's get you settled back into your room."

"Sounds good." Holt smiled at Barrett. He knew the trash bag wasn't heavy. Barrett was trying to help him out before he cried like a baby in the resort's lobby. "Can we hang out and have a beer or two?"

"No more beer for you, buddy. You need to dry out." Barrett grinned wryly. "We can hang out and drink some coffee."

"Yeah, that sounds great. See you all later." Holt grabbed his duffle from Alex and walked off with Barrett.

*** **Frey** ***

"Are you okay, *chackshosti*?" Sehoy wrapped her arm around her.

Frey didn't know what to do. He'd totally ignored her on the ride home. *Had she screwed up so badly that he didn't want to talk to her? Did he want to break up with her?* Frey crossed her arms around her stomach. *Had she lost her baby and Holt forever?* Frey watched Holt until he got in the elevator and replied with a mixed response.

"Yes, and no. I'm relieved he's back, but he isn't talking to me. He reconciled with Barrett, which makes me happy and filled with relief. But I don't think he has let go of his resentment toward me for abandoning him during our time of grief. I let him down, like his mom."

"You are nothing like his mom. You didn't let men beat him up." Sehoy pulled Frey around to face her.

"I let Barrett hit him a few times." Frey winced.

"That's different. You did not let Barrett hit him. You didn't even know Barrett had hit him until after it all happened. Besides, Barrett hit him because of his anger. I know in my heart, had you been there, you would have stepped in front of him and probably gotten hit yourself by accident. Those are very different situations. Never compare yourself to that horrible woman. You are nothing like her. Give Holt time. He loves you. He'll come around." Sehoy kissed her cheek. "You need to take care of yourself. Did you forget that you recently returned from the hospital?"

"I didn't forget." Frey touched her stomach while she assured her mom. It was wonderful to have a caring mother. That wasn't something Holt had until he moved in with them. She had almost taken that away from him. Frey felt horrible.

"I'll take her up." Tori grabbed Frey's arm. "We'll catch up with all of you later."

"Baby, I'm going to RUSH to check if they need me." Alex kissed Tori. "I'll come up as soon as I'm done."

"Your room or mine?" Tori wiggled her eyebrows at her.

"Look who's making jokes now." Frey smiled at her bestie. "Would it be okay if we went to my room? I'd like to take my pain medication and enjoy some TV before I go to sleep." Frey wanted to lie down and hoped the pain medication would dull the throbbing pain in her stomach.

"Of course." Tori escorted her upstairs and into her room.

Frey changed into cozy pajamas and settled into bed as Tori searched for something for them to enjoy.

"We should host a Girls' Night Out this time. I think it would do you some good to hang out with the girls. What do you think?" Tori came across a show and stretched out next to Frey.

"Sure. When?" Frey laid on her back, watching Tori.

"Saturday night? We can meet downstairs. They should bring their swimsuits and we can eat and drink outside. Say around six thirty since I work until five?" Tori looked expectantly at Frey.

"Sounds good," Frey smiled. "By that time, I won't be taking pain medication anymore, and a dip in the pool or hot tub sounds perfect."

"Yay!" Tori clapped her hands and grabbed her phone, texting like a crazy person in their GNO group chat.

"There it's settled. I can't wait. You need something to cheer you up and hanging with our girl tribe is always a blast!" Tori exclaimed, leaping onto the bed.

"Ow!" Frey scrunched up her nose as a burst of pain shot up her stomach.

"Shoot, I'm sorry. I forgot about your side. I'll go get your pain pills for you. Stay here." Tori got up and returned with pills and water.

"Tori," Frey asked when she sat up to take her pills, "do you think Holt will forgive me? Every time I think about our baby, I just want him to hold me. I can't lose them both." Frey's eyes watered.

"I know, honey." Tori laid down with Frey and held her. "I think you guys will be okay. In my heart, I truly believe he loves you. I can't imagine he could fall out of love with you so fast. You just need some time."

"Thanks, bestie." Frey scooted down, curling up under the covers. "Can we watch a show instead of a movie? I don't want to get hooked and miss the end of the movie once the meds kick in."

"Absolutely. I'll put on a sit-com and let you know how it ends tomorrow if you fall asleep." Tori found reruns of a show about friends that always made them laugh.

Frey watched roughly one and a half shows before dozing off. Her last thoughts were of Holt lying in bed holding her.

Chapter 54

Paying it Forward

Holt

For the past few days, Holt was not only working on repairing his relationship with Barrett, but working on himself. When Frey turned her back on him, all his childhood insecurities resurrected. He thought he'd gotten over what Betty had done to him, but then, when Frey shut him out, he'd regressed. Knowing how awful it felt to be treated like nothing, he wanted to help the shelter kids that visited Thunder on Fridays now that he was back in a good headspace.

Holt called Thunder at the AICC and asked him what time the boys were coming. Thunder was glad that Holt was going to come in and hang out with them. He told Holt those boys needed as many male mentors as possible to help them through their situations and he appreciated his help.

Excitement with a dose of anxiety ran through his veins as he pulled up at the cultural center. He looked forward to getting to know the boys so he could help them any way he could.

"Hey, Mark." Mark was sitting behind the lobby desk. "How's it going? Thunder said the shelter kids would be here?"

"Hey, man. Thunder told me you were coming." Mark stood and shook his hand. "They're in the storytelling room with Thunder." Mark pointed behind him. "Go around the tree and it's the first room on the left along the back wall.

"Sounds good. Thanks." Holt nodded and followed Mark's directions. He'd never been there before. The lobby area was spacious, with tall ceilings and a large tree in the center. *Who knew you could keep a live tree in the middle of a building? He supposed the skylights on the roof helped.*

Holt opened the door slowly. He heard Thunder telling them a story from the stage while the boys sat in a semi-circle facing him. Tori was sitting on the floor between the two youngest boys. He walked in and sat down behind the semi-circle.

"Today, we have a special guest joining us." Thunder stood on the stage and pointed at Holt. "Holt, would you come up here?"

All eyes turned to Holt. *Shit, he didn't realize Thunder was going to put him on the spot so quickly. Oh well, no time like the present to get to know these boys.* Holt stood, walked to the stage, and stepped up next to Thunder.

"Boys, this is Holt Adams. He is a security guard at the Rock 'n' Roll Resort & Casino. He is a friend of Alex and Frey. Holt wanted to get to know you all and possibly become a mentor for you guys if you all hit it off." Thunder placed his hand on Holt's shoulder. "When I call your name, please raise your hand so Holt knows who you are. I'll start from the oldest to the youngest. Tim. Luke. Kenny. Jimmy, and Bryce." All the boys followed directions, and it allowed Holt to put a face to the name. Holt could see why Frey was drawn to Bryce. He was the shiest and barely held eye contact. "The floor's yours." Thunder slapped his back and sat on the bench in the center of the stage.

Holt had every intention of asking them questions about themselves and leaving his story for another time. Until he looked at the boys' faces and saw the uncertainty reflected in their eyes. He was a stranger to them. They probably thought he was going to lecture them or tell them some bullshit about how they should feel. Realizing they probably didn't trust adults if they came from an abusive home, he decided to tell his story. Holt understood their wariness of him, but he hoped to change that.

"Hello, everyone." Holt smiled at the boys and took a quick deep breath to calm his nerves. This was one of the hardest things he'd ever done. He had never been a fan of talking about himself. They all looked like teenagers except Bryce. He was by far the youngest and looked to be around six years old.

"Let me tell you a little about myself and why I'm here. I grew up on what some people would say was the wrong side of the tracks." Holt heard some boys snicker. Yeah, he could relate. "My mom and dad divorced when I was young. My dad refused to believe that I was his son. He kicked me and my mom out and we moved to Florida. I never saw him again. In her depression, my mom turned to alcohol, drugs, and a string of loser boyfriends."

Holt watched his language since he was speaking to kids. Looking at the boys, he noticed they were watching him like a hawk, completely engrossed his story. Holt heard the door open and looked up to see Alex enter the storytelling room and sit behind Tori.

"Some of my mom's boyfriends made me their punching bag, and my mom didn't care. She would tell them to not hit my face so teachers and anyone that could help me wouldn't see the bruises. That was the first day that I started calling her Betty and not mom. Now some of you would feel sorry for me. I gotta admit, I felt sorry for myself, too. Then my life got a lot better when I met this little girl who stood up for me against a bully in elementary school." Holt heard more snickering, and he laughed.

"I know, right? This tiny wisp of a girl stood up to a gang of bullies for me." Holt smiled and shook his head, remembering that fateful day that turned his life around. "Then that little girl introduced me to her brother and the three of us became best friends. You all have met that little girl. Her name is Frey, and her brother is Barrett."

Bryce's little hand shot up. He had a question.

"Yes, Bryce. Do you have a question?" Holt smiled encouragingly at him.

"Yes, sir." Bryce nodded. "Isn't Frey's brother Chef Alex?"

Holt smiled, and Alex stood up and worked his way to the stage. All the boys shouted hello to Alex when they saw him.

"You're right, Bryce. Good job. Chef Alex is Frey's older brother." Holt placed his arm around Alex's shoulder as they stood together on stage. "But she also has a twin brother named Barrett."

"Chef Alex. Frey is a twin? Does he look like her? Are they close? Do they feel each other's pain?" The boys bombarded Alex with questions.

"Let's see if I can answer all your questions." Alex laughed. "Frey and Barrett are twins. Frey is one minute older than Barrett, which drives Barrett crazy. No, he doesn't look like her because they are fraternal twins. Yes, they are very close. No, they don't feel each other's pain, but they are sensitive to each other's feelings. I'll answer any more questions you have when you all come to the restaurant to eat lunch, but for now, let Holt finish his story." Alex smiled at Holt before looking at the boys and stating, "And by the way, we feel blessed that Holt came into our family. He will always be another brother to me."

"Thanks man." Alex hugged Holt before he left the stage and stood at the back.

"So, Frey, Barrett, and I became like the three musketeers. We went everywhere together. I hated coming home after school because I didn't know what I would find. So, Barrett and Frey invited me to go home with them every day. Mrs. Panther, their mother, would pick us up and take us to the resort. We all did our homework together, and I got to eat dinner there most nights, which was more food than what I got at home. Mr. and Mrs. Panther treated me like one of their children. They taught me about love, kindness, and how to treat someone." Holt sat down on the edge of the stage, dangling his legs. He wanted to be closer to the kids.

"I'm telling you all this about myself because I think I can relate to some of you. Our stories might not be the same, but they might be similar. I think we can help each other. Plus, I would love the opportunity to get to know you guys. So, what do you say to me, being one of your mentors?" Holt wasn't sure if his story helped them to accept him as a mentor, but he put out his hand for a fist pump.

Tim was the first one to jump up and fist bump him. "Thanks, man. It's nice to know we're not alone."

One by one, they fist bumped him. Thunder got up and jumped down by the boys.

"All right, let's bring it in," Thunder put his hand out and all the boys placed their hands over his. Holt and Alex laid their hands over the boys'. "To the family you get to choose. On three, give your best yell. One. Two. Three." Thunder said, and they all hooted and hollered before throwing their hands up in the air.

"Thunder, we enjoyed doing the Stomp Dance." Tim said as he looked around at the boys and Thunder. "We were hoping we could do that again with you."

"Absolutely. Let's meet around the tree." Thunder led them out to the tree.

Holt felt a tug on his pants, and he looked down. "Hey, Bryce. What's up?"

"Will you do the dance with us? Do you know how to do it?" Bryce crunched up his face in confusion.

Holt squatted down to his height. "Of course, I'll do it with you guys. Frey and Barrett taught me how to do it."

"Will you stand next to me and hold my hand?" Holt felt his heart swell hearing Bryce's words. *How could anyone not want this sweet young boy?*

"I would love to." Holt took his hand and was ready to stand up when Bryce threw his arms around Holt's neck for a tight hug. *Oh Yeah, this kid already had him wrapped around his finger. He would do anything for him.* Holt picked up Bryce and placed him on his hip, carrying him to the circle around the tree.

Everyone was lined up when Holt joined the group at the end of the line and set Bryce down. Alex led the dance for a few minutes before stopping to face the boys.

"I gotta go make your lunch, but lucky for you that you have Holt. He knows all our songs and can lead you in the dance. Holt." Alex waved at him to come over. "Why don't you and Bryce lead the boys?"

"I can lead with Holt?" Bryce's eyes bugged out.

"Yep." Holt led Bryce to the front and grabbed the rattle from Alex. "We're in this together now."

"Let's go Bryce! You got this!" Tim screamed and started chanting Bryce. The boys chanted with Tim. Holt looked down and saw Bryce beaming at everyone. *Yeah, he loved these boys.*

Holt and Bryce led the dancing until Alex came out and announced that lunch was ready. Everyone went to wash their hands and use the restroom before lunch. Holt, Thunder, Alex, and Mark let the boys get their food first. After Holt loaded up his plate, he noticed several tables were pushed together so they could all sit at one long table. He chose the seat next to Bryce. Holt noticed Bryce had a dessert fry bread not a taco one. Then he remembered Frey telling him Bryce didn't like the taco toppings on his fry bread. Alex must've remembered and made a special one for Bryce.

"Chef Alex?" Tim asked after he swallowed a large bite. "Do we get the dessert fry bread also?"

"Yup," Alex smiled. "I'll make those real quick after you finish eating."

The boys hooted and hollered with excitement.

Tim, Luke, Kenny, and Jimmy wanted to know about working as a security guard. Holt was happy to answer all their questions? Maybe someday they would want a job at the casino and Holt could guide them in the right direction.

"You know Mark" –Holt pointed at Mark near the end of the table– "is training to be a security officer for Thunder. He can answer some of your questions, too."

"Really?" Luke turned toward Mark. "That is so cool, man."

"Yep." Mark shook his head. "Bossman said I could. Since I'm in the process of getting my license, I'd be happy to answer any questions you guys might have. If I don't know the answer" –Mark signaled with a chin lift at Holt– "I can call Holt or Barrett, Frey and Chef Alex's other brother, and find out."

"Thanks, man." Luke smiled and continued eating.

It seemed like Mark was connecting with Luke. Bryce stayed next to Holt the entire time. He wanted to know more about his three musketeers' friendship with Frey and Barrett.

By the time the boys left, Holt felt lighter and happier. He'd felt a kinship with those boys. For the first time, he'd opened up to someone other than Barrett and wasn't embarrassed by his feelings or the things he lived through. Those boys understood and immediately welcomed him into their group. He was glad Frey had suggested for him to become a mentor to them. He truly believed they could all heal each other.

Holt spoke to Thunder about coming whenever the boys came to visit and going with Thunder when he visited the shelter. Holt also wanted to invite them to the resort so they could go swimming. He would speak to Sehoy and Osceola and get all the details worked out.

Chapter 55

Girls' Night Out

Frey

F rey was going stir crazy stuck in her room. The doctor's release papers said she wasn't allowed to work for at least a week, no heavy lifting, and must do "light walking" every couple of hours. Her parents, siblings, and Tori frequently visited to keep her company, play games, and walk circles around their floor. She wasn't the type of person to stay in bed and, after a couple of days, was eager to return to her daily routine.

It was difficult for her to go to Holt's room and talk to him because she always had someone with her. On the rare occasion she was alone and heard him, she'd hurry into his room to talk to him. But he'd make an excuse and leave. She was having little success in her efforts to communicate with him.

Feeling restless and depressed a week after her stabbing, Frey reached out to the girls and invited them over for a Girls' Night Out at the resort pool. She wasn't sure about going into the water, but she could at least dip her legs in and talk to her tribe. Hanging out with the girls was just what she needed to cheer her up.

Changing into her tankini for easier bathroom access, she laid on her couch in her living room, waiting for Tori to knock on her door. They had agreed to walk down together. Everyone else was meeting them downstairs.

Next week was Thanksgiving. It was the day she and Holt had planned to reveal their relationship to their family. Now, because of the last week, their relationship was nonexistent. At some point, she hoped to catch Holt alone and have a conversation with him. She missed him.

When Frey heard a knock, she got up, looked through the peephole, and saw Tori smiling on the other side of the door. Pulling the door open, she greeted her friend and held the door open for her to come in.

"Hi." Tori wore her yellow bikini. Frey was pretty sure Alex had not seen her in it yet. He likely would have requested her to switch to a one-piece. "Let's go."

"Uh, did Alex approve of your attire?" Frey waved her hands up and down in front of Tori.

"Did Holt approve of yours?" Tori sassed back.

"Hey, I covered up my stomach." Frey exclaimed as she stepped out and shut her door.

"Yeah, but your boobs are almost hanging out." Tori wound her arm around Frey's.

"I can't help it. I have big boobs." Frey always had a hard time keeping the girls in bathing suits.

"You have nice boobs. Don't sweat it," Tori said as she guided Frey into the elevator. "I like to say flaunt it if you got it."

"No, you don't," Frey shoulder checked her. "I have never heard you say that."

"You're right, I don't. My bestie does." Tori shoulder bumped her right back. Frey laughed because it was something she would say. Alex was right, she was rubbing off on her best friend. Not that she'd tell Alex that he was right.

Frey followed Tori to the outside tables. They had already pushed two tables together to accommodate six people.

"Uh, no." Frey heard Alex before she saw him.

Alex came up to Tori, spun her around, and with his hands on her hips, guided her back inside. "You are not wearing that."

"Alex, stop," Tori giggled while she tried to plant her feet and stop his momentum.

"Baby, why don't you wear a one piece?" Alex begged.

"I told you," Frey sing-songed from the table.

"You're going to be working throughout the whole time we're here. If anything happens, I know you will be the first one out to rescue me." Tori wrapped her arms around him.

"Fine, but I don't like it," Alex grumbled. Tori gave him a quick kiss. "We prepared a charcuterie board specifically for you ladies. I'll bring it out when everyone arrives. What do you ladies want to drink?"

"I'll take a frozen margarita," Frey declared, closing the drink menu.

"Me too," Tori sat across from Frey. "That sounds yummy and refreshing."

"You got it ladies." Alex headed to the bar.

"I knew he would lose his temper." Frey reclined in her seat.

"Yeah, well, I've successfully tamed the beast," Tori giggled, "for now."

"Hey ladies, what's up?" Maggie was the first to join them, followed by Isa, Sarah, and Gaby.

"Did all of you arrive together?" Tori asked, as they exchanged hugs.

Frey stood waiting to hug them after Tori. The only one in their group that was single was Maggie. She'd been dating someone, but it hadn't worked out. Maggie and Isa were best friends who met at the ad agency where they both worked.

"When everyone came to my house, Thunder and Grayhorse offered to drive us so everyone could drink." Isa announced to the group. "I informed my sexy hubby and brother-in-law that I could drive because I can't drink since I'm carrying Thunder's love child." Isa smiled and rubbed her belly. "But the boys insisted on joining us. They said they wanted to check out the casino, maybe gamble. I don't buy it, but that's what they said." Isa leaned over the table as best she could and whispered. "Since they don't gamble, I'm pretty sure they will be showing up to join us soon."

"Yep, they'll sneak out here eventually," Sarah winked at Isa, her sister-in-law.

"Well, if they stayed at my house, they'd be getting their hair done by Lucy," Gaby laughed along with all of them. Gaby was married to Matteo, Isa's brother. They had two beautiful little girls. Lucy, the youngest liked to braid Thunder, Grayhorse, and Alex's hair. The oldest Emmy was best buds with Tommy who was Sarah and Grayhorse's son.

"Ladies, I see you're all here." Alex held two charcuterie boards, one in each hand. "I'll set these down for you and Tiffany will take your drink orders." Tiffany set down Tori and Frey's margaritas and wrote everyone else's order.

"This looks so good." Maggie took a piece of cheese and wrapped it in salami. "Tori, I wish I had a personal chef like you."

"Maggie, you need to stop dating hooligans." Isa chose a piece of fruit.

Tiffany returned carrying plates and Isa's water.

"Hooligans? Who says that?" Maggie laughed.

"Ryan was a nice guy." Isa pointed a cracker at Maggie.

"Ryan was boring. I want some adventure." Maggie dropped her chin in her hand.

"No, you don't," Isa, Tori and Frey said at the same time.

"Okay, not like the adventures you guys have had. I want a guy that likes to have fun and do spontaneous things. Is that too much to ask for?" Maggie let out an exasperated sigh.

"And cooks," Tori filled in.

"And is good in bed," Isa blurted out.

"Fine, you guys have good men. It's my chance now. So, help a girl out." Maggie stuffed her mouth while they laughed at her. "I'm the only one without a partner now that Frey is with Holt."

Frey stopped laughing. "I'm not so sure Holt and I are still together. How did you find out about our relationship?"

Tori scrunched her face. "I'm sorry. I told them about your stabbing, Frey."

"Oh," Frey sighed, "that's okay. I'm glad you all know, because I don't feel like rehashing it. Did Tori mention I was pregnant and had a miscarriage?" Frey looked around and saw widened eyes and open mouths. *Nope, they didn't know.*

"No." Isa was the first to answer. "I'm so sorry. That must have been difficult. What can we do for you guys?"

These were the closest friends Frey had. She honestly believed it was best for everyone to know everything that had happened. They might help her get Holt back.

"I'll give you the short version of us. I've had a crush on Holt for a long time. Apparently, he's had a crush on me since high school, but Barrett made him promise not to date me." Frey rolled her eyes.

"What? Why?" Sarah looked confused. "I dated Grayhorse, and he was Thunder's best friend."

"Barrett didn't want Holt to treat me like another notch on his bedpost and was trying to protect me. He was also afraid of losing his best friend to me, and vice versa. So, Holt and I started dating about a month ago and kept it a secret. Which really pissed off Barrett when he found out." Frey reached for another slice of cheese.

"How did he find out?" Maggie asked after she took a sip of her drink.

"After Holt's mom stabbed me at the casino, they rushed me to the hospital for emergency surgery. When the doctor talked to my family and Holt after surgery, he told them he couldn't save the baby." Frey's eyes watered and she placed her hand on her stomach.

"Oh my God, Frey." Gaby covered her open mouth with her hands. "That's awful. Did you know you were pregnant?"

"Unfortunately, no. I'd been having morning sickness, but I thought it was from something I ate or drank the night before. I know I was stupid." Frey sighed.

"You were not stupid." Sarah stood up and knelt beside Frey. "I've been pregnant twice, and it still comes as a surprise when I find out because I don't always look at my calendar to check my cycle. Then again, I'm not sure why it surprises me, I can't keep Grayhorse off me." Sarah rolled her eyes.

"Is that stud constantly mounting his mare?" Maggie burst out laughing.

Frey appreciated Maggie's comment, lightening the mood.

"So, you haven't talked to Holt yet?" Tori raised an eyebrow. "It's been a week."

Frey harrumphed. "I've been waiting to get him alone, but one of us always seems to be busy."

"I would keep trying." Isa grabbed a cracker and pointed it at her. "You might have to corner him somewhere that he can't leave like I did with Thunder. Maybe late at night when he doesn't have anywhere to go or anything to do. That's what I did with Thunder when I needed to set him straight."

"Yeah, but a word of advice. Don't throw a rock at his window." Sarah stood and grinned at Isa. "I hear windows can be quite pricey to replace."

"Served him right." Isa humphed.

"Oh ladies, just send them to my house and Lucy will embarrass them with a new hairstyle." Gaby laughed.

"I don't know. I think they like Lucy's Hair Salon." Isa chuckled.

"I wouldn't know." Maggie took a dramatically deep sigh. "I've never been invited."

"Well, we'll change that." Gaby finished her drink. "Next time Lucy's Hair Salon is open for business, I'll let you know."

"Thanks, Gabs." Maggie smiled.

They all laughed at Maggie's craziness. Frey reached out for another piece of cheese and noticed all the food was gone. "Do you guys want more food?" All the ladies shook their heads.

"Let's go in the water," Maggie stood up and took off her cover up.

"I'm gonna sit on the side. I still have a dressing over my sutures." Frey followed the ladies and sat with her legs dangling in the pool.

"Can we stay in the shallow end?" Maggie asked while stepping in. "So, I can keep sipping on my margarita?"

"Sure, your drinks are in plastic cups," Frey nodded.

"Isa, I'm gonna get you a raft so you can chill." Sarah went to the poolside rental area and got a chair raft for Isa.

"Best sister-in-law EVER!" Isa shouted when Sarah dropped it in the pool. "Shoot, sorry Gaby." Isa winced.

"It's all good." Gaby smiled and shoulder checked Isa. "I didn't even think of getting you a raft."

"Sarah, Gaby, don't let me float too far away from everyone. I'm not sure I could get back." Isa said after she plopped into the raft.

Frey saw them all laughing. As she looked around, she realized this was exactly what she needed. They could all joke around with each other and no one got offended. If she wanted advice, they gave it. And when the mood got too heavy, she could always count on Maggie to make everyone smile.

Chapter 56

Overprotective Men...Gotta Love Them

Frey

Maggie, Tori, and Gaby swam away together while Sarah playfully pushed Isa around in the pool. Frey thoroughly enjoyed watching them goof off. Glad they could all come.

"It appears your friends have deserted you. Can I buy you a drink?" Frey's body jolted at the sound of the man's voice, who was crouching beside her.

"Oh. No, thank you. They'll be back in a few minutes." Frey looked back, pleading for Tori to return her gaze.

"I can't let a beautiful lady sit by the pool all alone. I'll keep you company until they return." He sat on his butt and dropped his legs into the water. "My name's Rob. What's yours?"

"Taken." Frey heard Holt's voice growl from behind them. Holt was standing in full uniform, feet apart, arms crossed, with a mean expression on his face.

"Oh, sorry, man." Rob bolted up faster than Frey thought possible. "I didn't know she was dating someone."

"Well, now, you do." Holt stared him down.

Frey watched the man flee from them to the other side of the pool.

"What the fuck are you wearing?" Holt grumbled.

"A bathing suit," Frey squinted up at him.

Holt squatted to her level before he responded. "Put a fucking shirt on. Your tits are on display for every man to see."

"You act as if you care," Frey said, turning toward the water and kicking her legs. Frey knew she was baiting him, but if he was so angry with her bathing suit, then he still had feelings for her. She could work with that, even if he was ignoring her.

"I do care," Holt said between gritted teeth. "I want you to be safe."

"I have enough brothers. I don't need another one," Frey grumbled.

"Well, you fucking have another one. Now put a damn shirt on." Holt whispered in her ear, since the girls were swimming toward them.

"I can't. I didn't bring one." Frey glared at him.

"Hey, Holt." Tori spoke up when she reached them. "How are you?"

Frey appreciated Tori's timing.

"Does your boyfriend know you're half naked in the pool?" Holt turned his venom on Tori.

"Hey." Frey backhanded him in the chest. "Your problem is with me. Leave her alone."

"For your information, Alex is watching." Tori nodded her head. "Look behind you."

Both Frey and Holt looked over and saw Alex squinting at them. Frey was doing a happy dance inside. Point for Tori. You go, girl!

Frey turned to Holt, ready to test his patience. "Cat got your tongue?" She smirked.

Holt leaned in and whispered in her ear. "Don't play with me or I'll spank your ass."

"Promises, promises," Frey mumbled.

"Hey, what's up?" Thunder and Grayhorse came to the pool wearing their swim trunks.

"Hey sexy," Sarah winked at her hubby.

The boys had officially crashed their girls' night. Frey didn't mind. They were fun to be around. Plus, they gave her a reprieve from her verbal sparring match with Holt.

In the water, Grayhorse approached Sarah, and she greeted him with a passionate kiss.

"Hey," Thunder smacked Grayhorse in the back of the head. "There are kids here. Besides, I don't need that burned into my retina." Grayhorse and Sarah laughed, and Thunder swam to Isa. "Hi, honey."

Alex also came over in his swim trunks. "I'm off for the night. Come here, gorgeous." Alex swam to Tori. Just a short while ago, Tori's only swimming technique was doggie paddling. Thanks to Alex's instruction, she could now swim short distances.

"I need to return to work. Alex will keep an eye on you." Holt stood.

"I can take care of myself. No need for someone to keep an eye on me." Frey wished Holt could stay there with her and enjoy the pool with their friends. She was positive he could've taken the night off. Sitting back, she pushed her chest out and kicked her legs in the pool.

"Yeah, right." Holt's parting words left a bitter taste in her mouth.

"Hey, I'll sit with you. Us single girls gotta stick together." Maggie put her fist up for a fist bump. "Aww come on, don't leave a girl hangin'."

Frey ignored Holt's growl and returned Maggie's fist bump. Out of the corner of her eye, she saw Holt glare at her before he walked away. He must not have been too happy with the single girl comment.

"I don't think he liked our single girl fist bump." Maggie covered her mouth and giggled.

"I think you're right." Frey took a sip of her drink.

"I like the way you pushed your girls out. It'll give him something to think about. It's a shame there're kids in the pool. You could've ripped your top off and dove into the pool. I bet he would've followed you." Maggie wiggled her eyebrows.

"Oh my God, Maggie!" Frey used her foot to push her shoulder. "I could never do that."

"Don't lie to me. You know you would. Especially if it was at night and no one was around. Nudge, nudge, wink, wink." Maggie poked her leg and winked at her.

"You are so bad," Frey laughed.

"Hang out with me, and I'll show you all my tricks." Maggie sipped her drink. "Ooh, maybe we can go dancing one night. Do you dance?"

"I love to dance, but I need to wait until this heals." Frey pointed to her side.

She would love to go dancing. Last time she danced other than their yearly pow-wows was at her high school prom. She remembered wishing that Holt would ask her, but he took another girl. That drive to prom was uncomfortable, to say the least. She didn't have a date—she was meeting her friends there. But Barrett and Holt had dates which they had to pick up...and they had to take a million photos with the girls and their families at the park.

Ugh...it had been so painful as soon as they got to the dance. She looked for her friends and left them. Avoiding them had been easy on a crowded dance floor. But when the slow songs came on and most people cleared out, it was hard not to see Holt and his date pressed close together. Her teenage heart broke a little more during every slow dance.

"Frey?" Maggie tapped her thigh. "Are you okay? I didn't mean to upset you. We don't have to go dancing. We can just go to a bar and get a drink."

"Sorry. I zoned out for a bit." Frey sighed.

"That look on your face was so sad. What were you thinking about?" Maggie finished her drink.

"Holt with another girl." Frey didn't want to go into the entire story now. Thinking of Holt with another girl always saddened her.

"I haven't known you guys that long, but I see the way he looks at you. I don't think you have to worry about him seeing someone else." Maggie crossed her arms on the edge of the pool and laid her chin on top. "I wish someone would look at me like that."

"Someday, some guy will. How could they not? You're funny, nice, and so full of life." Frey nudged her shoulder with her knee. "So, dancing?"

"Yep." Maggie nodded. "Just let me know when you're ready and we'll go."

"Where are we going?" Gaby asked Maggie. Matteo, her husband, was watching the kids and couldn't come with the guys.

"Dancin' girl!" Maggie grabbed Gaby's hands, and they began to salsa in the water.

Frey didn't know Maggie could salsa. I guess it paid off to hang out with Isa, who was Cuban. Impressive.

Seeing all the couples paired off in a loving embrace caused Frey to yearn for it to be her and Holt. She missed his kisses, hugs, dominance in the bedroom, but most of all his love. She hoped they could get back to the way they were, they just needed time.

Laughter and jokes filled the pool as they all enjoyed themselves. Frey didn't see Holt the rest of the night. It was probably a good thing, considering his bad mood. She knew she would see him at brunch tomorrow.

Chapter 57

Brunch Day Blues

Holt

L ast night, Frey had tested his patience. He knew he wasn't up to her standards, but did she have to wear such a revealing bathing suit to attract some other guy? After Alex got in the pool, Holt stayed away. It was by pure luck he had even seen her. He'd needed caffeine and went to RUSH for a cup when he saw that guy talking to her. His jealousy overpowered him, and without realizing it, he was stomping her way.

She had been right to get mad at him, but he couldn't help himself. Avoiding her was his best choice. A hard thing to do, considering they lived and worked in the same building. Fuck! He lucked out that she hadn't stormed into his room through their adjoining door after everyone left. She had a lock on her side, but he didn't—a future investment he might need to make.

Since he'd been home, he spent a lot of time with Barrett repairing their friendship. He knew he needed to talk to Frey. He just didn't know what to say. *Are we still together? Why did you throw our love away? Do you still love me?*

Today was going to wear on him because it was family brunch day and he always sat next to Frey. He'd tried to get out of going, but Sehoy told him he needed to be there. He delayed getting there by wandering around the resort and casino after his workout, hoping the empty seat wouldn't be next to Frey. Checking his watch, he saw that brunch started five minutes ago. It was time to suck it up and act like an adult. He didn't want to disappoint Sehoy.

As he walked into Savor, he noticed everyone was already seated and the only empty seat was beside Frey. *Son of a bitch!* He should have arrived earlier and sat in a different chair. He knew it would've caused some raised eyebrows because they always sat in the same seats, but it would've been worth a try.

"Good morning, everyone." Holt nodded and sat.

"Where have you been?" Barrett began passing the food around.

"I was walking around the resort and casino making sure everything was okay." Holt grabbed the Chicken Parmesan. It puzzled him why they still used the term brunch. Ever since Alex started preparing meals, they always had lunch items on the menu, not breakfast. He supposed it was from when they were young and Sehoy cooked. She prepared egg casseroles and kept sliced deli meat handy for sandwiches. "Sorry, I didn't mean to hold up brunch."

"You held nothing up, chakpootsi." Sehoy passed the spaghetti. "We just sat down. Ladies, how was your Girls' Night Out? Did everyone have a good time?"

"We had a lot of fun," Tori passed the rolls. "The guys eventually joined us in the pool. Thank you for letting us have it here."

"We are all family." Sehoy smiled at everyone around the table. "Next time, we must invite them and their families. I think the children would love to swim in the pool."

"We've been talking about that forever" –Tori rolled her eyes– "but haven't found the right date."

"What about having everyone over for Thanksgiving?" Sehoy's eyes brightened. Holt knew Sehoy would love to add more guests to her Thanksgiving table. Adjusting his leg, he bumped Frey.

"Sorry." Holt rumbled not making eye contact.

"It's okay." Frey whispered. "Are you ever going to talk to me again?"

"I've had things to do." Holt ignoring Frey and pretended to listen to the conversation at the table. *How could this girl that hurt him still mean so much to him?* He still loved her, but felt twisted up inside.

"I don't mind cooking for everyone. I'm off on Thanksgiving. Thunder is closing the cultural center because of the holiday," Alex said between bites. "Besides, I made a promise to Sarah to cook a meal and to Tommy that he could bring his friend Emmy and go swimming."

"Oh, Osceola, what do you think?" Sehoy gently rested her hand on his arm.

"I love the idea of having everyone here for a big family Thanksgiving. Tori, why don't you reach out to everyone and see if they can make it? Since Thanksgiving is only a few days away, they might already have plans. This will work out great. I need to talk to Thunder about expansion plans for our resort."

"We're expanding, *chacteka*?" Barrett glanced at his father.

"The tribal council wants us to add a couple of conference rooms to the resort. We are still in talks about where they will be added. We like what Thunder did with the cultural center and would like to get his opinion especially since he studied architecture." Osceola spoke between bites.

Holt thought that sounded like a good idea. Thunder had done a great job designing the cultural center. He could talk to Mark about working some extra hours as one of their security officers on the days or nights he was off.

"He is good at planning spaces. I can't wait to see what he comes up with." Barrett took a drink.

"Will we be adding a kitchen?" Alex inquired, looking up.

"Maybe. We'll see what Thunder comes up with." Osceola nodded.

Holt stayed silent throughout the conversation, trying not to bring attention to himself and Frey. The topic of Thanksgiving was ideal and kept everyone occupied. The anticipation grew as people eagerly discussed the schedule of events and calculated the expected attendance. So far, the head count was nineteen. Holt watched Tori pullout her phone and start texting.

"I just sent a message to all the ladies inviting them and their families. I'll call my parents when I get upstairs. I'll text Mark and Thunder separately. Osceola, I'll give Thunder a heads up and have him call you, if that's okay?" Tori looked around. "That's it right?"

"Thank you, *chackshosti*," Osceola smiled at Tori.

"As far as I can think." Alex kissed her cheek. "Good job, baby."

Holt cleared his throat and asked, "Could we invite the shelter kids?"

"I don't see why not," Osceola looked at Sehoy.

"We would love to meet them." Sehoy gazed into Osceola's eyes and held his hand.

Osceola and Sehoy had been married for over thirty years. With divorce running rampant, Holt liked to see the love shining in their eyes for each other. He'd craved that for himself with Frey.

Throughout the meal, Holt noticed Sehoy giving him questioning looks. Holt acted as if he didn't notice her. What did she want him to do?

"Holt, can you help me in the kitchen for a minute?" Sehoy stood and grabbed her plate.

"Of course." Holt grabbed his plate and followed her. "What can I help you with?"

"Can you go into the pantry and get me the powdered sugar for our dessert? It's on the top shelf and I can't reach it." Sehoy walked out of the kitchen.

Holt entered the compact pantry and examined the highest shelf. He didn't know why Sehoy sent him to get the sugar when this was Alex's kitchen, and he was sitting at the table with them. Sure, he was tall, but Alex was just as tall, and he knew where everything was. Checking the top shelf, Holt only saw small appliances and boxes of condiments, none of which were powdered sugar. "*Chatski*!" he called out. "I don't see the powdered sugar!"

Chapter 58

Mending Hearts

Holt

Turning to leave the pantry, he saw Frey being forcefully pushed into him and then the door slammed shut. Holt caught her before she fell. Both exchanged confused looks, unsure of what was going on. As the lock clicked shut, they realized someone had set them up. Turning around, Frey pounded on the door.

"Let us out!" Frey screamed.

"Neither of you are coming out of there until you talk and figure your shit out!" Alex yelled. "*Chatski's* orders."

"Really?" Holt moved Frey aside and tried the door. When it didn't budge, he rammed it with his shoulder.

"Don't you dare fucking break my door Holt! Sit your ass down and talk!" Alex hollered.

"Now what?" Holt threw up his arms. *What the hell was going on?*

"If we ever want to leave this pantry, we should probably start talking." Frey paced.

"We could wait them out." Holt leaned his back against the door and slid down to the floor, sitting with his knees raised and his hands hanging between his knees. *What were they thinking, locking them up in the pantry? What if there was an emergency and they forgot about them?*

"It's not even one and the dinner crowd doesn't start coming in until four." Frey stared at him like he was an idiot. *Well, shit, how was he supposed to know the restaurant hours? It's not like he worked in either of them.*

"They gotta come in to prep the food, right?" Holt rolled his eyes. *He had smart ideas. Why was she looking at him like that?*

"Not for another two hours! Plus, if I know Alex, and I do. He planned this with my mom, and he needs nothing from in here." Frey ran her hand over her hair. "Besides, I need to talk to you."

"No, you don't." Holt stayed seated. Placing his elbows on his knees, he became absorbed in his fidgeting fingers. He knew they needed to talk, but what if she still wanted to dump him? That was the main reason he had avoided her. He didn't want to feel that heartbreak again.

"Yes, I do." Frey got on her knees in front of him. She clung to his hands, capturing his attention. Glancing upward, her stunning brown eyes instantly mesmerized him. "Holt, I apologize. I can't say that enough. My intention was never to push you away."

"You didn't push me away, Frey—you threw me away, like trash." Holt corrected. His chest tightening, he was finding it hard to breathe. "You abandoned me when I needed you the most." *How could she have turned on him when he was always telling her he loved her?*

"I know, and I'm so sorry. I prioritized comforting Barrett and forgot about the impact it had on you. Abandoning you was never my intention. After calming Barrett down, I was going to come talk to you. Holt, I need you, and I don't want to live without you. I love you. We need to grieve for our baby together." Frey ended with her voice so low he had to listen closely to hear her.

Holt let out a slow breath, feeling relieved now that he knew she still wanted him. He pulled her in close, sitting her on his lap and positioning her legs around him. He needed to feel her body against his. The magnetic pull was too strong to ignore when she was this close. Holt placed one palm around her back and the other behind her head holding her against his chest.

"I'm so sorry about our baby. But maybe it's a good thing in the end. I'm not sure I would be a good father. My father was never around for me." Holt mumbled into the side of her hair.

Frey moved back and grasped his face with both hands. "That's bullshit. Look at me, Holt Adams." Holt gazed into her eyes. "You are the best man I know. Despite facing many challenges, you only resort to violence when defending yourself or your loved ones. Hell, you allowed Barret to hit you at least twice that I could tell, because you felt bad for hurting him by lying to him. You know, right from wrong. You're honorable, loyal, giving, and caring. Someday, you will be an amazing dad."

"How do you know, Frey?" Holt was desperate for her answer. Barrett had told him he would make a good dad, but he wanted to hear it from the woman he loved.

"Because you've had good examples, like my dad. Osceola may not be your biological father, but he raised you like his son. You've also witnessed exceptional men who work here that are amazing fathers. You've seen their loving interactions with their children." Frey leaned her forehead against his.

"What if I fuck up?" Holt gripped her waist tightly.

"We all fuck up. I'm sure sometimes my dad wished he had done something differently, but the great thing is you have my dad to help guide you." Frey gave him a light kiss. "I'm sure I will fuck up, too. There's no manual for raising kids, but with love and teamwork, we can navigate it together." Frey leaned back and stared at him. "Can you still love me after everything I said?"

"Sweetheart, I will always love you." Holt would never stop loving her until he drew his last breath. Even then, he hoped to love her and be with her in the afterlife. Their love was limitless.

"But?" Frey started trembling and crying. "Did I lose you?"

"My love for you will never waver, but please promise me you won't abandon and reject me like that again. I can't bear to experience that twice. It's too hard on my heart." That's what hurt Holt the most. He wanted to trust that she would never leave him again. It might take some time, but he was hopeful.

"I promise, I won't ever do that again." Frey wrapped her arms around his neck and held on tight. "Holt. I miss our baby," Frey mumbled.

Holt held her tightly against his chest. She was his lifeline, his soulmate. They would have to comfort each other and let go of the grief.

Holt pictured himself rocking their baby to sleep. In his mind, their baby was a little girl that looked like Frey. When she cried at night because she was hungry, Holt would pick her up and bring her to Frey to breast feed and lay next to them, enjoying every moment he could be with them. If Frey didn't want to breastfeed, then he would give her a bottle so Frey could sleep and relax. Thinking about all those lost moments he would never have with his baby flashed through his mind bringing him to tears. He would be a hands-on dad and help with diaper changes, feedings, temper tantrums, anything his little girl needed. He could picture her as a little toddler with cute pigtails and a sassy attitude just like her momma.

They were both trembling in each other's arms. So much pain leaking out with their tears that they soaked Holt's shirt. When their trembling stopped, Holt rested his head on top of hers and ran his hand over her back. He continued to comfort her until their breathing went back to normal. They'd needed this moment with each other to think about what could've been and lay their baby to rest.

Holt brushed her hair away from her face, raised her head, and used his thumbs to wipe her tears. "Sweetheart, I will always miss what could have been. But I want to spend forever with you. We can keep using whatever form of birth control you want until we get married and when the time is right, we'll talk about starting a family."

"You want to marry me?" Frey's smile quivered.

"I always wanted to marry you. Ever since you rescued me from those bullies at the water fountain. My love for you has never wavered. Even after everything that's happened between us, I want you with me forever." Holt kissed her deeply. "I love you more every day. You are my everything."

"I love you too, Holt." Frey gifted him with one of her bright smiles that lit up her eyes with happiness.

"I meant to tell you I went to the cultural center and met the shelter kids. When they were all sitting on the floor staring at me wondering who I was, I decided to tell them my story. You were right. We can help each other. I'm going to mentor them, but I gotta admit I also took a special liking to Bryce. I now understand how you fell in love with him so quickly. He wrapped himself around my heart too." Holt hugged her. Maybe Bryce could have a future with them someday now that they were staying together.

"Oh, honey. I'm so happy to hear you say that." Frey kissed Holt.

The sweetness of their kiss was transforming into an intense craving. It had been a long time since they had made love. Frey was grinding against him on the floor. Engaging in make-up sex here was not his preferred choice.

"Frey," Holt said between kisses while he held her hips in place. "Let's go back to my room."

"Okay." Frey whispered longingly.

Holt got to his feet and helped Frey stand.

"You good?" Holt cupped her face.

"I'll be better when you're inside me." Frey smiled and pushed her hips against his.

"Done." Holt grabbed her hand and pounded on the door. "Alex! We're good. Let us out!"

Holt noticed the door unlocking and spotted Alex on the opposite side.

"Took you long enough." Alex slapped Holt on the back and hugged Frey.

"We weren't in there that long," Frey giggled.

"If you think two hours is not long, okay?" Alex laughed. "Everything's good?"

"Everything's outstanding," Frey said, wrapping her arm around the hand she was holding. "Holt's going to teach me all about make-up sex."

"Oh man, really? I didn't need to hear that." Alex placed one hand on his hip and the other pinching between his eyes while Holt and Frey laughed at him.

"Gotta go." Holt pulled Frey out of the kitchen.

Holt couldn't believe Frey had said that to her brother. Ultimately, this ended up being the most amazing Sunday Brunch ever.

Chapter 59

Thanksgiving Morning

Frey

Holt and Frey were inseparable for the days leading up to Thanksgiving. Frey had gone back to work on Tuesday for just a few hours and Holt always stayed by her table, guarding her. She was sure over time he would become less protective. Okay, who was she kidding? He probably wouldn't, but Frey loved having him close. Now that they were always together at night and Winston was staying in jail, Frey removed the chair from under the adjoining door to Tori's room.

Thanksgiving Panther style was underway. They were expecting thirty-three people for Thanksgiving Dinner including the five shelter boys. Gaby, Aurora, Sarah, and Isa offered to bring a dish, but Alex wasn't having it. He was ecstatic to be cooking for everyone. Alex closed Savor for their meal. But at six they were opening it to the public for a special Thanksgiving menu. Bernie offered to work so Alex could enjoy some family time after the meal.

Dyani, Tall Bear, and Lizzy (Tori's parents and sister) flew in from South Dakota with Spirit-of-the-Eagle last night. Tori's family didn't want to stay in Tori's old room—too many terrible memories. Therefore, Frey gave her room to Tori's family, and she stayed in Holt's room. Lizzy, Tori's younger sister, was fine sleeping on the couch because she could watch cable TV into the night. Thunder wanted to spend more time with his Uncle Spirit, so he stayed with them.

Frey was excited to have so many friends and family come over to give thanks, that she volunteered to do the table seating and set up. Everyone was told to bring their bathing suits so they could enjoy the pool after their feast. Of course, the casino was also open to the adults and the public. Frey anticipated Tori would struggle to keep her dad, Tall Bear, away from the casino.

Thanksgiving was a busy time in the resort and casino. They never shut down. Their employees who worked today could eat a Thanksgiving meal for free and got paid time and a half.

After a great night of lovemaking with her man, they had taken a shower together—to conserve water, Holt had said. She called bullshit because after getting him off in the shower and fucking her brains out, partaking in mutual orgasms, she was pretty sure they ran more water than if they had showered separately. But she wasn't complaining. It was a mutually satisfying shower.

Frey got out before they started another round. Holt was hard to resist. Plus, she needed to get dressed and start setting up downstairs. The seating chart Frey made was on the bed while she analyzed it—again. *Should she have just let everyone sit where they wanted? Would they hate their assigned seats? Would they get mad at her?* Frey wanted everyone to enjoy themselves. Wanting a second opinion, she texted Tori and asked her to come to her room.

Holt had just gotten out of the shower with a towel wrapped around his waist. He looked yummy. Too bad Tori was on her way.

"Get dressed." Frey eye fucked him from his toes to his lips. "Tori is on her way."

"Then stop looking at me like that," Holt grumbled as he undid the knot on the towel and let it drop to the floor. "Are you sure you want to let her in?"

"No, but I need to talk to her." Frey stared at his cock and licked her lips.

"You're killing me, sweetheart." Holt strolled to her, grabbed her face, and kissed the hell out of her. Just when it started getting good, she heard the knock on the door.

"Later," Holt mumbled against her lips and strode off into his closet to get dressed.

Frey stood in the room with her hands on her hips as she stared up at the ceiling and took some deep breaths. He was destroying her. The knocking now turned into pounding, snapping her out of her sexual haze.

"Frey, Holt," Tori yelled, "are you guy's descent?"

Frey swung the door open and smiled. "Yes, bestie. Sorry, we were a little busy."

"I bet you were." Tori pointed to her neck. "Nice hickey, by the way."

"Aw, shit." Frey slapped her neck. She knew exactly where Holt had put it. Last night, he fucked her hard and sucked her neck until he came. He was proud of himself for marking his territory. Frey threatened to mark him up, but Holt loved the idea. So instead, Frey playfully slapped him on the chest and told him not to put it in a visible place again until after they were married. She didn't want her dad or brothers to have a heart attack. They had to know Holt and Frey were having sex, but that was just a visual they shouldn't see. "I'm gonna have to cover that up before mom and dad see it. Follow me. What I need to show you is in the bedroom." Frey strode away.

"I bet it is," Tori giggled.

"Since when did you get such a dirty mind?" Frey turned and laughed.

"Since I met you and hooked up with your brother."

"Hey, Tori," Holt stepped out of the closet fully dressed.

"Hi Holt. I'd ask how you're doing, but from the huge hickey on the side of Frey's neck, I'd say you're doing great." Tori grinned.

Frey's mouth dropped as she stared at her friend, who was once an innocent young lady and would never joke about sex.

"I'm doing great." Holt walked up behind Frey, placed his hand on her belly, and pressed her against his chest. Kissing her hickey before resting his chin on her shoulder.

"Okay." Frey placed one hand on Holt's forearm and pointed to the seating chart mounted on the foam core laying on the bed. "I need your opinion. What do you think? I'm gonna put it on an easel downstairs when we go down there."

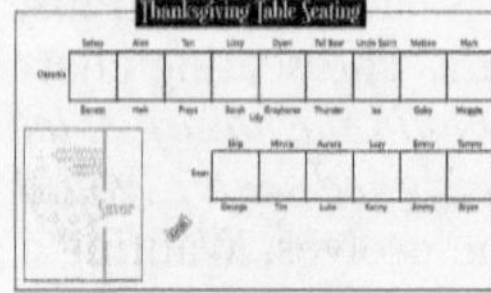

"It looks great, sweetheart." Holt kissed her cheek.

"Do you think everyone will be fine with the seating arrangements I made?" Frey turned to him, biting her lip.

"If they don't, let them know they can switch their seats." Holt pulled her lip free of her teeth and pulled her in for a kiss. "No one will care. The most important thing is that we are all together."

"You are so smart." Holt's words soothed her and helped her realize this was about everyone being together, not where they were sitting.

"Okay, I know I'm in your bedroom and all, but let's focus and get back to work." Tori smiled at them. "I love saying that since Frey always interrupted me and Alex."

"You would." Frey pulled away.

"Payback's a bitch." Tori grinned.

"Not my payback, sweetheart," Holt whispered in her ear before slapping her on the ass. "You like mine."

"Oh, my goodness, what did he say to make you blush so hard?" Tori grabbed her arm.

"Nothing," Frey said breathlessly, watching Holt's sexy ass in his tight jeans as he walked away. Turning when he reached the doorway, he winked at her. Her man was so fucking hot!

"Hey." Tori snapped her fingers in front of her face. "Snap out of it. We have a lot of work to do. And for the record, I agree with Holt. If they want to switch seats, let them. But I like the layout."

"Thank you." Frey grabbed the board and followed Holt. "I'm gonna go downstairs and set it up. Are you coming?"

"Yep, right behind you." Tori followed Frey. "Alex said he would put out some finger foods that we could eat while we get Savor ready for our dinner."

"Perfect, let's roll," Frey walked through the door that Holt was holding open for them.

Chapter 60

Thanksgiving Dinner

Frey

"Hey, Frey." Isa walked in with her family. "Everything looks great. Where can Thunder put our bags with our suits for the pool later?" Isa gave her a hug.

"Thunder, follow me." Frey waved her hand. "We're going to put them in the security offices behind the lobby desk, but let's go this way." Frey led him to the kitchen.

"Hey, Thunder," Alex came over to greet him. "I'm so glad you guys could come."

"We wouldn't miss your cooking for the world. Hey, Holt. Nice to see you again." Thunder shook Holt's hand. "Thanks for inviting the shelter kids. Tim said they were all excited to come. Not only do they love Alex's food, but getting to swim in a pool is quite a treat for them. They don't get to do that very often, if at all."

"It's our pleasure." Holt nodded. "I'm glad they could come. I love hanging out with them."

"I think they loved hanging out with you. Thank you for sharing your story. You're welcome to join us anytime. Tori can let you know when they are coming. It's usually on Fridays."

"Sounds good. I'm sure Frey would love to join us also." Holt draped his arm around Frey's waist.

"Absolutely." Frey beamed at Holt and Thunder. "Okay, let's get back to work. Everyone is showing up. Thunder, I'm putting you in charge of letting everyone know where to put their stuff, so let's go." Frey waved her hand.

"Bossy little thing." Thunder looked at Holt.

"Just the way I like 'em." Holt winked at Frey.

"Good man." Thunder chuckled and followed Frey through the kitchen into the security room.

Frey pointed to the room. "Now that you know how to get here, you can help the others when they bring in all their stuff."

"I'm on it." Thunder put the bags down and they returned to Savor.

"Isa, you can help me, and Tori let everyone know where they are sitting," Frey slid between them. "If they don't want to sit there, they can move."

"This chart looks great, Frey." Isa pointed to it. "The kids will love sitting away from us." Frey was pleased with her hard work, considering the compliment came from a professional Graphic Designer.

"I don't know." Frey heard a voice behind her. "I love sitting with beautiful women." Frey turned and saw Tim, Luke, Kenny, Jimmy, and Bryce.

"You're crazy." Isa hugged Tim.

"Frey," Bryce shouted and ran to her. Frey knelt and caught him in a tight hug.

"How are you, Bryce?" Frey squeezed him. "I've missed you." Looking over her shoulder, she saw Tori covering her mouth with tears in her eyes. "Tori, can you get Holt?" Tori nodded and scurried away.

"I heard you met someone very special to me." Frey held Bryce by his hips when he dropped his arms.

"I did?" Bryce scrunched up his nose. "Who is it?"

Holt had perfect timing.

"Hey, Bryce," Holt squatted down to Bryce's level and smiled.

"Holt! You're here." Bryce pulled away from Frey and hugged Holt.

"So, you like Holt?" Frey looked between them, waiting for Bryce's reaction.

"I do. We're friends." Bryce turned to face Frey but kept his arm around Holt's neck. Then, with his other hand he held it for a fist bump. "Right Holt?"

"Yup." Holt nodded, and fist bumped Bryce. Frey couldn't stop smiling. They were so cute together.

"You want to come with me and help the guys in the kitchen? Alex wants to say hi. He's our chef today so he can't leave the kitchen," Holt stood and extended his hand out to Bryce.

Bryce took Holt's hand, and they swung their hands all the way to the kitchen. Frey stood up and watched them disappear into the kitchen. She knew they would hit it off.

"Boys," Frey turned to the rest of the boys, "if you want to hang with the guys, they are all in the kitchen."

"Nah, we want to hang with the pretty girls. Do you ladies need any help?" Tim smiled. Frey shook her head. Tim was such a charmer.

"You can help us finish placing all the silverware," Tori jumped in. "I'll show you where it is and how to set it."

"Sounds good." Tim faced the boys. "Let's help Tori."

Knowing some of their experiences, Frey's respect for them grew with each encounter. These were well-behaved children who faced unfortunate circumstances. With some great mentors and lots of love, they could achieve anything they wanted.

"*Hola, niña*," Aurora, Isa's mom, surprised Frey with a kiss on the cheek. She needed to stop daydreaming. She hadn't heard her arrive.

"How are you doing?" Frey hugged Aurora.

"I'm doing great now that Holt and I made up."

"I am so happy for you." Aurora smiled and cupped Frey's face. "I'm gonna go help your mom in the kitchen." Frey met Aurora at a Girls' Night Out when they did their nails. Sometimes Aurora didn't join them because she watched the kids, but that night, the boys took the kids to the park so Aurora could join them.

"Hi everybody," Sarah ran up to Frey, Tori, and Isa for hugs. "This is going to be so great, and I didn't have to cook anything."

"Alex said he was happy to return the favor." Tori smiled and watched Emmy, Tommy, and Lucy go to the table and sit. "Grayhorse, find Thunder in the kitchen. He'll tell you where to put your bags and the car seat."

Frey watched Grayhorse unbuckle Lilly and hand her to Sarah. Grayhorse gave her a hug, then grabbed all his stuff and kissed Sarah on his way out. "I'll be back *wíŋyaŋ mitáwa*."

"Miss me?" Lizzy grabbed Tori from behind.

"I'm so glad you're here." Tori turned and squeezed her sister.

"Everyone, check the seating chart to see where to sit.," Isa motioned to it.

Thunder, Grayhorse, Barrett, and Holt came out to take drink orders.

Frey saw an elderly couple walking toward Sarah, so she made her way over there.

"Minnie, Skip," Sarah greeted them as they walked in. "Grayhorse and I are so glad you could come." Oh, now Frey remembered Sarah mentioning them.

"Frey, this is Minnie and Skip." Sarah turned to face Frey." They live next door and are great adoptive grandparents to Tommy and Lilly." Sarah introduced them.

"Thank 'ya fer invitin' us," Skip hugged Sarah. "Nice to meet ya' Frey. Where'r my kids?"

"Skip!" Tommy was jumping out of his seat, yelling. "Over here! You're sitting at my table."

"Gotta go say hi," Skip walked away, heading toward Tommy.

"Thank you, Frey, so much for inviting us." Minnie grasped her hand. "We really appreciate the invite. Can I help your mom in the kitchen?"

"I think they're all set, but thank you." Frey squeezed her hand. "I'm glad you could come."

"Ah, my Lilly," Minnie took Lilly from Sarah's arms. "I got her. You can socialize with your friends."

"Thanks Minnie," Sarah kissed her cheek.

From the little interaction she just had with Skip and Minnie, she could see how much they all meant to each other. Sarah was lucky to have them, especially since her parents died when she was in high school, and Thunder was in college.

"Boo!" Frey watched Isa jump when Maggie scared her.

"Mags! Don't do that. I'm pregnant." Isa slapped her arm.

"Yeah, yeah, yeah. What's the worst that can happen? You'll pee yourself?" Maggie laughed at her own joke while Isa glared at her. Frey loved watching the two of them. They loved to tease each other.

"If I peed myself, you're cleaning it up because I'm having a hard time bending down." Isa shrugged.

"So dramatic," Maggie sighed.

"Hey, where are all the men?" Mark asked when he approached their little group.

"Why? We're more fun." Maggie wiggled her eyebrows at him.

"Yes, you are." Mark held up his hands. "But really, where are they?"

"In the kitchen," Frey answered.

"Barefoot and pregnant!" Maggie giggled. "Where they should be."

"Have you been drinking?" Mark raised an eyebrow.

"Nope, this is my natural self." Maggie shoulder bumped him.

"Run Mark, run," Tori pushed him toward the kitchen. "Run while you can. Go join the man tribe."

They all laughed, watching as Mark jogged away, turning around with a very confused look when he reached the kitchen.

"Did someone call the best police team on the force?" George and Sean came in full uniform. "We might get called, but wanted to stop by for dinner. Can't pass up an opportunity to eat Alex's food." George walked up to Isa for a big hug. "How are you, honey?"

Thunder was George's mentor when he was a shelter boy and had lived with him until he found an apartment he could afford. Frey knew Thunder and Isa thought of him like a son.

"Deputy George!" came Thunder's booming voice from the kitchen. "Are you manhandling my wife?"

"I sure am. She's so exceptional I might just steal her away," George kept holding her and they laughed at Thunder as he approached them. George let go when Thunder got to him and give him a man hug with a few slaps on the back.

Frey had heard that George was the first shelter kid Thunder mentored. Perhaps one day Holt could form a similar bond with one of boys currently at the shelter. Bryce came to mind.

"Okay," Sehoy shouted to everyone. "Have a seat. Dinner is ready."

As everyone took their seats, they passed the plates around the table. When they filled their plates, Osceola got up from his seat.

"I would like to make a toast to all our family and friends here today. We are so blessed to have you all with us. Please take a moment to close your eyes and think of something you are grateful for." Everyone closed their eyes for a few seconds. "Make sure you tell that someone you are grateful for them. I am grateful for my beautiful, loving wife, Sehoy; fantastically talented chef son, Alex and his wonderfully kind fiancée, Tori; protective son, Barrett; strong daughter, Frey; and last but certainly not least, our loyal son, Holt. My heart is full of love for all my family and friends here today."

"Here, here!" everyone lifted their glasses for the toast.

Frey squeezed Holt's thigh.

"Can I have everyone's attention?" Holt stood, pushing back his chair. "As some of you might know, Frey and I have been on a rollercoaster ride of emotions. But we pulled through with the help of our family and friends." Holt placed his hand on Barrett's shoulder. Barrett handed him something and Holt got down on one knee. A ripple of murmurs and gasps disrupted the silence.

"Frey. I have loved you since you saved me from bullies by the water fountain in elementary school. You possess all the qualities I've always desired in a wife: intelligence, kindness, forgiveness, assertiveness, and sassiness. I look forward to starting a family with you and having many children. Although they can never replace the child we lost, we still have so much love to offer. You mean everything to me—you are my heart, my soul, my everything. I wanted all of our family and friends to be present and witness our love. Will you do me the honor of becoming my wife?"

Throughout the entire speech, Frey held her face in her hands. Tears fell from her eyes. She gave a nod of agreement.

"I need the words, Frey," Holt mumbled.

"Yes, yes! I will marry you!" she choked out.

Holt slid the ring onto her finger, stood, and embraced her tightly as they kissed. Cheers and congratulations filled the room. Each person took a turn embracing them and admiring Frey's new round solitaire ring set on a silver band. The ring was simple, yet gorgeous. This was exactly what Frey would have chosen if she had to pick.

As soon as everyone was seated, Holt leaned in and whispered. "I love you."

"I love you too. When did you buy this?" Frey loved her ring and couldn't stop staring at it.

"Barrett and I went a couple of days ago. I wanted his opinion." Holt kissed her cheek. Frey leaned around Holt and tapped Barrett's thigh.

"Thank you for being a part of my ring and the engagement."

"It was my pleasure. You're both stuck with me now." Barrett winked at her and brought her hand to his lips for a kiss. "I love you, sis."

"Love you too, bro."

The tables buzzed with lively conversations. They all agreed on dessert after swimming. Just as George and Sean finished eating, they received a phone call. Sehoy promised to save them a slice of pumpkin pie if they could come by later. They agreed.

Following dinner, they used the lobby restrooms to switch into their swimming attire. Aurora, Minnie, Sehoy, and Dyani sent them all off while they cleaned the dishes and cleared the table. Frey and Holt stayed behind to change out the linens and reset the tables for their guests.

Chapter 61

Thanksgiving Pool Party

Holt

Holt couldn't help himself; he was grinning from ear to ear after Frey accepted his proposal to marry him. Considering he was alone and intoxicated a few days ago, he couldn't have asked for a better Thanksgiving. Everyone pitched in to clean up dinner before going to the pool.

Lucy styled Thunder, Grayhorse, and Alex's hair while they hung out in the pool. Holt, Barrett, and Mark were glad they had short hair as they watched. While Barrett's was longer than Holt's, it was still shorter than the other men's.

Maggie and Frey approached them, saying, "Don't feel like you were saved from Lucy's Hair Salon." Frey embraced Holt and said, "That little girl has a lot of creativity, as Barrett discovered on Halloween."

"She did something to your hair. How?" Mark looked shocked. Holt had already heard the story.

"That little peanut stood my hair up with hairspray and pipe cleaners to look like the branches of a tree," they all laughed. "My damn hair was so spiky and stiff it took for fucking ever to wash all the hairspray out. I don't know how you girls do it."

"Aww, you looked so cute." Frey poked her brother.

"Did you get photos?" Maggie wiggled her eyebrows. "If not, I've heard Tommy takes lots of photos. I want to see them."

"I think Mark and I are safe. We barely have enough hair since we keep it so short," Holt and Mark fist bumped.

"Oh, don't worry." Gaby said as she walked by. "If she can't do your hair, she'll do your nails."

Holt and Mark whipped their heads around, looking at each other, then Gaby.

"Are you shitting us?" Mark dropped his mouth open. "She can't paint my nails. The guys at the security training facility would give me so much shit. I'd never live it down."

"Then I guess you better grow your hair.' Gaby winked at him and swam away.

"Is she fucking with me?" Mark asked Maggie.

Maggie shrugged. "I don't think so, Fabio."

"Maybe she'll do a pedicure and we can hide it with our shoes," Holt murmured.

"Hi," Lucy swam up to them. "I'm Lucy. Can I do your nails?"

"Oh, shit!" Mark said before realizing he had cussed in front of a child. Frey watched Maggie smack him upside the head. "What was that for?" Mark glared at Maggie while Lucy giggled.

"Cussing" –her eyes widened meaningfully– "in front of a child."

"Sorry, Lucy." Mark groaned.

"Why do you guys have short hair?" Lucy tilted her head, looking at them.

"So, you can't braid it," Mark mumbled, earning him another smack upside the head from Maggie.

"Woman, stop hitting me." Mark said through gritted teeth. "I almost dropped my beer in the pool."

"Well, stop saying stupid shit," Maggie immediately covered her mouth with her hands. "Sorry, Lucy."

"Hah." Mark pointed at Maggie.

"Don't you dare slap me upside the head." Maggie glared at him.

"I wouldn't dare." Mark took a sip of his beer.

Frey, Holt, and Barrett were biting their lips, trying to keep from laughing out loud. Holt's gaze was darting between Mark and Maggie the whole time.

"I think I need a swear jar near you guys," Lucy smirked at them. Then she turned around and screamed for Thunder. "*Lekší*, do you have any swear jars at the cultural center?"

Thunder fixed a stern gaze at everyone near Lucy. It would've been scarier If he didn't have so many the wet braids all over his head. "No *toján*, but I promise to buy you one and you can charge them."

"How much can I charge them?" Lucy swam to Thunder.

Holt and the rest of the group locked eyes in astonishment.

"As much as you want, honey." Thunder kissed her cheek and smiled at Holt.

"You can't charge Holt." Bryce swam up to Holt and held onto his shoulder. "He's my friend."

Bryce had captured Holt's heart as well as Frey's. They'd already discussed adopting him. But before talking to Bryce, they wanted to speak with Thunder and the shelter. If adoption wasn't possible, they didn't want to get his hopes up.

"Okay, Bryce." Lucy nodded. "I was only going to charge Mark and Maggie. They are the ones with the potty mouth."

They all burst into laughter. Holt heard Mark say, 'That little girl is something else' before he smiled and took a drink.

"Aw come on sweet girl." Maggie swam to Lucy, who was still in Thunder's arms, and started tickling her. "You love me."

"*Lekší*, make her stop." Lucy was wiggling in Thunder's arms so much he backed up and lifted her up above his head like the baby lion in that kid's movie.

"The queen has spoken," Thunder belted out. "No more tickling and beware of the swear jar."

"Fine, but I'm taking your woman." Maggie grabbed Isa's hand and stuck her tongue out at Thunder.

"I love you, *Lekši*," Lucy wrapped her arms tightly around Thunder's neck when he brought her back down.

"I love you too," Thunder kissed her cheek.

Holt hoped to someday experience that kind of love from a child.

Frey

Frey approached Maggie and Isa, giving Holt some male bonding time with Bryce. Her heart filled with warmth to see how happy Holt was with Bryce.

"What's going on? Why did you drag me away from my sexy hubby?" Isa asked Maggie.

"Can I join you guys?" Frey stood between them.

"Of course." Isa sat on the step and leaned back.

"I'm thinking of getting another job," Maggie blurted out.

"No." Isa looked alarmed. "Why?"

"Because Ryan is driving me crazy. Despite knowing I'm not interested in dating him, he continues to bother me. Now he's telling his buddies that I used him," Maggie sighed. "They always give me the evil eye whenever I see them at the front desk."

"I'm sorry, Mags," Isa grabbed her hand. "I kept pushing you toward Ryan. I didn't know what was happening. That's a case of harassment. We can write them up."

"No!" Maggie pulled her hand away. "That will only make it worse."

"But I don't want you to leave. I'll miss you," Isa whined.

"Yeah, but for how long," Maggie smirked at Isa. "Once you have the baby, are you going to keep working at Teramar?"

"I'm not sure." Isa took a deep breath and stared at Thunder. "I really want to stay home with our baby. Thunder said I don't have to work. We can cut back on our spending and set up a budget. So, I thought about doing some freelance work from home. I have several contacts that don't use Teramar. Or I could stay with Teramar and work from home. I need to talk to my boss."

"Either way" –Maggie smirked– "you won't be there full time."

"You're right. If I could start my own company, I'd hire you. I'll miss you." Isa hugged Maggie.

"Maggie, I think we just hired some staff, but I could ask my mom?" Frey offered.

"That would be great. I'll start looking around at other places as well." Maggie took a sip of her drink.

"Hey wait! I can talk to Thunder," Isa blurted. "With Mark in training to become his security officer and Thunder focusing on marketing, Tori might benefit from having an assistant."

"Oh, my goodness, that would be great!" Maggie set down her drink and hugged Isa. "Ask him later. I don't want him to be on the spot in front of everyone."

"Okay," Isa chuckled.

"I'm taking my woman back," Thunder reached out and pulled Isa off the step and into his arms. "You've had her long enough. Besides, it's getting late. Time to go home."

Everyone unanimously declared it "The best Thanksgiving EVER" before they said their farewells. After their last friend departed, Holt and Frey headed to his room. They showered quickly and got into bed after undressing. Frey nestled in Holt's arms while he lay on his back.

"This was the best day of my life," Holt mumbled and kissed the top of her head while he ran his hand down her back. "I love you."

"I love you too, fiancée," Frey kissed his neck.

"I like the sound of that." Holt rolled them over and gazed into her eyes. "Thank you for agreeing to be my wife. I promise to love you until we grow old and leave this earth. You are my everything."

Chapter 62

Epilogue...8 Months Later

My Cup Runneth Over...Frey

F rey was brimming with excitement. Today was the day she would become a mom. Another incredible milestone in her life after their crazy, scary wedding. After the wedding, they began the adoption procedure to bring Bryce into their family. The entire adoption procedure lasted about eight months, just like their lawyer had advised them.

During the last six months, Bryce had been living with them. Holt moved into Frey's room and Bryce took over Holt's room. At first, since it was a new place, Bryce slept with Holt and Frey. The first few days Holt teased her about having blue balls, but then he got creative. He would ask someone in their family to watch Bryce for a morning or an afternoon so they could spend some time alone. Which wasn't hard to do because everyone loved that little boy.

Frey only worked two days a week. On those nights, Tori or another family member would come over and watch Bryce for a few hours before putting him to bed. After about a month, Bryce enjoyed falling asleep with them, but loved rolling around in his own king size bed. So, once he fell asleep, Holt moved him into his room and left the closet door ajar.

Early this morning, they had their final adoption hearing in front of a judge. All her family had been there and clapped when the judge threw down the gavel and announced Bryce's new name. Bryce Panther. Not only did Bryce have a new name, but after Betty's attack, Holt asked Osceola if he could change his last name in honor of the only father he'd ever had. Frey remembered that day vividly. Holt and Frey went in search of Osceola and found him with Sehoy in the security office downstairs.

"Chacteka, can I talk to you for a minute?" Holt gripped Frey's hand tightly. Frey rubbed his forearm.

"I'll get out of your way. We're done with lunch." Sehoy stood and picked up their left-over containers. "I'll see you later." Sehoy bent down and gave Osceola a kiss. It always warmed Frey's heart to see the love shining in their eyes when they looked at each other. She wanted that with Holt for the rest of their lives.

"Chatski, stay. Please." Holt choked the words out. Frey looked up at him and switched her hands in his so she could rub his back. His breaths were coming in faster now. She was afraid he would pass out before he talked to her parents.

"Chakpootsi, what's wrong? You look pale." Osceola stood and grabbed his shoulder. "Come. Sit." Osceola pulled a chair out for him.

Frey nudged Holt toward the chair and stood behind him keeping her hands on his shoulder. Gently Frey massaged him, and his body began to relax.

"I have a question to ask both of you and I hope I don't make you mad." Holt glanced up at Frey and she smiled at him. Frey was positive nothing about this question was going to make her parents mad. She had told Holt that, but his old childhood fears were eating away at him.

"You can ask us anything and it won't make us mad." Osceola and Sehoy sat down facing Holt and held hands.

Holt took a deep breath, held his hands in his lap, and glanced between Sehoy and Osceola. Frey saw his leg bouncing and continued to rub his shoulders. She knew this question was hard for him to ask because deep down, he was afraid of rejection.

"You both have been the only mother and father that have ever cared about me. You brought me into your home and showed me what love is. I don't know what would have happened to me without you." Holt shook his head and looked at his hands.

"You are not your parents," Sehoy spoke sternly. "You are a smart, caring, and strong young man. You are a survivor and I know those instincts would've kicked in. I'm sorry for what you went through, if I could take it away I would. But if I'm being honest, we got to love and care for a very special boy who filled our hearts with joy every day he was with us."

Frey's eyes watered and, as she glanced down at Holt, she saw a tear running down his cheek.

"Thank you." Holt reached up and wiped his cheek. "I love you both, too."

"So, what is this question that you want to ask us?" Osceola sat forward in his chair and patted Holt's knee.

"I would like to ask you if I could take your last name?" All the words came tumbling out of Holt's mouth. Frey smiled at her parents while she watched their mouths drop. Sehoy covered her mouth with her hands and cried. Osceola stared at Holt, stood, and pulled Sehoy into his arms.

"I'm so sorry, chatski. I didn't mean to upset you." Holt bolted up from his chair. "I...I've never wanted to be an Adams but have longed to be a Panther." Holt looked down at the floor. "I hate my last name and everything it stands for. If this is too much to ask of you and you don't want me to take your name" –Holt deflated– "I understand."

"Honey, I think those are tears of joy." Frey came around and wrapped her arm around Holt's waist.

"Are you sure?" Holt looked down at Frey and mumbled.

"Oh, yeah." Frey smiled at him and shook her head.

"Chakpootsi, we would be honored to share our name with you." Osceola continued to rub Sehoy's back while she wiped her tears and turned to Holt. "We always wanted that, but we didn't want to force it on you. Of course, you can change your last name to Panther. We've always considered you family."

Sehoy opened her arms wide and pulled Holt into her arms. "We love you."

"I love you, too," Holt leaned down and tightened his hug.

Frey was crying so many tears of joy she had to keep wiping her face. She'd told Holt her parents would be honored to share their last name with him, but he'd still been nervous.

Holt stepped back and draped his arm around Frey's shoulder. "Thank you for this. It is the greatest gift you could give me. Well, except for your daughter."

"Hey, snap out of it." Tori snapped her fingers in front of Frey's face. "The shelter kids are here, and we have a lot to do before they get here."

"Sorry." Frey blinked and walked over to the boys. Tim drove them so they could celebrate with Bryce. After presents and cake, they were all going swimming in the resort pool.

"Tim, I'm so glad you could come and bring the other boys. I didn't know how the other boys would feel about us only adopting Bryce." Frey hugged him.

"It is hard for them, but they are so happy for Bryce. He's the youngest and needs parents so he can enjoy his childhood. We all want that for him. Besides, we may not live with you guys, but you are always inviting us over." Tim smiled at Frey.

"You guys are welcome here anytime." Frey kissed Tim on the cheek and was surprised when he blushed. Frey had never seen him blush before. "Can you and the boys help Isa and Maggie hang the streamers?"

"Sure thing." Tim grinned and walked toward them.

Frey was glad the boys came. It would be a great surprise for Bryce.

After the hearing, Holt told Bryce the guys were taking him out for ice cream for some male bonding and all that. Bryce was so excited he never questioned why Frey wasn't going. Frey and the girls went back to the resort and decorated the family living space on their floor so when Bryce stepped out of the elevator, they could surprise him and welcome him home.

They were almost done. String from the helium balloons hung down from the ceiling and other non-helium balloons littered the floor. Tori was in charge of the balloons, and she went a little crazy. She'd been blowing them up all week and storing them in her and Alex's room so Bryce wouldn't see them.

Alex baked a cake for Bryce that said, "Welcome Home, Bryce Panther" and several of their friends bought him toys and books. Instead of buying Bryce a toy, Frey and Holt had gotten him something they could enjoy as a family. She couldn't wait for him to open his box inside of another box. As they were putting on the final touches, Frey's phone buzzed with a text message from Holt.

"Oh, they're here." Frey announced, and all the girls gathered in front of the elevator. The shelter boys stood next to Emmy and Tommy. Lucy was bouncing with excitement next to Aurora. Sarah was carrying Lilly and standing next to Isa, Maggie, and Gaby. The gang was all there to welcome her little boy. Frey stood in front of the group filled with anticipation.

"Surprise!" everyone shouted when the elevator doors opened. Holt walked out holding Bryce's hand.

"Is all this for me?" Bryce looked up at Holt. Holt squatted down and grabbed his shoulders.

"It sure is. We wanted to show you how happy we are that you're a part of our family. Welcome home, son." Bryce flung his arms around Holt's neck and hugged him so hard Frey was afraid he'd cut off his circulation.

With tears in her eyes, Frey walked over and bent down, hugging both Holt and Bryce. "We love you, Bryce."

Bryce stood back and looked at Frey. "I love you too, mom" –then he looked at Holt– "and dad." His smile lit up his entire face. They did another family hug and Frey looked at Holt over Bryce's head. They both smiled at each other. All they knew about Bryce's parents was that they were drug addicts who signed their birth rights over to the state. Bryce had never called them mom and dad before. Frey's heart was bursting with love toward her son.

"Let's open presents." Lucy screamed in the background.

Frey laughed as she watched Lucy approach Bryce and pulled his hand toward the cocktail table filled with presents.

"Okay." Bryce went with her. "Wow! Are all these presents for me? I've never gotten presents before, not even on my birthday." Bryce turned and looked at Frey and Holt. Holt had his arms around Frey as they watched his eyes bug out.

Frey's heart froze for a second. From this day forward, she would make sure every one of his birthday's was a celebration. Her son would know he was loved and wanted.

"They sure are. Start with whichever one you want first." Holt tightened his hold on Frey and pointed toward the presents. Frey sat in front of Bryce handing him whichever gift he pointed to. Bryce opened every card, was excited about every present, and thanked the person that gave it to him. She was so proud of him.

When he got to the last one from Frey and Holt. He opened the first box and raised an eyebrow. "Mom? Dad? You got me a box. I guess I can use it as a chair in my room." Smiling, he hugged Frey and Holt. "Thank you."

Everyone in the room chuckled.

"It's not just a box," Frey smiled at him. "Open it up."

"Okay." Bryce turned back to the box, opened it, and screamed. "You got me Mickey Mouse! I've never had one." Bryce pulled him out and hugged his new toy.

"Open the envelope." Holt smiled.

Bryce opened the envelope and pulled out three colored bracelets. "These are really cool. Is mine the green one?"

"Yep. That's your favorite color, right?" Frey asked.

"It sure is. Thanks." Bryce grabbed his and gave the others to Frey.

"Do you know what that is?" Frey smiled.

"It's a bracelet. I love it."

"Well, it is a bracelet." Frey chuckled. "But it's also your ticket to get into Walt Disney World. The three of us are going next week and spending four days at one of their resorts."

"Really?" Bryce's eyes widened.

"Oh, Bryce. You're going to love it. It's my favorite place!" Lucy jumped up and down, clapping.

"Thank you, mom and dad." Bryce threw himself into their arms.

Frey and Holt shed more tears of joy as they held their son.

"You're welcome, *chakpootsi.*" Holt murmured and Frey kissed the top of his head.

"Bryce. Look." Lucy came over and tugged at his shirt. "Alex made you a cake."

"Really?" Bryce sounded shocked as he followed Lucy. *Silly boy*, Frey thought, *of course his uncle Alex would make him a special cake.*

"What do you think, big guy? Do you like it?" Alex stood next to him, looking at the cake.

"Mom and I have to try it first before we can tell you if we like it." Bryce grinned.

"I can see I'm gonna have my hands full with anything I cook for you and Frey." Alex ruffled Bryce's hair.

"Yep." Frey gave Bryce a high five.

"Alright, alright, you two. Let's cut this bad boy and see if you like it." Alex grabbed a knife and cut a piece, placing it on a plate for them with two forks.

Frey and Bryce ate a piece and looked at each other as if they were thinking.

"Well?" Alex placed his hands on his hips and watched them.

"Yummy," Bryce said at the same time Frey said. "Delicious."

All the kids hollered their excitement and waited for their piece of cake. They looked at all of Bryce's gifts while they devoured their piece. When they finished eating, they all went downstairs to swim in the resort pool.

Frey kept watching Bryce as he played with his friends. Today was the happiest she'd seen him since they met each other. Looking around, she felt blessed to have such great family and friends. This was what life was all about. She'd married the love of her life, and they'd adopted a wonderful son.

Tonight, she had a surprise for Holt. She was late with her period and immediately took a pregnancy test. She was three weeks pregnant.

*** 9 Months later ***

Frey gave birth to boy/girl fraternal twins.

Chapter 63

About this Story

Neri

Being a teacher, I taught a lot of kids who were living in broken homes. In this story, I wanted to touch on bullying, a bad divorce, addictions, and adoptions. I had several students who over the years shared their stories with me. Holt is not one child's story, but a mixture of different children.

Children are resilient, but the more love and care they are shown the more they blossom. Mental health is very real for some kids, and they struggle with how to handle situations. If you ever have the honor of being a mentor or sounding board for a child in need, please be there for them to listen and not judge. It will mean the world to them to know they have someone in their corner.

Thank you for reading Holt and Frey's story. I hope you enjoyed it as much as I loved writing it. I shed many tears with this book because it took me back to different children and their situations. They all hold a special piece in my heart—I will never forget them. I hope they achieve any goal they dream of and find joy in their lives.

Chapter 64

Special Thanks

Neri

Thank you to my Beta reader, Michelle. Your support means everything to me.

Special thank you's to Deputy Bryan Wright and Deputy Nathan Lebon. Deputy Wright answered so many of my questions about arrests and consequences, while Deputy Lebon gave me a tour of our county corrections facility (jail) filled with loads of information. These two exceptional deputies were very kind, respectful, and extremely helpful. I would be remiss if I didn't mention Corrections Deputy Archavette Word. Yes, she is a real correctional facility deputy, for giving me suggestions about future storyline ideas. It was a pleasure meeting you.

I'm lucky to have Doctor Dan as one of my family members that I could go to for his medical advice. Medicine is not my forte and without him, I would not have known the damage a knife wound to the stomach could inflict.

I could not have written this book without the help of several people. If I got anything wrong or applied creative license, it is my doing.

As always, I must express my gratitude to McKenzie Gibel, my chosen 4th child and favorite book editor. You truly push me with every book I write to be better. Now when I write I can hear your voice in my head when I'm doing something wrong like "floating heads" and "POV". I couldn't have done any of this without you. We consider ourselves blessed to have you in our lives.

Chapter 65

About the Author

Neri Lopez has worn many hats as a stay-at-home mom of triplets, graphic designer, and high school teacher (Spanish, Art, and Digital Design/Graphic Design). She lives in Florida with her husband, grown kids, and their fur babies Mocha and Chewy. She is a crafter of all trades including, jewelry making, knitting, crocheting, sewing, scrapbooking, and painting.

Neri loves to hear from her readers. If you want to reach her, use the information below.

Website: https://www.sirenbookandcraft.com

Sign up for her mailing list and you will receive a FREE digital Red Path bookmark. Neri sends out a newsletter every two weeks.

Email: sirenbookandcraft@gmail.com

Facebook: Neri Lopez – Author

Instagram: @neri_lopez author

This Path Series will have six books and one novella, so stay tuned for future book launches.

Book 1: Red Path

Book 2: Unconquered Path

Book 3: Wagering Path

Book 4: Unexpected Path

Book 4.5: Wedding Novella: Double Trouble Path

Book 5: Twisted Path

Book 6: Blue Path